Rupert James is a fashion and celebrity journalist.
He lives in London and is married to a barrister.

He is also the author of the critically acclaimed *Silk*.

Also by Rupert James

Silk

Published in the United States by Cleis Press Inc.,
2246 Sixth St., Berkeley, CA 94710.

Printed in the United States.
Cover design: Scott Idleman/Blink
Cover photograph: foxline.com.ua
First Edition.
10 9 8 7 6 5 4 3 2 1

Trade paper ISBN: 978-1-57344-812-3
E-book ISBN: 978-1-57344-826-0

STEPSISTERS

RUPERT JAMES

CLEiS
PRESS

This book could not have been written without the input, conscious or otherwise, of the hundreds of actors, producers, directors, writers, editors and publicists I've encountered in 25 years as a journalist. It's inspired by all of them, and based on none of them.

Five Years Ago

Chapter 1

Elizabeth put down her knife and fork. 'Married?' she said, through a mouthful of roast chicken. 'You can't get married.'

'On the contrary,' said the Professor, 'I can, and I will.'

'But mother's only been dead for . . .' Elizabeth scanned the ceiling, calculating. Her younger brother Christopher looked from his father to his sister like a spectator at a tennis match.

'Two years, this April,' supplied the Professor. 'Thank you. I am aware of the fact.'

'Well, then,' said Elizabeth, as if this clinched the matter, and started eating again.

'And what would you consider a suitable period of mourning? Five years? Ten? Or would you prefer me to remain celibate for the rest of my life?'

'You're being ridiculous,' said Elizabeth.

'No,' said the Professor, with maddening calm, 'if anyone at this table is being ridiculous, it is certainly not me.'

'Are you going to tell us who it is? Or does Chris already know? I suppose, as usual, I'm the one who's been kept in the dark. Is that it?' She jabbed her fork towards her brother. A pea shot across the table, like a bullet.

'Don't look at me,' said Chris. 'I didn't know.'

The Professor interrupted, as if unaware that his son was speaking. 'Her name is Anna. I've been . . . what's the right term? Seeing her? I've been seeing her for about six months.'

'Six months! God, you hardly know her.'

'And she is the best thing to happen to me for a very long time.'

'Oh well, that's charming,' said Elizabeth, her mouth full. She swallowed, making it easier to say, 'And I suppose that means better than me getting a first. Or getting accepted to do a PhD. Or getting engaged to be married. Or had you forgotten that?'

'All of those things are very fine,' said the Professor, cutting a roast potato into four precisely equal parts. 'It goes without saying that you two are the most important things in my life.'

'It certainly *does* go without saying,' said Elizabeth, 'because you never say it.'

Chris started eating as fast as he possibly could, eager to get away from the table and up to his room. He had the perfect excuse – exams were only weeks away, and even revising would be preferable to this.

'Anyway,' said the Professor, 'I would like you to meet her.'

'And what's so special about this one?' asked Elizabeth, as if her father had had a string of girlfriends since his wife died. 'Why the sudden rush to marry her? Oh God, you haven't got her into trouble, have you?'

Chris nearly ejected a mouthful of wine through his nose, and got the disapproving glare that should have been directed at his sister.

'As you're determined to make a big joke out of this, we'll leave it there. Silly me for thinking that my children might take an interest in their father's happiness. I certainly won't make that mistake again. We shall go our own merry ways.'

Elizabeth was torn between the desire to say 'as you wish,' stand up, fold her napkin and walk out of the house, and the need to hear the juicy details of her father's hitherto-unsuspected sex life. Curiosity got the better of her. She could always storm out later.

'All right, all right. I'm sorry. Go on. You're getting married, Father? How wonderful! Who's the lucky lady?'

'That's more like it, although I would remind you that sarcasm is the lowest form of wit. Her name is Anna, thank you very much for asking, she's forty-three years of age . . .'

'*Forty* . . .' Elizabeth stopped herself just in time, dabbed her lips with her napkin and said, 'I'm sorry. Do please go on.'

'Yes, forty-three. Some years my junior, but still old enough to be your mother.'

'She won't be my . . .'

The Professor held up a long, slender, white hand, the same hand that quelled unruly students in his famously over-subscribed ethics seminars. Even Elizabeth, who had lived with the Hand all her life, shut her mouth. 'I am saying neither that she is your mother, nor that she in any way replaces your mother.' The Professor used 'neither' and 'nor' in the same way that other people swore, to create emphasis. 'I am simply making the point that I am not marrying a gold-digging bimbo.'

'So what is she? Not another philosophy lecturer, please. One of those in the family is quite enough.'

The Professor laughed. 'No, I haven't sunk quite that low yet. She's actually a florist.'

Elizabeth and Chris looked at each other, then at their father. 'A florist?' they said, in unison.

'Yes. Some people are, you know.'

'What sort of florist?' asked Elizabeth.

'The sort that sells flowers, funnily enough. Is there any other?'

'No, I suppose not. I'm just having difficulty imagining what you find to talk about with a florist.'

'You'd be surprised.'

'And how did you meet? I suppose you just popped into

her shop and . . .' A sudden, unwelcome realisation dawned on Elizabeth. Her father bought flowers for one purpose only these days. 'Oh, God. You didn't.'

The Professor looked shifty for a second, then straightened himself in his chair. 'I know this is going to be hard for you, but you must accept the fact that I can't live the rest of my life in a state of emotional deep freeze. Yes, if you must know, I went into a flower shop to get some roses to put on your mother's grave, and that's where I met Anna.'

'Well, that must have been an interesting icebreaker. Hello, my good woman, I need some roses for my wife's grave, and while you're at it, how about dinner? She must have seen you coming.'

'Okay,' said the Professor, putting his knife and fork on his plate at 45 degrees to the table edge. 'I'll leave you in peace. I'm sure you two have some sniggering to do.'

He got up, pushed in his chair and left the room, closing the door quietly behind him. They'd argued again: so much for Elizabeth's resolution to get through the weekly visit without incident. But it was her father's fault, springing a marriage on her like that. His fault, as usual.

Listen to yourself, she thought, as Chris gobbled the roast potatoes that his father had left, mashing them with gravy and stuffing them into his mouth. You're always blaming other people. It's always the Prof's fault that we argue, never yours. It's Chris's fault that he can eat unlimited numbers of roast potatoes without gaining an ounce, while you're still overweight despite months of dieting. It's even Mother's fault that we're in this mess, arguing and resenting each other. She was the one who got cancer and died and left us in the lurch.

None of it's ever your fault, is it, Elizabeth?

Chris got up to leave. 'Sit right down,' said Elizabeth.

'I've got to revise.'

'Did you know about this?'

'No.'

'What do you mean, no? You live under the same roof as him. Are you really trying to tell me that you haven't noticed anything going on?'

'He doesn't tell me anything. We hardly speak. I sometimes wonder if he remembers who I actually am.'

'But she must have been here.'

'Maybe.'

'Come on. Have you met her or not?'

'I might have done. I don't remember.'

'God, how many women has he had coming and going?'

'None. One. I don't know. Yes, I suppose I have met her. I just didn't remember her name. And I certainly didn't know that they were . . . you know.'

'Did she stay over?'

'How the hell should I know?'

'Oh, you know. Little things. Like, for instance, she was still here for breakfast. Or there were tights in the laundry basket. Or the sound of creaking and moaning from the master bedroom.'

'That's disgusting.'

'Too right it's disgusting, but that's what we're talking about. Late-flowering love. Our own father entertaining some . . . woman. In his bed. In *their* bed.' Elizabeth hated herself, but it was like pulling at a torn nail – she couldn't stop, however much it hurt.

'Stop it.'

'What did she look like?'

'I don't know.'

'Are you really as bloody stupid as you look?'

'Fuck off.'

'Is she short? Tall? Fat? Thin? Is she pretty? What colour hair? Come on, Sherlock, you must have noticed something.'

'Well, if she's the one I'm thinking of, she's . . . let me see. Quite short.'

'Hah! I knew it! She's a midget.'

'She had reddish hair.'

'A ginger midget. Oh, this just gets better and better. Full complement of limbs?'

'Yes.'

'Oh well. Pretty? Ugly?'

'I don't know. Not bad. Well dressed. Shawls. Jewellery.'

'A hippy ginger midget. What sort of accent?'

'Normal.'

'You can do better than that. Posh? Common? Northern?'

'Like yours. Normal.'

'Oh, you're hopeless.'

'Maybe if you hadn't pissed Dad off so much, he might have actually told you about it himself.'

'And how do you expect me to react?' Elizabeth's voice was getting higher, despite her efforts to control it, in the euphoria of cruelty. 'I've just heard that my father is marrying a woman I've never met, barely two years after my mother died. Well, whoopee. Hurrah. Zip-a-dee-doo-dah.'

'She was my mother as well.'

'And I suppose you're all in favour of the match.'

'I don't mind. Let him get on with his life.'

'It's like you don't care.'

'Don't say that,' said Chris, suddenly flushing, his eyes wet. 'You know I care. I miss Mum every day.'

Elizabeth was suddenly sorry, and put an arm round him. 'I didn't mean it. It's just a shock.'

The thrill had gone, and she felt like crying. It had been like this ever since their mother died – lashing out, then regretting it. Since before, even. When Susan had got ill, was that when it began? Or earlier, perhaps, when Elizabeth became aware of the cracks in her parents' marriage. The civilised coolness in public, the quiet rows in private, nothing shouted, nothing thrown, never in front of the children. Chris had no idea about all that, or so she hoped.

'Nothing he does is going to bring her back, is it?' said Chris. 'So let him marry this woman. It can't make him any more miserable than he already is.'

'Is it really that bad?' Elizabeth hadn't lived at home for a long time. 'I thought you got on OK.'

'We're in the same house. That's all we have in common.'

'Right. And if he gets married?'

'At least someone might talk to me.'

'I talk to you.'

'You're never here.'

'You can come and see us any time you like.'

'That's the trouble,' said Chris. 'It's "us". It's not you. It's always you and Nick.'

'You like Nick.'

'I know I do,' said Chris, who considerably more than 'liked' his brother-in-law-to-be. 'He's great. But I can't talk to him about . . . stuff.'

'I don't see why not. He's perfectly OK about you being gay.'

'I don't mean that.'

'Then what?'

'Stuff about Mum and Dad. Personal stuff.'

'Go on, then. I'm here now.'

'I don't want to now.'

'Oh, for God's sake. I wish I'd never come. Between you and Father, this place is a bloody madhouse.'

'Go home to your fiancé, then.' Chris shrugged her arm away, and rose to leave.

Elizabeth took a deep breath, and tried to calm herself. 'I'm sorry, OK? Let's talk about it. Father is getting married. We don't know anything about her, except that she's a hippy ginger midget.'

'She's not,' said Chris, but at least he was smiling.

'So I assume that she's some ageing tart who wants to get her hands on Father's money. And, by the way, Mother's money, seeing as that's where most of it comes from.'

'Maybe he's marrying her because he likes her. Can marriage make people happy? Discuss.'

'Oh yeah? And why would he suddenly conceive this strong attraction to a florist?' She made it sound like a euphemism for prostitute. 'She's got him where she wants him, I've no doubt. Used her womanly wiles to secure a proposal of marriage. Father is a very attractive proposition to a woman of a certain age. He's got a good job, status, property, money. A certain amount of fame.'

'Only in academia.'

'Perhaps she's an intellectual ginger midget.'

'She didn't seem it.'

'All right, then. Let's assume she's not a keen follower of the latest developments in post-structuralism. She'll have taken one look at this place and the pound signs will have flashed up in her eyes.'

'Is that why Nick loves you, then? Because you're going to inherit half of it when Dad dies?'

'What a horrible thing to say.'

'But it's all right for you to say it about the woman Dad wants to marry.'

'That's different.' It was, wasn't it?

'Well, I just hope you're all very happy. You and Nick, Dad and this woman.'

'Anna.'

'Anna.' They both tried the word out, as if tasting a new brand of sweet. 'Yes. I hope you all live happily ever after, and I hope that someone will buy me a new suit for the weddings.'

'Oh my God,' said Elizabeth, 'the wedding. When's it going to be? Did he say?'

'No. He didn't get a chance, thanks to you.'

'Damn it. He'd better not try and upstage me.'

'What do you mean?'

'You know perfectly well what I mean. Me and Nick. It's all set for November.'

'That's ages away.'

'Exactly. And supposing Father and this Anna decide to sneak in before us?'

'Is that what this is all about, then? Spoiling your special day?'

'That's not the point.'

'You're angry with Dad because you don't want to share the limelight.'

'You're so bitchy sometimes, Christopher.'

He got up. 'I'm going to revise.'

'Go on, then. Run away from it. Leave me to deal with everything, as usual.' A classic Miller row was brewing, and it was when they were both angry that Elizabeth and Chris most looked like sister and brother. Their faces grew pale, with spots of high colour on their cheeks. Their grey eyes flashed through fringes of blond hair, their eyebrows contracted into a deep frown. Chris, who preferred to avoid confrontation unless severely provoked, was about to tell his sister exactly what he thought of her when the doorbell rang and saved them from a major slanging match.

'That'll be Nick,' said Elizabeth, glad of an exit line. Chris pounded up the stairs to his bedroom, slamming the door behind him.

Elizabeth could see her fiancé's silhouette through the frosted glass of the front door. Her heart beat faster, her fingers trembled as she opened the lock. He still had that effect on her even after almost two years. She took a deep breath, closed her eyes for a moment and cleared her throat.

'Hello.'

'Hi Betty-Boo,' he said, pushing past her, pressing against her, his upper arm making contact with her breasts. 'How was it? Old man behaving himself?'

She closed the door and raised her face for a kiss, which he bestowed as if it were an afterthought. 'I'll tell you later. Shall we go?'

'Where's my little friend Christopher?'

'He's upstairs revising. Don't torment him.'

'He loves it. Let me go and say hello. Make the poor little bugger's day.'

'Please, Nick . . .' He was up the stairs, two at a time, before she could say any more.

Nick Sharkey was one of those people to whom genetics have been unnecessarily generous. In less sensitive times he'd have been called Creole, combining the best qualities of an Oriental mother and a British-West Indian father. He had high cheekbones, long, hooded eyes, a strong jaw, a large, sensitive mouth and regular nose, the whole covered in skin the colour of caramel. His thick black hair fell into whatever was the most desirable hairstyle of the week, without benefit of grooming. His body was naturally, effortlessly athletic. And, as Elizabeth knew – although she had very little to compare it with – he was perfectly proportioned in all departments.

When he walked into a room, Elizabeth experienced a rush of blood to the head, and blushed. Chris experienced a rush of blood a little further down.

Nick burst into Chris's bedroom without knocking. 'Caught you wanking again, Little Brother?'

Chris was, in fact, doing nothing more exciting than studying a media studies coursebook, but he looked guilty, as he always did when he saw Nick. Even for a permanently horny seventeen-year-old, there was something uncomfortable about fancying your sister's fiancé.

'Shut up' was all he could think to say, but his face expressed the adoration he could not express in words. Nick put his arm around Chris's neck, held him in a headlock and rubbed a fist over his long, curly blond hair. 'Still as pretty as ever,' he said, exaggerating his London accent. 'If I was stoned, I might not be responsible for my actions.' Chris struggled, and there was a lot of the sort of physical contact that is described as 'horseplay'. Why does he do this, thought Chris, as his hands pushed against Nick's rock-hard stomach. Is he not getting it at home?

Finally, he broke free, and placed his media studies coursebook face down in his lap, to cover his embarrassment. 'You all right, then?'

'Yeah, I'm all right. I'm always all right.'

'Come to take her away?'

'Yeah. She getting on your nerves?'

'No more than usual.'

'Poor little Chris. Always up here with your nose stuck in a book.' He grabbed the media studies, flicked through it and tossed it on the bed, losing Chris's place. Chris crossed his legs, hoping that nothing was visible. 'You ought to get out more. Haven't you got any nice boyfriends?'

'No.'

'What a bloody shame. You'll never be seventeen again, you know. Wasting it all on a box of tissues.'

'I'm all right.'

'I bet you are.' Nick grinned, showing a set of perfect white teeth with slightly elongated canines. 'Well, I can't spend the rest of the afternoon hidden away up here, however much you might like me to. Time to take the trouble and strife home. See what the latest wedding plans are. You know, all the important stuff.'

'Okay, Nick. See you soon.'

'Be good. And if you can't be good, tell me all the gory details.' He stood up, winked and disappeared.

Downstairs, the Prof and Elizabeth were exchanging frosty farewells. Nick extended a hand, which the Prof shook without enthusiasm.

'How's work, Nick?'

'Not bad, thanks. Yeah. Fine.'

'Still . . .'

'Riding motorbikes for a living. Yeah. Sorry about that. Haven't taken over the Bank of England or anything. But thanks for asking.'

'Come on, you,' said Elizabeth with a smile, as if the whole conversation were just a bit of manly banter. She knew perfectly well that it was not. She had tried to convince her father a thousand times that Nick was only working as a motorcycle courier until he got his break as a photographer or an artist. The Prof was unconvinced, and occasionally hinted, in that careful, inoffensive way of his, that Nick was a parasite.

'And how are things in ethics?' This was Nick's oldest and least-welcome joke. 'Or have you moved to Thuthex?'

'Goodbye, Daddy,' said Elizabeth, feeling guilty for her behaviour and eager to make peace. 'Thanks for a lovely lunch. I'll call you soon.'

'Please do. We need to talk.' He held open the door and nodded at Nick, who always felt that the Prof was checking him for stolen silverware.

Elizabeth waved through the car window. The Prof was standing at the front door, a prosperous, serious man of property – and the house, with its large, flat, creeper-covered facade, seemed to look back at her, too. It was still 'home', the house where she'd grown up, the gravel drive and leaded windows, the clipped conifers and neat lawns, a big fat chunk of her inheritance tucked away behind the grime and bustle of the Finchley Road.

'What the fuck was that all about?' said Nick, relighting a half-smoked joint as they drove away from the house.

'I wish you wouldn't.'

'What? Oh, for Christ's sake, don't start that again. Open the window if you don't like it.'

'How was your day?'

'Fantastic.' He meant the opposite, and she knew it. It was a long time since Nick had joined her at the family Sunday lunch. The convenient fiction was that he was 'working' on his various projects. In fact, this meant sleeping, smoking and watching football. 'The Old Man's his usual charming, friendly self, I see.'

'Yes.' It was easier to agree with Nick than to defend her father.

'What is his problem? Not getting enough, I reckon. Like your brother. That house must shake on its foundations when those two get going. Like father, like son.' He took a puff on his joint and placed it in the ashtray, taking his eyes off the road. Elizabeth knew better than to object. 'Wankers, both of them,' he added, in a smoke-cracked undertone.

'As a matter of fact,' said Elizabeth, 'at least one of them has been getting his oats.'

'What? My little Christopher? Don't tell me he's finally got someone to shove it up him.'

'No. My father.'

'You're kidding.'

'I'm not. And what's more, he's marrying her.'

'He's . . . what?'

'Getting married.' She saw Nick's jaw muscles working.

'This is a joke.'

'I wish it was.'

'Fuck.' He slammed his hands on the wheel, and the car swerved. Elizabeth hissed as she drew breath, her feet seeking imaginary brake pedals.

'I don't see why *you're* so angry about it,' she said, although she suspected. 'He's *my* father.'

Nick changed his tone. 'I know, baby. I'm sorry. It's you I'm thinking about. I mean, after your mum . . .'

Hearing her own arguments in another mouth made Elizabeth feel ashamed of herself. 'I suppose it is nearly two years now.'

'It just seems so selfish.'

'That's the Prof for you. Can't see much outside his ivory tower.'

'So who is she?'

'Her name's Anna. According to Chris, she's a redhead.'

'A redhead . . .' There was a note of speculation in Nick's voice, as if he was weighing up the benefits of having a redheaded mother-in-law. 'And how old is she?'

'Forty-something.'

'Right.' Nick was not above flirting with women at least twice his age. 'So when are we going to meet her?'

'Don't know. Soon, I suppose.'

'Find out.'

'I will.' Why was he so interested, all of a sudden? The prospect of another woman on whom to exercise his charms? Or the desire to assess the threat to his wife's dowry?

'A new mum, eh . . .'

'Don't say that.'

'Why not? That's what she'll be. A stepmother.'

'A wicked stepmother, maybe.'

'Wicked? Yeah . . .'

Elizabeth didn't like the relish in his voice, and let the subject drop, turning her face to the open window, trying to breathe fresh air as the car filled with cannabis smoke.

They got home without mishap, and without speaking. Elizabeth had a headache – wine with lunch, arguments with the family, worrying about Nick, passive smoking – and wanted to sit in front of the TV with a cup of herbal tea. Nick had other ideas.

'Come on, Betty-Boo,' he said, the moment they were indoors, putting his arms round her waist and pressing himself into her backside. 'I've been waiting all day.'

'I'm not really in the mood,' she said. 'Can't it wait?'

'I don't know. Let's have a look, shall we?'

'Nick . . .'

'Hang on a tick.' He unbuckled his belt, unbuttoned his fly with one hand, turned Elizabeth around with the other. 'Let's see what he says.' He pulled out his cock; it didn't look particularly patient. 'Go ahead, ask him.'

Elizabeth, for all her interest in feminism, particularly as it applied to the development of the nineteenth-century French novel, on which she was doing her PhD, could never say no to that. She dropped to her knees.

Nick leaned against the wall, put his hands on Elizabeth's head and wondered just how much of a threat this new mother-in-law would be.

Chapter 2

By the time everything was shoved into Anna's old red Peugeot, there was no rear visibility whatsoever: the boot, the back seat and the parcel shelf were piled high with black bin bags containing clothes, shoes, toiletries, CDs, mobile phones in various states of repair, and yet more clothes and shoes. Earlier that morning, Anna had searched the house, convinced that there was some sort of luggage hidden away, but in the end they'd scooped everything up into plastic sacks and shoved it in any old how. Anna knew that her daughter's idea of 'unpacking' would simply be to empty everything out in the middle of her bedroom floor and let gravity take its course, so what was the point in squandering money she did not have on fancy suitcases?

It was high time Rachel left home; she was nineteen, after all, at which age Anna had already been living independently for two years. She was a student, too – and weren't students supposed to live in squalid flats that they trashed during drug-fuelled parties? Certainly the students Anna partied with in the 1970s had done so. But children grew up slower these days, thought Anna, and for all Rachel's new-found sophistication (she learned *that* at drama school, at least), she was still a child. Perhaps leaving home would help her to grow up. The last thing Anna wanted, as she embarked on her second marriage, was a child hanging around.

'Is this safe?' asked Rachel, nervously biting her lower lip. They'd moved house dozens of times, but leaving home was a different matter, and she was jumpy. 'Can you actually see anything?'

'I'll just drive very slowly,' said Anna, checking her eye make-up in the otherwise redundant rear-view mirror as they pulled out into the traffic of Kilburn High Road. 'Don't worry. I know what I'm doing. Here, hold this.' She pressed an embroidered hessian tote bag into Rachel's hands. 'I can't reach the handbrake.'

'Watch out!' A Royal Mail van, travelling at twice the speed limit, swerved to avoid them. 'He almost hit us!'

'Don't exaggerate, darling.'

'If we get there in one piece, it'll be a miracle.'

'Well, if you'd prefer to take a taxi, that's just fine.' Anna stopped the car halfway out of the junction. 'Go ahead.'

'Mum, please.' Horns were being honked. 'Let's go!'

'Right.' The car lurched forward, almost went into the back of a taxi, and finally they were driving fairly normally towards town. If a policeman stopped them, Anna could probably sweet talk her way out of it. She usually did.

'So, will your new flatmates be there? I'm dying to meet them.'

'I expect so. But don't feel you have to . . . you know. Hang around.'

'And miss the chance to meet my darling daughter's new best friends? Are you kidding? What's the matter, darling? Ashamed of the old bag?'

'Don't be silly, Mum.'

'What, then? Afraid that I'll turn the boy's head?'

'You might be barking up the wrong tree there, Mum.'

'Oh, darling,' said Anna, with a sigh. 'Don't tell me he's gay. I mean, I know it's drama school and everything, but come on. There must be some straight ones.'

'There are plenty of straight ones, thank you very much.'

'Oh, goodie.'

'Only I don't care to live with them.'

'Don't care to? Aren't we getting a bit grand all of a sudden? I can't think where you get it from. Certainly not from me.'

'No. You're common as muck.'

'Am I, indeed? Well, come on, then. Tell me all about them.'

'There's not much to tell,' said Rachel, who was so tired of competing with her mother for the attention of her friends that she had only agreed to this lift because she couldn't afford the alternative. 'They're on my course.'

'I know that, darling. But who are they?'

'Natasha and Mark. She's a very good singer. He's a . . . Well, he's interested in all sorts of things.'

'Oh. I know the sort.'

'What's that supposed to mean?'

'Nothing, darling. Go on. Is he good-looking? They usually are, damn them.'

'Yes, I suppose he is. But please don't try to convert him. You'll only end up embarrassing me.'

Anna put a heavily ringed hand to her breast. 'Me? Embarrass you? I don't know what you mean.'

It's little wonder I've been drawn to the theatre, thought Rachel, with her for a mother. 'Anyway, they're very nice.'

'Nice? Oh dear.'

'And I'm very grateful to them for letting me move in. It's a lovely flat.'

'So you keep saying. How you're going to afford it, I do not know. You're not expecting me to come up with the rent, I hope.'

'Don't worry about that. It's all taken care of.'

'Sounds murky.'

'It's not.' It was, actually – the flat belonged to a businessman friend of Mark's, who was working in Dubai for a couple of years, and who let Mark flat-sit in return for a comfortable berth on his occasional return visits. The mornings after Mark's 'rent nights' were notable for his more-than-usually distracted behaviour in class.

'Which way now?'

'Down here. Go round Regent's Park. Then we cut off into Camden.'

'Oh look! There's that house we used to live in, remember?'

'Where? We never lived round here, did we?'

''Course we did. One whole summer. Must have been around '90, '91.'

'I was only four.'

'I suppose you were. Seems like yesterday. Oh, time has a cruel way of speeding up as you get older.'

'Is there any borough of London we haven't lived in?'

'Yes, thank God, Tower Hamlets, and you should be very grateful that your old mother has never sunk quite that low. Here we are. This must be the turning. Dear old Camden Town. I could tell you a few stories about Camden Town.'

'I'm sure you could.'

'But listen, darling,' said Anna, placing her hand on Rachel's knee – the car swerved to the right, but she didn't notice, 'if things don't work out, you only have to call and I'll come and rescue you.'

'I'll be fine.'

'I hope so, darling, I really do.' Anna pulled up at a crazy angle to the kerb. 'Never mind me, rattling around all alone in that ghastly old mausoleum. You spread your wings. Enjoy yourself while you're still young.'

'Spare me the sob story, Mum. You're never alone for long.'

'Oh!' The hand went to the breast again, and this time Anna had to disentangle a large turquoise ring, set in cheap silver, from a string of amber beads around her neck. 'I almost forgot to tell you, and you've just reminded me.'

'What? You're moving again?'

'Well, that's part of it. I'm getting married.'

'Married?'

'Yes. Married.' Silence fell, and the car rolled gently back a couple of feet, resting against the bumper of a silver BMW. 'Oops!' said Anna, and put the handbrake on. 'Isn't that a hoot?'

'Were you planning to tell me?'

'I just did, didn't I?'

'Right. Well, I must say, Mum, your timing is as brilliant as ever.'

'There's no need to make a big song and dance about it, Rachel. I happen to have met someone I like and he wants to make an honest woman of me, and you can take that look off your face right now.'

'Well? Who is he?'

'Oh, he's the most marvellous man,' said Anna, removing the ring, which refused to separate itself from her beads, and letting it dangle like a pendant, where it would remain for months. 'He's a professor, you know.'

'Of what?'

'Something terribly clever that I really don't understand, psychiatry or something. We shall be Professor and Mrs Anthony Miller. How do you like that?'

'Anthony Miller.'

'Yes, darling. Obviously, I call him Tony.'

'And what do I call him? Assuming you were planning to introduce us.'

'Whatever you like, darling. You'll love him, and he'll love you, I'm sure.'

'Hmmm.' Rachel had unpleasant memories of some of her

mother's former boyfriends who had 'loved her' a little bit too much, and obliged her to keep her bedroom door locked. 'How old is he?'

'Madly old,' said Anna, opening the car door. 'Hadn't you better ring the bell?'

'How old? Oh God, Mum, you haven't latched on to some horrible old geezer, have you? Is he rich?'

'No I haven't, he's in his sixties, but it's true, he's not short of a bob or two, and quite frankly after all I've been through, I think I deserve a bit of comfort.'

'And when are you getting married?'

'Quite soon.'

'Have you set a date?'

'Not yet, darling, no.'

'This is . . . I mean this is *real*, is it, Mum? It's not just one of your ideas?'

'It's perfectly real, thank you, and I don't know what you mean by my *ideas*. We're just waiting till we've told everyone that needs to be told.'

'Meaning who? His wife?'

'Very funny.' Anna started pulling bin bags out of the back of the car, piling them up on the pavement. 'His wife is dead, as a matter of fact. I was referring to his children.'

'His . . . children?'

'Yes, darling. A boy and a girl, just like your new little friends. You're going to have a family at last. Isn't that nice?'

'How old are they?'

'Oh, they're . . . Let me see . . .'

'You must know. I mean, you have met them, haven't you?'

'Not yet, no. We're not rushing into anything.'

'Right. I see. Well, do keep me posted, Mum. And if you move house, please try and remember to tell me the address.'

'Oh, very funny. Anyway, as soon as you're settled, we're going to have a lovely big family get-together.'

Rachel felt too much, all at once. Surprise at the news, of course, although it was quite in character for Anna to 'forget' such things. Excitement mixed with fear at the thought of siblings, something she'd longed and prayed for all through her lonely childhood. She was popular now, beautiful and maybe even talented, but as a child, forever on the move, always the new girl in the class, awkward and gawky, she learned to fear the cruelty of other kids. 'Lovely,' she said. It was easier to be sarcastic than to tell her mother how she really felt.

The car was empty. 'Please try to be happy for me just once, darling. This means a lot to me.'

'Mum, if you like him, and he's got money, and he's not a drunk or a pervert or a thief, I'll be as happy as you could possibly want me to be. Now, come on. Help me lug this stuff up the steps.'

'With my back? Anyway, here comes the cavalry.'

The front door of the mansion block burst open, and Natasha and Mark came rushing down the steps in a flurry of colour and squeaks and flapping hands.

'Darling, you made it,' said Natasha, kissing Rachel on both cheeks and leaving smears of dark plum lipstick wherever she went. 'Welcome to the madhouse.'

'You must be Anna,' said Mark, who had marginally better manners. 'We've heard so much about you.'

'Christ,' said Anna, putting on her huskiest voice, 'that sounds like my cue to leave.'

'Goodbye then, Mum,' said Rachel. 'Thanks for the lift.'

'Look after my little girl,' said Anna, getting into the car and seesawing her way out of the parking space. 'Good luck!' She waved her rings out of the window, and kangaroo-hopped along Parkway.

'My God,' said Mark, 'she's even better than you described her. What was she wearing around her *neck*?'

'Don't ask,' said Rachel. 'Now, help me get this crap upstairs.'

'And then we'll open a bottle of wine,' said Natasha. 'I think we'll need a drink by then.'

'Unpacking' was an organic process, and by the time Natasha was pouring wine for everyone, the room that was now Rachel's resembled the aftermath of a rather chic jumble sale. Her notion of housekeeping was to have everything within easy reach – and, given that her bed consisted of a mattress on the floor, she could get anything she needed simply by rolling. There were drawers, and a wardrobe with plenty of hanging space, but that was a project for another day. There were more important things on the agenda.

'Married?' shrieked Natasha, putting on a Duke Ellington album too loud for normal conversation. 'You're joking, right?'

'No, I think she really means to go through with it.'

'Will we all be invited?' Natasha sketched out a dance step on the wine-stained carpet. 'I love weddings. Marvellous DUOs.'

'What?'

'DUO. My favourite thing. Dressing-Up Opportunity.'

'Last time she went to a wedding she wore a kind of stripper outfit,' said Mark. 'Caused a riot.'

'It was not a stripper outfit. It was a very tasteful basque with a tutu and stockings.'

'Certainly went down well with the best man. Or on the best man, was it?'

'Shut up, you.' Natasha stopped dancing long enough to neck her wine. 'So, tell all. Who's the lucky feller?'

'He's a professor.'

'Eeeeew!' said Natasha and Mark in unison, putting their fingers down their throats, pretending to gag. 'How ghastly!'

'Is he good-looking?' asked Mark. 'Would I like him?'

'I don't know, darling,' said Rachel, 'as I haven't had the honour of an introduction.'

'My God, Rachel, he could be anyone,' said Natasha. 'He could be some kind of conman. Or a serial killer. Like Acid Bath Haigh. Marvellous.'

'Look, if anyone's going to murder my mother, it will be me, thank you very much. He's a psychologist or something.'

'A psychopath? I told you.'

'And he's got two children. A boy and a girl.'

'What's the boy like?' asked Mark, refilling everyone's glasses and emptying the ashtray. 'Is *he* good-looking?'

'Is there any member of my new family you don't want to shag?'

'Probably not. Is there a grandfather? He might be hot.'

'I don't even know how old the kids are. They could be tiny.'

'Even Mark wouldn't stoop as low as paedophilia,' said Natasha, slurping from the rim of her overcharged glass.

'All right,' said Rachel, 'here's an idea. You can both come to the wedding. One of you can seduce the grandfather, the other can seduce the son, and I'll have a crack at my stepfather.'

'Incest!' screamed Natasha. 'How madly fashionable!' She started Charlestoning.

'Well, he's supposed to be a psychologist, isn't he, so incest should all be part of a day's work.'

'Is it incest?' asked Mark. 'I don't suppose it matters, as long as he's fit.'

'Right,' said Natasha, who had reached the limit of her interest in someone else's life, 'where are we going?'

'Are we going out?' asked Rachel. 'On a Sunday night?'

'Of course!' said Natasha. 'It's still the weekend.'

'But college tomorrow. Nine o'clock lecture.'

'Oh, please,' said Mark, 'we'll worry about that in the morning. Come on. Let's go into Soho.'

'I'm tired. I'm going to bed.'

'Boring,' chorused Natasha and Mark.

'Boring or not, I'm going to get an early night. I need my beauty sleep.'

'Hah! We'll soon break you of these disgusting habits,' said Natasha. 'You've got to come out. It's the law.'

'I'm sorry. Learning that I'm about to have a new daddy has exhausted me. Go and have fun. And try not to wake me up when you drag some man home at five o'clock in the morning.'

'What kind of a slut do you take me for?' asked Mark. 'I always go to the gentleman's house.'

'If he has one,' said Natasha. 'What about that time you woke up on the Embankment with a bottle of cider in one hand and a . . .'

'Thank you, Madam,' said Mark, slapping Natasha hard on the arse. She feigned outrage. 'Sure you won't come, Rachel? Save me from a fate worse than death?'

'Another time, thanks. See you at college.'

'Swot,' said Natasha, flouncing off to the bathroom to replace the lipstick that was now smeared across faces, glasses and cigarette ends. 'We'll soon drag you down to our level.'

'I don't doubt it. Goodnight.'

It was past two when Natasha and Mark got home – their idea of an early night – and nearly three by the time they'd crashed and flushed their way to bed. It didn't matter: Rachel was awake. Sleep would not come. A strange bed in a strange house? Perhaps. Homesickness? Unlikely; she'd been dreaming of this day ever since starting at drama school, waiting only for the opportunity. What, then, was making her mouth dry and her stomach turn over?

She's getting married.

It shouldn't matter, should it? Anna was hardly a conventional mother, and nothing she did would surprise Rachel. She'd coped with worse. A turbulent infancy, her father kicked out when she was five, returning occasionally to spend the night, or to fight with Anna, to give his daughter inappropriate presents in lieu of forgotten birthdays or, if he was drunk, to cry or hit her. She got to know the signals, and learned when to stay in her room. When they finally divorced, and the judge ordered him to keep away, Rachel was glad. She was better off without a father.

So why, now, was she so excited? Surely it would be just another in that long line of hopeless, feckless drunks that Anna, with an unerring instinct for disaster, had taken up with over the years. It would be all roses for six months, during which Rachel would be neglected. And then she'd have another six months of tears and depression before Anna bucked up and moved on. This would be no different.

But it was. She'd kept it so quiet; discreet, almost, which was uncharacteristic. And they were actually getting married. The 'M' word had never been mentioned, not since Mrs Anna Hope reverted to being Ms Anna Bates. Perhaps this really was the One. And he had children, and money, and that could change everything. And it was with those uneasy, hopeful dreams of a future of security and family that Rachel finally fell asleep.

Chapter 3

Her students were not responding very well to *Madame Bovary*, which Elizabeth usually regarded as a sure-fire crowd-pleaser. Back in her undergraduate days, *Madame Bovary* had hit her like a bolt of lightning from some literary Olympus; she and her friends debated and dissected Emma's corpse over endless cups of coffee and bottles of supermarket plonk. Today's group sat like dazed cattle on their way to some corporate abattoir, marking time in the university until, equipped with the relevant piece of paper, they shuffled into the cold, fetid air of the slaughter-house. What would Flaubert have made of them? Or Zola? If only Elizabeth were a novelist herself, she'd have something to say about this bovine generation . . .

'Come on, now. Does the word "feminism" mean anything to any of you? Please put that phone away. You know they're not allowed in classes.'

'It's on silent.'

'I'm waiting.'

The phone offender, who resembled a cow even more than the rest of them, sighed deeply, as if some part of her soul were being torn away from her, then sat motionless, staring into space, perhaps digesting the cud in her second stomach. Elizabeth fought back a desire to slap her pale, round cheeks.

'What did you think of the ending, then? If the story of Emma's adultery didn't move you, surely her death . . . ?'

Four pairs of eyes scanned the middle distance.

'You did get to the end of the book, didn't you? Sean,' she

said, turning to the one student who could usually be relied on to break the silence, 'come on. Emma's death. Some reaction.'

'It's tragic.'

'Good. Tragic. Let's talk about that,' said Elizabeth, seizing on the word like a drowning woman grasping a lifebelt. A rather leaky, perished lifebelt, but it might get her safely to the end of the hour. 'In what way does Emma's story conform to the ideas of tragedy that we've discussed in relation to, say, Shakespeare?' She snuck a look at her wristwatch; Christ, another forty minutes to go. At this rate she'd be chucking them out at quarter to, and nobody would be more relieved than her.

'Well,' said Sean, a bullet-headed young man who got through life on a combination of good looks and a carefully cultivated working-class accent, 'she dies.'

'Yes, indeed, she dies. But more precisely, she ceases to live, to exist. "*Elle n'existait plus*" is how Flaubert puts it. Is that tragic? A simple termination of existence? What does Flaubert want us to think? Is he not, in a horrible way, laughing at Emma? Laughing at our sentimental, romantic need for a tragic heroine?'

The grim certainty that none of them had actually read the book fell over the room like a cold fog. Time, thought Elizabeth, to get the conversation on to more general topics. They would never be any good. They would never engage with books in the passionate, life-changing way that she had. They were duds. It did not occur to her for one moment that the fault might lie, not with the students, but with their teacher.

'So,' she said, shifting her position, recrossing her legs, 'let's talk about the meaning of adultery in the modern world. Does it still matter? Princess Diana, for instance?'

Tiny flickers of light kindled in those large, wet, bovine eyes, and Elizabeth knew that they would all make it through another week.

Theatre history was the least popular component of the Alderman's drama course, largely because it involved some reading, rather than just showing off by impersonating emotions that one had never actually felt. Rachel liked it more than most of her fellow students because a) she found it quite restful and b) she fancied the tutor, an intense young Irishman with curly black hair and ice-cold blue eyes who found it impossible to disguise his more-than-educational interest in her. This extra-curricular warmth often expressed itself in stern reprimands, to which Rachel responded meekly, with flaming cheeks and wet eyes; oh, Colin may say that she would never make an actress, but what did he know? He was the one who couldn't pretend, not her.

Today they were studying the Restoration period, and attendance was rather meagre, despite the fact that Colin had told them the previous week that Restoration comedy was 'all about sex'. Rachel, Natasha and Mark had flicked through *The Country Wife*, looking for 'the good bits', and ended up prancing around the living room pretending to be whores and dandies, then painting their faces white, applying cupid's-bow lipstick and beauty patches made out of sequins, going out to a club and saying 'Zounds' to anyone who offered to buy them a drink. Natasha, who entered into the role of a Restoration whore more convincingly than the others, introduced herself to everyone as 'Demelza Jollop' and did not come home that night. That was their preparation for a class on Restoration comedy.

Now Colin, who was far too slim and athletic to be a college lecturer, and who filled a pair of jeans to perfection, was droning on about 'libertinism' and the emergence of women on to the professional stage. Rachel found herself wondering if he ever went out, and what he would say to her if they met, by chance, one night in a bar. Would he throw aside the professional mask, tell her that he'd been unable to sleep ever since he first saw her in his class and whisk her off to some remote Irish crofter's cottage – did they have crofters in Ireland? – where they would wear sweaters and go for long bracing walks on the beach before making wild elemental love in the seaweed . . .

'Anyone? Come on, I know that ten o'clock in the morning is the crack of dawn for most of you, but imagine how much worse it will be when you're touring around provincial secondary schools in the back of a transit van.'

The class tutted and grumbled and cast bitter looks at each other; *they* were not going to be the sort of actors who resorted to such desperate measures to get their equity cards. *They* were going to be spotted by agents and casting directors in the big autumn production, and might not even bother to graduate from the stupid bloody course because they would be too busy with photo-calls and interviews to promote their upcoming role in . . .

'Okay. If you won't volunteer, I'll do a bit of casting myself. Ben, you can be Horner. For those of you who haven't found time in your busy schedules to actually read the play, he's the dirty shagger who gets all the women. Rachel, you're Lady Fidget, who is hot for him. Paul, her husband Sir Jasper, and Joelle, Mrs Squeamish. Act four, scene three. The famous china scene. Page two hundred and twenty, if any of you actually have the book. But what do you know? I've photocopied it just in case.' He handed out the parts. 'Now, stand up and try to look as if you know what it's all about.'

They stumbled through the scene, breaking down over un-familiar words, reading each other's lines, failing entirely to convey any meaning, let alone comedy. Rachel and Ben, the two best-looking students in the class, brought to the flirtation between Lady Fidget and Horner all the sexual frisson of a DSS waiting room.

'Stop! Stop!' cried Colin, as they dragged towards the end of the scene. 'Does anyone have the faintest clue what this is all about? What they mean by "china"?'

Cast and audience regarded him blankly.

'I don't know why I bother with you lot.' When Colin got angry, his face darkened, and his cold blue eyes flashed out with more brilliance than usual. Why was he wasting his time here, wondered Rachel? He could be having so much *fun* . . .

'You. Rachel. What do you think Lady Fidget means when she say "let him come, and welcome, which way he will"?'

'I don't know.' She brought the blood to her cheeks, felt her eyes moisten on cue, and looked down at the floor.

'*Come*. Does that word have any meaning other than to arrive?'

There was a certain amount of shifting and sidelong glancing.

'Ah. A light dawns. And when she says "we women of quality never think we have china enough", what is she referring to? A Spode tea service?'

The students looked at each other, then stared at the martyred Rachel.

'I'm waiting.'

'Cock?' volunteered a voice from the back of the class.

'Eureka!' shouted Colin, slapping his forehead. 'Cock, it is. Yes, they had it in the seventeenth century, you know. And the other thing, too. Why do you think the bloody play is called *The Country Wife*? Now, let's try it again, bearing those important facts in mind. And Rachel?'

'Yes?'

'If you could concentrate on something other than being professionally beautiful, that would be a great help.'

'I . . .' She forced the accumulation of salt water in her lower lid to spill down her cheek like a real tear. 'I'm sorry.'

Colin blushed, this time in shame, rather than anger, and the class proceeded. Whether Rachel had learned anything about Restoration comedy was open to debate, but she'd certainly taken a great step forward in her acting.

Back in the Queen's College staffroom, Elizabeth furiously spooned instant coffee into a mug. 'They're so bloody stupid,' she said. 'I mean, *Madame Bovary*, of all the books in the world, failed to get them going. What do they want? Why are they even here?' She took four biscuits from the communal tin; damn these students for making her fat!

Her colleague Charlotte, who had been working on a PhD about the literature of female monasticism for seven years and still showed no sign of submitting it, sighed and shook her head. 'It's not about results, Elizabeth. It's about process.'

'Process? What do you mean, process? They don't even read the bloody books. How can they proceed if they don't read?'

'Given the fundamentally patriarchal structure of the university, are you surprised that nobody reads? Tell me, how did the women in the class respond?'

'They picked their nails and played with their mobile phones.'

'You see? The female voice has been effectively silenced in this institution. Just as, in a way, Emma Bovary was silenced. Notice that Flaubert calls her *Madame* Bovary – denying her even the luxury of an identity, seeing her only as the possession of a man. Flaubert did more to oppress women than possibly any other writer.'

They had been over this before, and Elizabeth had no desire

to hear Charlotte's interesting ideas about the sexist nature of just about everything except a few medieval nuns. 'Well, anyway,' she said, pouring boiling water on to the coffee, 'at least it's a good incentive for me to finish my PhD and get a job.' The words were out before she had a chance to call them back; the idea of completion was anathema to Charlotte, who was determined to be a full-time academic for the rest of her life.

'You're miles away from completion,' she said. 'You've only been doing this for a year.'

'Nearly a year and a half.' Throwing herself into her PhD had been a welcome respite from her grief at her mother's death. 'And I don't intend to take more than three.'

'You can't be serious. How can you possibly engage with the subject in sufficient depth in three years?'

'Apart from anything else,' said Elizabeth, 'I need to start earning some money.'

'But there's teaching!' They were paid twenty-five pounds per class. 'Papers!' If, as occasionally happened, someone in the department broke into print, they were usually content with complimentary copies by way of payment.

'I need a salary.'

'There are bursaries!'

'No. A salary. A wage. I'm getting married.'

This was another sore point, as Charlotte regarded marriage as an implied criticism of everything she stood for. In the real world, thought Elizabeth, this bitter virgin would never be my friend – but here, where kind words are in such short supply, she's all I've got. The rest of the staff in the department regarded her, if they regarded her at all, as either a fool or a threat. There was a certain amount of muttering about nepotism, even though her father's professorship was in another subject in another college; it was all part of the University of London, and that was enough to get tongues wagging. Anthony Miller cast a long shadow.

Elizabeth had thought of using her mother's maiden (and professional) name – Barnard – but that would only make matters worse, as if they'd only accepted her because she was the daughter of a highly regarded, tragically dead novelist. 'Are you related to Anthony Miller?' was bad enough, but 'are you related to Susan Barnard?' would be even worse, and would entail all sorts of painful explanations about how she felt about her mother's untimely death from cancer, how she regarded her small but significant literary output, whether she was going to follow in her footsteps, if there was anything left unpublished for the critics to pick over. And, worse still, the unspoken question, 'What do you do with all the money?' For, ever since her mother's debut novel (the first of only two) had been translated to the screen, a surprise hit on both sides of the Atlantic and the launchpad for two subsequently massive Hollywood careers, the money had been coming in abundance. It all went to the Prof, but the Prof, despite their differences, was always open-handed. Elizabeth already owned a flat; all of her peers were renting. She could afford to keep house with Nick, to plan her wedding to Nick, indeed to afford the luxury of Nick at all, as he was bringing very little into the household by the time he'd spent his courier earnings on dope. The economic independence of women loomed large as a topic in her research – indeed, the tragedy of Emma Bovary would be discussed in those very terms, regarding sexual commerce as the disempowered woman's only currency – but it was something Elizabeth had never had to consider seriously outside the study.

Unless, of course, someone came and took it all away, remembered Elizabeth with a sudden chill. Tonight was the night that she would meet her new stepmother.

'What's the matter?' asked Charlotte, scrutinising Elizabeth's face. 'You look like you've seen a ghost. I'm sorry, but when I say that the entire French realist tradition is a construct of gender imperialism, I'm not having a go at you personally.'

Elizabeth realised that Charlotte had never stopped talking.

'I'm sorry,' she said. 'Miles away. I just remembered something.'

'What?'

'My father is having his new girlfriend and her daughter round for dinner tonight.'

'Your . . . what? Professor Miller has a . . . a . . .'

'A girlfriend. Yes. Shocking, isn't it? And him the head of a philosophy department. You'd have thought he could do without.'

Charlotte, who had met the Prof once or twice and had the most enormous intellectual crush on him, looked bilious. 'Well, I'm . . .' *Disappointed* was the word she should have said, but instead she said 'looking forward to hearing all about it.' In her long, lonely sessions in the archives, Charlotte allowed herself to wonder if the Prof's obvious admiration for her mind might ever develop into something more like a warm companionship. She was, after all, some years older than his daughter. There was nothing wrong with such an affection. She wouldn't expect it to be physically expressed. The mutual admiration of two great minds, drawn together by a love of words and ideas . . .

'She's a florist, apparently,' said Elizabeth. 'God only knows what they find to talk about. Although I'm afraid that talking may not be the basis of their relationship.'

'Right.' Widowhood was all very well, but the idea of sex, at least for a professor, seemed to Charlotte like a betrayal. 'Well, jolly good luck to you all.' She bundled up her papers and trudged off to teach another group of indifferent students about the wonders of medieval religious poetry. Elizabeth listened until the squeak of her well-worn walking shoes had faded down the long corridor to the seminar room.

'What does *he* know?' said Mark. 'Nothing. He's just a frustrated actor himself. They all are. Why else would they be teaching here? He knows you've got more talent than he has and he can't stand it. Wanker.'

'I don't mind that much, really,' said Rachel, fishing in her handbag for her keys. 'Colin only picks on me because he likes me.'

'Well, why don't you do something about it?'

'What, shag him? No thanks.'

'I would. He's gorgeous.'

'I thought you said he was a wanker.'

'He is. But he's a gorgeous wanker.'

'God, you're shallow. I suppose that's why we get on. Ah! Here we are.' She let them into the flat.

'You should take advantage of your looks, you know,' said Mark, following like a dog at her heels. 'If I looked like you, I'd have a different man every night.' He was currently working a high-fashion road-mender look, shaven head and stubble, rolled up shirtsleeves and pulled-down jeans, with acres of bum cleavage on show. He might have passed muster, but for the shaped eyebrows.

'Thank you, darling, I suppose that's meant to be a compliment, but I do have certain standards. And tutors are definitely off the menu.'

'Picky picky, get no dicky,' said Mark. 'If I was a girl, I'd be a complete slut. I'd have two a night, one at each end.'

'Why stop at two?' said Natasha, stumbling out of the bedroom, where she'd been sleeping off the night before. Some of Demelza Jollop's make-up was still on her face; the rest was presumably all over various pillows. 'The great advantage women have over gay men is that they have three holes. Morning, darlings!' She wove her way to the bathroom.

'Oh, she's disgusting,' said Mark. 'Mind you, she has a point. So, where are we going tonight?'

'I don't know where you're going,' said Rachel, tipping the contents of her bag into the middle of the living-room floor, 'but I'm going to meet my new daddy.'

'The professor? Well you kept that very quiet. Oh, can't we come? Please? Natasha!' he shouted, but couldn't make himself heard. 'She's meeting her new family tonight and refuses to take us with her. Come on,' he said in lower tones. 'I thought we were going to share them.'

'Another time, Mark.' Rachel started removing her make-up, dropping the used cotton wool pads on the carpet. 'Tonight I'm going to be on my best behaviour. Have you got any nail varnish remover?'

'It's in the bathroom. She'll be in there for hours.'

'Never mind.' Rachel looked at her fingernails; they were chipped, but not disastrously so. 'I'll have to go like this.'

'So who's going to be there?'

'Me and my mum.'

'Oh, the divine Anna. I love your mum.' Anna had called at the flat on various pretexts and, while Natasha couldn't stand her, Mark was her number-one fan. 'I bet she's got him just where she wants him.'

'No doubt,' said Rachel, 'if she thinks there's money in it.'

'Is he rich?'

'Rich, and infatuated,' said Rachel. 'The two qualities my mother looks for in a man.'

'Darling, does that mean you're going to be rich as well? Can we go on holiday?'

Natasha emerged from the bathroom, her dressing gown gaping. 'Holiday? Where are we going on holiday? Oh, I desperately need a holiday. After last night I need complete rest.'

'Wow, was he really that good?' asked Mark, and the spotlight shifted from Rachel's new family to Natasha's Restoration romp.

Rachel slipped out of the living room and took possession of the bathroom. She pulled her hair back and tied it in a ponytail. Her face was clean enough, but she washed it with soap and water, rubbing with a flannel to bring some colour to her cheeks. She flossed and brushed and ran her tongue over her teeth – large, regular teeth that earned her the playground nickname 'Horseface', which was marginally preferable to 'Muppet' (on account of her big mouth) or 'Twiglet' (skinny legs). Her looks were still a novelty. Some time around her sixteenth birthday, the insults had stopped and the compliments began. Rachel could see little difference between the face in the mirror and the bug-eyed, big-lipped kid of fifteen, but it was impossible to ignore the effect she had on men. They bought her drinks, stared at her in the street, begged for her number. At college they asked her for dates. She mostly held back – afraid, perhaps, that it was just another playground prank, that after she accepted they would all point and laugh and scream, 'Only joking, Muppet!'.

Tonight at least there was little danger; tonight she wanted to be liked, not adored. She brushed out her hair, dabbed the tiniest amount of eyeshadow on her upper lids and, satisfied that she looked like the girl next door, set off to pick up her mother and meet her new family.

Chapter 4

The Millers were on time; they were always on time. A table for five was booked for seven o'clock, and the Prof led his two children through the door at one minute to. They were seated immediately, and ordered drinks. Half an hour later, they were still waiting for the rest of their party.

Anna and Rachel were always late. This time, the old Peugeot had a flat tyre, and since neither mother nor daughter had a clue how to change a wheel – 'that's what men are for,' said Anna – it took them a while to find an obliging van driver who, greatly encouraged by Rachel's cleavage, had the flat off and the spare on in less than twenty minutes. All might yet have been well, but that twenty minutes gave Anna enough time to rethink her outfit, and she left Rachel waiting in the car while she threw clothes around her bedroom for half an hour and emerged, looking very pleased but not noticeably different, ready to set off.

So they arrived at the restaurant at ten to eight, by which time the Prof had sent half a dozen increasingly frosty texts. 'They're on their way,' he said, every time his children so much as raised an eyebrow. 'It's not Anna's fault, she had a puncture.'

'I hope she's not late for the wedding,' said Elizabeth, who was making rather too free with the wine; she was more nervous than she liked to admit. The prospect of having a new mother and a new sister, while appealing in theory, was fraught with danger. Supposing Anna really was a gold-digger, and intended to swindle the Prof out of his money – and, more to the point, to deprive her and Chris of their inheritance? Women who married for money were tarts, weren't they? While Elizabeth was a passionate advocate of the rights of fictional characters of a hundred years ago, she found it hard to square her beliefs with the real and present danger of a conniving stepmother and her no-doubt-grasping daughter, their beady eyes trained on the Miller family fortune. Her mother's money. *Her* money. Hers and Chris's.

'There's no wine left for our guests,' snapped the Prof, signalling to the waiter for another bottle. 'I would appreciate it if you could try to be sober when they get here.'

'*If* they get here,' said Elizabeth, burying her nose in the glass; the Prof always chose good wine, and this was no exception, something light and lemony that made one feel like celebrating. Perhaps this was how he'd wooed and won the fair Anna. Intimate dinners in expensive restaurants, laying out his wares like an ageing bowerbird attracting a hen.

'They're on their way! Chris, for God's sake,' said the Prof, turning on his son as he always did when he wanted to avoid an argument with his daughter, 'you could at least have ironed that shirt.'

Chris, who knew the routine all too well (and who, besides, had bought the shirt ready-crumpled), just said, 'Sorry, Dad.' There was no point in arguing. The Prof could win every argument – that, after all, was his job.

Just as the Prof's fingers were poised to send another glacial text, the door opened and the mood changed, as if spring had succeeded winter. Anna came first, a head of frizzy red curls, a flash of rings and a clatter of beads, a brightly coloured piece of Indian cloth threaded with silver and hung with tassels slipping off her shoulders. She waved to the Prof, who beamed in a way Elizabeth had never seen before. And it was then that every eye turned to the door, every breath was held, even the tinkling piano seemed to stop for a moment as, apparently in slow motion – but this, thought Elizabeth, must be an illusion – the most beautiful young woman she had ever seen in her life walked into the restaurant, a point of stillness and grace in Anna's clashing, jangling wake. She stood in the doorway, her lips slightly parted, looking around with half-closed eyes, as if she were short-sighted (too vain to wear glasses, wondered Elizabeth) and then, when she identified the Millers, opening her mouth in a smile.

Such a smile does not come along often. It was big – almost too big for the face. The lips formed a perfect elongated heart shape, framing bright white regular teeth, so clean and shiny they could almost be dentures. Behind them was a tempting, velvety suggestion of tongue, of soft tissue, of warm, wet pink-ness. Elizabeth, the Professor, even Chris could hardly fail to respond; Rachel was sexually attractive to an unprecedented degree, and had she not been so apparently unaware of the fact, her very entrance into the room might have seemed like a form of aggression. And then she broke the spell, ran her fingers through her hair – dark, glossy hair that fell like the tail of a well-groomed pony – and joined her mother at the table.

Anna was talking nineteen to the dozen, recounting the saga of the puncture, their timely rescue by some knight of the highway, the terrible traffic up the Finchley Road, interspersing it all with greetings and introductions and little remarks about the restaurant, but nobody was listening. Her voice was drowned out by the white noise of Rachel's beauty.

'Hi,' said Rachel, and suddenly all seemed clear again, 'I'm sorry we're late.' She fixed the Prof with her deep blue eyes – blue eyes with brown hair, it's so unfair, thought Elizabeth – and held out a hand. 'I'm Rachel. I've been looking forward to meeting you so much.'

The Prof, still standing, didn't know what to do, and stared like a startled rabbit at the hand, as if it might be dangerous. For a moment, Elizabeth thought of stories she had read in the papers about daughters who stole their mother's boyfriends.

'How do you do,' said the Prof, snapping out of it. 'I'm Tony. This is my daughter, Elizabeth, and my son, Christopher.'

Anna sat next to the Prof, of course, between him and his son. Rachel, whether by accident of design, was between Elizabeth and Chris. She immediately turned her attention to her sister-to-be.

'Mum's incapable of getting anywhere on time,' she whispered, while Anna made loud appreciative noises about the Prof's choice of wine. 'I'm sorry we're so late. You must think we're awful.'

Well, one out of two ain't bad, thought Elizabeth, who had taken an instant dislike to Anna, but was finding it hard, despite her best efforts, to resist the charms of the daughter.

'She had to go back in to change,' said Rachel, 'but as usual, she's managed to make herself look like a drag queen at a jumble sale.'

Chris sniggered into his drink, and Rachel leaned towards him. 'Check out the back of her dress,' she said. 'The price tag's still on the label. Sale, of course.'

'Well,' Anna said brightly, 'isn't this nice. All the family together.' She raised her glass. 'Here's to us,' she said, and took a big gulp without waiting for the ritual chinking. She's more nervous than she's letting on, thought Elizabeth, and well she might be, the old harridan. She looks like Colette on a bad day. How did she manage to produce such a daughter?

Something by way of a response was needed, but the Prof seemed to be struck dumb, and so Elizabeth stepped into the breach. 'Thank you very much, Anna, and it's wonderful to meet you both. We've been looking forward to it, too, haven't we, Chris?'

'Yeah,' mumbled Chris, who had just caught sight of the sale label as Anna rearranged her wrap, and was turning a nasty shade of purple. Rachel was pinching him under the table, the two of them acting like children.

The Prof was still goggling and smiling. Anna, on the other hand, was staring coolly at Elizabeth through those over-made-up eyes, and for all the blobs of mascara, the lines of eyeshadow leaching up into the wrinkles, it was clear that this was not a woman to be taken lightly. She was assessing Elizabeth, weighing her up, perhaps doing some kind of SWOT analysis.

'And what do you do, Elizabeth?' she asked, tilting her head to one side for a well-practised 'interested' look.

'I'm doing a PhD.'

'Oh.' Anna sounded dismayed. 'I never know what to ask next. In what, or on what? Does it matter?' She addressed the question to the Prof, who blinked as if just awoken from sleep.

'Sorry?'

'Does one do a PhD *in* something or *on* something, darling?'
Darling?

Elizabeth didn't wait for an answer. 'I'm researching the influence of early feminist thought on the French realist novelists of the nineteenth and early twentieth century,' she said, but before she'd finished, the Prof said:

'Interesting question. Both, I suppose, would be applicable. One researches a subject, so it is *on* something, at least we must hope so. But one is attached to a department, and thus *in* it, although many of my PhD students are in so infrequently that one wonders . . .'

'I'm in the English department at Queen's, even though my area of specialism is French, but I'm teaching right across the curriculum . . .'

'Queen's? That's not where you are, is it, Tony?'

'No, I'm at Royal.'

'How confusing. I get so muddled.' Anna rearranged her beads, and looked up at the Prof with a little-girl-lost look.

'It doesn't really matter,' said the Prof, to whom it mattered a great deal; he'd lectured both his offspring a thousand times on the relative merits of the London colleges. 'Royal and Queen's are both excellent institutions.'

'I love queens,' whispered Rachel to Chris, setting him off on another giggling fit, 'don't you?'

As Chris shook with laughter at her side, Anna looked up adoringly at the Prof, and the Prof beamed generally at the entire table, Rachel thought that this was going to be easier than she had feared. The men she could manage, provided her mother didn't drink too much and make a fool of herself. It was the daughter she would have to work on.

A serious-looking woman, her age difficult to guess – could be thirty, except that didn't quite work with a teenage brother. Could be twenty. Dressed badly, without confidence, from the high street. Hair badly cut, doing nothing for her rather round face. Intelligence in the eyes, and good manners, but something hard and angry underneath. She would not be a pushover. Rachel would have to try harder with this one.

'French novels?' she said, turning from brother to sister. 'I loved *Madame Bovary*. Is that one of them?'

She had hit the bullseye with a single shot.

'Oh, it's *the* one,' said Elizabeth, turning grateful eyes on her. 'It's the book that got me interested in the first place. I must have read it ten times, and it still startles me.'

'Yes,' said Rachel, who had seen a recent television adaptation and very much fancied the actor who played Léon. She wondered how anyone could be 'startled' by a book, but she caught the idiom. 'It's so audacious,' she said; 'audacious' was a word frequently bandied about at drama college. 'I mean, at the time, it must have been . . .'

'Oh it was,' said Elizabeth, who appeared to be refocusing her eyes. Rachel was used to this. When people met her, they saw nothing but her looks. A few carefully chosen words of more than two syllables usually prompted this kind of re-appraisal. *Perhaps she's not just a pretty face . . .*

'I'd love to play Emma,' said Rachel, finding the name and hoping it was right. She could see from the movement of Elizabeth's eyebrows – sadly unplucked – that it was.

'Of course,' said Elizabeth, 'you're an actress.'

'Only in training,' said Rachel. 'I've got a lot to learn, as my tutors keep telling me.'

'Where are you?'

'Alderman's.'

'Alderman's!' She sounded surprised, damn her, as if she'd expected Rachel to say, 'I'm doing the occasional night class at an adult education institute'.

'Yes. I was very lucky to get in,' said Rachel, who had breezed through her entrance audition, and in truth had earned a place the moment the selection panel saw her photograph. 'It's a very good school.'

'One of the best, I believe. Well done.'

'It's a start.'

'So you really want to be an actress, do you?'

'Oh yes,' said Rachel, who wanted to be an actress only because her looks seemed to demand it. 'It's my passion.'

'I wish my students were more like you. They seem to enrol in degree courses by default, because it's expected of them. Only today I was teaching a class . . .'

Elizabeth's face stiffened as she talked; perhaps, thought Rachel, she doesn't have many friends. Perhaps I can thaw her out a bit. With a bit of a makeover, she might even be quite fun. Not the same kind of fun as Natasha and Mark, but quieter, softer, more thoughtful. A welcome break from the chaos of the flat. She'll have to talk about something other than books, of course, but that can be arranged.

Then Rachel heard the words 'my fiancé', and started paying more attention.

'Oh! You're engaged? How exciting!'

'Yes. We're getting married in November.'

'Ah.' That explained some of the bitterness; she was being upstaged. 'And who's the lucky man?'

'Nick. You'll love Nick. Everyone loves Nick.'

'Well, I can't wait to meet him. What does he do?'

Elizabeth dreaded this question. 'He's a photographer, really, but he's doing all sorts of different stuff at the moment.'

'Wow. A photographer.' Rachel gushed like a fan. 'I love photography.'

The waiter was hovering. Nobody had even looked at a menu. 'Oh, you order for us, Tony darling,' said Anna, looking up at her husband-to-be. 'You do it so well.'

The Prof, who prided himself on such things, rattled off a list of dishes without reference to the menu. The waiter nodded approvingly.

'So,' said Anna brightly, when the waiter had gone. 'Have you asked them?'

'Er, no,' said the Prof. He rarely said 'er'.

'Right. Here goes, then.' She clasped her hands in front of her and leaned forward. 'We'd very much like it if you'd all come to our wedding in May.'

'May?' said Elizabeth. 'That's only a few weeks away.'

'Yes,' said Anna. 'Isn't it marvellous? He's absolutely swept me off my feet.'

'But . . .'

But I'm getting married in November, how dare you spoil my plans?

'I know, there's so much to organise, and that's why I'm . . . that's why *we're* hoping that you'll all pitch in and lend a hand. First of all, obviously, we need witnesses, and who better than our two lovely girls?'

'You mean . . . us?'

'Of course. It won't be a massive ceremony or anything, just something very simple at the registry office, we thought, didn't we?'

'Yes,' said the Prof, looking uncomfortable.

'Maybe twenty or so friends and family. Just the inner circle,' said Anna. 'But then a lovely party. Wasn't that the idea, Tony?'

'At the house, of course.'

'*At the house?*' said Elizabeth.

'Where else? We've got plenty of space. And the garden, if it's fine.'

'I see.' The house where my mother lived. Where the last party we held was after her funeral.

'And then, of course, a little honeymoon.' She lowered her voice. 'He's whisking me off to Paris for a long weekend. How romantic is that?'

Not very, thought Elizabeth; we're having two weeks in Cuba.

'And then, in July, when everyone's broken up . . . Well, you'd better say it, Tony. It was your lovely idea.'

The Prof swirled a glass in his hand, and stared into the whirlpool of wine. 'We'd like you all to come with us.'

'Where?' said Chris and Rachel together, and immediately started sniggering again.

'Cape Cod,' said the Prof.

Cape Cod – where they had been on family holidays when Elizabeth and Chris were small.

'You remember Cape Cod, don't you, Elizabeth?'

'Of course.' Elizabeth could feel her lips compressing, but could not help herself. The whole of the peninsula was redolent with memories of her childhood, her mother. 'Lovely.'

'I hoped you'd be pleased,' he said, looking relieved. It seemed unfair to rain on his parade.

'Yes. It would be lovely. Of course, I'll have to see if the dates work. I mean, I'll have to ask Nick.'

'I'm sure he can get the time off,' said the Prof. Rachel intercepted a look between father and daughter. There were cracks in the family facade, secrets to be discovered, confidences exchanged – perhaps on holiday? She had only known her new family for twenty minutes and already her things were falling into place. Holidays, confidences, laughter and wine . . . Perhaps her mother had found the right man after all. Their luck was changing.

The waiter arrived with a steaming dish of mussels, and the party addressed themselves to the business of eating.

Chapter 5

As the spotlight shifted from Elizabeth and Nick to Anna and the Prof, it was very hard not to feel upstaged. Elizabeth fought it, and ploughed ahead with the arrangements for her own wedding, but somehow the sparkle had gone. The dress she'd chosen, which seemed like a classic at the time, now looked frumpy as it hung in the wardrobe. The venue, a club in Notting Hill where Nick occasionally DJ-ed, seemed like a provincial pick-up joint. She never questioned her choice of husband – loving Nick was the bedrock of her life, the one truth that could never be doubted – but even he couldn't stop going on about the all-expenses-paid holiday to Cape Cod, which seemed to interest him much more than the fortnight in Cuba they'd booked for their honeymoon.

'Babe, a free holiday is a free holiday, no matter where it comes from,' he said, as she wrestled with a leg of lamb that seemed to be all fat. 'Never look a gift horse in the mouth.' He put his arms around her waist, kissed her on the back of the neck, which was rather inconvenient as she was attempting to get the joint in the oven. Two key members of the wedding party – her 'best woman' Kate, and his best man Alan – were coming for dinner, and she wanted to show that everything was still perfect. But the meat was fatty, and the pastry for the apple pie, which required a cool touch, refused to roll out properly under her hot hands. The finished result would look more like crumble.

She wriggled out of Nick's grasp, and got a blast of hot, smoky air from the open oven door. 'There,' she said, 'that's in. Now I can relax.'

'You need to, love. You're a bundle of nerves.'

'Glass of wine?'

'Thought you'd never ask.'

He threw himself on the sofa – it was a combined kitchen, dining room and lounge, far from ideal, but better than nothing – and waited to be served.

'What's she like?'

'Who?'

'Your new mum, of course. Would I like her?'

'I don't think I've got too much to worry about.'

'And the daughter?'

This was the question Elizabeth had been dreading. 'Revoltingly pretty. And she knows it.'

'Oh yeah? I'll be the judge of that.'

She sat on his knee, looked into his hooded eyes. 'If I didn't know better, Nick Sharkey, I'd think you were rather too interested in your new sister-in-law.'

'Nah,' said Nick. 'You're the only girl for me, sweetheart.' His accent plummeted down the social scale; Nick rather fancied himself as her piece of rough, despite the fact that his father was a civil servant and his mother the youngest daughter of a once-wealthy county family. They'd divorced years ago, which was convenient for Nick; it didn't suit him to be the well-educated son of a cash-strapped middle-class family. He preferred to play the plucky urchin who'd pulled himself up by charm and talent.

'And don't you forget it, my lad,' said Elizabeth, who was happy to go along with the illusion. It was Nick's laddishness that first attracted her when they met, she a final-year student still reeling from her mother's death, he the promising young photographer that she'd met at a gallery show in Shoreditch. He swept her off her feet with his dropped Hs and glottal stops, and by the time she met his mother – a thin, birdlike woman with the strangled vowels of the Royal Family – it was too late. She loved him. Within a month of meeting, they were inseparable, within a year they were living together in the flat her father had paid for, and now they were months away from marriage. The Prof suggested they should wait until Nick 'found his feet', but Elizabeth told him not to be so old-fashioned, she could support them both. To herself she admitted that if they waited until Nick found his feet, she'd be looking at a very lengthy engagement, and while she never doubted his talent for photography, she was well aware that days went by in a haze of dope smoke without a shutter being clicked. Nick's interest in work waned while she was paying the bills. One day he'd surprise them all, she thought, or at least hoped. But for now she loved him with the passion of first love, and could hardly complain that he spent his days resting when he had so much energy for her at night.

'Cape Cod,' he said, running a hand along her thigh. 'Supposed to be posh, isn't it?'

'It is posh.'

'Sounds nice.'

'Oh, you'll love it.' That sounded sarcastic, she realised a little too late. She had to be careful to avoid any suggestion that Nick was a parasite. 'I mean,' she said, in a brighter voice, 'the landscapes are fantastic. You'll get some wonderful photos.'

'Yeah,' he said, but the hand had gone from the thigh, and he was groping in his pocket for his rolling gear.

Please don't get stoned before dinner, she thought, trudging back to the kitchen to start work on the potatoes. Nick strolled out to the garden, and lit up.

Kate arrived first, took off her coat, put on a pinny and started helping with the vegetables. Kate was a cross between a surrogate mother and an older sister, someone Elizabeth had known most of her life, and on whose honest advice she could always rely. She'd been a student of her mother's when Susan was still teaching creative writing, before the success of the first novel and the long hiatus that preceded the second. Kate, twenty years younger than her mentor and ten years older than Elizabeth, started as a student, became an acolyte, an assistant, a sort-of-manager and then, during the hasty organisation necessitated by Susan's illness, her literary executor. Along the way she also became, by necessity, a friend of the family. It was Kate who kept things together when Susan was dying, who drove Elizabeth to and from the hospital and, later, to the registrar's office, the undertaker's, the cemetery. Kate handled the press and the publishers, appointed a new agent and, in the years since Susan's death, made sure that the books remained in print and profitable. At one point, Kate was at the house so much that Elizabeth wondered if she might soon be calling her Mummy, but she remained nothing more, and nothing less, than a loyal friend. She was the first to congratulate Elizabeth on her degree, on her postgrad place, on her engagement. Kate was reliable and solid, in every sense of the word, rather thick round the middle and plainly dressed. Above all, she was cheerful – and in a family where feelings were disguised and their expression avoided, she was a breath of fresh air.

'Where's Nick?' she asked, whipping the skins off carrots with deft strokes of the peeler. 'Working?'

'He's in the garden.'

'Oh,' said Kate. 'Gardening. That's nice.' Elizabeth couldn't see her face, but assumed she was smiling.

'How's Neil?' Kate's husband did something very sensible with software, and the children, four and one, were happy, affectionate little creatures without a hang-up between them. Kate managed to feed them, keep the house clean, manage the Susan Barnard estate and, in between times, knock out a couple of extremely successful novels that were as far removed from her mentor's rarefied literary output as possible.

'Oh, he's fine. We're all fine. I sometimes think your mother would be disappointed with the way I turned out,' said Kate. 'I'm so ordinary.' Not like Susan Barnard, who, the critics all agreed, was extraordinary, whose 'searing' psychological account of a woman who grapples with the idea of sexually abusing her own father went on to be a 'shattering' Hollywood film and sold 'staggering' amounts. Whose erratic approach to motherhood meant that her children adored her, worshipped her even, but sometimes didn't actually like her. Whose husband felt shut out by her intense interior life, and took refuge in work and – if the whispered rows Elizabeth had overheard were to be believed – in affairs.

'I'm sure she'd be very proud of you,' said Elizabeth, although she knew it wasn't true. Susan would have hated Kate's books, their glossy covers and jaunty narratives. If something wasn't about Susan Barnard, she wasn't much interested. She could be fiercely, impulsively affectionate when the mood took her, but it took her less and less in later life, and not at all after the cancer got a grip. When she lay dying, she shrank from her children's touch.

'Anyway, I'm very proud of *you*,' said Kate. 'You're doing so well. A good job and a lovely man. And a wedding on the way. I can't wait.'

Good old Kate, thought Elizabeth. At least she has the good manners to be excited. They discussed the wedding plans for a while, and very soon the vegetables were peeled and chopped and sitting neatly in pans of salted water. Things seemed to go more efficiently when Kate was around.

'So,' she said, pouring them both a glass of the wine she'd brought, and ignoring the fact that Nick, whose job this should have been, was still 'gardening'. 'Have you met them?'

'Who?' asked Elizabeth, knowing perfectly well.

'Your new family, of course. Come on, I'm dying to hear all about it.'

'Seems that's all anyone's interested in.'

'Of course! You're not jealous of the attention, are you, Liz?'

Elizabeth laughed as if it was the most ridiculous idea in the world. 'Well, Anna's all right. Not at all the kind of person I would have imagined my father going for, but there you are.'

'Clever?'

'No, not particularly.'

'Good. It'll do Tony no harm to have a sensible, cheerful wife who doesn't have her head in the clouds. No disrespect to Susan, but there's only room for one intellectual in a marriage.'

'She's certainly cheerful,' said Elizabeth, thinking of Anna's gaudy outfit and her loud, cackling laughter. 'And she puts a smile on the old man's face.'

'Thank God. And the daughter?'

'Ah.' Elizabeth didn't have a ready response to this one. She'd approached the idea of having a sister with a mixture of distaste and trepidation, as if this interloper had no right to be part of the family. But after a couple of hours in Rachel's company, Elizabeth had thawed, and by the end of lunch, both she and Chris were eating out of her hand. She was beautiful, spontaneous, surprisingly awkward and showed a very flattering sense of awe towards Elizabeth's academic achievements. 'She's nice enough,' she said, wondering why she had to be so mealy-mouthed. 'Time will tell.'

'Are you seeing her again?' asked Kate, but then the doorbell rang.

'That'll be Alan,' said Elizabeth, hurriedly putting her drink down, straightening her skirt and touching the back of her hair. Kate watched her with a half-smile. 'What?'

'He has that effect on everyone, I suppose.'

'I don't know what you mean.'

Nick beat her to it, and from the entrance hall she could hear the booming voices of male bonding.

'Mate!'

'Mate!'

Nick ushered Alan into the kitchen. 'Here he is, ladies. The one you've all been waiting for, Mr Alan Southgate.'

Standing in the doorway together, the pair of them looked like an advertising executive's idea of twenty-first-century laddishness. Nick was all dark skin and stubble, floppy hair and open shirt, revealing smooth muscles. Alan was crisp and neat, his hair freshly barbered, his chin recently shaved, the strong neck disappearing in the collar of a dazzling white shirt. When they smiled, Elizabeth half-expected a product name to appear in front of her eyes. Whatever it was, she would have bought it.

'Elizabeth,' said Alan, stepping forward with open arms. 'As gorgeous as ever.' They embraced, but his lips did not touch her face. 'Kate.' He took her by the upper arms, and made kissing noises near each of her ears. 'How lovely to see you.'

'Lovely to see you, too, Alan.'

'Come on, mate, I want to show you this bike I've found on e-Bay,' said Nick, grabbing beer from the fridge. 'It's wicked.' They pounded up the stairs, leaving the women gazing after them.

'Sure you chose the right one?' said Kate, noticing her friend's flushed cheeks and sparkling eyes. 'It's not too late to change.'

'Don't be ridiculous. Besides, any chance I ever had of being Mrs Alan Southgate is long gone.'

'Really?'

'Of course. Why would you say a thing like that?'

'I sometimes get the impression that Alan is the loyal swain type. Standing aside because he wants you to be happy. Because he believes that you don't care for him in that way.'

'That's ridiculous,' said Elizabeth, busying herself with the oven. 'Alan has his pick of the most beautiful women in the world.'

'He might like you for other reasons.'

'I don't know whether to be flattered by that, or offended.'

Kate held up her hands. 'All right! I'm only joking.'

'I hope so,' said Elizabeth, and they talked of other things. But it was not so easily put aside. Alan's success was one of the many things that threw Nick's underachievement into stark relief.

Elizabeth always knew Alan would go far, ever since she met him at university, five years ago. It wasn't just his looks, although at eighteen he already looked like a movie star. He had brains as well as beauty, and they became friends through an intense love of literature. Elizabeth couldn't quite believe it when the best-looking man in the college sought her out, and for a whole term she waited for him to make a move – in vain. When he started dating another girl, she was disappointed but relieved; their friendship continued all through that relationship, and the next, and the next. Alan never confided in Elizabeth, and she never asked for details. It was this, perhaps, that attracted him as much as anything. By the time they were twenty-one, and both on their way to first-class honours, Alan was so ridiculously chiselled that women, men, children and dogs became playful and skittish in his presence. He was already a star of the drama society, and went straight from university to the Bristol

Old Vic to train as an actor, where it quickly became apparent that he was as talented as he was handsome. Within weeks he had an agent, and before the first year of his course was over he'd been given special leave to appear in a First World War movie that was being shot in Shepperton. In uniform as a heroic, doomed young officer, his brown hair cut short, parted at the side and slicked down, he looked too beautiful to live. He died halfway through the movie; audiences spent the remaining hour wondering if he'd really been as beautiful as he seemed, and went back to find out. The movie was a hit, and Alan could have gone straight to Hollywood to spend ten years starring in romcoms. Instead, he completed his course, walked into a job at the Royal Shakespeare Company and resisted further film work until he was good and ready.

Which was round about now.

In the years since they left college, Elizabeth was surprised that her friendship with Alan showed no sign of tailing off. He'd already been linked with some of the most beautiful actresses in the land, and was occasionally photographed on red carpets with very famous women from across the Atlantic, but somehow he always found time for Elizabeth. He invited her to all his first nights, to the dressing room, even out to dinner after the show. He kept in touch with postcards and emails when he was on tour. Between jobs, he organised trips to the seaside or dinner in town, always his treat. By rights, Elizabeth thought, she should have been relegated to the status of fan/former friend, by now – but Kate was right. Alan was loyal. When Nick appeared on the scene, Alan went out of his way to be his friend, too. He took an interest in Nick's plans and, more to the point, seemed to believe in them. Not all of Elizabeth's friends had been so accommodating. And when it was first suggested that Alan might like to be best man, he accepted eagerly. Nick was flattered; none of his friends had an international profile.

He's doing it for me, thought Elizabeth – and perhaps she was right, but if Alan was just playing a role, pretending to be Nick's best mate for the sake of appearances, he was doing a very convincing job of it. She could hear them upstairs, laughing and chatting over Nick's computer, and she did not want Kate's insinuations to spoil the picture.

Dinner was fine, as long as Nick was eating. He shovelled the food into his mouth in huge forkfuls, his cheeks stretched, his throat working as he swallowed, his hands always occupied with cutting and tearing the next chunk. While Nick gorged – and not an ounce of fat on him, thought Elizabeth – the others talked. There was much to catch up on: the wedding plans, of course, and news of the Prof's intentions, and then there was Alan's exciting new project, an episode of a long-running TV crime drama in which he would play a psychologically disturbed young man who attempts to set fire to a tower block. There was news of Kate's children – the older could read already, and the younger was walking – and of her books, which sold as fast as she could write them. Between the three of them, they had enough news to keep going for hours. But then Nick laid down his knife and fork, stifled a burp in his napkin and then, slumping in his chair and crossing his arms over his chest, proceeded to scowl and sigh.

'So, Nick,' said Alan, always quick to pick up a cue, 'how are your plans coming together? Anything to report?'

This was the point in the evening at which things could go either way. Nick could respond positively, tell the company about his current photographic project, and do it with such enthusiasm that they left half-believing that he would one day break out of his dope-induced lethargy and actually become the breadwinner in the family. Or he could respond negatively, taking each well-intentioned question as a veiled insult, and spoil everyone's appetite for dessert.

Elizabeth put on an expression of cheerful optimism, as if to say, 'Oh, there's such jolly lots to tell!', and tried to catch Nick's eye. He avoided hers, and the seesaw lurched downwards.

'No,' he said, lowering his brows so that his eyes were almost invisible.

'There's that job you're doing for Geoff and Paul,' volunteered Elizabeth.

'Yeah. Great. Painting and decorating. Thanks for reminding me.' This was not how he'd pitched it to her; back then, it was 'visual merchandising', and something Nick thought he might be rather good at. Now it sounded like the kind of cash-in-hand gig that only the desperate would take.

'I didn't mean it like that,' said Elizabeth, feeling suddenly sick, but Kate came to her rescue with a change of subject. 'You know, Elizabeth, you should try your hand at a bit of journalism. The money's not bad, and you'd be so good at it.'

Nick opened his mouth to speak – he may have been sulking, but that didn't mean he didn't want to be the centre of attention – but one stern look from Kate was enough to shut him up.

'Oh, I don't know,' said Elizabeth, 'I don't think the department would . . .'

Nick got up, pushing back his chair, and slouched out of the room. 'Going for a smoke,' he mumbled, which meant a joint.

'Okay, darling,' Elizabeth said brightly, trying not to see the glance that passed between Kate and Alan.

'But, really,' said Kate, 'you've got to start looking beyond your PhD. I hate to say this, but the world is full of people with

PhDs and very little else. If you're going to start earning some decent money . . .'

'I was hoping that they might actually ask me to stay on,' said Elizabeth. 'I like the teaching,' she lied.

'I could put you in touch with a couple of editors.'

'I don't know.' There was a wobble in her voice, and it wasn't caused by professional indecisiveness.

Alan got up, and made a tactical retreat. 'I fancy a pint,' he said, as if nothing had happened. 'I'll see if I can drag Nick down the Red Lion. We won't be long.'

He left, and Elizabeth started fussing with plates. When the table was clear and the dishwasher loaded, she poured more wine and rejoined Kate at the table.

They sat in silence for a moment, drinking and thinking.

'I'm only going to say this once,' said Kate, 'and then I promise to shut up on the subject for ever. But you are absolutely sure, aren't you, that you want to marry Nick? I mean, really marry him, for richer for poorer, till death do you part, and all that jazz.'

'Yes.'

'Because if you had any doubts about the subject, now is the time to . . .'

'I'm sure, thank you.'

'Right.'

They drank in unison, each counting the ticking of the clock, wondering who would break the silence first.

'Well,' said Kate, after thirty seconds had passed, 'I'm very glad to hear it. Nick's a wonderful man and I'm sure you're going to be very happy together.'

'Me too,' said Elizabeth, forcing her mind to focus on the image of Nick's naked body moving above hers, his lips on her neck, his legs pushing hers apart.

'And while the boys are down the boozer,' said Kate, 'perhaps you and I can discuss what you want to do for your hen night. No, don't look at me like that. You're having a hen night, whatever your stuck-up colleagues think about it. If they don't like it, don't invite them.'

'As long as there aren't any male strippers,' said Elizabeth.

'Strippers! It had never crossed my mind. But now you come to mention it . . .'

Chapter 6

'So what's she like?'

'I don't know. Ordinary.'

'Ordinary? Yuk! I bet she's fat.'

'No, she's not particularly fat, as such.'

'Oh, stop being kind,' said Natasha, gluing on a second pair of false eyelashes. 'She's a blob.'

'She's not.' Rachel laughed, trying not to smudge the lipstick she'd just applied. 'She's just . . . curvy.'

'Hey, Mark!' Natasha shouted, a mascara wand poised in mid-air, ready to cast an evil spell, 'the new stepsister is a fatty!'

'Shut up, Natasha! She's not!'

'Oh God,' said Mark, coming into the living room in a T-shirt so tight you could see what he'd had for dinner, 'trust you to marry into an ugly family.'

'I'm not marrying anyone. Anyway, who says they're ugly?'

'Go on,' said Natasha, viciously stabbing the wand into the tube, 'I bet they are. Ugly, ordinary, boring, ghastly people.' She applied the mascara with a whipping movement of the wrist, emphasising each word. 'Not.' Whip. 'Like.' Whip. 'Us.'

'The son's kind of cute.'

A cute son was almost as interesting as an ugly daughter; more, potentially. 'How old is he, is he fit, would he like me?' asked Mark, joining the girls at the mirror and hunting through the piles of cosmetics for some concealer.

'He's younger than us.'

'I can do young. Go on.'

'Curly blond hair. Big blue eyes with long eyelashes.'

'Like mine?' said Natasha, batting her falsies; you could feel the breeze a yard away.

'Darling, there's nothing left of yours, just stumps,' said Mark. 'If you ever left the house without make-up, people would flee in terror.'

'Good job I never do, then.'

'Go on about the son. When do I get to meet him?'

'Not until I've got him entirely under my spell, thank you very much. I don't want you muscling in on my territory.'

'God, you're so selfish. Oh shit,' said Mark, 'what colour is this stuff? Terracotta?'

'It's for tanned skin, you stupid poof,' said Natasha. 'Now you look like you've got impetigo. Not a good look.'

'Got any wet wipes?'

'Just put it all over your face, darling.'

'It's concealer.'

'Problem?'

'Oh fuck off,' said Mark, spitting into a tissue and dabbing at the orange blobs under his eyes. 'I hope it's going to be dark at this party.'

'What makes you think anyone's going to be looking at you?' Natasha took a swig from a half bottle of vodka, wiped lipstick from the rim and passed it to Rachel. 'Come on. Time for lift-off.'

'Haven't we got any tonic?'

'Tonic?' Natasha looked mortally offended. 'We don't have tonic in this household, darling. Nobody has malaria.'

'But I don't like neat vodka . . .'

'Oh, please.' She shoved the bottle at Rachel's mouth. 'Take it and drink it. Unless you think you're better than we are all of a sudden. With your *new family*.'

'All right.' Rachel sipped.

'Take a swig! Or are we suddenly too grand now that our new daddy is a professor?'

Rachel rolled her eyes, and tipped the bottle back. Vodka ran down her cheeks and chin, burned her tongue, and slipped down her throat. She shuddered, and swallowed.

'That's better. I can't stand lightweights.' Natasha was applying another coat of lipstick. 'Darling, will there be any drugs at this party?'

'Of course,' said Mark. 'You don't think I'd invite you to a party without drugs, do you? My friends have class.'

'Class A, I hope. I'm absolutely desperate' – Natasha put a tissue between her lips, pressing them together, blotting – 'for a big fat line of coke.'

'You just had one. Our last one.'

'That was hours ago, darling. Mama needs more.'

'God, you're turning into such an *addict*,' said Mark, taking the bottle. 'You want to watch yourself. Nobody loves a junkie.'

'I'm not a junkie. I'm a society cocaine fiend.'

'Without the money to do it properly, unfortunately.'

'Well? With looks like mine, a girl doesn't need money.' Natasha checked herself in the mirror – she looked, by now, like late-period Carol Channing – and liked what she saw. 'Right. Face ready. Time to dress. I'm doing bugle beads tonight. Madly flapper.'

'Mad old slapper,' said Mark, under his breath, and caught Rachel's eye in the mirror. 'It's not fancy dress,' he said out loud.

'Darling,' said Natasha, 'every party is fancy dress. Life is fancy dress. Come on. It's a DUO. Let's all go Roaring Twenties. Bright Young Things. Vile Bodies.'

'Nothing vile about my body,' said Mark, holding his stomach in and admiring his contours in the mirror. 'As some lucky man is going to find out tonight.'

'What are you wearing, Rachel?'

'This.' She gestured down at a plum-coloured velvet top, cut low at the neck, and short, tight black skirt.

'Oh,' said Natasha, her mouth turned down in disapproval, 'I assumed that was just your getting-ready look.'

'You don't look nearly enough like a common prostitute for Natasha's liking,' said Mark. 'She wants everyone to dress as if they're on the game.'

'You certainly do,' said Natasha. 'You couldn't look more available if you stuck a red light on the end of it.'

'Well?' said Mark, flexing. 'I am available. Extremely available.'

'Come on, darling,' said Natasha. 'At least put on a pair of fishnets or something. It's a party, not a funeral.'

Rachel rummaged in a pile of lingerie, wondering what kind of funerals Natasha had been to, and eventually came up with what appeared to be a pair of fishnet tights. She held them to her nose and sniffed; they seemed clean enough, in that, like everything in the flat, they smelled of cigarette smoke.

'Will these do?'

'I suppose they'll have to. Someone zip me up. Come on. Let's get a move on – pharmaceuticals await.'

The party was somewhere around the back of Kings Cross station, in a large eerie mansion that was earmarked for demolition. Once upon a time it had been a gracious home, possibly the venue of just the sort of bright young parties that Natasha dreamed of attending; now, with the last owners long gone, it had become a temporary venue, the walls covered in graffiti, the stair carpets ripped and sticky, the toilets insanitary beyond belief. Nobody minded much. You could piss in the street or out of a window, and nobody had eaten enough in the last forty-eight hours to pass solids. Drug use was so prevalent that you could simply chop out a line on any flat surface and consume it in public. If you insisted on privacy for more intimate acts – and not everyone did – there were dozens of rooms upstairs where once, perhaps, children and servants slept. Now they were places of assignation, some lit romantically by candle stumps, others by orange sodium lamps shining in through broken window panes. One more really good party might save the developers the trouble and expense of demolishing the place themselves.

'Oh, this is boring,' said Natasha, reclining on a filthy old couch as if it were a Second Empire chaise longue and she a *grande horizontale.* 'Someone say something *amusing.'*

'You've had too much coke, darling,' said Mark, perched on the arm and sipping champagne from a plastic cup. 'You're becoming jaded.'

'Jaded. Yes, I rather like that. Jaded. I think it suits me.' She put an arm behind her head and exhaled smoke through her nose. 'Let's go somewhere else.'

'Not yet. I have prospects.'

'Ooh! Where!'

'Don't stare. Over there by the door. Tall. Red T-shirt. Jeans.'

'The bald one?'

'Shaved, not bald.'

'Oh, aren't they all? Get up close, you'll see that stubble is drawn on with an eyebrow pencil. He's bald as a coot. Fifty if he's a day.'

'Oh fuck off.' Mark smiled sweetly. 'He's looking over. Don't embarrass me.'

'Coo-eee!' Natasha waved a little finger. 'There. Now he's coming to talk to us. I don't know what you'd do without me.'

The bald man approached, smiled weakly and continued to the bar.

'You put him off!'

'Please! You can do that all by yourself.'

'I was doing very nicely until you started coo-eeing.'

'Well, then, follow him! Go and talk to him! Tell him I've got mental problems and you're my carer. He'll like that, he'll think you're nice.'

'Oh shit. He's talking to someone else. Let's go. You're right, this is boring. Where's Rachel?'

'Over there. Surrounded by a throng of men.'

'God damn it, how does she do it?' said Mark. She makes no effort at all.'

'Rachel, in case you hadn't noticed it, is exquisitely beautiful. Next to her, I feel like an absolute hag.'

'You are an absolute hag. To be precise, an absolute fag hag. Come on. Let's go to Soho.'

'Not again. Why do we always have to go to Soho?'

'Where else is there?'

'I sometimes wonder,' said Natasha, and this time the dis-illusionment in her voice was not entirely feigned, 'if this is really *all there is.*'

Mark finished his champagne, crumpled the plastic cup in his fist and tossed it over a shoulder. 'Isn't it enough? Let's go.'

One of Natasha's false eyelashes was starting to peel off, hanging diagonally from its remaining patch of glue, but she didn't notice. The effect was to make her look even more drunk than she already was.

'Darling, we're going,' she said, laying a hand on Rachel's shoulder. The six handsome, well-dressed men who surrounded her barely gave Natasha a glance. 'Or would you rather stay? Hi. I'm Natasha.' Not much response. 'Hello! Yes, over here!' She waved. 'Another person in the room!' They were looking now. The eyelash detached itself, and landed on her bosom. People stared. 'That's better. Rachel, darling, we're going on. Supper in Soho, perhaps a night club. Will you join us? Or are you . . .' She gestured around the circle. All six men tried to look a little taller, a little better-looking.

'Oh, no, of course I'll come.'

'Where are you going?'

'I'll give you a lift.'

'Sounds like fun.'

'A lift? That would be very kind. Have you got room for my friends?'

The volunteer driver looked crestfallen. 'Oh . . . sure . . . how many?'

'Two, darling,' said Natasha, taking his arm. 'We never let her out of our sight. Come on, boys. Look lively. Soho, here we come.'

They ate in a bistro on Frith Street – six of them, the three flatmates plus three hopeful suitors, the others having given up the chase. 'One each,' said Natasha, rather too audibly, as they sat at the table. There was a lot of jostling for the seats near Rachel; Natasha and Mark were elbowed out to the ends.

Natasha ordered three courses: wine, wine and more wine.

Everyone else ate; Rachel heartily.

'She doesn't put on an ounce,' said Mark in the ear of the one he'd decided was 'his'. 'It's so unfair.' He picked at his garnish. 'I have to be so careful . . .' A detailed explanation of his nutritional programme was drowned by laughter; Rachel had said something moderately amusing.

'Oh, that's funny!'

'Yeah, that's just how it was.'

'Good God,' said Natasha, to no one in particular, 'it's like having dinner with Joan Rivers.'

Two of the suitors were bankers; the other worked for a cancer charity. They took turns to tell Rachel about their jobs, while she looked interested and Natasha and Mark exchanged satiric looks down the length of the table. Natasha was about to say 'this is boring' for the second time, and initiate a move to somewhere so loud that conversation would be impossible – preferably with lights so low that nobody could see just how much more beautiful Rachel was – when things started to get interesting.

'Good God,' Natasha said, as a dark, curly-haired man in tight blue jeans and a dark blue shirt walked into the restaurant, 'it's Colin from college.'

'No!'

'Where?'

'There! He's seen us! He's coming over.'

'Hi!' Colin said to Rachel – and nobody else. 'I thought it was you. Fancy running into you like this.'

'She's with us,' said Natasha, whose eyelids were starting to get tired with the effort of lifting all that glue. 'And what, may I ask, is a nice boy like you doing in a dump like this?'

Colin scrutinised her for a moment, half-smiled and said, 'God, is that Natasha under there? Then where's . . . ah, there he is. Hiya, Mark.'

'Hello, Sir.'

'Well, I couldn't walk past without saying hello.'

'Right.' Rachel was blushing, looking at her napkin as if it were the most fascinating piece of cloth since the Turin shroud, glancing up with huge, wet eyes.

'So, have a nice . . .'

'Oh for God's sake,' said Natasha, grabbing a chair from a nearby table. 'Join us for a drink.'

'I won't, thanks. We're just on our way home from the theatre.'

'Oh,' said Natasha, 'are we?' She craned her neck to survey the street, trying to identify Colin's date, or mate.

'Yes,' said Colin. 'Some people, believe it or not, do actually go to the theatre. For fun. Try it some time.' He walked towards the door. 'Night, Rachel.' He waved, and was swallowed up by the Soho tide.

'*Night, Rachel*,' echoed Natasha and Mark in horrid, sing-song voices.

'Anyway,' said the man on Rachel's right, 'we're rolling out the Hong Kong project next month, so it's exciting times for me.'

'Simply riveting,' said Natasha, standing up and dropping her napkin on to the table top. 'I'm sure we'd love to hear all about it, another time. But right now, my friends and I are going to a chic little club that, I'm terribly afraid' – she sighed, and lowered her head – 'you gentlemen would simply not be allowed into. Goodnight. It's been fun. No, really. Ripping.'

She took Mark by one hand, Rachel by the other, and pulled them, giggling, into the street.

Half of the Kings Cross party had ended up in the same Wardour Street basement that Natasha, Mark and Rachel now entered, like Norma Desmond and her two sensible friends, down a long staircase lined with cracked mirrors. They were immediately engulfed, bought drinks, shouted at, jostled and squeezed (it may have been dancing) until the music got so loud and the drinks so powerful that it was no longer possible to say whether anyone was having a good time or not. In fact, it was no longer possible to say anything much. Natasha's tongue had gone numb through a combination of cocaine, champagne and violent kissing with a man who looked as if he may have recently been released from prison. Mark was on the dance floor, or what passed for one, furiously sucking his teeth and screwing up his eyes, stamping in time to the beat, stopping occasionally, when he had mustered enough saliva, to lick the face of an ageing skinhead who looked like the night's best prospect.

Rachel was at the bar, with a terrible headache – she had stopped drinking alcohol when they left the restaurant – wondering if she dared brave the night bus back to Camden on her own.

'Rach!'

'Ben?' The best-looking boy in class, Horner to her Lady Fidget.

'Rach!'

'Ben!'

Further conversation was impossible. They went up to the street for some fresh air.

'Wondered where you'd disappeared to.'

'We got taken out for dinner.'

'All right for some. I'd like to take you out for dinner.'

'That would be lovely.'

'Are you with anyone?'

'Only Natasha and Mark. Looks like I'll be going home alone. As usual.'

'I'll take you home, if you like.'

'That's very kind.'

'Well, I . . .' Ben had the bashful-little-boy routine down pat. He was an appealing combination – a dark, handsome young man who, sometimes, looked about fifteen years old. He wore old black wool sweaters with holes in them, the sleeves way over his hands, and drew strange tribal designs on his arms with magic markers. In fact, he was from a perfectly nice background and had been to a grammar school, but nobody need know that.

'If it's not too out of your way,' said Rachel. 'You will be able to get home all right, won't you?'

'Of course, I can walk from there,' said Ben, who was not used to the brush-off, even as charming a brush-off as this, and preferred Rachel to think that this was all in a night's work.

'In that case,' said Rachel, stubbing out her cigarette and taking his arm, 'I'm ready.' Ben felt her skin against his, through an artful hole in his sweater, and hoped she'd change her mind on the bus.

She didn't.

They kissed goodnight at the door – a long kiss, a great kiss, the kind of kiss that was much more satisfying than any of the things that Natasha or Mark would be doing over the next few hours of consciousness – but still only a kiss, nothing more.

'Goodnight, Ben,' said Rachel, her arms still round his neck, looking up into his eyes – all pupil, just a thin ring of dark brown iris. 'That was very sweet of you.'

'Mmmmf,' said Ben, who couldn't trust himself to say any more.

'See you in the morning.'

'It *is* morning . . .'

You're right . . . It's not really worth your going home, is it? Why don't you just come in and we'll . . .

'So it is. Well then, see you later. Thanks ever so much. You're a gentleman.'

I am, thought Ben, damn it. 'G'night.'

He stomped off on the long, long walk home, and Rachel let herself in to the empty flat with a soft smile on her lips.

Chapter 7

Nobody was particularly looking forward to the party, apart
from Elizabeth, who had planned it, and for whom celebrating
Nick's birthday was a sort of sacred duty. Nick wasn't interested: another year passing was just a reminder of the fact that
he wasn't yet successful. Chris wasn't looking forward to it; after
disastrous results in his mock A levels, he didn't want any
distractions from revising – and being around Nick was the
very worst sort of distraction. The Prof and Anna were officially delighted to be invited, but had already agreed on a
codeword that would enable them to leave after no more than
an hour. Rachel was looking forward to having a nose round
Elizabeth's flat and meeting the famous fiancé, who would
doubtless be a fellow academic in a cardigan and baggy trousers.
She planned to stay for half an hour, then make her excuses
and go on to a party in Bethnal Green to which *everybody*
was going, including Ben and Colin and half a dozen other
boyfriends-in-waiting.

But things changed.

First of all, Rachel heard that Alan Southgate was going to
be at the party. Now, in theatrical circles, even those circles as
remote from the stage as Rachel moved in, the name of Alan
Southgate was something of a touchstone. He was the British
actor most likely to make it. He'd made an effortless transition
from drama school to movies to the legitimate stage, and if he
could do it, then why not any of them? Obviously, neither
Rachel nor any of her peers had seen him in a theatre, but they

had all seen the films and TV, they kept up with his romantic life through the medium of magazines, and several of them claimed a tenuous connection to him. Mark, for instance, said they went to the same hairdresser, and called him 'Alan' in conversation. Natasha had slept with a man who'd slept with a woman who'd slept with Alan Southgate, and sometimes she looked a bit misty when she saw his picture, as if they'd had sex by proxy. And now Rachel was actually going to meet him at a party, as his equal, not through some desperate bit of stage-door johnnying but because it just so happened that he was her soon-to-be stepsister's best friend. And that was a hell of a lot closer than sharing a hairdresser.

Chris was planning to avoid Nick, be nice to his family and slip away unnoticed as usual – but then Nick greeted him with an open-mouthed kiss, and a flash of taut brown abdomen above his low-slung jeans, and Chris suddenly decided that all work and no play made Chris a dull boy.

The Prof and Anna were so delighted by the sight of all their children getting on so well that they forgot all about the codeword, and ploughed into the buffet instead.

Nick hadn't yet made up his mind which way the party would go. People were giving him presents and fetching him drinks, which was nice, Alan Southgate was calling him 'mate' and Chris was following him around like a love-struck puppy. But still, every conversation inevitably got round to 'How's work going?', at which point Nick could either lie or make a joke or, if he felt so inclined, cause a scene. He knew what they thought of him – the Prof, Kate, even Alan – a work-shy dud, sponging off Elizabeth, already twenty-five and no sign of a career, no money of his own, the photography a convenient fiction to mask his essential uselessness. But he was as good as any of them. He'd show them one day. But for now, the only power he really had was to create a row and storm out and ruin the party for them all. That would make them treat him with a bit more respect. Maybe that was the thing to do.

And then he saw Rachel.

In a cartoon, his eyes would have shot out of his head, his heart would have leaped from his chest and his tongue would have fallen to the floor with an audible clunk. Birds would have tweeted round his head, wings would have sprouted from his heels and he would lay himself at her feet to be walked all over. In fact, they just said hello when Elizabeth introduced them, their eyes met for a few seconds and Rachel looked away. Nick watched her through lowered lids and long black eyelashes, exhaling audibly through his mouth, as if he were smoking. Something – pheromones, perhaps, or what the Prof might call elective affinity, or just good old-fashioned lust – marked each out to the other. From that point on, there was no one else in the room. Elizabeth, Anna, the Prof, Chris, even Alan Southgate, faded and blurred. Rachel and Nick alone stood out in sharp focus and 3-D technicolour, hyper-real, crackling with mutual awareness.

It was in neither of their natures to make the first move; Nick was used to being fancied and, if he wanted someone, had only to wait. Rachel, too, was beginning to relish the effect her looks had on men and enjoyed making them do all the running. So, after that first fateful frisson, they turned in opposite directions and started to circulate with rather more animation than before. Time, and their own irresistibility, would do the rest.

Nick, who understood female psychology in an intuitive way, turned his charms on Chris. If a woman thought that you might be a bit gay, Nick knew, she was much more likely to let down her guard. And so he whispered in Chris's ear, allowing his stubble to tickle the unfortunate boy's jaw line. He put a manly hand on Chris's shoulder, and felt the knees buckle. He made him fetch drinks, and intimated that wine in the afternoon always made him feel horny, which was possibly not the most appropriate thing to say to your own fiancée's brother but which had the desired effect. Chris was luminous with desire, like a beacon; surely Rachel could not fail to notice?

And she did. Rachel's heart hammered in her chest, and she felt short of breath. It was an unfamiliar and unpleasant sensation. She had liked plenty of men before: Colin the tutor, for instance, or sweet Ben – but this was not *liking*. This was like standing on the edge of a precipice and feeling an urge to jump.

She focused on Elizabeth, who had just gone up immensely in her estimation. A woman who could marry a man like that must be something special. Natasha, for all her phoney sophistication, never held a man for more than a week. Rachel's romantic experience was limited to dating and what was once called 'petting' – a fact she concealed from her flatmates. Despite many offers, she was still a virgin. Elizabeth, only four years her senior, seemed like a woman of the world by comparison. Someone to look up to. A big sister. For the first time, Rachel could see advantages to having a family.

'I love your flat,' she said, brushing a strand of hair behind her ear. 'I'd like a place like this one day.'

'Oh, it's . . . Well, thanks. It is lovely.' Elizabeth, who was a few inches taller than Rachel, looked down at her kindly. 'I'm very lucky.'

'You certainly are,' said Rachel, in a schoolgirlish tone. 'I mean, wow! He's absolutely gorgeous!' She whispered the last word, and finished it with a giggle.

'God, not you as well. Everyone fancies Nick.' There he was, across the room, terrorising Chris as usual; she'd asked him not to torment the poor boy. But at least he was smiling and joining in; at one point, Elizabeth feared that he'd spend the whole party smoking dope in his bedroom.

'Did you make all this food? It's delicious.'

'Oh, it was easy, really. I mean, Nick helped a lot, obviously.' He hadn't. 'I'm glad you like it.'

Kate was hovering, waiting for an introduction. Elizabeth found herself unexpectedly reluctant to share Rachel.

'I must introduce you to some people. This is Kate, my very best friend.' Out of the corner of her eye, Elizabeth noticed Charlotte pulling a sour face. She'd deal with that later. 'Kate, this is Rachel, who's going to be my sister.'

'Oh, hello,' said Rachel, clumsily and rather charmingly juggling a glass and a plate so that she had a free hand to shake. 'It's lovely to meet you.'

'Must be strange, having this whole new family suddenly foisted on you,' said Kate. 'I hope you're coping.'

'Well, it's a bit terrifying.'

She's never been terrified in her life, thought Kate. 'Let's go and get drinks, and let Elizabeth play hostess for a while. Besides,' she said, steering Rachel towards the kitchen, 'I want to hear all about you. You're at Alderman's, aren't you?'

They disappeared into the kitchen. Alan was immediately at Elizabeth's side.

'So that's Rachel.'

'Yes. Pretty, isn't she?'

'Very.'

'Oh dear. That sounds ominous.'

'Bit young for me, Liz.'

'But give her a couple of years, is that it?'

'Never say never.'

'Go ahead, marry her. What would that make you? My stepbrother-in-law? Isn't life complicated?'

'Oh, I think it's quite sweet,' said Alan. 'I wish my dad would do something of the sort. Miserable old bastard, in his ivory tower, still blaming my mum for the divorce, even though he was the one who . . . Well, never mind that. But don't blame me for not being the marrying kind.'

'So many actresses, so little time, is that it?'

'Actresses?' Alan screwed up his face. 'No, thanks. Had enough of them to last me a lifetime. Too much like hard work.'

'You're out of luck, then.'

'Don't tell me . . .'

'Drama school.'

Alan passed a large, strong hand over his smooth, pale brow. 'Blast,' he said. 'I feared as much. Oh well. The wedding's off. Mine, that is. Not yours. Although it looks like you've got competition.'

Chris's face was red, his eyes shining, veins standing out in his neck as Nick whispered something in his ear.

'Oh, for God's sake,' said Elizabeth, as if she'd just caught a toddler sticking its fingers into an electric socket, 'I've told him not to do that a hundred times.' She went over to rescue her brother. Alan was instantly pounced on by Anna, who had surrendered the Prof to Charlotte's over eager interrogation.

'God, darling,' said Anna, in her cracked, cabaret-bar voice, 'it's all getting a bit too intellectual for me. I don't suppose a charming young man like you would get a drink for an old crock like me.'

'With pleasure, madam.' Alan produced a bottle, rather like a conjuring trick. 'Fizz do?'

'Rather.' Anna held her glass at the appropriate angle. 'So, who are you, and where do you fit into the picture, and please tell me that you're not gay.'

Alan laughed; this was obviously the only person at the party who didn't know who he was. 'I'm Alan, I'm an old friend of Elizabeth's, and no, to the best of my knowledge, I'm not gay.'

'Well that is a relief, I must say. Cheers. Don't get me wrong, I've got nothing against them, I mean, how could I, I've been surrounded by gay men all my life for some reason, even went out with a few as it turned out, but it doesn't do much for a girl's self-esteem when the good-looking ones are more interested in each other.'

'Oh, I'm sure that . . .' said Alan, about to produce a compliment, but Anna interrupted.

'I don't go to parties any more,' said Anna. 'I mean, parties were *parties* when I was younger. Not like this, standing around and being polite and *chatting*. It was all dancing and drinking and what we used to call *getting off*, which makes me sound ancient, doesn't it?'

This was obviously a cue. 'Not at all. People still get off.'

'Bless you, my darling. Of course, my heyday was a long time ago now. You know, the . . . well, the eighties.'

And the rest, thought Alan, but just smiled and nodded.

'My daughter's a chip off the old block, mind you. Of course, she doesn't tell me the half of it, but I can guess. Sex and drugs and all sorts. We didn't need drugs in my day. Well, perhaps a whiff of this and a dab of that. Do you do drugs, darling? If you don't mind my asking?'

'Certainly not,' said Alan. 'I'm a clean-cut kind of guy.' He smiled, showing all his teeth.

'Well, good for you.' She put a hand on his arm. 'Now, you must excuse me while I rescue my poor dear Tony from that . . . person. Before she bores him to death. I don't want to be a widow before I've even married him.'

She moved away in a jangle of beads and a haze of perfume. Alan watched as Elizabeth prised her brother away from her fiancé, noted the look of deadly sibling hatred that blazed out of Chris's eyes and then, when he stomped out of the room, decided to follow him.

Rachel, in the kitchen, was starting to feel like a fox at bay. Nothing Kate had said was in any way hostile, and yet, somehow, she felt that the dogs of suspicion had caught her scent. Kate didn't respond to Rachel's charms. The little-girl-lost routine didn't make her motherly. The ladette act didn't inspire confidence. The questions kept coming and coming.

— So, have you got a boyfriend?

— And what exactly do you see yourself doing in five years' time?

— Elizabeth's lovely, isn't she?

— When are we going to meet your friends?

They were all the questions that a mother might have asked – a more motherly mother than Anna, that is, one for whom her child's well-being was the prime consideration. Rachel was tongue-tied, and drank too much, and then, when she saw that Kate was monitoring her alcohol consumption, filled a glass from the tap and drank that. She was dying for a cigarette, but nobody else was smoking; it didn't seem to be that type of party. From the kitchen window above the sink she saw Elizabeth and Nick walking out into the tiny back garden, where he lit up.

Any minute now, thought Rachel, Kate's going to say, 'I saw the way you looked at Nick. What's your game?' She felt guilty without having done anything wrong. Time for a change of subject.

'So, anyway,' said Rachel, interrupting yet another question, 'what about you? What do you do?'

'Oh, I'm a writer.' So casual, as if they were all artists of one sort or another. 'I was a great admirer of Susan's.'

'Oh.' *Susan?*

'Yes. You know.'

Damn her eyes, her all-seeing eyes.

'I don't think I . . .'

'Elizabeth's mother.'

Clang! *The woman your mother is supplanting.* 'Ah. She was a . . .'

'A wonderful writer. And a wonderful woman. We all miss her.'

If Natasha had been there, she'd have told the bitch to fuck off, possibly thrown a drink in her smug face; a party wasn't a party without a fight, Natasha often said. But Rachel wasn't the brawling type. 'Yes,' she said, lowering her eyes, 'I'm sure you do. So sad.'

'And your father.'

'My . . . Oh, yes, of course. I miss him terribly, too.'

'Is he . . . ?'

For a hysterical moment, Rachel considered saying, 'Yes, he was taken from us far too soon', but Kate looked like the type that would check. 'He ran off when I was very small. I never really knew him.' Kate looked interested, and clearly wanted more, but Rachel was seized with a sudden urge to flee.

'Would you think me awfully rude,' she said, not caring much one way or the other, 'if I just went and joined Elizabeth in the garden for a crafty fag? I know it's disgusting and I'm trying to give it up, but . . .'

Kate looked out of the window, registered the presence of the happy couple, and said, 'Of course, go ahead,' with just a tilt of the eyebrow that said, to Rachel, by now morbidly sensitive to every facial tic, 'I know your game.'

Why am I letting her make me feel this way? Nothing's happened. He's Elizabeth's fiancé. Of course he's good-looking, anyone can see that, and of course I want to get to know him, he's one of the family. But that's all. It's Elizabeth I should be making an effort with. It's Elizabeth I like.

But Elizabeth was coming back indoors, leaving Rachel alone in the garden with Nick. She squinted in the sunshine and rummaged in her pocket for cigarettes.

'Allow me,' said a dark brown voice from a figure silhouetted by the sun. A packet of cigarettes was offered, and a light.

'Thank you.' She inhaled, then shaded her eyes the better to see him. 'Ah! Hello! It's you.'

'Yeah. It's me.'

'Happy birthday.'

'Cheers.' He put the cigarette to his lips as if kissing the filter. Smoke curled up before his eyes, into his floppy black fringe. 'It is now.'

'What?'

'Happy.'

'Ah.'

They smoked.

'Rachel, isn't it? The daughter.'

'Yes. And please don't say you've heard so much about me.'

'I haven't.'

'Oh.'

'In fact, she's been unusually silent on the subject.'

'Obviously I didn't make a very good impression.'

'Hmmm.' They moved a pace or two towards the house, out of sight of the kitchen window. 'Chris told me you were beautiful.'

'Did he?' A squadron of butterflies took flight in Rachel's stomach. Whatever was happening was happening too fast.

'Chris tells me everything.'

'I see.'

'And he's right.'

'Is he?'

'Yeah. You are. Beautiful.'

'Thank you.'

'I'm a photographer, you know.'

'Wow.' He's flirting with me. And they're watching from indoors, Rachel thought.

'I'd love you to pose for me.'

'Would you?'

'Yeah.'

I must stop this. I must say something to put him off.

'Well, perhaps we can do something about that one day.' No! That's not what I meant to say!

'Hope so.'

She wanted to kiss him, to run her hands up his shirt and down his trousers, into the warm, hairy darkness. She felt light-headed. It could have been the cigarette, but it wasn't and she knew it. It was desire – the hot, tormenting desire that left Ben panting on her doorstep, that made Colin's face darken, his brows contract, as if in anger.

She had never felt it before, and she was not at all sure she liked it.

He watched her, his face giving nothing away, his eyes hooded.

You know. I know. Let's just get this over with.

The doorbell rang, suddenly very loud.

'Excuse me,' he said. 'Duty calls.'

She finished her cigarette alone. When she returned to the party, Nick was standing with Elizabeth, his arm round her waist, in animated conversation with the new arrivals, suddenly the perfect host. Rachel didn't know who to talk to: Chris was nowhere to be seen, and Alan Southgate, whom she wanted to impress, had disappeared. Anna was clinging to the Professor. Kate watched Rachel like a hawk as she crossed the room. How much had she seen? Suddenly, that party in Bethnal Green seemed very attractive, but Anna took possession of her and soon she was being interrogated by the Prof, her mother answering on her behalf. She did not have to look to where Nick was laughing and kissing people and opening presents. She could feel him, a tangible source of heat, as if someone across the room had opened an oven door.

Upstairs in the bedroom, where Chris had gone to breathe deeply and calm down, he was now deep in conversation with Alan, who seemed to be taking a sudden and profound interest in his well-being.

'Passing exams is just a question of attitude,' Alan was saying, sitting back on the bed with his legs a yard apart. 'As long as you sound like you know what you're talking about, they'll fall for it.'

'Is that what you do?'

'Yes. It's called acting.'

'Right.'

'Just a question of letting people believe what they want to believe.'

'Sounds like a useful skill.'

Alan looked him straight in the eye. 'It is.'

Chris was young and inexperienced, but not so dumb that he didn't sense the meaning behind these words.

'So is that what . . .'

Alan stood up. He was a good six inches taller than Chris. 'How old are you now, Chris?'

'Seventeen. Eighteen next month.'

'Next month.' Alan did some rapid calculations, and then he said, moving forward, 'Well then, happy birthday in advance,' and kissed Chris on the lips. Their mouths opened, Alan's hands moved to Chris's back and drew him in, and they kissed as if they had waited for this moment and nothing else for the last five years.

'I think it's going awfully well,' said Elizabeth, her arm through Nick's, surveying the party. Rachel was in animated conversation with Anna and the Prof, Kate had drawn Charlotte into her literary circle, where she was now cheerfully demolishing anything written after 1500, and the buffet had been gratifyingly laid waste.

'It's lovely,' said Nick, squeezing her waist, where there was a little more to squeeze than either of them would have liked. But what did that matter where there was love?

'I'm off,' said Alan, appearing behind them in the doorway. 'Thanks for a fantastic party. If I have any more to drink, I'll be forgetting my lines.'

'Of course.' Elizabeth disengaged herself, and stretched up to kiss him; at the last moment, he turned his head and offered his cheek, not his lips. 'What are you giving them tonight?'

'*All's Well That Ends Well*,' he said. 'I'm Bertram.'

'Oh!' said Elizabeth. 'The swine! I'm sure you'll be marvellous.'

'Thanks. Come and see it any time. It's a mess, but I'm good.'

'Who the fuck is Bertram?' asked Nick, after Alan had left. 'I hate all that stuff. You know I don't know what you're talking about.'

'He's a man who marries a woman he doesn't love,' said Elizabeth.

'Silly bastard.'

'He changes his mind in the end,' she said, but Nick did not hear her, and went to carry out his duties as host.

'Drinks, anyone?' he said, popping the cork on another bottle of champagne, and making his way towards the Professor.

Chapter 8

'Well, I don't care if I don't get the part,' said Natasha. 'Nobody pays any attention to first-term productions. They only do them because they think they have to. It's the graduation shows that matter.'

Rachel, Mark and Natasha were drinking coffee in the college refectory, dissecting their auditions for *The Rivals*. Rachel thought she'd done rather well; she'd certainly spent enough time preparing, when the others were out drinking. Mark sleepwalked through his audition with his usual lack of commitment, and would be content to be 'guest at party' as long as he got to wear a wig. Natasha, who was excited when the production was first announced, soon cooled when she discovered it wasn't a stage adaptation of her favourite Jilly Cooper novel. She gave the worst audition of all, and was eager to bury the whole project.

'Anyway,' she went on, 'Charlie never got cast in a single college production and look at him.'

Charlie Evans – the one recent Alderman's alumnus who had achieved the kind of fame that most of the students could understand – was a source of pride and a thorn in the side of the college authorities since his triumph on a TV talent show. On the one hand, student numbers rocketed when it became known that he was a Alderman's graduate. On the other hand, his road to success was hardly in keeping with the school's philosophy. Attending the bare minimum of classes, and disrupting even those, Charlie used his college place as a launchpad for affairs with anyone – staff, student, visiting agent or guest lecturer – whom he thought could give him a leg-up in return for a leg-over. Instead of following the approved career path – getting an agent, paying his dues in rep before landing a coveted guest role on *The Bill*, where that dialect training would come in handy – Charlie cut his final exams to attend the TV audition, where he took off his shirt and sang 'I'm Too Sexy'. He never returned to Alderman's, and the rest was celebrity history. For now, he was a pop star, selling a lot of records and doing PAs up and down the country – but as long as he kept the torso in shape, the world was his oyster.

'But Charlie's not an actor,' said Rachel. 'Don't you want to be an actor?'

Natasha and Mark looked at her as if she'd farted. 'An actor?' said Mark. 'God, hark at her.'

'Nobody wants to be an actor, darling,' said Natasha. 'I want to be a star.' She rolled her eyes. 'A star!'

'Well, I'd quite like to be an actor,' said Rachel, doggedly. 'I mean, this is a drama school.'

'Good luck to you,' said Mark. 'But it seems such a waste. With your looks, you don't need talent. You just need a good agent.'

'Or a rich husband,' said Natasha. 'Just think of it. You'd never have to lift a finger.'

'And how am I going to find a rich husband if I don't parade myself on a stage?' said Rachel. 'I mean, the sort of parties and clubs we go to aren't exactly dripping with millionaires, are they?'

'You had a bloody good try though, didn't you?' said Mark.

'Yes, and you two scared them away.'

'Oh darling, they were *boring*,' said Natasha, to whom this was the unforgivable sin.

'Rich men often are, I suppose,' said Rachel, thinking about Nick, who clearly didn't have a penny to his name. 'If I want excitement, I can stick my fingers in an electric socket.'

'Speaking of boring,' said Natasha, 'how's the new family?'

'Oh, you know. Stuffy. Rich. Nice.' She'd given only the sketchiest details of the party, and certainly hadn't mentioned Nick. 'We're all going on holiday together.'

'Yuk,' said Natasha. 'Where? Bognor?'

'Cape Cod.'

'Where's that?'

'America.'

'America?' said Mark, who was impressed by anything transatlantic. 'Wow! When?'

'July.'

'Sounds great . . .'

'Sounds madly dull,' said Natasha, staring into her coffee.

'And what are you doing that's so much more exciting?'

'Oh, didn't you know? Mark and I are going on tour.'

'Well . . .'

'Yes we are, Mark. We're taking our show on the road.'

'What show?'

'The cabaret show that we're doing. Aren't we, darling?'

'We haven't actually got any bookings yet.'

'Oh,' said Natasha, waving her freshly varnished nails, 'that's a minor technicality. I told you, darling, I *know people*. We'll get gigs at festivals. Clubs. It's going to be fabulous.'

'What exactly are you going to do?'

'Sing. Dance. Tell jokes.'

'It's kind of in the planning stages at the moment,' said Mark. 'I mean, we've got the costumes together.'

'It's going to be very Bob Fosse,' said Natasha, who had seen *Sweet Charity* at an impressionable age. 'We'll come on as sort of post-modern sluts with heavy eye make-up and ripped stockings . . .'

'I'm going to rouge my nipples,' said Mark.

'It'll be very decadent,' said Natasha. 'Very Weimar.' She also loved *Cabaret, natürlich*.

'And what will you actually sing?'

'You're just jealous,' said Natasha. 'We'll be on tour and you'll be bored out of your mind in that Cod place, wherever it is. When you come back we'll be stars, darling, and you'll just be another drama student. Well, don't say I didn't warn you.'

'I wouldn't dream of it,' said Rachel. 'I wonder when they'll tell us who got the parts?'

'They said tonight,' said Mark who, for all his future cabaret stardom, still wouldn't have minded being 'guest at party'.

Kate pulled a few strings, and one day, much to Elizabeth's surprise, she received a call from *the Daily Beacon* arts desk asking her to review a play. 'Our regular critic's ill,' said the commissioning editor, 'and you come highly recommended.'

Elizabeth needed a date. Nick hated the theatre on principle, it was 'boring and middle class', he said, remembering childhood trips with his parents for which he was forced to wear a blazer and tie. Kate, with two small children to feed and wash, was unavailable for evening engagements, and Chris was locked in his room revising. It was far too modern for Charlotte, and Alan was working in a much bigger theatre.

Then inspiration struck. Why not ask Rachel? She was an actress, or about to be, and it would be a good opportunity to get to know her better. 'I know it's a bit of a cheek asking at such short notice,' Elizabeth said on the phone, 'but they only just rang. It's nothing very exciting, just a small venue above a pub . . .'

'I'd love to,' said Rachel. 'It would be nice to have a night off studying.' In fact, she didn't want to sit around the flat listening to Natasha and Mark planning their career in cabaret, waiting for the phone call that might come if she'd got a part in *The Rivals*. Better to be out, phone off, at least doing something vaguely related to her chosen career, rather than drinking lukewarm homemade martinis and waking up with another hangover.

She took care over her appearance, toning down the make-up, pulling her hair back into a ponytail and dressing in jeans and a white shirt. She still looked like something from the pages of *Vogue*, but she couldn't help that. It would be the first time they were alone together, and Rachel wanted things to go well. Women, she was learning, tended to resent it when she got too much male attention.

'Thanks so much for this,' she said, kissing Elizabeth on both cheeks. 'It's really exciting. I can't afford to go to the theatre as much as I'd like to, so this is a treat.'

'My pleasure,' said Elizabeth. 'What would you like to drink?'

'Just a Coke, thanks. I want to concentrate.'

Elizabeth, who had been on the point of ordering a bottle of white wine, bought two Diet Cokes instead.

'Do you know that man over there?' she said, when they had settled at a table. 'The one who's looking at you?'

'Who?' Rachel peered across the bar.

'Him in the black sweater. Tall. Raising his glass towards you right now.'

'Never seen him before in my life.'

'Oh.' Elizabeth raised her eyebrows. 'I see. Perhaps it's a case of mistaken identity.'

'I suppose so,' said Rachel. 'Now, tell me all about the play. What are we seeing, who's in it, who's directing it and, most importantly, what are you going to say about it?'

'I don't know until I've seen it.'

'Right. Of course. Do you know anyone in it?'

'No.'

'So you can be honest, then.'

'I'd be honest even if I did.'

'Wow. You're brave.'

Elizabeth, to whom the idea of writing a dishonest, partisan review had never occurred, was shocked. 'Just doing my job,' she said, sounding even to herself like a prig. 'Anyway, let's see what it's like. I think they're going in.'

The play was appalling, two hours of self-regarding pathos about how great it was to be Northern. Elizabeth hated it.

'Well,' she said, when she'd finally managed to get a drink in the post-show scrum, 'what did you think?'

'I . . . I'm not really sure . . .'

'Come on. Love it, or hate it?' Elizabeth hadn't yet decided which way she'd jump. Obviously, it was a load of rubbish, but it might just prove a convenient stick with which to beat the West End.

'The actors were good,' said Rachel.

'Yes. But the play.'

'Oh, well, the play . . .'

'Did you think it was perhaps a bit . . . naive?'

'I suppose so.'

'But not without a certain amount of passion and intensity.'

'No . . .' said Rachel, wondering if she should have said 'yes'. The clothes had been terrible, and of the four actors, at least two had split ends, the other two had forgotten their lines, and she was pretty certain that the lighting effect at the end (it was meant to signify a chip-pan fire) had gone wrong.

'The question is, does one encourage a new talent even if the play is not without flaws, or does one maintain some kind of critical absolutes?'

'I suppose you just say what you think,' said Rachel, 'and make it quite funny so that people might actually read it.'

'Yes,' she said, filling their glasses. 'That's one way of looking at it.'

'I can't wait to see your name in print,' said Rachel. 'I'll tell everyone it's my new sister.'

'Will you?'

'Oh yes. I'm ever so proud.'

'Right.' Elizabeth drank. 'Well, cheers.' She thought for a while. 'And you. What about you? How are things going?'

'Oh, don't,' said Rachel, clasping her hands so the knuckles went white. 'I had an audition today. I daren't turn my phone on in case there's a message.'

'What, you mean they might have told you already?'

'Yes, but . . .' She fished her phone out of her handbag. 'Would you mind looking?'

'Are you sure?'

'Please. Then just say "yes" or "no".'

'Okay.' Elizabeth turned the phone on, waited impatiently for bars and beeps and nearly jumped out of her skin when the words 'voice message' appeared on the screen. She listened.

'Yes,' she said, at length.

'No!'

'Yes. You've got Julia.'

'Oh.' Rachel's shoulders slumped, and she looked crestfallen. 'I hoped for Lydia.'

'But Julia's a marvellous part!'

'You know it?' said Rachel, truly astonished.

'Of course! It's a classic! Lydia gets all the flashy lines, it's true, but Julia can steal the show.'

'Steal the show . . .' The idea of theft appealed. 'How?'

'You don't need me to tell you that.' Elizabeth nodded across the room, where the Man in the Black Sweater was still lurking and looking. 'Just be yourself.'

'I see.' Rachel fiddled with the elastic band that held her ponytail, pulled it out and shook her hair over her shoulders. 'Watch this,' she said then, running her hand from her forehead back over her head, cleared the dark brown cascade from her face.

The Man in the Black Sweater looked poleaxed.

'What's he doing?'

'He looks as if he's just come in his pants, quite frankly,' said Elizabeth.

'Works every time. Perhaps I should just do that when I walk on stage.'

'Yes,' said Elizabeth, wondering if she could ever pull off a similar trick – because it must be a trick. 'A star is born.'

'How's Nick?'

'Wha . . . ? Oh, Nick's fine. He's working tonight. He sends his love.' It was not a figure of speech; he really had asked Elizabeth to send Rachel his love. His manners, she thought, were definitely improving.

When the post-show drink was drunk, neither was ready to call it a night. 'Do you fancy a nightcap?' asked Rachel, when the pub was closing and the last few drinkers were leaving. They'd worked their way through two bottles of wine since the curtain went down, and were feeling elated. Elizabeth, who not only had to teach classes in the morning but also had to file her review by lunchtime, started objecting, but Rachel added, 'There's a really fun little club in Kings Cross that we could go to. It's on the way for both of us. Come on, please. I'm having such a good time, I don't want to go home. Anyway, we're celebrating!'

'Yes. Your role. Congratulations.'

'Oh, that.' Rachel drained her glass. 'I wasn't thinking about that.'

'Then what?'

Rachel looked at Elizabeth, her eyes sparkling. 'The fact that we like each other. Not because we have to. Not just to please our parents. But because we really do. Don't we?'

'We do,' said Elizabeth, feeling an unexpected lightness of heart. 'Come on, then. Kings Cross, it is. You can help me write the review. And if I turn up to class tomorrow stinking of liquor, well . . . They probably won't notice.'

'Call in sick!'

Elizabeth laughed; when she laughed, thought Rachel, she looked a lot better. Younger.

Arm in arm, they set off in search of a taxi.

'So, how did you two meet?'

'Oh God. It was a long time ago.'

It was well past two, and they were into their third bottle of wine. The review was partially written on the back of the programme, and there had been much merriment over comments and phrases that would have landed Elizabeth, and her publisher, in the libel courts.

She's not as stupid as she looks, thought Elizabeth, sniggering at one of Rachel's jokes.

She's not as boring as she looks, thought Rachel, watching Elizabeth laugh.

Then they passed on to personal matters, and a quick rundown of their relationship history. Rachel dismissed her own in a few sentences ('Lots of boyfriends, no one serious, don't have time, never met "the one"') before quizzing Elizabeth in great detail over her history with Nick. 'You two seem to be so . . . solid,' she said, remembering how Nick's eyes had burned into her, even while he was playing the perfect host at his birthday party. 'That's what I want from a relationship. Someone who's there for me. Someone I can trust.'

Elizabeth had drunk enough to feel that this was true, and felt better about Nick than she had done for months.

'I know how lucky I am. Sometimes, when I wake up next to him, I have to pinch myself, even after all these months.'

'Was it love at first sight?'

'Lust at first sight, certainly.'

'Well, yes. I mean . . .' Rachel felt herself blushing.

'It was at a party. I saw him across a crowded room. It was such a cliché.'

Just like me, Rachel thought. 'Sounds romantic.'

'He was at my college. He was doing a postgrad photography course, I was finishing up my masters, but we had friends in common. I went to his graduation show. It was amazing. He was the star of his year. Everyone said so.'

'I bet.'

'Anyway, I asked our mutual friend who he was, and before I knew it, we'd been introduced and we were chatting away like old friends. We spent the night together and . . . that's it. Pretty much every night since.'

'How long?'

'A couple of years. I was in my final year. It was a difficult time for me; my mother had just died, I was revising for my finals, and I was spending a lot of time looking after Dad and Chris.'

'And then along came love.'

Was that sarcasm in her voice? Elizabeth scrutinised Rachel's face, but found nothing there. Her own doubts, perhaps; the lingering suspicion that it had all happened too quickly with Nick, too easily. She had never questioned it.

'Yes,' she said. 'I know it's very corny.'

'Not at all. I just wish it would happen to me.'

'It will,' said Elizabeth, feeling a rush of generosity and gratitude. No one else made her feel this good about the man she was going to marry.

'So,' said Rachel, 'tell me all about him. He's a photographer, right?'

'Yes. Or will be one day, when he gets a break.'

'I'm sure he will.'

'Yes.' Elizabeth's brows contracted, a line forming between them. 'The thing is with Nick,' she said, 'he never had much of a family life. Didn't always go to school. He finds it hard to apply himself.' How much should she tell her? He coasts through life on charm and good looks, he never looks for work, I've taken more photos in the last twelve months than he has. If my father weren't rich, I'm not sure if we'd be getting married . . .

She swallowed her doubts with a mouthful of wine. 'But, of course, it's a difficult business to break into. Like acting, I suppose,' she said, happy to change the subject.

'I'm determined.'

'I bet you are, too.' Elizabeth saw the way men looked at Rachel; that was money in the bank.

'I get it from my mother. She usually gets what she wants.'

'Indeed.'

'Oh,' said Rachel, 'I don't mean in a bad way. She really loves your dad.' Anna had said no such thing; *grateful* would be nearer the mark. 'Anyway, I'm happy for her. And it takes her off my hands, thank God.'

'I'll drink to that.'

'And without her,' said Rachel, 'I wouldn't have met you.'

Something passed between them: confidences, vulnerability, an awareness that each complemented the other. A feeling that they might be good for each other. That they might be friends.

It was enough for one night. 'Time for your beauty sleep,' said Elizabeth, 'not that you need it.'

'And time for you,' said Rachel, after a yawn so wide that it could have engulfed the wine bottle, 'to go home to that man of yours. You lucky thing.'

Nick was grumpy when Elizabeth clambered into bed, mumbling, 'fuck off' when she tried to kiss him, but he woke up when she went under the covers.

'How was your night?' he asked, leaning back on a pillow, his arms behind his head. Elizabeth looked up, disengaged her mouth for long enough to say, 'lovely' and carried on.

'How was Rachel?'

He wasn't usually this conversational during sex; in fact, he rarely asked anything much about her life at all.

'She was great, thanks.'

'Yeah,' said Nick, slipping a hand into Elizabeth's hair and closing his eyes. 'I bet.'

It didn't take long. As Nick started to come, and she pulled her mouth away to finish him off by hand, it occurred to Elizabeth that it had been a long time since he'd actually made love to her. When was it? She tried to remember, casting her mind back as Nick tensed and moaned. Since the party? Or before? Since the Prof announced his marriage? When? Suddenly, it seemed to matter.

Chapter 9

Anna was late for her own wedding, of course. Not marriage-wreckingly, ceremony-cancellingly late, but late enough to make the Prof think that he had been jilted at the registrar's desk. Everyone was sitting there waiting, long after they'd been called into the Garden Room, and there was much nervous glancing at watches and checking of mobiles, before the registrar beckoned the Prof over and asked him, in hushed tones, if there was a problem.

'No, of course not,' he said with a scowl; it was unfair to take this out on the poor woman, who after all was only doing her job and had a timetable to keep to, and God knows that the Prof of all people respected a timetable, but it was not in his nature to be nagged by anyone. 'I told you. She'll be here.'

'We can only hold the room for another five minutes, Sir,' said the registrar, her smooth, bland face giving nothing away. Oh God, thought the Prof, she's seen this happen a thousand times, some old fool rushing into a hasty marriage, inviting his whole family to witness his degradation.

And then, just as Elizabeth caught his eye for the hundredth time, goggling and shrugging her shoulders, just as he expected to hear the slow-hand clap and the chorus of 'Why are we waiting?', the door burst open, Rachel almost fell through it, smiled, gave a big thumbs-up and stood aside to permit the blushing bride to enter.

There were no trumpets, no Mendelssohn, no Wagner, just an explosion of flowers, a clatter of heels on parquet and there she was – Anna Bates, with nothing but debts and a daughter, about to become Anna Miller, with a considerable fortune and a couple of extra kids. And a husband.

Most of the flowers were gathered into an extravagant bouquet, which the bride clutched at waist level. Some of the flowers – and there were an awful lot of flowers, the whole shop full, by the look of it – were arranged in Anna's hair, which had been twisted up on top of her head for the occasion, serving as a launchpad for a fantasia of lilies and gerberas, red and orange and pink, a cross between a bridal wreath and an old-fashioned rubber bathing cap.

The Prof felt momentarily dizzy with relief, and had to lean on the desk for a moment before he could stand up straight, gather his thoughts and remember that this was the woman he was planning to spend the rest of her life with. She was chronically late, she dressed like a woman half her age and she didn't have a penny to her name – but she made him feel alive for the first time in two years. Or longer. She made him laugh – and there had been precious little laughter in his marriage to Susan. Not all of that could be blamed on the cancer. Of course, Susan was the love of his life, the mother of his children, his soulmate – but fun, she was not. Theirs had been a marriage of true minds, everyone said so, but sometimes the Prof had wished he could come home to a cooked dinner and some light-hearted conversation before an agreeable roll in the hay at bedtime.

That was not Susan's idea of married life. She preferred debates to chats, spent an increasing amount of time in her study and gave up anything like a sex life shortly after Christopher was born. Little wonder that the Prof sought comfort with colleagues on conferences, and the occasional fling with a postgrad student. Nothing serious; he was married, after all, to a highly regarded novelist, and could not afford to let the side down. Just a little light relief . . .

Anna was different. Anna liked food, she liked wine, and she liked sex. She had no interest at all in the academic world, accepted the Prof as her intellectual superior and got on with the business of enjoying life. He was not blind to her gaudy taste in clothes, her tendency to shriek after a few drinks – but, after the long cold years of marriage to Susan, Anna was like a holiday in the sun. Even with her flowers and her shoes that didn't match her skirt and her eyeshadow that did, she was *alive*. She mouthed 'sorry', and fiddled with a gerbera that was coming out of her headdress, falling over her forehead like a floppy orange pompom. The Prof's heart beat a little faster, and he felt a smile spreading across his face, relaxing the muscles that had been tensed with worry and embarrassment.

Rachel slid into the empty chair beside Chris, and immediately dug him in the ribs with a sharp elbow. 'She looks like something out of Dr Seuss,' she whispered, as Chris stared at his knees and tried not to laugh. Their heads rocked down towards the floor, and Elizabeth's disapproving sidelong glance did not help matters.

There was some business at the desk, to which Rachel was oblivious, until Elizabeth's piercing '*pssst*' and a jab in the knee recalled her to her senses. They were asking for the witnesses. Rachel and Elizabeth stood, and moved to the desk, all trace of mirth or annoyance wiped from their faces.

My two girls, thought Anna, trying the idea out for size; it had not really occurred to her until now that she might have any maternal responsibility for her husband's children, and she wasn't at all sure that she liked the idea, having made such a hash of things with Rachel. Wasn't at all sure that she liked the children, come to that; Elizabeth found nothing to say to her, and Christopher, for all his good manners, seemed entirely too shy and self-absorbed. But she wasn't marrying Tony for his children, nor for his money, despite what everyone thought. She was marrying him because, after years of bohemian freedom, strings of lovers and marvellous parties, she was tired, and he offered a refuge. Yes, it was a refuge that only money could buy – if he didn't have the nice big house, the salary and the status, the dinners and the hotels and the honeymoon on Cape Cod, she might have been less eager to sign her name. But even without the trappings of wealth and success, Anthony Miller was a rock – and Anna needed a rock. To cling to, to hide beneath, sometimes to throw at other people.

The solemn formalities completed, the Prof slipped an arm round Anna's waist, kissed her on the lips and beamed at the assembled well-wishers while Elizabeth and Rachel bent over the desk to affirm that they had witnessed the above. Nick looked at the pair of them – sisters now – and couldn't help thinking that Rachel had by far the better arse. But his choice was made, and his own wedding was hurtling towards him like a well-oiled machine that he had no way of stopping. Marriage to Elizabeth would give him everything he wanted – for now. Money, a home, status, connections. An attractive sister-in-law was the cherry on the cake.

The Prof and Anna kissed, and everyone applauded. That's me in a few months, thought Nick. A married man. And then the Prof could sneer all he wanted. With a ring on his finger, Nick was next of kin. Elizabeth would have him, for richer, for poorer. Nick had no intention of being poorer.

The girls turned round, holding hands. Rachel whispered something in Elizabeth's ear, and Elizabeth smiled – a big, open, beaming smile that Nick could not remember seeing on her face for a long time. She, in turn, whispered in Rachel's ear, and there was laughter – God, the girl's mouth was big, her teeth white – and then a hug and a kiss. Both of them, thought Nick in a flash, but dismissed the idea before it had even fully formed. He shook Chris's hand and put an arm around his shoulders. There was one member of the family, at least, who Nick had exactly where he wanted him.

Why does he do this to me? thought Chris, felling the warm weight of Nick's arm on his back. At a wedding, of all places? He wanted to get up, to run away, but he was stuck to his seat, incapable of movement. Nick had only to wink and cock his head towards the door and Chris would follow wherever he led, to fulfil those fantasies that disrupted his revision.

I shouldn't be thinking of these things at my own father's wedding, he thought, closing his eyes and trying to banish the vision of Nick standing over him, looking down with a smile.

'Chris.'

He opened his eyes; it was Alan standing before him.

'Hi.' They hadn't spoken since the afternoon of the party, when they'd kissed in Elizabeth's bedroom. 'How are you?'

'Fine, fine.' Alan looked quizzical. 'Congratulations. You have a new mother.'

'Thanks, I suppose.'

'He'll have a brother-in-law come November,' said Nick, tightening his grip on Chris's shoulder. 'Ain't he the lucky one?'

'I should say so,' said Alan, raising an eyebrow. Chris felt faint, made his excuses and went into the garden, where a crowd was gathering around the newlyweds.

Rachel ran up to him, kissed him on the lips and said, 'I've got a brother, I've always wanted a brother, and now I've got one!' She grabbed two glasses from a passing tray. 'Watch and learn.' She drank deeply, sloshed the champagne around her mouth and swallowed. 'Oh! That's better! I thought I was going to *die* in there. I don't know why. Am I a bad person, laughing at my own mother's wedding?'

'No, I don't think so, I mean it was quite . . .'

'Oh God, here comes that Nick again,' she said, 'following me around like a bad smell. Come over here. Let's go and charm some old people. He won't follow.' She took Chris by the arm, and pulled him towards a gaggle of uncles and aunts. 'Hello,' she said brightly. 'I'm Rachel, Anna's daughter. I don't know who any of you are, but I have a feeling we might now be related.'

Nick watched her at work, and noticed, with his photographer's eye, the occasional, tiny, easy-to-miss glances in his direction.

Making sure I'm there . . . he thought.

'Well, then,' said Kate, coming up beside Elizabeth as she stood on the patio steps, looking out over the growing crowd on the lawn, sipping champagne and nibbling canapés, 'you next.'

'Yes, I suppose so,' said Elizabeth. 'It all went rather well, didn't it?'

'Once the bride had turned up, yes.'

'She makes Dad happy.'

'And that's all that matters.'

'Yes,' said Elizabeth, with what sounded to Kate suspiciously like a sigh. 'Shall we join the merry throng? I don't know about you, but I need a drink.'

Kate took her arm, and walked her down the steps, glancing across to where Nick stood, alone as usual, leaning against a wall, looking simultaneously predatory and available. She followed his eyes, and was not surprised to see on whom they rested.

Chapter 10

With love's middle-aged dream safely despatched to a hotel in Kensington, the young people gathered at the town hall doors and decided to carry on celebrating. 'But where?' asked Elizabeth, and Nick drew breath to suggest a club in Notting Hill where he occasionally played records (and where he got a small commission for bringing people) before he realised that all eyes turned to Rachel.

'Soho, of course,' she said, and was already calling someone on her phone. Nick shrugged, took Elizabeth by the arm and said, 'I don't want to go to some shitty West End tourist trap.' He was annoyed with Rachel for avoiding him all afternoon, for being more popular than him, for being another one of 'them' when he was quite certain, on that first meeting, that she was going to be on his side, among other places.

'There, that's settled,' said Rachel, dropping her phone in her bag. 'We're on the guest list at First Class.'

'Sounds good to me,' said Elizabeth.

'It's a fucking gay club,' hissed Nick in her ear.

'Don't come if you don't want to,' said Elizabeth, still smiling, disengaging herself. 'I'm sure we can manage without you.'

There was nothing to be gained by an argument, still less by staying away, and so Nick swallowed his objections, made a mental note of yet another grudge and promised himself that at least he wouldn't pay for any drinks.

'Taxi!' shouted Rachel, and about five black cabs converged on the street in front of her, the drivers jumping out to open doors. She stopped, giggled, looked at them in turn as they sucked in their stomachs and stuck out their chests, and eventually chose the oldest and most decrepit of them all.

'You,' she said to Elizabeth, grabbing her by the arm of her expensive but rather ill-fitting suit, 'are coming with me.' She bundled her into the back of the cab, and shouted, 'family only!', pushing Chris in front of her, throwing herself in between them and slamming the door, leaving the rest to fend for themselves. 'London's glamorous West End, please, driver!' she said, grabbing a hand in each of hers, whooping as the car sped off down the road, making Elizabeth wonder just how much champagne she had drunk.

Nick, Alan, Kate and Charlotte followed behind them. It was not a happy company, and would have been miserable in the extreme had not Alan and Kate kept up a flow of polite small talk. Nick and Charlotte looked out of their respective windows, each hating the other, each resenting Elizabeth for putting them through this, wondering why they had not had the guts to stand up and say no, I'm going home, I've had enough.

In the family carriage, however, things were getting very jolly long before they entered the London Borough of Westminster. Rachel had produced a small silver hip flask from her handbag – Natasha dropped it in there when she set off, 'Just in case of emergencies, darling' – and all three had taken a good mouthful of vodka, enough to make the night ahead seem thrilling, the cab too slow, the company the best in the world.

'Sisters, sisters,' sang Rachel, as the old boy in the front nodded in time and cast twinkling glances in the rear-view mirror, 'there were never such devoted sisters.' She squeezed both their hands, and both squeezed back, thinking, for the first time in their lives, that having a family could be fun, rather than something to be endured.

By the time they reached Charing Cross Road and tumbled on to the pavement, Elizabeth and Chris even felt that they loved each other, not in a 'well, s/he is my sister/brother, of course I love her/him' way, but in a warm-stomached, shoulder-shivering kind of way that made them wonder why they hadn't done this sort of thing more often.

Rachel dragged them down Shaftesbury Avenue, up Greek Street, along Old Compton Street, into a maze of streets that neither of them knew well, despite living in London all their lives, and which she seemed to know like the back of her hand. 'The others,' said Elizabeth. 'Hadn't we better . . . I mean, do they know . . .'

'We don't need them,' said Rachel, 'and anyway, I'm sure at least one of them knows where First Class is.' She giggled. 'What do you think, Chris?'

Chris threw his head back and laughed, conscious that heads were turning as they walked along the street – turning in his direction, not Elizabeth's, not even Rachel's. He felt high, as if each step bounced him three feet into the air.

'Hey!' Alan's voice was behind them. 'Wait for us!'

'Told you,' said Rachel in Chris's ear, and then, 'you're blushing! So I *am* right!', but didn't stop to explain. 'Hello darlings,' she said, sounding to herself like Natasha on one of her rabble-rousing nights. 'Welcome to the jungle. Lead on, kind sir.' She curtsied to Alan.

'I don't know the way,' he said, but turned into a narrow passage off Dean Street, muttering something like, 'down here, I suppose, isn't it?'.

'Gosh,' said Rachel, '*quelle surprise* that you would know something like that, Alan.'

'And here I shall leave you,' said Alan, holding the door open. 'Goodnight, Elizabeth.' They kissed on the cheek. 'Goodnight,

Chris.' They shook hands. Everyone objected. 'No, I'm afraid I have to meet my agent,' he said, pointing up the road, 'at the Groucho.'

'Well that tells us,' said Rachel, and her attention was caught by screams from within the club. Natasha and Mark came scuttling through the crowd, hands clutching drinks held high above their heads. She screamed back, and joined them, pulling Chris with her.

'Not my sort of place, either,' said Charlotte, who hated loud music, crowds, fashion, sex, make-up and fun on principle. 'Thanks for a lovely . . .'

Nick pushed between her and Elizabeth. 'Christ,' was all he said, before he was absorbed in the crowd.

'Do you want me to stay? I don't mind,' said Kate, 'but it looks to me as if you're fully occupied.'

'Thanks, I . . .'

'I'll take Charlotte home.' Charlotte was clutching her handbag as if she expected to be mugged, at the very least.

Kate kissed Elizabeth on the cheek, murmured, 'Call me tomorrow' in her ear, and led Charlotte to the relative safety of Leicester Square tube station. 'Lovely to see you,' she said, making it clear that they would not be sharing a train, or any unkind reflections on the day's events. 'I shall get the bus.'

She waited until Charlotte was out of sight, and hailed a cab. There were some advantages to being a popular novelist, after all.

In the noisy, underlit cube that was First Class, several hundred men and a peppering of their female friends competed for air and attention while sucking down gallons of sugary alcoholic drinks that the bar staff handed out free to their friends, charging strangers through the nose. Rachel pressed a bottle of something cold and white into their hands, and said, 'Sister, brother, I want to introduce you to my two very best friends in the whole world.' A woman who looked like the Bride of Dracula slithered off a barstool, extended a long, pale hand, the fingernails painted dark purple, looked at them through heavy-lidded, world-weary eyes, and then spoiled the illusion by hiccuping loudly and saying, 'Oops!' in the voice of a tired three-year-old.

'This is Natasha,' said Rachel, 'or what's left of her. Wonderful singer, dancer, actress . . .'

'And lush,' said the young man beside her, squeezed into a T-shirt that was designed for someone with a physique far better than his. 'I'm Mark. Pleased to meet you.' He shook hands with Elizabeth, dropped her quickly and turned his attention to her brother. 'You must be Chris. About bloody time, too, I've been asking her for weeks where she's been hiding you,' he said, and whisked him away to the other end of the bar. Chris looked back at his sister, and might have shouted for help, but the vodka was still doing its work, and this was all part of the adventure, a foretaste of life after A levels, after leaving home, a life to which Rachel was the gatekeeper.

Natasha remounted her stool with difficulty, and turned back to a bored, blank-looking young man with a shiny face who was half-listening to her, half-listening to Madonna, mouthing along to the lyrics and occasionally essaying a dance move that he had learned from repeated viewings of her videos.

'This is fantastic,' said Elizabeth, with a slightly hysterical tone in her voice. 'You know all the best places.'

'I wouldn't describe this as one of the best places, exactly,' said Rachel, 'but it's a good place to cadge drinks. We never pay for anything here. Unless *she* disgraces herself again.'

'There was something I wanted to ask you.'

'Hey Rachel,' bellowed Natasha, swinging around on her stool and only keeping her balance by throwing her drinking arm up towards her face, where some liquor sloshed into her mouth. 'Tell him. I'm fucking fabulous, aren't I, darling?'

'You are. Fucking fabulous.'

'See? I'm fucking . . . Oh.' The young man had wandered off. 'Where'd he go? Oh, for Chrissakes.' She slithered after him, falling forward on shoes that were not designed for walking.

'Sorry about Natasha,' said Rachel, 'but really, she is very talented.'

'I'm sure she is. Now, there was something I wanted to . . .'

'Rachel!' A young man with spiky black hair, a moth-eaten black jumper, and three days' stubble. 'At last!'

'Ben!' They kissed. 'What the hell are you doing here?'

'Looking for you, of course. What do you think?'

'But how did you . . .'

'Intuition. Besides, where else in town can you get free drinks?'

'Ha ha. Mark told you, I suppose.'

'He might have done. Sorry, I'm interrupting.'

'Ben, this is my new sister, Elizabeth. We've been related for . . .' She looked at her watch. 'About five hours now.' She put an arm round Elizabeth's waist. 'Elizabeth, this is Ben. He's playing Captain Jack in *The Rivals*. The best-looking boy at Alderman's.'

'Oh,' said Ben, looking down at his feet, then up through long dark eyelashes, corrugating his forehead – but he didn't deny it. 'Hi.' They shook; a couple of his fingernails were painted black.

'He's straight, believe it or not,' said Rachel. 'And he's stalking me.'

'I wouldn't call it stalking, exactly.'

'What, then? You hang around in gay bars for your own amusement?'

'Jealous, Rachel?'

'In your dreams.'

This dialogue went on in the same vein for some time, while Elizabeth looked around for Nick. She couldn't see much; the place was packed with men, most of them a good deal taller than her, and for all she knew Nick could have left, could be buying drugs in the toilets, could be . . . well, anything, really.

'I'm just going to look for Nick', she said, but Rachel wasn't listening, far too busy with her make-believe argument with her make-believe stalker. He was a perfect match for her. They had the same colouring, the same ability to look great in cheap and, in his case shabby, clothes. The same assurance that they were the best-looking person in the room. It made so much sense. Elizabeth was pleased to discover that Rachel had such a nice little boyfriend stashed away – although she had never mentioned him. Pleased, and rather relieved.

She pushed through the crowd, away from the bar, looking for brown skin in an open-necked black shirt, stripey skin-tight trousers, pointed Chelsea boots, heavy black hair falling into the narrow eyes . . . But everywhere she looked the skin was too orange, the trousers uniformly denim, the hair cut so short, she suspected an outbreak of nits. But no Nick.

Her stomach turned over; he was up to no good.

'Don't be ridiculous,' she said to herself. 'You trust him, don't you?' She stood on tiptoe, strained her eyes. 'Well you're marrying him, so you'd better trust him.'

'Talking to yourself? First sign of madness, babe.' Nick's arms slipped around her from behind, his lips found the nape of her neck, and her knees went weak.

'There you are!'

'Here I am.' He pressed into her. 'Every inch of me.'

'So I see. Who's been floating your boat?'

Some bloke over there with a big bag of weed. 'Just you, Betty-Boo. Come on. Let's go home.'

'I can't. Not yet.'

'Can't?' He pushed harder. 'Or won't?'

'Don't be silly, you know I want to, but I can't just leave them to it.'

'I see.' He pulled back. 'Family comes first, as usual. And now you've got even more family to prefer to me.'

'That's ridiculous and you know it.'

'Do I?' He spun her round, like a ballroom dancer, his large hands skimming her waist, pulling her in.

'All right. Let me finish my drink and say goodnight to Rachel.'

'Go on, then. But hurry up. We've wasted enough time on that little . . .' He was going to say 'prick tease', but at the last moment changed it to 'princess, for one night.'

'Be nice to her,' said Elizabeth. 'She's young.'

I'll be more than nice to her, thought Nick, as Elizabeth walked away from him.

'Oh, you can't go!' said Rachel. 'Please stay for another drink.'

'You're busy, and I'm tired.'

'I'm not busy in the least. I can see this one every day of the week at school.' She made it sound as if they were both twelve years old. 'How often do I get to celebrate having a new family?'

'No really, I must.' Elizabeth nodded towards Nick. 'Sorry.'

'I understand. I can't compete with that, you lucky girl.'

'Call you later.'

'Elizabeth,' said Rachel, as her new sister walked away, 'what was it you wanted to ask me?'

'It'll keep,' said Elizabeth, feeling the fun of the evening draining away like water from a leaky bucket. That surge of happiness that had pushed her to the brink of asking Rachel to be her bridesmaid had gone. 'Have fun. Love you.' She blew a kiss, and joined Nick, who took her hand and pulled her, none too gently, to the door.

In a shady nook furnished with soft couches, Chris was being pumped for gossip, none too gently, by Mark.

'Come on, there must be more about him than that. Have you ever seen him naked?'

'He's just a friend of my sister's. I don't know him that well.'

'Oh, listen to him,' said Mark, to an eager audience who had gathered when the words 'Alan Southgate' were spoken. 'So blasé. Well, is he as good-looking in the flesh as he is on screen?'

'I suppose so. I've never really thought about it.'

'Well, I've heard he's bi,' said someone who looked very much like Mark, and had this on good authority from a friend of his hairdresser who had done make-up on a TV show that Alan had appeared in. 'Shags anything that moves, they say.'

'Is that true?' demanded Mark, sounding like a prosecuting barrister.

'I've no idea!' said Chris, remembering the force of Alan's kisses, the firmness of his hands clutching at his arse. 'I told you, he's just a . . .'

'Friend of your sister's,' they chorused. 'I thought she might bring him here,' said Mark, turning his mouth down. 'Obviously, they're not such great pals as all that.'

'Oh, he was here,' said Chris. 'Didn't you see him? Dropped us off at the door then had to go on to a meeting at the Groucho.'

'The Groucho?' Five heads popped up and turned, as one, in the direction of Dean Street, like star-struck meerkats. 'Come on!'

'Oh, no, please don't,' said Chris, clasping his knees. 'He won't like it.'

'Don't bother,' said Mark. 'They don't let the likes of us in there. Bloody elitist places, I can't stand them. At least I'm true to myself and my community.' Given half a chance, he'd have been behind the smoked glass, preferably cordoned off by a velvet rope, but nobody had as yet extended the invitation. 'The Soho House is just as bad. I've been in all of these places.'

'Yeah, serving canapés you have,' said one of his lookalikes.

'That's all you know,' said Mark, and a lot of squawking ensued. Chris, who was not as yet well practised in the art of public bitching, laughed in the right places, looked around and noticed that he was being watched by a man who looked as if he might have been in the army. He blushed, looked away, looked back, and this time the man was closer; it was like a game of What's the Time, Mr Wolf?

'That man,' Chris whispered in Mark's ear. 'He's staring at me.'

'Where? Oh! Are you sure it's you he's looking at, and not me?'

'Well, I don't . . .'

Mark attempted to smoulder; Soldier Boy looked away.

'Oh, him,' said Mark, when it was clear he was not the object of interest. 'He's in here all the time. Anyway, there I was in Soho House with Jude Law on one side, and Jonny Lee Miller on the other . . .'

Nature called, and Chris made his way to the toilet. As if by magic, Soldier Boy materialised beside him.

'What's he been telling you about me?' he asked, in a husky London voice that made Chris think of fruit and veg stalls.

'Nothing . . .'

'That's all right, then.' He unbuttoned his jeans. 'My name's Phil.'

Do we shake hands at this point, wondered Chris, who was having difficulty urinating. 'Hi. I'm Chris.'

'All right, Chris.' Phil turned towards him; it seemed that he had not come to the toilet for the conventional reason. When he nodded towards a cubicle, Chris found himself following.

Nick was more than usually amorous when they got home. Perhaps, thought Elizabeth, as he kissed her on the neck and put his hand up her skirt before they'd even got their coats off, being at a wedding has reminded him of how much he really loves me. This was how it was in the early days, when he'd been insatiable and insistent, breaking down her maidenly modesty with sheer willpower, giving her a crash course in what sex was really all about, until she was just as enthusiastic as he was. Since that first fine careless rapture, they'd settled into something more workaday – but nobody can live on caviar all the time, thought Elizabeth. You have to have bread and butter as well.

Tonight, however, promised to be the full gourmet experience. He unbuttoned her blouse, unfastened her bra, his dextrous fingers making quick work of the job, and was sucking on her breasts as she leaned against the hall wall, watching their reflection in the mirror. What a fool I was to worry, thought Elizabeth. Of course everything is all right. We've just been through . . . what? A bad patch? Is that what it was? And then all thought went out the window as Nick lifted her skirt and pulled down her pants. She was hobbled, her upper body restricted by the half-removed garments, and when he led her to the bedroom, she hopped and stumbled behind him. He lay down on the bed, pulled her on top of him, and spent the next hour making up for lost time.

When Rachel realised that everyone had left – she didn't realise that Chris was actually still on the premises, although behind closed doors – and that Natasha was far too pissed to notice anything, she decided that the time had come to reward Ben for his faithful attentions over the last few months. And so, in the middle of an increasingly earnest discussion about the nature of acting, the technicalities of his performance as Jack Absolute, and his ambitions to do 'gritty new work', Rachel said, à propos of nothing, 'is your flatmate at home?'

'What?'

'Your flatmate. Whatsisname.'

'No. He stays with his girlfriend most weekends.'

'Good.'

'Why?' Ben's eyes brightened in hopeful expectation.

'Because you're taking me home tonight.'

'Home? My home?'

'No, the mental home.'

'Right . . . I mean, really? You're going to . . . ?'

'Yes. Come on, quick. Before I change my mind.'

He whisked her out the door so fast, she left a drink unfinished. As they disappeared into the Soho streets, Natasha's hand reached out, found the glass and brought it to her lips.

Chris emerged from the gents, his face burning – he'd run the gauntlet of furious stares from a queue of men waiting to use the cubicle for their own purposes, sex or drugs or even its intended purpose – but with a spring in his step. Was it this easy, really, to get what you wanted? Soldier Boy was not exactly boyfriend material, and when it was all over he'd been in a hurry to get away, which suited Chris just fine, but as sordid experiences went, this certainly beat wanking over dog-eared photographs of his sister's fiancé.

He looked around for a friendly face, but Rachel was nowhere to be seen, Elizabeth and Nick had disappeared, and when Mark saw him, he very pointedly turned away and started sucking on a straw. Time to go home, then. Chris left the club, not really knowing where he was, and without a map, but it was not yet eleven o'clock, the tubes would still be running, and he had enough money in his pocket for a ticket. He vaguely thought about looking for the Groucho Club, about which he'd heard so much, and where Alan Southgate might or might not be in a meeting with his agent. But one adventure was enough for the night. After a few wrong turnings, he found his way to Leicester Square and took a train north.

'You won't tell everyone about this, of course,' said Rachel, as she and Ben shared a post-coital cigarette. It was not a request, or even a question. 'I can't stand all that.'

'I won't if you won't,' said Ben.

They lay in the darkness, watching the glowing tips of their cigarettes, both glad that they had done what they had done, neither willing to admit that it meant more than the inevitable attraction of two beautiful people.

I have lost my virginity, thought Rachel. And about time, too. It had been ... pleasant, she supposed, was the word to describe it. Ben had enjoyed himself, obviously, and it was nice to be appreciated. Good practice for the future. A rehearsal for the real thing, when it came along,

She lay awake for hours, seeing Nick's face against the darkness of the room.

Nick was asleep now. He fell into sleep after sex like a man falling over the edge of a cliff, one moment attentive and awake, the full beam of his sexual allure shining on her, the next a dead weight from beneath which Elizabeth often had to struggle.

Elizabeth listened to Nick's steady breathing and felt the sweat drying on her temples, felt the warm soreness on her breasts where his stubble had scratched her. All was well. Her father was married and therefore off her hands, work was going well, she had a promising new sideline in journalism – that review had been well received, and more was on the way – and, best of all, she had a new sister. With Rachel around, things were just more fun. And, to cap it all, her relationship with Nick, which in a few short months would be formalised by law, was as good as it had ever been. Perhaps better.

Without waking him, she crept out of bed, located her handbag, which she had dropped just inside the flat door, and found her mobile phone.

There was something she had to do – something she'd meant to do in the club, and which she must do now, while the thought was fresh and bright in her mind.

She found Rachel's number, and composed a message.

She'll get it in the morning if she's sleeping now, thought Elizabeth. Or, more likely, she's still in that crowded club, and won't even know.

The silence of Ben's room was shattered by the beep of an incoming text.

'That's mine,' they both said, immediately reaching out in the darkness, but it was Rachel who found the little envelope sign.

'Oh, how sweet,' she said.

'What?'

'She wants me to be her bridesmaid.'

''Snice,' said Ben, and turned over.

'I suppose the children are all right,' said the Prof, lying in bed beside his new wife. 'It feels strange leaving them like this.'

'They're adults,' said Anna, who was wearing a new nuptial

nightie and was unimpressed by the turn the conversation had taken. 'Now, come here, Husband.'

'Ah,' said the Prof, 'Mrs Miller.' He took her in his arms, got a face full of lace-sheathed bosom and dismissed all thoughts of Elizabeth and Chris.

Just before midnight, Chris put his key in the lock of the Miller family home. The house was dark and silent.

Chapter 11

The house on Cape Cod belonged to a former colleague of the Prof's, 'Uncle John' to Elizabeth and Chris in their early childhood, now a hugely successful author of what the Prof privately dismissed as 'pop philosophy', and a regular guest on television shows in the United States. He and his second wife lived in New York City, and went down to 'the cabin' to entertain about once a month; for the rest of the time it stood empty. 'The cabin' was, in fact, a substantial five-bedroom saltbox house, and just one of four separate buildings that stood on the property, which made up a sort of compound between the busy little town of Barnstable and the sea. As children, Elizabeth and Chris had crossed the sandy road hand in hand to play all day on the beach under the watchful eye of the lifeguard, while their parents discussed ideas with Uncle John and his first wife, long since divorced, working their way through several shakers of martinis. Those were idyllic days, always sunny, with Mother joining them for a swim, or Uncle John taking them in his motor boat across the narrow sound to the pristine beaches of Sandy Neck, where you could run and run and never see another soul. For Chris, the memories were pure and untainted, blue skies without a cloud, the neighbours' kids always happy to play, the Prof too busy to criticise him. Elizabeth remembered the awkwardness of drunken adults, the rows between Uncle John and Auntie Renee that were already pitching them towards the divorce courts, but those shadows only served to emphasise the light.

And so, when they arrived en masse at Boston airport and piled into hired cars bound for the Cape, Elizabeth and Chris had an agreeable sense of homecoming.

Anna was nervous; would she match up to the memories that still haunted the place? What would John make of her? Could she charm him as effectively as she'd charmed Tony? Rachel and Nick, both of them heartily sick of hearing about the Good Old Days, long before the plane had even landed, took refuge in snide asides about the 'Yanks', and soon had a repertoire of private jokes that sustained them through the exclusive bonhomie of the Miller clan and well beyond.

'Here we all are,' said the Prof, as they gathered in the big stone-floored kitchen of the old wood house. 'The family together, just as it should be.'

'It's like the Waltons,' muttered Nick, and Rachel dug him in the ribs.

'I hope,' said the Prof, as if he were beginning a lecture, 'that this will be a chance for all of us to get to know each other properly, to coalesce, as it were, not just as a group of people brought together by a happy circumstance, but as a unit, a clan, a tribe, perhaps, just as the indigenous Wampanoeg people whose ancestral territory this is . . .'

'Oh Christ,' said Rachel, who was desperate to get into the sea, 'how long is this going to take?' But she said it very quietly, for only one person to hear.

They slipped away, with some show of getting luggage from the car, but nobody paid much attention.

'. . . because, as those ancient cultures understood so well, what is family but a shared sense of values, a link formed not through consanguinity but through even more fundamental notions of community, what the Greeks called . . .'

'Shall we have a drink?' said Anna, leaving the Prof's jaw biting at the air. She might never know what the Greeks called it, but that, thought Anna, was a small price to pay. Uncle John was arriving in a matter of hours, and she could not face him without at least half a bottle of wine inside her.

'Of course, my dear,' said the Prof. Elizabeth wondered how long it would before he started objecting to these interruptions; for now, he obviously still found them charming. 'I bought champagne at the airport. It won't be very cold, but . . .'

'I think warm champagne is lovely,' said Anna, grabbing the carrier bag. 'Now, where do you imagine they keep glasses?'

'Silly old fart,' said Nick, hoisting the heaviest of the cases (Anna's) out of the boot. This showed off his upper body to good advantage. 'When he gets going, there's no stopping him.'

'I think he's sweet,' said Rachel, half-watching him, half-looking towards the end of the road, where tarmac gave way to sand and grass and a worn set of wooden steps leading down to the water.

'Sweet! See how you feel at the end of next week.'

'Oh, come on,' she said, enjoying the feel of sand scuffing under her pumps. 'It's going to be fun.'

'Yeah?' Nick reached up to close the boot, his shirt riding up to expose his midriff. 'Well, I'm pleased to hear it.'

'I can't wait to get into my swimsuit and . . .'

'I can't wait for you to get into your swimsuit, either.'

'Oh, stop it!' She giggled, put a hand over her mouth. 'You're terrible.'

'And you've got two whole weeks to find out just how terrible. Now go on. Take this.' He handed her a powder-pink shoulder bag that contained nothing heavier than clothes, but she managed to totter under the weight and had to grab his arm for support.

'Oops,' she said, looking up into his eyes. The sun was behind him, catching a few hairs sticking up on his head, but it was easy to read his expression.

'Any time,' he said. 'You can . . .'

A loud pop interrupted him, and whoops of delight from within.

'They're playing my song,' said Rachel. 'Come on. Champagne.'

Nick watched her as she walked up the path to the house, her denim-clad backside wiggling from side to side. Nick felt thirsty, and followed her.

They dined together that night: all six of the Miller clan, plus Uncle John and his new bride Tamara, who used a job as a TV researcher as a launchpad to her real career of wife. She was substantially younger than John, Anna noticed with some relief – considerably younger than her, in fact, and much more obviously stupid. Her hair was bleached, her taste in clothes made Anna look chic and her conversation was vacuous and grating. John didn't seem to mind. The Prof raised his eyebrows, and nestled up to Anna, feeling proud, or perhaps relieved, that he'd chosen a more appropriate mate. Anna resolved to be kind to her hostess, whose delight in her husband's wealth was the most honest thing about her.

The two professors sat at either end of the long, well-worn dining table, a real English antique, according to Tamara, 'Just like John!' Anna, Rachel and Tamara sat down on one side, Elizabeth, Nick and Chris down on the other. All the couples were sat together, which meant that Nick could stare at Rachel across the table to his heart's content, and reach to his right to pinch Chris on the leg if he felt like causing even more trouble. Rachel and Tamara soon got talking about clothes and celebrities, Uncle John and the Prof caught up on the latest developments in post-structuralism, while Elizabeth tried to carry on a conversation with her stepmother, somewhat hampered by her father's voice booming down the table in her left ear, and Chris, as usual, was left out altogether, fending off Nick's interfering fingers and wondering if it was true, as he had read, that Cape Cod was a homosexual hot spot. His thoughts drifted, and while the rest of them shrieked and gabbled, he was back on his knees in a Soho lavatory.

'. . . Chris?'

'Huh?'

'John's asking you a question.'

'Oh sorry, Dad. What?'

'For God's sake . . .'

'Don't, Tony,' said Anna, putting a hand on the Prof's arm. 'The boy's tired. Uncle John was asking you, dear, how your exams went.'

'Oh, not bad, thanks,' said Chris, who felt certain that he'd failed every one. His heart hadn't been in the revision, and he had coasted through his A levels in a sort of trance. He was dreading the results – or dreading his father's response to them.

'And what's next, young man? University?'

'I don't know.' This earned a glare from the other end of the table. 'I think I might take a bit of time to . . .'

'Oh, these bloody gap years,' said the Prof, shaking his head. 'Don't tell me you want to travel to Machu Picchu and find yourself.'

He doesn't talk to anyone else like this, thought Chris, only me. 'No. I thought I might get a job for a while. Earn some money.'

'Good idea,' said Anna, but was interrupted by an explosive noise from her husband.

'And what sort of job are you going to get?' asked the Prof. 'Tell me that.'

I'm going to become a male prostitute, thought Chris.

'I don't know. I'll work in a shop or something.'

'A shop?'

'Oh, honey,' said Tamara, 'I used to work in a supermarket, and it was fantastic. You can make real good money, and it's an education in itself. Don't you listen to what these old men tell you. You learn more sitting behind the till in Walmart than you do in some old library.'

'If that's true,' said John, 'then it makes rather a nonsense of our work.'

'Oh, sure,' said Tamara, flapping a hand. 'You keep doing what you're doing, guys, and bring home the bacon. But you, sweetheart,' she said, dabbing her lips on a napkin and leaning over to touch Chris's hand, 'you just do what you gotta do. That's my advice.'

This was the only positive parental advice Chris had received in recent years, and he took it to heart. When Nick's pinching fingers sought his bare leg again, he did not push them away.

Elizabeth was whispering to her father. 'For God's sake, Daddy, leave him alone. It's not easy for everyone.'

'Ridiculous,' muttered the Prof, filling his mouth with lobster salad. 'A supermarket!'

'It wouldn't do you any harm to come down from your ivory tower once in a while, Professor Miller,' said Anna. 'You're altogether too out of touch with reality.'

'Stop ganging up on me,' said the Prof, rather enjoying the feeling. 'He's big enough to take care of himself.'

Rachel tried to avoid Nick's eyes, which wasn't easy, given the seating plan, but she did not want to give Elizabeth any reason to think that she was encouraging his attentions. They were not unwelcome – Nick was without a doubt the most attractive man she had ever met, and her brief affair with Ben had given her a taste for sex. But on a family holiday? Under his girlfriend's nose? When she was meant to be the *bridesmaid* . . .

'And what about you, honey? When are we going to see your name in lights?' Thank God for Tamara, thought Rachel, turning her attention to the left, but running her fingers through her hair just to make sure that Nick kept watching.

'Oh, I don't know about that,' she said. 'I'm only at college.'

'I hear great things,' said John. 'Your reputation precedes you.'

'What?'

'You made quite a splash in *The Rivals*, I gather. Wonderful play. Comedy. So difficult,' said John.

'Oh,' said Rachel, wondering who on earth in the Miller party would bother to say anything so positive about her. 'Well, it was all right.'

'Don't hide your light under a bushel,' said John. 'Elizabeth says you stole the show.'

Elizabeth, of course. 'Well, that's very kind of her, but I don't think . . .'

'You did, you were great,' said Elizabeth. 'I was very proud of you. The girl who played Lydia was outclassed.'

'Thank you. Not everybody thought so.'

'My daughter is a professional theatre critic, I'll have you know,' said the Prof, somewhat sarcastically, disapproving of journalism as a distraction from academia, 'so she must be right.'

'We're doing it again at the beginning of next term. It's quite a big night. The agents come, apparently.'

'Well, here's to you, sweetheart,' said Tamara, raising a glass. 'You'll be on Broadway before you know it, and I'll be proud to say that I know you.'

*   *   *

By common consent, there were no more dinners for eight around the antique English table. The company divided first along generational lines, then subdivided into couples, leaving Rachel and Chris very much in each other's company, which suited them both. As the youngest members of the party, they were natural allies; for Chris, it was the first time he'd had a real confidante, someone with whom he could share secrets and discuss problems.

He told her about the man in the First Class toilets.

'What was his name?' asked Rachel, as they lay on the beach beside the embers of a fire, on which they had toasted marsh-mallows, thinking this very American, and being appalled by the result. A chilly wind was starting to blow off the sound, making the seagrass whisper.

'Phil,' said Chris. 'That's all I know about him.'

'You're as bad as Mark.'

'It's the first time I've ever done anything like that.'

'Will you see him again? Don't tell me – you didn't get as far as exchanging numbers.'

'I was going to look for him, but then I thought better of it.'

'Don't tell me. There's someone else.'

'No,' said Chris, thinking of Alan. 'There's no one else.'

'Your time will come.'

'What about you and this Ben?' Chris had confided in Rachel, and now it was her turn.

'He's just a friend.'

'Really? Can I have him, then?'

'Go ahead. I don't have time for that sort of thing.'

'Pull the other one. I've seen the effect you have on men.'

Rachel giggled, and put a hand over her mouth. 'I can't help it. Have you seen the way he stares at me?' They both knew who she was talking about. 'It's embarrassing! I hate him!'

A log collapsed, sending up a shower of sparks, and there behind them, like a conjurer behind a curtain, stood Nick, in a pair of baggy skater shorts and nothing else. He was dripping.

'Oh,' said Rachel. 'Talk of the devil.'

'I'm freezing.' Nick dropped to the sand and reclined on one arm, the dying light of the fire illuminating his torso in flickering relief.

'Been for a dip?' asked Rachel, in a cut-glass English accent.

'Yeah. Needed to cool off.'

'It's really quite chilly for the time of year, I find.'

'Oh yeah?'

Chris felt like a gooseberry, and wanted to leave.

'Where's Elizabeth?' asked Rachel.

'Indoors, talking to Uncle Bloody John, as usual. Leaving Tammy-Faye to paw me. That's why I had to go for a swim.'

'She get you all worked up, sport?'

'Oh yeah. She's just my type.'

'Funny,' said Rachel, 'Chris and I were just discussing that very question.'

'And what might that be?'

'What *is* your type?'

'You know.'

'I'm quite sure I don't.' She sounded like something from an Ealing comedy.

A stronger gust blew ash and sand in Chris's eyes. 'Ow. Shit,' he said, glad of an excuse to make it back to the house. Neither Rachel nor Nick tried to help.

'Getting colder,' said Nick. 'I've got goosebumps.'

'Yes, you have.'

'Fancy a walk along the beach?'

'Don't you need some clothes?'

'Do I?'

'I suppose not.'

'Come on.'

It was dark past the three or four other houses that made up the shorefront community, just the light of the moon and the stars, the gentle, muffled clang-clang of rigging on the masts of pleasure boats. Nick put his arm around Rachel's waist.

'I still haven't taken your picture, have I?'

'No, you haven't.'

'I want to.'

'I know.'

'So how about it?'

'I don't think you have your camera with you at the moment,' said Rachel, 'unless you're hiding it somewhere.'

'No, love, that's not my camera.'

'I thought it might not be.'

'Want to . . .'

'Hello!' Anna's voice, floating across the sand from fifty yards away. 'Who goes there?'

They sprang apart like opposing magnets.

'Only us!' trilled Rachel, wondering how much her mother had seen. The Prof could be relied on to notice nothing.

'Lovely evening, isn't it?' said Anna, who was wearing a kaftan that she'd found on a day trip to Provincetown. She scrutinised her daughter's face, but gave no sign of what she read there. 'We've been all the way to the marina and beyond. It's so romantic.'

'Yes,' said Rachel, avoiding her mother's eyes. 'It's lovely.' She shivered. The Prof took off his cardigan and put it around her shoulders.

'Oh, thank you.' It came down to her knees, and over her knuckles. She turned up the collar.

'Time we all got back to the house, I think,' said Anna, brightly. 'I don't know about you, but I'm ready for a little nightcap.'

Nick melted back into the shadows. Anna, Rachel and the Prof walked back to the house. Nothing more was said.

Chapter 12

'Damn it. I can't go to your next performance.'

'Why not?'

'Because I'm reviewing for the paper on Saturday night.'

'Oh.' Rachel sounded genuinely disappointed. 'Well, you've seen *The Rivals* before. It's just nice to know you're there.'

'I'll make sure Nick comes,' said Elizabeth. 'To lend you moral support.'

'Great.' The kind of support Nick had been offering Rachel throughout the holiday, and in increasingly lurid texts since they got back, was anything but moral, and Rachel's resistance was getting low. She'd held out for the holiday, much to his obvious chagrin, but now they were no longer surrounded by the family there were no more excuses. She was caught in the fierce glare of Nick's desire, like a rabbit in headlights. 'What are you reviewing?'

'Some bed-hopping farce in the West End. Not my cup of tea. But they seem to like sending me out to do all the things that nobody else wants to do, and if I can get a foot in the door, you know . . .'

'Of course. There's a cast party after the show, if you fancy it.'

'Oh,' said Elizabeth, 'I'd love to, but I have to file.'

'It's okay. It'll just be the usual drunks. I'll put in an appearance and sneak off early. I need my beauty sleep.'

'Good girl. See you Sunday, anyway.'

'Lunch?'

'At Dad's as usual. Love you. Bye.'

'Bye.' The line had gone dead. 'Love you, too,' said Rachel, quietly.

But this was a lunch date that Rachel was destined to miss.

'I wish you were coming with me,' said Nick, stepping out of the shower and towelling his hair. Elizabeth was at the dressing table, wrapped in a dressing gown, choosing earrings. He lifted up her hair, kissed her on the back of the neck. 'I won't know what to say to anybody. What's the play about again?'

'Don't be silly,' she said, feeling shivers down her spine. 'You'll understand it. It's not that difficult.'

'I don't have your heducational hadvantages,' said Nick in his best cockney accent. 'I don't know anything about theatre.' He pronounced it with an F. 'But 1 like seeing the pretty ladies in their fine dresses.'

'You sound like Dick van Dyke. Now stop it, I've got to get ready.' She watched his buttocks describing figures of eight as he walked into the bathroom. This play had better be good, she thought, and was already sharpening a few barbed phrases in case it was not. 'Marriage is no laughing matter,' she said to herself, 'at least, not in this woefully unfunny farce.'

Nick stepped into a pair of black Calvin Kleins, a gift from Elizabeth that resembled a jockstrap more than conventional pants, and turned from side to side, surveying the effect. Yes, he thought. She will approve.

Natasha regarded her flatmate's triumphant return to the role of Julia as one hell of a Dressing-Up Opportunity, and although the agents would be there to see Rachel rather than her, she was damned if she was going to let the evening go by without making an impression of her own. First of all, she covered her entire face in a green-tinted moisturiser; she had noticed to her horror that she was getting a bit florid, which she put down to some kind of food intolerance rather than alcohol abuse, and this was supposed to tone it down. Before the green had really had time to soak in, she started plastering on the foundation; at present she favoured a super-pale biscuit colour, which, mixed with the green, gave her the look of something dredged from the canal.

'Where's my lash technician?' she screamed above the getting-ready CD, one of Mark's interchangeable house mixes. 'I need glue.'

Mark was getting good at this, which was just as well, because Natasha's hands had a tendency to shake.

'Close,' he said, straddling her knee and offering the glued-up lashes to one eye, then the other. 'Now don't move, don't speak, don't even breathe.'

'Can I smoke?' she croaked out of a pea-sized hole in the side of her mouth.

'Of course you can smoke,' he said. 'I don't want to kill you.'

'I don't suppose *she* is here, is she?'

'Of course not. She's at the theatre.'

'She's never here.'

'Not during *your* waking hours, perhaps.'

'Is she fucking someone? That Ben, for instance?'

'I don't think so,' said Mark, testing a lash. 'Sit still.'

'Then who?'

'She doesn't tell me everything.'

'Well, she barely speaks to me. Ever since the summer, she's been quite unmanageable. Really, you know, I think we might have to get rid.'

'Don't be ridiculous, she's going to be a star and I want to say we shared a flat for ages and ages. Okay. Open. Perfect. I'm a genius.'

'You are, darling.' Natasha surveyed the results, and approved. 'I don't know what I'd do without you.'

'Die, probably. Now come on. Put some bloody clothes on. Curtain's up in an hour.'

'Don't rush me.' She stepped into an elasticated, sequinned tube, black at the top, fading through grey to silver at the bottom. It reached, at a stretch, above the nipples and below the crotch, but she would spend the rest of the evening pulling it up and down in order to reveal all.

'Is that it?'

'Of course not, silly.' She put on a pair of stripper heels. 'There. Ready.'

'Oven ready, by the look of it,' said Mark, and they teetered out into the night.

Rachel put the final dusting of powder over her stage face, brushed a little off her bare shoulders and went over her lines for the final time. Of course she had them by heart; she repeated the part to herself every day, at least twice, but you never knew when stage fright would hit, and she had yet to get used to that uncanny sensation of being watched. During the first run, three performances at the end of term, she'd dried badly once, and had to be rescued by Ben, who seemed to know everyone's part just as well as his own, and had steered her back on course. That would never happen again.

The affair with Ben had petered out by unspoken mutual consent at the end of the summer term. Rachel saw, without surprise, that he had upgraded to a casting director who had several continuing TV dramas in her gift; Rachel herself was being hotly pursued by Colin the tutor, who could hardly wait for her to graduate so that his extracurricular interest in his star student wouldn't lead to instant dismissal. Rachel did nothing to encourage him, and precious little to discourage him, either. It was nice to be adored.

She looked at herself in the mirror. This was not a full-on period production of *The Rivals*, much to everyone's disgust; they had all been looking forward to wigs and bustles and beauty patches, believing that anything written before 1960 was a great excuse to raid the dressing-up box. Colin, who was directing the piece, insisted on its 'modernity', and hence decreed that everyone should wear 'heightened street clothes' and minimal make-up. Having noticed the way Colin stared at her mouth, she covered her lips in the brightest, glossiest, pillar-box-red lipstick that money could buy. When she made her first entrance, she knew where every man in the house was looking. True, Lydia had the lion's share of the lines, but Rachel didn't need to talk to get attention. Colin, while approving of her performance on dramatic grounds, writhed in jealous agony in the wings. When Julia and Faulkland had their big fight in act three, and Rachel had to rush off in tears, she found herself on more than one occasion running straight into the protective arms of her director.

Certain technical aspects of the art of acting were beyond her, but Rachel knew how to get a reaction. Despite the fragility of her appearance, which made men like Colin want to protect her, she was about as subtle as a Trident missile. While she was on stage, nobody could think of anything else but what it would be like to be her, or be with her. While the actress playing Lydia chattered and capered and showed off her comic timing, Rachel stood still and felt the lust.

And tonight would be special. Nick would be in the audience. She blotted her lipstick, rearranged a strand of hair and adjusted the top of her dress to show a little more shoulder. The American tan was fading; her skin looked like marble. He would notice that, with his photographer's eye. He had taken a few shots on Sandy Neck one afternoon, the wind in her hair, her shoulders bare, 'publicity shots for you', he said, touching the side of her face to turn her towards the light. She felt a shock from his touch, down her neck to her stomach. She had never felt that way when Ben touched her.

It would be so easy to do. Just sit back and let nature take its course. The brakes were off, the juggernaut rolling closer and closer, ready to smash the House of Miller to rubble. Without lifting a finger, she could destroy Elizabeth's marriage, her mother's marriage, tear her new family into pieces, enslave one man and break half a dozen hearts.

She felt her power, as intoxicating as vodka or cocaine. She had only to let it happen, to do nothing, and everything would change.

Could she stop it even if she wanted to? I'm not a bad person, she said to the mirror. I don't want to hurt anyone. I love Elizabeth, in a way. But this . . . I have never felt this before. I am not in control.

I can't help it.

Nick watched the play like a man watching television with the sound down. He didn't much care about the story, which seemed inconsequential to the point of idiocy, and very soon got annoyed by people laughing in all the right places, as if something funny had been said. Only Rachel held his attention, but it was not her performance he was concentrating on.

He was weighing in his mind the pros and cons of moving from one stepsister to another, and wondering if he could effect the transition without fatally screwing up his financial position.

There was no doubt which side his bread was buttered on; Elizabeth owned a flat, she had a job, and was making a few bob on the side with her journalism. More to the point, she stood to inherit a big chunk of money when the old man finally popped his clogs. But that could be years away; the Prof could have another twenty-five years in him, by which time Nick would be fifty-odd, and well past taking advantage of what the money could do for him. He and Elizabeth would be celebrating their silver wedding anniversary, they'd have a bunch of kids, possibly even grandchildren, and she'd have nagged him into getting a proper job long ago. He'd be a fat, balding middle-management type, using hookers in hotels, wondering what could have been if he'd had the courage to take the plunge all those years ago.

Rachel, on the other hand, was an unknown quantity. She was gorgeous, of course, and that counted for a lot; Nick wanted more than anything else to shag the living daylights out of her, especially when he saw her simpering and pouting on stage, thinking she was so bloody clever. But she was also broke. Her mother might inherit a good deal of the Prof's money, and that would come to Rachel – but Anna was even younger than the Prof. By the time she died, Nick might be in his sixties – the Prof's age. It didn't bear thinking about.

But there was something that told Nick that, despite her present circumstances, Rachel was a good bet. She already looked like a star, and given the right breaks, she could be out-earning all the rest of them put together in a couple of years. And if he, with all his promise, hitched his wagon to her star, then couldn't he too ride to glory? With Rachel's money and connections, his dreams might become reality. He'd get the girl, he'd get the gold and he'd get what he wanted more than anything – the status that success bestows. It was the one piece missing from his puzzle. He had looks, he had talent, of that he was sure; all that was missing was status. Power. Position. Elizabeth could give him some of those things. Could Rachel give him more?

* * *

The performance went well. Colin was delighted, kissed Rachel on the lips and gave her a huge bouquet – much bigger than the one he gave to Lydia. There was muttering and sniggering in the dressing room; some people wouldn't speak to Rachel, while others suddenly wanted to be her best friend. She changed as quickly as possible, stuck a couple of Colin's roses in her hair and put on her party dress, a simple green silk shift that she'd picked up for a song in the Zara sale. On her, it looked like couture.

Colin, Chris, Natasha, Mark and Nick were hovering around the dressing-room door. Colin glared at everyone else, wishing he could whisk her away to a restaurant somewhere. Chris went to kiss her, but was thrust aside by Natasha, who threw her arms in the air, screamed, 'You're fabulous!' and steered Rachel on a lap of victory around the bar. She was quickly surrounded by admirers.

Nick knew that he had no need to compete with the others; he'd seen exactly what Rachel's eyes were doing when she walked into the room, her pupils flitting about until they found him. He only had to wait, and make his move. He retreated to the other end of the bar, got a beer and lit a cigarette.

A good-looking young man moved in beside him, an unlit cigarette in his hand. 'Any chance of a light?'

'No.'

He watched Rachel do a full circuit of the room, clockwise, moving away from him at first, but always checking to see where he was. She passed from one group to the next, gathering a larger following with every step, until the party resembled a conga line. There was a lot of kissing, a lot of jockeying for position. The dark-eyed, dark-haired man in the denim jacket who was staring at her like a starving dog in a butcher's window was gradually elbowed to the back of the line. Bad move, pal, thought Nick, assuming this was his only serious rival.

Eventually, she got close enough for Nick to eavesdrop. Among the 'fabulous' and 'marvellous' and 'darlings', he caught what sounded like a serious business proposition.

'Who's the lady with the shoulder pads?' asked Nick, when Rachel finally landed at his feet.

'Important casting agent.' She sounded out of breath.

'Oh, yeah. How important?'

'Important enough to piss everyone else off.' She surveyed the room. 'See how they're all staring at me? If looks could kill . . .'

'That's because you're talking to the best-looking man in the room.'

Rachel feigned confusion. 'Where?'

'Right here, baby, and you know it.'

'Oh, aren't you full of yourself?'

'Yeah. And wouldn't you like to be?'

Chris came over at the wrong moment. 'Want a drink, Rachel?'

'Oh, I . . .'

'I'm getting the drinks in,' said Nick, without offering to include Chris in the round. He took the hint, and walked off.

'That was rude.'

'Three's a crowd.'

'I thought he was your friend.'

'He's Elizabeth's brother.'

'So?'

'And I don't want him telling her what's happening.'

'And what, exactly, is happening?'

'You know,' said Nick. 'We're leaving this party right now, and I'm taking you back to your place. And when we get there . . .' He leaned towards her ear and told her exactly what he intended to do.

'I'll get my coat,' she said, feeling strangely numb.

It started in the taxi: kisses, hands on legs, on breasts, on crotches. The taxi driver had seen it all before, of course, but even he thought these two were going for it, and put his foot down in order to save his upholstery.

They made it to the front door without actual penetration taking place, and disengaged for long enough for Rachel to get the key in the lock – not easy when Nick was humping her from the rear – and, once inside, they collapsed to the floor, tearing at each other's clothes, until they were both naked. Rachel manoeuvred them into her bedroom, and locked the door. Natasha and Mark wouldn't be home for hours, as long as the bar didn't run dry, but she was taking no chances. She concentrated on the practicalities of what she was doing; it made it easier to blot out the bigger issues.

Once in bed, he took her by storm. Ben had treated her reverently, like an *objet d'art*. Not so, Nick. His big, square, brown hands grabbed her arse and lifted her in the air, forcing her to wrap her legs around his waist, locking her ankles in the small of his back. While his fingers entered her from the rear, his mouth was locked on to her breasts, sucking and biting, never hard enough to hurt, but far from gently. She could feel his cock pressing against her, ready to slip in.

'Wait, baby,' he said, dumping her softly on the mattress, then hooking his jeans from the floor with his big toe. There was a condom in the pocket, and he tore the packet open with his teeth. One, two, three swipes of his hand, and he was ready.

Rachel leaned back on her elbows, opened her legs and thought of the destruction she was about to unleash with this one simple act. It was too late to stop now.

Chapter 13

The clock was ticking, the wedding getting closer and closer, and Elizabeth immersed herself in the preparations. They were an excellent distraction. Questions like, 'Do the shoes match the dress?' or 'Have the caterers got enough vegetarian meals?' were much easier to deal with than 'Is the man I'm marrying an attractive but ultimately worthless sponger?' or 'Is he being unfaithful behind my back?' It was hard, at this late stage, to realise that she'd never really trusted Nick. In the first rush of love, she took so much for granted; now, as a bigger reality appeared on the horizon, her mind was clouded with doubt. Was he losing interest in her? Taking her and her money for granted? Looking elsewhere for excitement? Elizabeth had no concrete reasons for thinking so. He'd been going out with his friends more than usual, but that was to be expected so close to the wedding. It was natural for him to enjoy his last few weeks of bachelorhood. That's all it was. Perhaps Elizabeth had last-minute jitters herself, and was looking for problems where none existed. All the same, she made a point of satisfying Nick in bed as often as possible, working on the principle that a man who is getting it at home is far less likely to stray. On the good nights, she fell asleep almost immediately afterwards, exhausted by her day job, her evening job and her bedtime duties. On the bad nights she lay awake, wondering if Nick had been less enthusiastic than usual and, if so, whether that was due to a) excessive dope consumption or b) the fact that he was getting it elsewhere. As the wedding approached, the bad nights started to outweigh the good.

She desperately wanted to confide in someone – but who? The Prof was out of the question; she'd never gone to him with personal things, and besides, he made it quite clear at the outset that he disliked Nick, and would greet any misgivings on her part with unalloyed delight. Chris was just a kid. Anna was hopeless, too; Elizabeth would never admit any weakness to her. Normally, she'd have taken her troubles to Kate, but since that awkward Sunday afternoon in the kitchen, when Elizabeth had insisted that she was marrying the right man, she didn't feel she could go crawling back and say, 'Actually, Kate, I'm not so sure'. Alan was Nick's best man, which ruled him out, and Charlotte was so fundamentally opposed to the whole idea of marriage that she would only get a lecture from her on the benefits of the celibate life.

That left Rachel – her stepsister. She'd listen and give advice and comfort, make Elizabeth feel good about herself. She'd laugh Elizabeth out of her foolish fears. Yes, Rachel was the one to turn to. That's what sisters are for.

One Saturday morning, a week before the wedding, Elizabeth and Rachel went shopping for a bridesmaid's dress.

'What about green?' said Elizabeth, as they stood in Debenhams, surveying rack after rack of clothes that she would never dare to try on.

'Green? Absolutely not. You never wear green to a wedding. Terrible bad luck.'

'I've never heard that one before.'

'I think blue or grey,' said Rachel.

'Oh no, not grey . . . Oh. I see.' Rachel whisked something off a hanger – it looked like a dishrag until she held it up against herself, when it was suddenly transformed into the most alluring garment of all time. The pewter colour of the silk came to life, reflecting light off Rachel's curves. 'If I just put a belt round it,' she said, pulling it in at the waist, 'I think it could work. Oh, and look!' She pulled out the label. 'It's marked down by seventy-five per cent! What a stroke of luck.'

'How come I never find things like that?'

'You don't look in the right places.' She put the dress back on the rack. 'I'm sure we can do better.'

'Oh, I don't know. That was lovely . . .'

'Yes, but what about this?' Rachel found a little suit, royal blue with white piping, the sort of thing that Elizabeth considered frumpy but which, on Rachel, made one think of Jackie Kennedy. 'That could be fun. Are we doing hats?'

'You're going to be the belle of the ball,' said Elizabeth, seeing an opening for the subject she wanted to discuss. 'I'll have to watch you around my husband.'

'Oh, don't,' said Rachel, turning towards a full-length mirror and surveying the effect of the suit. 'He's terrible!'

This sounded innocent enough, and Elizabeth had a lovely vision of all her anxieties evaporating in the bright light of truth. 'What do you mean?'

Rachel had been debating whether or not to put an end to this ridiculous affair, and had actually had as many sleepless nights as Elizabeth, although some of them for slightly different reasons. Nick was a bastard, she could see that – he might as well carry around a big neon sign to that effect. He was a coward, a cheat, he was lazy and dishonest. And all that mattered while he had his clothes on. But as soon as they were together, things changed. It wasn't just his body – although it was by far the most beautiful thing that Rachel had ever seen, and made her slightly sick just thinking about it. It was how he made her feel. Of course, he was a wonderful lover; that was no surprise. He knew exactly what to do, and he enjoyed doing it. But there was more to it than that, some mysterious magic that he worked on her. When they were apart, she was all too aware of his faults, and of the terrible risks she was running, the pain she was causing to others. But when they were together, none of that mattered. The danger turned her on. The sense of surrender was intoxicating. She felt, with Nick, as if she were falling from a great height, and there was nothing she could do about it. The pain of a guilty conscience enhanced the pleasure of doing wrong. Even now, standing in front of a mirror in Debenhams' womenswear department, modelling a suit that she would wear once and then consign to the dressing-up box, she was starting to feel that giddiness, that sense of falling . . .

'Oh, he's just such a flirt,' she replied, hoping that her red cheeks did not give her away. 'You know what he's like.' Better to admit to a little than to nothing at all.

'Yes, he's certainly got a roving eye.'

And a roving cock, thought Rachel, with a sudden, vivid memory of what that errant member had been doing to her just twenty-four hours ago during one of their afternoon trysts. She felt breathless, and thought she might have to sit down. 'Yes,' she said, 'but I'm sure that's all.' This didn't sound good; it was weak and confused, as if she were hiding something. 'So what do you think: the grey or the blue?'

'They're both lovely,' said Elizabeth, who had insisted on paying for whatever Rachel chose. 'I hope he's not been . . . hassling you, has he?'

Rachel thought back to the campaign of seduction that began when they first met, the siege that lasted through the entire fortnight on Cape Cod, the final push that broke down her resistance at the after-show party. Hassling was really not the word for it.

'Nothing I can't handle, thanks,' said Rachel, and then, realising that this sounded too much like a confession, added, 'worst luck.

If he wasn't marrying you, I'd have been very tempted. But I'm not like Natasha.' Better to sell her friend down the river than to admit to anything herself. 'I don't try to steal other people's boyfriends.'

'Does she? How rotten.'

'Oh, yes. She's had a few off me.' Rachel thought of a few cast-offs who had been hoovered up by the less discriminating Natasha. 'I never introduce her to anyone I'm interested in now. That's why I haven't told her about Colin.'

'Who's Colin?' Elizabeth's eyes lit up; job done. 'You didn't tell me about a Colin.'

'He's my . . . Well, it's awkward.' It certainly was awkward, as Colin had been pestering her with phone calls and letters, and was becoming a liability even at college. Let Elizabeth think he had succeeded.

'Oh, go on. I won't tell a soul, I promise.'

Rachel whispered in her ear. 'He's my tutor.'

'What, at Alderman's?'

'Shhh! Yes. Isn't it awful?'

'Well well well. You're a dark horse, Rachel Hope.'

'I didn't want to do it,' said Rachel, saying the right words about the wrong person. 'I know it's wrong and we're going to end up hurting people. But he just wore me down. He's so gorgeous, I couldn't resist any more.' She felt a sense of rising hysteria. 'And the sex,' she added, 'is fantastic. He's the greatest lover I've ever had.'

'Wow.'

'Oh, yes,' said Rachel. 'I just don't think I can give him up.'

'Well, I suppose when you find someone like that, you just have to follow your heart.'

'Yes,' said Rachel. 'That's rather how I feel. So, come on. Grey, or blue?'

'Whichever you like,' said Elizabeth, who felt so grateful that she would have paid for both.

'I'd like you to choose.'

'Well then, let's go for the blue.'

'Good choice,' said Rachel. 'Now can we have a drink?'

Nick was quite happy to go without a stag night; an evening out with the boys was an evening he couldn't spend with Rachel. But for appearance's sake, he allowed Alan to take him out for dinner, the groom and best man doing a bit of last-minute bonding. He was surprised when Chris turned up as well.

'Sent you to keep an eye on me, has she?'

'No,' said Chris, who had barely spoken to Nick since giving his marching orders on Cape Cod. 'Alan invited me.'

Well, thought Nick, as long as Alan's paying the bill, I don't care who he invites. It was nice to be seen in public with a celebrity. It was something Nick intended to get used to, one day. It didn't matter that his girlfriend's little brother tagged along, staring at Alan with stars in his eyes, the way Nick himself used to stare at him. Nice of Alan to ask him. Unless, of course, there was more to it than that . . .

Dinner went well enough. Alan chose a restaurant in the West End where he knew he would not be pestered by star-struck fans. They met for a drink at the Groucho, and from the moment the barman greeted them, Nick was on his best behaviour. This was what he wanted – the easy access to the private clubs, the relaxed familiarity of the staff, the nods and waves and how's-it-goings from people that he had only ever seen on television. Alan ordered champagne, and from the very first sip, they were off and running. Nick talked at length about his plans, his photography projects, and said very little about his forthcoming marriage. Alan occasionally interrupted with an anecdote from studio or location, some titbit about a famous friend, some deli-cious piece of insider info that just had to be true, you couldn't make it up. Chris sat and watched, sipping at the champagne that he was only just old enough to drink. When Alan caught his eye, Chris no longer looked away.

Thus launched, they made their way to the restaurant, where the good mood lasted until they were well into their main course, and Nick had started drinking more heavily.

'A toast,' said Nick, rather too loudly. Alan recharged their glasses and hoped that this hadn't been a big mistake. He wanted to come to this restaurant again, and people – impor-tant people – were already looking at them.

'Here's to you and Eliz—'

'My last night of freedom,' said Nick, rather inaccurately, as the wedding was still three days away, but the meaning was clear enough. 'From now on it's the old ball and chain for me. Cheers.' He raised his glass, and drank deeply, not seeing the look that passed between Alan and Chris.

'Yeah, cheers,' they murmured, feeling uneasy, hoping that Nick would go to the toilet soon so they could discuss him.

'She's a fine woman, Elizabeth,' said Nick, finishing his glass and smacking his lips. 'Very good at what she does. You know. Very *clever*.' It did not sound like a compliment. 'She'll make a very good *wife*.'

'Yes,' said Chris, 'I'm sure she will.'

'Oh yes, everyone thinks so, don't they? Everyone thinks I'm very lucky.'

This sounded dangerous to Alan, who wondered aloud if anyone was thinking of having a dessert or coffee or anything or should they just get the bill and –

'I know what everyone says,' continued Nick. 'They think I'm not good enough for her.'

'Oh come on, Nick, nobody thinks that.'

'Yes, they do. I know what the old man thinks of me. Thinks I'm a waste of fucking space.'

People were frowning and whispering around them, including a journalist whom Alan had charmed the pants off a couple of weeks ago. He smiled at her rather weakly, and wished he'd never brought them here.

'That's not true at all.'

'They don't know anything,' said Nick. 'I could tell you a thing or two . . .' He stopped suddenly, and closed his mouth. 'Is there anything left in that bottle?'

'Yes, sure,' said Alan, pouring the rest of the wine into Nick's glass; at least if he was drinking, he was not talking, and when they got him to a club the music would be so loud that he could rant and rave to his heart's content. He waggled his fingers at the waiter, and the bill appeared.

'So, Chris,' said Alan, in an unnaturally bright voice, 'what's happening in your world? Any news?'

'I've got some work experience with a . . .'

'Oh, work ekshperience,' said Nick, his lips dripping with wine. This was getting awkward; Alan produced his credit card, anything to hasten their exit. 'Your family is only interested in work, work, work. When do you find time to have fun?'

'Well, I've got to do something with my life,' said Chris, and immediately wished he hadn't.

'Oh, right. *Right*. Meaning I haven't, I suppose.'

'I didn't mean that at all.'

'You're just the same as your bloody dad. You think I can't get a proper job.'

'Come on, Nick,' said Alan, 'nobody's having a go at you.'

'Well you weren't always so bloody fussy were you, Chrissie-Wissy.'

'I don't know what . . .'

'Couldn't keep your bloody hands off me, could you? Got you all going, haven't I?' Nick hiccuped loudly. 'You and your sister and your bloody stepsister. All want a bit of it, don't you?'

He stood up, grabbed his crotch and then, before he could do anything really disgusting, staggered slightly and grabbed the edge of the seat. 'I'm going outside for a fag,' he said. 'Don't be long.'

'Christ,' said Alan, when Nick was safely out of earshot 'Is he always like this?'

'Dunno. Last-minute jitters, I suppose.'

'What's all this about you and him?' Alan leaned across the table. 'Should I be jealous?'

'Jealous? You? I don't think so.'

'Have you and he ever . . . you know.'

'Of course not!'

'Good.'

Chris frowned. 'What's so good about it?' Since that long-ago encounter in a club toilet, Chris had been unhappily chaste.

'I don't want to share you.'

'You . . . what?'

'Why do you think I asked you tonight?'

'Because you felt sorry for me, I suppose.'

Alan smiled, his teeth dazzling white. 'Let's get rid of Nick,' he whispered, 'and I'll show you just how sorry I feel.'

Nick returned, bumping into furniture and earning furious glances from fellow diners. Alan helped him into his coat and bundled him out of the restaurant.

'Time for a club,' said Nick, putting an arm round Alan's shoulder and dragging him down Shaftesbury Avenue. 'The night is young.'

Chris followed, wondering where he would be sleeping. And wondering, in the back of his mind, what Nick meant about 'your bloody stepsister'.

While the stags were at bay in Soho, the hens were enjoying a Girls' Night In at Kate's. Her husband had taken the children to see their grandparents for a couple of days, leaving the coast clear for the orgy of white wine and chocolate to which she had invited Charlotte and Rachel.

'Oh God,' said Elizabeth, at about nine o'clock, 'I shudder to think what the boys are up to.'

'Probably best if you don't know,' said Rachel.

'I don't suppose there's much to worry about,' said Kate, without adding 'as long as Rachel stays where I can see her'. 'Nick's not the lap-dancing type, is he?'

'I shouldn't have thought so,' said Elizabeth, with a giggle, 'but you never know, do you?'

'I should hope he isn't,' said Charlotte. 'You know what those places are? They're *entrepots* for human-trafficking networks. Girls are kidnapped in small rural villages in the former Soviet states and . . .'

'More chocolate, anyone?' said Kate, who recognised the beginning of a long and thoroughly depressing feature she'd recently read in the *Guardian*.

' . . . form of slavery, and many of them disappear completely. I've been getting quite involved in a group that's trying to reach out to some of these women and . . .'

'Please, Charlotte, this is supposed to be a party.'

'You can't turn a blind eye to these things,' she said, 'they're happening all around them and if we don't make our voices heard –'

Kate turned up the stereo. 'Oh, I love this one,' she said. '"Girls Just Wanna Have Fun."'

'We are all contributing to the problem, we're as bad as the men who pay these girls for sex . . .'

Rachel stood up. 'Anyone for a drink? I've got a bottle of champagne in the fridge. I think the time has come.'

'Marvellous idea.'

'I'll get the glasses,' said Elizabeth, and the three of them got up, leaving Charlotte to discuss the human-trafficking problem with Cyndi Lauper.

'Let's ring them up,' said Rachel, 'and compare notes.'

'Bad idea,' said Kate. 'We don't want them to think we don't trust them.'

'Oh, but I'm dying to know what they're up to. I bet they're pissed.'

'Well, we'd better try and catch up,' said Kate, opening the champagne. 'Here you go, Liz. And I'll just go and pour some for Charlotte.'

'Leave her for a moment,' said Elizabeth, pushing the kitchen door shut with her toe. 'Let's have our own little party in here for a moment. Cheers, girls.' They drank. 'Here's to friendship.'

'Friendship,' repeated Rachel, and her phone rang. She glanced at it quickly, saw who was calling and swiftly put it back in her handbag.

Nick vetoed the first club that Alan proposed on the grounds that it was boring, and the second because he had fallen out with the manager over a small financial misunderstanding, and at half past ten they were wandering through Soho with no idea of where to go, as lines formed outside any places that looked halfway decent. In the end Alan despaired, and said,

'Well, I'm sorry, I don't know what to suggest. Chris, any ideas?'

'The only clubs I know are gay clubs,' said Chris, 'and I don't suppose anyone wants to go there.'

'Oh, come on,' said Nick, 'we might as well. After all, I'm not going to pull tonight, am I? At least you'll have a chance.' He grabbed Chris in a headlock. 'Lead the way!'

Chris took them to a club Mark had told him about, an unassuming little pub on the edge of Covent Garden with a huge subterranean dance floor that was already packed.

'This'll do,' said Nick, and headed for the toilets in search of drugs.

Alan stood close to Chris, their shoulders touching. 'It only seems like yesterday that you were a shy little teenager who wouldn't say boo to a goose.'

'Sorry to disappoint you.'

'I never said I was disappointed. Want to dance?'

'Love to.'

'Come on, then.'

Twenty minutes later, Nick came barging through the crowds, looking much more animated. 'All right, lads? Having a good time?'

'Where have you been?'

'Had to make a couple of calls.' He winked.

'I'm going to the bar,' said Alan, and wove his way through the bodies. Heads turned in his wake.

'That's his closet blown open,' said Nick, with a leer. 'Fucking hell, mate, if looks could kill, you'd be dead.'

'What do you mean?'

'They all hate you 'cause you're the one that's shagging Alan Southgate.'

'No, I'm not.'

'Looks like you will be before the night is over, lover boy.'

'Don't be stupid.'

'Hey, it's okay,' said Nick, holding up his hands. 'I won't tell on you if you don't tell on me.'

'What would I tell anyone about you?'

'Nothing, mate. Nothing, nothing. Let's just say we'll keep it in the family, eh?'

'I don't understand.'

'You're not meant to.' He took a fresh pint from Alan. 'Ta very much. Right, you two. Much as I'd like to join you, I've got other fish to fry.' He downed the pint in one, his throat working, streams of beer running down his chin. 'Don't tell the missus, lads.'

'Are you going?'

'Yeah. Things to see, people to do. Have fun. Tell me all the gory details. Thanks for a great night, Al.'

He strutted across the dance floor without looking back.

'I really ought to be going,' said Rachel. 'I've got a busy day tomorrow.'

'It's not even midnight,' said Elizabeth. 'You can't go yet.'

'I must. I've got a meeting with a casting director tomorrow and I can't turn up looking like something the cat dragged in.'

'Oh, please stay for another.'

'It's OK, Rachel,' said Kate. 'You go if you need to. Hope it goes well.' Strange she didn't mention it before . . .

'Thanks. Look after the bride.'

'Don't you worry about me, darling,' said Elizabeth. 'I can look after myself.'

'Course you can,' said Rachel, and kissed them both goodbye. Charlotte, who was asleep on the sofa, she ignored.

She was making the call before she even got out of the building.

* * *

'You don't really want to stay here, do you?'

'Why not? It's fun. The music's good, and . . .'

'I thought we might go somewhere.'

'Oh.' Chris felt his stomach turn over. 'Where?'

'My place.'

There it was, at last, the direct offer from the man that everyone else in the club would give their right arm to sleep with. And Chris hesitated. Was sleeping with his sister's best male friend the right thing to do? Shouldn't he be worrying about the things that Nick had been hinting at all evening?

Alan whispered, 'Please'. They walked out of the club and straight into a taxi.

'Did she suspect?'

'Of course not. I'm not stupid.'

'What did you tell her?'

'The truth.'

'What?'

'Don't panic. I told her I've got an important meeting tomorrow. Which I have.'

They were naked in Rachel's bed, with the whole night ahead of them; Elizabeth could hardly get annoyed if Nick stayed out late on his stag night. He kissed her on the neck, on the breast.

'We shouldn't be doing this,' she said, but she did not push him away. 'It's not right.'

'You want to stop?'

'We ought to.'

'Yeah.' He kissed her some more, 'But do you want to?'

'I don't know . . .'

'Right.' He moved down her stomach. She opened her legs and felt his face between them.

'But when you're married . . .'

'Mmmmfff.'

'We'll have to stop.'

'Look,' said Nick, coming up for air, 'if you don't mind, could we not talk about my marriage right now? Maybe I'm just being fussy, but it kind of puts me off.'

'But what if . . .'

'Oh, for God's sake,' said Nick. 'You're getting as bad as she is. Do you want this, or don't you?'

'Yes. I do.'

'Then do me a favour, darling, and shut the fuck up.'

She did as she was asked, and soon forgot all about Elizabeth, all about her meeting with a casting director, forgot everything except the feeling of Nick inside her and the sensation of falling and flight.

She woke in pitch darkness, convinced that she'd heard someone moving around the room. Nick was beside her, breathing deeply. She lay still for a while, listening, then drifted off to sleep again. When next she woke, dim light was filtering through the curtains, and Nick was pulling on his jeans.

'Got to go, love,' he said, bending down to kiss her forehead. 'I'll call you.'

He crept through the silent flat, and let himself out into the cold, twilit streets of Camden Town.

Chapter 14

'Of course, you realise that everybody knows, don't you?'

'Knows what?' Chris had promised Alan not to tell a soul, and he was as good as his word, so unless people in the club had been talking . . .

'About Rachel,' said Mark, folding his arms and narrowing his eyes.

'Oh.' Chris felt like sticking his fingers in his ears, shouting, 'I can't hear you' and running out of the café. There were less than seventy-two hours to go before the wedding, and this was not a good time to have his suspicions confirmed.

'I mean, she's not been very discreet.' Mark was enjoying this, and had clearly invited Chris for coffee simply to wallow in the dirt. 'When we got in last night, they were at it. You could *hear* them.'

'Oh, God. Please don't say anything.'

Mark put a hand to his chest. 'What do you take me for? I'm not a gossip. But I just wonder what you think of it.'

Chris was about to give his opinion, when he realised that Mark hadn't actually said who Rachel was 'at it' with. He might be trapped into confirming something that Mark only suspected. 'It's none of my business,' he said.

'Absolutely, absolutely! That's what I say. Live and let live. I mean, if that's what they want, well, that's up to them, isn't it?'

He's not saying the word 'Nick', thought Chris. He doesn't know for sure. He suspects, but he doesn't know.

They moved on to other matters, like what they were going to wear to the party, what were the chances of pulling and so on, when the door jangled open and there stood Natasha, her hair matted, last night's make-up smeared around her eyes. She was wearing one of Mark's T-shirts, a gaudy number featuring various Hindu deities, and a grubby pair of tracksuit bottoms.

'Ah, there you are! Get me a coffee, for God's sake.' She sat down, rummaged in her bag and brought out a battered box of soluble aspirin. Mark placed a large espresso in front of her, and she dropped two pills into the black liquid, which foamed and hissed. She downed it in one, and smacked her lips.

'That's better. Now, let me tell you something.'

'What?' said Chris and Mark in unison, both knowing all too well.

'Well, I had to get up in the night to go pee-pee,' said Natasha, 'and I took a bit of a wrong turning.'

'She's always doing that,' said Mark. 'The other week I found her trying to climb into the washing machine at four o'clock in the morning. She gets confused.'

Natasha waved her hand in his face, jangling her tarnished bangles. 'It's not my fault if the rooms move about during the night. Anyway, I accidentally went into Rachel's room.'

'Oh, yes.'

'And you'll never guess what I saw.'

'I have a horrible feeling that we will,' said Mark, while Chris stared glumly at his feet.

'Well, what are we going to do about it?' said Natasha. 'I mean, it's not right. She shouldn't be. Not with him. It's immoral.'

'Since when has that bothered you?' said Mark. 'I thought you had embraced immorality as a lifestyle. Or was that last week?'

'I'm just saying, because I care about Chris.' She put a hand on Chris's arm; they'd only met about three times, but she was well into the earth mother role.

'What's it got to do with me?'

'She's your stepsister.'

'What about her?'

'She's fucking Nick.'

It was out. 'Oh.'

'Your sister's fiancé.'

'Yes.'

'Who she's meant to be marrying the day after tomorrow.'

'I know.'

'Well? What are we going to do about it?'

'You keep asking that,' said Mark, 'as if you're going to burst in there with a shotgun or something.'

'It's an idea.'

'You're just jealous because he wasn't interested in you.'

'Oh, and I suppose you're not?'

This went on for some time, giving Chris a chance to think. Should he tell Elizabeth? It was far easier to let sleeping dogs lie, especially when the dogs in question were sleeping with each other. But what would he say when, in six months' or a year's time, Elizabeth found out for herself – and found out that her brother had known all along? How would she feel, then – her marriage in ruins, betrayed by her own stepsister and, apparently, by her brother, her own flesh and blood? No, he would have to tell her. It was his duty to tell her, even if it meant cancelling the wedding, falling out with Rachel, destroying Elizabeth's relationship with Nick, breaking up their home and facing the wrath of his father, who would doubtless blame Chris for the whole thing.

Was it worth it? Wasn't it easier to gamble on Elizabeth never finding out? Nick was devious enough to keep it under wraps, and Rachel wasn't stupid. Perhaps it was just a last-minute fling, it would blow over before the wedding, a moment of madness best forgiven and forgotten.

'I'm sorry, but I'm not just going to sit back while she steals another woman's husband from under her nose!' Natasha bellowed, lighting a cigarette. 'It's disgusting. It's a betrayal of everything I stand for.'

'Big on the sisterhood all of a sudden,' said Mark. 'Have we been reading *Cosmopolitan* again?'

'Fuck off. You're all the same. You hate women. Misogynists, that's what you are. You disgust me.'

'And you disgust me, too. Another coffee?'

'Absolutely.'

Elizabeth, in a rush of bridal modesty, decided to spend the night before her wedding at her father's house, giving her a chance to bond with her family, concentrate on her grooming and plan the last few little surprises that would make the day special. She'd ordered a vintage Daimler to collect them from the reception, because Nick was keen on old cars, and she'd booked (at great expense) a famous DJ to play some records for half an hour; these things, she knew, would please her husband, and get their marriage off on the right foot.

Nick begged her not to go, and then, when she was safely out of the door, texted Rachel with the words 'the coast is clear'. He then set about preparing a little surprise of his own, although it was not for Elizabeth. He set up a tripod in the corner of the bedroom, where it could be easily concealed by curtains, and fixed a small digital video camera to the top of it. He rigged another in the wardrobe. Both of them were invisible, and both of them were focused on the bed. The guy he'd borrowed the gear from assured him that they were easy to operate; you had only to switch them on, and they would run untouched for up to four hours. That was more than enough for what Nick had in mind.

It was just a bit of fun, he told himself, something to look back on when he was a middle-aged, married man, a step up from a dog-eared Polaroid in the wallet. The affair would be over soon enough. Even if it survived the wedding, it would peter out afterwards. Nick liked Rachel a lot, and if she had more to offer by way of money and status, he might have considered trading up. But not now. The timing wasn't right. Elizabeth was still a better bet. Maybe the marriage wouldn't last, but it would do for now. And it was far too late to back out. He'd have one more night with Rachel, and if it was to be their last, Nick wanted to make it a night to remember.

And while memories were all very well, a digital video was so much better.

He turned the cameras on, lay back on the bed and bounced around, just to check that everything was working.

It was.

Rachel did not like putting herself in other people's power – call it the result of a broken home – but Nick was an irresistible force. That last night before the wedding – and it would be their last night too, surely – he was more than usually masterful. He turned her this way and that, arranging her limbs, determined, it seemed, to use every inch of the mattress before it became, once and for all, the marriage bed.

She surrendered to the experience, disengaged her brain and went along for the ride. There would be plenty of time for regrets and repentance. Tomorrow she would be the loving stepsister, the dutiful bridesmaid in her conservative blue suit, her hair up in a chignon, and if there were any suspicious marks on her neck or bosom, well, Natasha had some top-quality concealer, so thick it could cover a multitude of sins.

This is how it ends, she thought, as they made love for the third time. He was insatiable, as if he, too, knew that it was over. And when I see him tomorrow, marrying another woman, how will I feel? Will there be pain, or just relief? Can I sit there and smile and make conversation and congratulate Elizabeth? Can I give this up – this feeling of completeness, of surrender? Rachel knew perfectly well that Nick was a bad man, that what he was doing to Elizabeth he would do to her without a second thought, and she disliked him for it. Hated him, even. But the hate did not stop her from feeling this way about him: loving him, if you could call it that. From feeling, as she thought about tomorrow, that something was being torn out of her by the roots.

Finally, it was over, and they lay side by side, barely touching.

'Nick.'

No answer.

'Nick.' She prodded him with a toe.

'Hmmfff?'

'Are you awake?'

'Wha'ssit?'

'We need to talk.'

'Go to sleep.'

'I can't.'

'Please . . .' He rolled towards her, put an arm across her chest. 'Tired . . .'

'I'm worried about tomorrow.'

''S'okay.'

'It's not. I feel awful.'

Nick snuggled up; to Rachel's astonishment, he was hard again. She reached down and grabbed him. Perhaps if they could just keep fucking, morning would never come.

'Gerroff . . .'

'Oh, come on. One more time.'

He opened his eyes. 'Look, love, we've been doing it solidly for over four hours. That's enough.'

'Is it?'

'Yeah,' he said. 'Can't do more than four hours.' He kissed her on the jaw, turned over and, to Rachel's consternation, seemed to be laughing.

The wedding day dawned bright and sunny, not bad for November, and Elizabeth, who had not slept a wink on her final single night, took this to be a good omen. Everything was in place, all she had to do now was get to the town hall, say, 'I do' and enjoy her big day. She was marrying the love of her life, she had wonderful friends and a loving family – a wonderful extended family – and for a few moments she simply lay in bed, looking at the light creeping across the ceiling, feeling like the luckiest woman in the world.

There was a tap at the door. 'Can I come in?'

'Of course.' Chris sat on the edge of the bed, and she pulled back the covers so he could get in, just as he used to when he was little, or in the aftermath of their mother's death. She had never felt as close to her brother as she felt now. She had love to spare.

'Hello little brother,' she said. 'Come for a cuddle?'

'Come for a chat, really.' His voice was troubled.

'What's the matter, darling? Has something happened?'

'No. I'm fine.'

'Right.'

'It's just . . .'

'What?'

'Oh, nothing. I just wanted to tell you how happy I am for you.'

Elizabeth put her arms around him, and gave him a big kiss. 'Thanks, Chris. That means a lot to me. I know I haven't always been here for you . . .'

'No, really, it's not that.'

'But things are going to change now. My story is over. I've got my happy ever after. It's time to concentrate on you now. We need to find you a —'

'Please, don't start,' said Chris, who felt that they were straying on to dangerous ground. It was bad enough that her bridesmaid was screwing her fiancé; Elizabeth really didn't need to find out that her brother was getting it off the best man as well. 'I'm fine.'

'I just want you to experience what I'm experiencing.'

'That's very kind of you,' said Chris, hoping that he never experienced anything of the sort. 'Well, I just came in to wish you all the best, really.' He moved away from her, got out of bed. 'It's going to be a busy day, and I probably won't have time to talk to you again. So I just wanted to say . . .'

Your husband is unfaithful and you haven't even married him yet.

'To say that I love you and I'm very happy for you.'

'Awww, thanks, Chris.' Elizabeth got out of bed, stretched, picked at the elasticated waistband of her tartan pyjama bottoms – not exactly bridal wear, but comfortable and warm. She had something special for tonight. Nick was going to love it. 'Yeeeuch, look at the state of me.' She stood in front of the mirror, sticking out her stomach and screwing up her face. 'There's a lot of work to be done before I'm fit to be wed.'

'I'll leave you to it, then,' said Chris, closing the door softly behind him. His sister was singing 'Chapel of Love'.

He went to the bathroom and surveyed himself in the mirror. 'I can't tell her,' he said to his reflection, as the muffled strains of Elizabeth's happy song sounded from down the landing. 'I just can't.'

*   *   *

The phone rang at ten o'clock, just four hours before they were all due at the registry office. Kate answered.

'It's Rachel.'

She sounded ill.

'Hi, Rachel. What's the matter?'

'Something awful has happened.'

'Oh God. Are you okay?'

'No, I'm fine, it's just . . .' She coughed and cleared her throat. 'Sorry. I've just had a call from this casting director.'

'What?'

'I mean, they want me to come in and see them right now.'

'You can't.'

'That's what I told them, but . . . I don't know what to do.' Her voice wobbled. 'It's the chance of a lifetime. If I turn this down, they'll never look at me again.'

'If you stand Elizabeth up on her wedding day, I don't think she'll ever talk to you again.'

'I know!' wailed Rachel. 'What should I do?'

'You should explain to this casting director that you have a prior engagement. I'm sure they will reschedule.'

'You don't understand.'

Kate thought she could understand all too well. 'Have you spoken to Elizabeth?'

'No.'

'I suppose you want me to tell her, is that it?'

'Oh, would you?' said Rachel, as if Kate had already offered. 'I just don't think I can face her.'

'No. I don't suppose you can.'

Silence for a moment, then a small voice. 'Do you think I'm awful?'

Kate did not answer that, but said, 'Rachel, is there something that you need to tell me?'

'No.' That sounded decisive enough. 'I just feel awful about letting her down.'

'Well, she will be very upset.' I'm not going to let her off the hook, thought Kate. 'You know how much it means to her.'

'But you'll be there, won't you? And you'll explain. I'll get to the party as soon as I can.'

'If you get out of your meeting in time, of course,' said Kate, 'but somehow I wouldn't be surprised if it overruns.'

Bitch, thought Rachel, who had been keeping this excuse up her sleeve. 'Look, I'm really sorry,' she said, trying to keep the animosity out of her voice, 'but I've got to go. The car's here.' She couldn't resist embellishing the lie. 'They've sent a car for me, you see. That's how important this is.'

She hung up, her heart pounding. The panic that had gripped her when she left Nick was starting to subside. She had made a decision. She could not go to the wedding, could not sit quietly while he married Elizabeth. She would scream or cry or faint. Something would happen. She wasn't that good an actress. Better to lie to them all one last time than to ruin everything. Just one lie, and then it was over. Forgotten.

Nick checked over the tapes, and was very satisfied with the results; even in low light, the images were unmistakable. He tried freeze frame; yes, that was good. Better than he'd expected. A little bit of digital jiggery-pokery and those images would be good enough for print. He extracted the tapes, put them in a padded envelope along with his dope stash, looked at the clock and realised that he'd better get a move on. He took a long, slow bath, smoked a big, fat joint and dressed for his wedding day.

Chapter 15

Kate walked up the hill to the Prof's house mulling over Rachel's desertion, for such it surely was. Even actresses don't blow out family weddings for the sake of a casting – especially not on a Saturday. It was suspicious. If this happened in one of my novels, thought Kate, it would mean the character had something to hide – and in Kate's fiction, that something was nearly always an affair.

She had mistrusted Rachel from first sight: too pretty by half, and doesn't she know it. Too aware of her attractiveness to men – to one man in particular. And if she was doing something so bad that she couldn't face the family at Elizabeth's wedding, there were certain conclusions just begging to be drawn. She was lying, ergo she was having an affair, and there was only one kind of affair that could explain her decision to stay away from the wedding.

Nick.

As Kate arrived at the house, she had argued herself into a terrible state of foreboding.

Chris was drinking coffee at the kitchen table. His morose expression did nothing to reassure her.

'Only me,' said Kate. 'Where's Liz?'

'Upstairs getting ready,' said Chris, sounding glum.

'And your dad?'

'They've gone shopping. Anna decided she didn't like her hat.'

'Right. Chris . . .'

He got up, slopped his coffee over the table and said, 'shit'. Kate grabbed a cloth and wiped up the mess. 'Sorry,' he said. 'I'm so clumsy today.'

'Is something the matter? You look like you're going to a funeral, not a wedding.'

'I feel like it, too.'

'Ah.'

He knows something, Kate thought.

'Chris.'

'Yes?'

'Is anything the matter?'

He sat down again. 'I don't know.'

'Is it something to do with the wedding?'

'Yes.' He sounded wretched, as if he might start crying. Kate put an arm round his shoulders.

'Chris, if something's wrong, you'd better tell me about it.'

'I can't.'

'Is it . . .' She took a deep breath. Once it was said, there was no going back; a chain of events would lead inevitably to the wreck of Elizabeth's happiness. Was it any of her business? 'Is it to do with Rachel?'

'I don't know what to do.' He sighed so deeply, Kate felt his ribs creak. 'Oh, God. It's Nick.'

'Has she said anything to you?'

'Of course not.'

'But . . . I mean, you are absolutely one hundred per cent sure, aren't you?'

'Her flatmate walked in on them.'

'Shit.'

'Precisely.'

'Right,' said Kate, rinsing out the cloth under the tap, hanging it to dry, and then, because they were there, wiping up a few mugs and plates and putting them away in cupboards. 'We have to do something then, don't we?'

'Do we? I was kind of hoping that we could just . . . You know, let it work itself out.'

'She's going to find out. We've got to tell her first.'

'Oh, Christ. How?'

The bathroom door slammed, and they heard footstep thudding across the landing, a voice from upstairs. 'Is that Kate?'

She sounded so happy; how could they possibly burst her bubble? 'Hi Liz. Do you want a coffee?'

'Love one.'

'Okay,' said Kate, pouring. 'Coming right up.' She held the mug between her hands, inhaling the steam, her eyes closed for a moment, and then she said to Chris, 'Right, you. Come on. We're going up there.'

It was just after eleven o'clock when Kate and Chris mounted the stairs with heavy feet and heavier hearts to deliver the *coup de grâce* to Elizabeth's wedding plans. If they'd kept their mouths shut, in three hours she would have been Mrs Nicholas Sharkey, soon to be joining the ranks of mums at the school gates, letting her work slip and slide, a happy housewife who might never know that her husband was unfaithful. It would have been so much easier to turn back.

'Hi darling.' The two women kissed the air; Elizabeth's make-up was half-done, her hair carefully pinned up. She was still in her dressing gown.

'Hi Liz. You look lovely.' Shit, thought Kate, that was a stupidly encouraging thing to say. 'Here's some coffee.'

'You don't mind if I just carry on putting on my face?'

'Of course . . .' Chris stood in the doorway, as if contemplating a quick getaway.

Kate took a deep breath. 'I spoke to Rachel this morning.'

'Oh,' said Elizabeth, dabbing the mascara wand around her eyes. 'Is she okay?'

'No.'

The wand stopped in mid-dab. 'What's the matter?'

She suspects.

'She can't make it today.'

'What?'

'She . . . well, she said she's got to see a casting director.'

'You're joking.'

'No, I'm not. Am I, Chris?'

'No.'

Elizabeth put down the mascara, and turned away from the mirror. 'What's going on? Why are you both looking at me like that?'

'There's something you need to know, Liz. I'm sorry, but I've got to tell you.'

Elizabeth's eyes darted around the room and rested on the coffee cup. She picked it up, held it close as if she needed its warmth.

'Please don't . . .'

'Nick and Rachel are having an affair.'

Silence. Elizabeth sipped the coffee, which was too hot, and scalded her tongue. 'Ow. Fuck.'

'I didn't want to tell you, but they haven't been very careful. Other people have found out.'

'Don't be ridiculous. You know what Nick's like. He's the world's worst flirt. Come on, Chris, tell her.'

'I'm afraid it's true. They've been −'

'And you just come in here on the morning of my wedding to tell me this, do you? You didn't ever think it might be a good idea to mention it beforehand and let me sort it out for myself?'

She doesn't sound very surprised, thought Kate. 'We didn't really know. Not till now.'

'And what . . .' Elizabeth swallowed hard. 'What happened now?'

'They were . . . Go on, Chris.'

'They spent the night at Rachel's flat. Natasha saw them.'

'That drunk,' said Elizabeth. 'You don't believe what she tells you, do you?'

'I'm sorry, Liz,' said Kate. 'I couldn't let you go ahead with the wedding without telling you.'

'You've never liked Nick, have you?' It was an accusation rather than a question.

'That's got nothing to do with it.'

'Oh, I think it has.' Elizabeth's voice was getting higher, her face red. She turned back to the mirror and resumed her make-up, jabbing the mascara into her eyes. 'The minute some jealous bitch starts spreading a rumour about him, you swallow it hook, line and sinker. Well, I'm sorry, but I don't believe it. I'm sure you came here thinking that you were being very noble and doing the right thing and all that jazz, but I know Nick better than anyone and I know he's not doing . . .' Her voice cracked, but she got it quickly under control. 'What you said he's doing. He's not. I know he's not.'

'Darling, I'm sorry . . .' Kate reached out to touch her shoulder, but Elizabeth spun round, her eyes red, one of them watering where she'd hit it with the brush.

'Get off me! Please! Just leave me alone! I can deal with this! I can't believe you. You . . .'

'You can't pretend it's not happening.'

'Ridiculous.'

'Then why do you think Rachel suddenly can't make it to your wedding?'

'Because she's . . . What did you say?'

'Seeing a casting director. On a Saturday.'

'Well, then.'

'You believe her?'

'Why not?'

'Then ask her. Talk to her. Get her to explain it in person.'

'All right,' said Elizabeth, slamming her coffee mug down on the dressing table. 'I will. What's the time? Oh, that's fine. Plenty of time for me to accuse my bridesmaid of sleeping with my fiancé. Yes! I'm sure we can clear that little misunderstanding up in no time, and still be at the registry office with hours to spare. Thank you so much for bringing it to my attention.' She shoved things into a bag, threw her dressing gown into a corner and pulled a sweater over her head. It caught on her hair grips, and smudged her make-up. 'Come on, then. Let's go.'

'Where?'

'Round to Rachel's, of course! Let's catch them in the act. It's not far. Very convenient little love nest, wouldn't you say? Yes, come on, both of you. Kate, you can drive, if you'd be so kind. Perhaps Nick will still be there, and we can ask him as well. I know it's unlucky to see each other before the wedding but on this occasion I'm willing to break with tradition.' She stood in the middle of the room, her eyes blazing. 'Well? Ready?'

Kate and Chris followed her downstairs, casting guilty looks at each other, like conspirators. But the deed was done, the knives thrust in, and all they could do now was watch.

Mark answered the door, and only saw Chris at first, which was no accident, as Kate and Elizabeth were standing out of sight. As soon as the door was open, they surged past him and up the stairs.

'Wait,' said Mark. 'You can't go in. She's not here. She's not well. For God's sake,' he said, turning to Chris, 'what have you done?'

Rachel was in bed, alone, thank God, but not looking much like a woman who was about to have an important meeting with a high-powered casting director. She was wearing an old black V-neck sweater, her hair was tied back with a scrunchy and her eyes were puffy with lack of sleep, or crying, or both. She heard the door slam, feet thundering up the stairs, and for a moment she pulled the duvet over her head, sinking into the warm darkness.

But this would not do. This looked bad.

She threw the duvet back, jumped up and grabbed a hair-brush. It was filthy, full of her hair, and she started nervously pulling it out. The door burst open.

'Oh, hi,' she said, as if a morning raid by your stepsister and her matron-of-honour were the most natural thing in the world. She dropped a handful of old hair on to the floor, and started brushing.

Elizabeth was dumbfounded; nothing, short of the sight of Nick's naked buttocks pumping away between Rachel's thighs, could have confirmed her guilt more than this brazen coolness.

'Rachel,' said Kate, pushing into the bedroom behind the momentarily paralysed Elizabeth, 'we need to talk to you.'

'Do we?' She carried on brushing. 'Go on, then. I'm listening.'

Chris and Mark stood on the landing. The bedroom door closed.

'Is it true?' asked Elizabeth, at last.

'Is what true?'

'Don't make me spell it out.'

'I'm terribly sorry,' said Rachel, in an actressy voice, 'but I don't have the faintest idea what you're talking about.'

'You . . . What do you . . .'

'Listen,' said Kate, 'there's no point in beating about the bush. You and Nick. Come on. Tell the truth.'

'Nick?' said Rachel, pressing a finger to her forehead, as if trying to place him. '*Your* Nick?'

'Yes, my Nick. The man I'm supposed to be marrying today.'

'Oh, him.'

'Listen, you little bitch . . .' Elizabeth stepped towards her, but Rachel stood her ground.

'You mean your Nick who's been hitting on me from the first moment we met? Your Nick who kept sneaking off behind your back when we were on holiday to get me alone? Nick who kept telling me that he was making a mistake marrying you but it was too late to back out because he didn't want to hurt your feelings? That Nick?' Elizabeth stared into space, the veins on her neck standing out.

'That's enough, Rachel,' said Kate, taking Elizabeth's arm and trying to lead her from the room.

'Oh, I see. You just thought you'd pop round and accuse me of seducing Nick and then walk out, is that the idea? I see. Fine. Off you go.'

'Thanks, we're leaving. I'm sure you have to get ready for your big appointment.'

'Oh, sod off, Kate, you're so bloody—'

'How could you do this to me?' Elizabeth's voice was a ragged wail, bubbling through tears and snot. 'How . . . how could you?'

Something flickered in Rachel's eyes, but she said, 'It was easy, really. When someone wants you that much, the difficult thing is to say no.'

'And what were you planning to do?' said Kate. 'Carry on behind her back? Did you think she wouldn't find out?'

'I never gave it a moment's thought,' said Rachel. 'As for Nick – well, I wouldn't know. Have you asked him?'

'I don't know where he is,' said Elizabeth in a pitiful, little-girl voice.

'I imagine he's at home, getting ready for the wedding.'

'The wedding's off, you little cow,' said Kate. She put an arm round Elizabeth's shoulders, and led her from the room.

'Right,' said Rachel to their backs. 'I assume one of you will inform him.' The door slammed, and she stood quietly for a while, breathing steadily, focusing her mind on calming the panic. No, she would not let it come. It had happened, it was over, she had survived. She need never speak to these people again.

It was not quite the performance she'd intended to give, not quite the role she'd intended to play, but it had worked. The cord was cut, and if she concentrated hard, she felt no pain, no guilt. After a few moments, she carried on brushing her hair.

Kate took the weeping Elizabeth to the car, loaded her carefully into the passenger seat and drove away at speed. She put her to bed, and explained to the Prof that there had been a change of plan. The Prof didn't understand, and so Kate was obliged to go into details.

Chris lingered on the stairs back at Rachel's flat, unsure of what to do. There was Rachel at the top, the villain of the piece, the woman who had broken his sister's heart. Elizabeth had gone without him. Mark was in the kitchen, hoping for a good gossip. Another door opened upstairs, and Natasha staggered out, her hair wound up in multicoloured foam rollers, a fag in her mouth and a drink in her hand.

'What's all the fucking row?' she croaked, and disappeared into the bathroom.

Chris decided to get the bus. The traffic was heavy, but he was in no hurry to get home. After all, he had nothing to do for the rest of the day, as it turned out.

*   *   *

'What has your daughter done?'

'Hmmmm?' Anna was having a bit of trouble with her corsage, and didn't look up to see the expression on her husband's face.

'Rachel. Did you know?'

'Sorry, darling, could you just help me with . . .' Now she looked up. 'Oh. What's the matter?'

'Your daughter. And Nick.'

'What? Don't be ridiculous.'

'I haven't actually told you anything yet.'

'I know what you're suggesting. You don't have to spell it out. And the suggestion is completely ridiculous. She wouldn't.'

'Wouldn't what?'

'What you're saying.'

'What am I saying?' The Prof looked angry.

'Just a God damn minute,' said Anna, and then stabbed her thumb with the pin she was using to fix her corsage. 'Shit.' She sucked blood. 'Look what you made me do.'

'Well? What have you got to say about it?'

'Are you *accusing* me of something, Tony?'

'No, my dear.' His voice was as cold as ice. 'I merely seek information.'

'*I merely seek information.*' She impersonated him, tightening her mouth to a tiny puckered O. 'This isn't a research project, buster. This is real life. Now will you please tell me . . .' She threw the corsage on to the floor; there was blood smeared on the white petals. 'What is going on?'

'Elizabeth has locked herself in her room, where she is crying as if her heart were breaking. Kate informs me that she has just found out that Nick has been carrying on, with your daughter.'

'Her name is Rachel. And I thought she was our daughter now.'

'She's no child of mine.'

'Oh, I see,' said Anna, standing up. 'This is all my fault, is it? Some man who can't keep it in his pants for reasons that are all too abundantly clear has a roll in the hay with Rachel and it's *my fault*?'

'What reasons might those be?'

'For Christ's sake, Tony, just look at her! Look at him! Why do you think he's marrying her? For her looks? I don't think so!'

When Chris finally got home, the house was quiet, and he thought for a wonderful moment that everyone had gone out. He went into the kitchen and looked out over the garden; the sun was already declining, the shadows lengthening, and there was the faintest of mists in the shafts of light that slanted over the lawn. He stood still, listening to a blackbird singing. And then there was a creak from upstairs, the sound of the toilet flushing, the pad of feet, a door closing. He listened more intently.

They were there, then, some or all of them, in separate rooms, not speaking. Elizabeth would be in bed. The Prof would be in his study. Anna could be anywhere, or perhaps she'd gone out; the house was never this silent when she was around.

He was hungry, and made himself a sandwich, tiptoeing from the refrigerator to the table. In his effort to make no sound at all, he knocked the lid of the mayonnaise jar on to the floor, where it seemed to clatter and spin for about five minutes.

His father appeared at the door, his face pale.

'I suppose you knew all about this,' he said. 'Were you planning to tell us?'

Chris picked up his sandwich, said, 'excuse me' and left the house.

Chapter 16

At ten o'clock in the evening, Elizabeth should have been leaving her wedding reception in a chauffeur-driven limousine, bound for the airport. Her bags were packed for a fortnight in Cuba – two weeks of sunshine, sex and planning their future. Instead, ten o'clock found her alone in bed in her father's house, shivering despite two duvets, a blanket, pyjamas, a dressing gown and a fistful of paracetamol.

Nick, too, was alone, in what would now never be the marital home, unpacking his honeymoon things and replacing them with a few hastily selected essentials. The Prof had paid a visit and informed him, in the most glacial tones, that tomorrow the locks would be changed, and that any attempt to remove Elizabeth's property from the flat would be regarded as theft. Everything else would be sorted out by the solicitors. There was no need for further contact between Nick and Elizabeth. He did not say why. He made no reference to what had happened, to the cancelled wedding, to Elizabeth's unfortunate discovery; they both knew exactly what he was talking about. Nick tried to protest, to say it was all a big misunderstanding, but the Prof silenced him with one magisterial gesture of his long, white hand.

'You will, I trust, have the decency to leave without causing a fuss. I assure you it will be very much in your interests to do so.' For a moment, Nick wondered if he was going to be offered a pay-off. 'The consequences of any unpleasantness at this stage would be extremely costly.'

He left without another word.

Nick shouted and swore for a while, then started sorting out his underwear. What had happened? Who had talked? They had been careful, hadn't they? Surely Rachel hadn't blabbed. He thought of calling her; she'd be in pieces, whatever had taken place.

But he called no one. He needed time to think. His world had turned abruptly upside down, and he must not make any sudden decisions. Let Rachel miss him for a while. He knew how she'd be feeling now – guilty and tearful, angry enough to lash out and blame him. Better to disappear for a while, speak to no one, and then, when the dust had settled, see what could be salvaged from the wreck. He fastened his suitcase, took one last look around the flat and walked to the tube station. He had places he could disappear to.

Kate left Elizabeth when she was sure she wasn't going to harm herself, and gave Anna and the Prof strict instructions that they were to call her straight away if there was any cause for concern. She had to deliver these instructions twice, as the unhappy couple weren't speaking to each other, weren't even able to be in the same room as each other. Kate went home to her husband and children and exhausted herself cooking a large meal and then, when all the washing-up was done and the kids were put to bed, lay on the sofa with her husband's arms around her and watched a horror movie.

Chris walked out on his father before he could be blamed for everything, spent a few hours wandering around Hampstead Heath and then, when it started to get cold, switched on his phone. There were dozens of messages, most of them from Mark, which he deleted unopened. But there was one from Alan, to which he replied immediately, and by ten o'clock the two of them were lying in Alan's bed, discussing the fact that, while they were very sorry about Elizabeth's predicament, her loss had been their gain, because if they'd spent the evening being nice to people at her party, they probably would never have ended up like this. They spent the rest of the weekend together, seeing no one, which was how Alan seemed to like it.

Rachel stayed in her room, numb with shock, until early evening. She tried repeatedly to call Nick, but there was no reply. She needed to talk to him, the need like a claw tearing at her insides, to hear words of comfort, to be told that it was all worthwhile, that whatever pain they'd caused to others didn't matter because they could be together. To be told that he loved her, had loved her from the first minute he saw her, and he didn't care what the world thought as long as they had each other. To be taken away from this terrible quiet nothingness, the ordinariness of her room, the sound of her flatmates' feet creaking up and down the stairs, the listening and whispering at her door. She flicked through magazines, smoked cigarettes, waiting for a tsunami of grief that never came.

She called and called until her battery was nearly flat, and then turned her phone off and put it in her dressing table drawer.

Whatever happened, she said to herself, was not my fault. I never had a choice. There was never a moment when I decided to do one thing or another. I was powerless. Things simply happened. They blame me for this, but they might as well blame the moon for causing the tides.

She slept for a while, awoke at seven and opened her door. Within minutes, Natasha and Mark were sitting on her bed asking her what had happened. It was easier, and a lot less painless, to turn the whole disaster into an amusing drama for an audience of two, with herself as the wronged heroine. And they gobbled it up, like vultures at a kill.

They had a gig that night at a cabaret showcase in Farringdon, where 'absolutely all the important TV people go,' and it didn't take much to persuade Rachel to come with them. Anything was better than sitting at home waiting for a call that never came, waiting for tears to overwhelm her. Feeling sorry would change nothing. Going out and getting drunk might at least stop her from feeling any sense of responsibility.

And so to Farringdon they went. The gig was in a renovated pub near the railway line, and while Natasha went ahead to announce their arrival, Mark and Rachel lugged in the costumes and equipment. The *artistes* disappeared into the dressing room, and Rachel found a seat at the bar. She ordered a glass of wine. The barman took his time, and she was about to say something when he returned, and placed a bottle of champagne in an ice bucket in front of her.

'That's not . . . Sorry, but, what . . .'

'The gentleman over there,' said the barman with a nod, 'asked me to send it over.'

Rachel squinted across the bar. Who would send her champagne? Surely not . . . Nick? Yes, of course, she thought in a flash, he's found out where I am, he's come to sweep me off my feet, and . . .

'I hope you don't mind,' said a cultured, older voice. 'I am not in the habit of buying champagne for young ladies to whom I haven't been introduced.'

He was tall, perhaps in his forties, well dressed in a sports jacket, an open-necked shirt and dark trousers. He had short brown hair peppered with grey, nice blue eyes and a natural-looking suntan.

'My name's Gerald,' he said, extending a hand.

'Hi,' said Rachel, pushing back her hair. 'I'm Rachel. Thanks for the drink.'

'Are you here on your own?'

'No. I'm with friends.' She made a sketchy gesture towards the stage.

'You probably think I'm trying to pick you up.'

'It had crossed my mind.' And you're welcome to try, she thought. She could do with the distraction, and he looked rich.

'In a sense, I am.' He filled her glass with champagne.

'What sense might that be, then?'

'Are you, by any chance, an actor?'

'Oh.' She took a sip; it was delicious. 'Yes, as a matter of fact, I am.'

'Performing tonight?'

'No. I'm just here to support some friends.'

'Ah. Good. Between you and me,' said Gerald, leaning closer, 'most of this cabaret stuff bores me to death. But it pays to keep an eye open. You never know what you might find.'

'Are you in the business, then?'

'Television,' he said, and left it at that. They talked of other things – Rachel's training at Alderman's, plays and film and TV shows that he had seen and she hadn't, and Rachel was just beginning to get bored when further conversation was drowned out by the opening chords of 'If My Friends Could See Me Now' on Mark's horribly overamplified keyboard. Heads turned to the stage, where Natasha was twirling around, a blue chiffon neligee floating out around her.

'Christ,' said the casting agent when the sound had been controlled, 'what fresh hell is this?'

'They're my friends.'

'Oh dear. I hope you're better than they are.'

'Well, I don't sing.'

'Neither does she.'

They drank champagne while Natasha squawked her way through a *Sweet Charity* medley, and when she got to 'Where Am I Going?', Gerald said 'back to the drawing board, I hope, as soon as possible'. Rachel tutted and applauded. 'But it's a good question,' he said, as Natasha took bow after bow. 'Where are we going?'

'Where did you have in mind?'

'Have you eaten?'

'No. And now you come to mention it, I'm starving.'

'Then you will allow me to take you for dinner. There's a nice little French place near Smithfield, where they always look after one.'

Rachel, feeling very much in need of being looked after, slipped off her barstool and out of the club, while Natasha and Mark discussed what they could do for an encore.

Elizabeth needed sleep more than anything in the world, but sleep would not come. She lay awake in a sweat of confusion, reminding herself of those fictional Victorian heroines who conveniently developed brain fever whenever life got too much for them. She saw herself taking to her bed for the rest of the winter, worrying her family half to death before sitting up one fine spring day, as a robin sang at her window, and deciding that, after all, she might take a bowl of light broth.

To her own and her father's surprise, however, she got up on Sunday morning at eight o'clock, had a shower, got dressed and started making breakfast. She was brisk and efficient, not at all the tragic heroine that she might have been, the only indication of her recent disappointment being a thin-lipped determination not to discuss the events of the last twenty-four hours. She gave the Professor toast and coffee and orange juice and boiled eggs; she even made a tray for Anna and left it outside the guestroom after tapping discreetly on the door. She said nothing to her father about the question of separate beds and he, out of sheer gratitude, talked about a paper he was giving at a conference in Montreal in a couple of weeks. They did not mention Nick, or Rachel, or even Chris, who had not come home last night. They said nothing about the financial disaster of the venue hire, the caterers, the embarrassment of guests turning up for the wedding only to find that it had been cancelled. No, as far as Professor and Miss Miller were concerned, none of these things mattered. Nothing had happened.

The doorbell rang. Elizabeth froze.

'I'll get it,' said the Prof. 'Don't worry. If it's . . .'

'Yes.' She couldn't bear to hear his name. 'Thanks.'

It wasn't Nick. 'It's all right!' shouted the Prof from the hall. 'It's only Charlotte.'

Charlotte entered the house with head thrust forward, her shoulders hunched, like a small, cardigan-wearing bull entering a china shop, clutching a bundle of files under her arm.

'I thought you might like some marking to do,' she said, staring at the toast crumbs on the kitchen table. 'I know that whenever I have problems, it always helps to lose myself in work. These were in your pigeonhole.'

Elizabeth felt dangerously close to laughing. 'You went in on a Sunday?'

'I often go in on a Sunday. It's so quiet.'

'Right.' Charlotte put down the folders, and stood awkwardly, shifting from foot to foot. 'Well, thanks. I appreciate it. I'm sure it will . . .' Elizabeth's voice whooped upwards, but she paused and brought it back down. 'I'm sure it will help.'

'You're better off without him, you know.'

Elizabeth had been wondering who would be the first person to say these words. Of course, it had to be Charlotte. 'No doubt,' she said. 'But still . . .'

'He wasn't good for you. He was standing in your way.'

'Thanks, Charlotte.' If she says that Rachel has done me a favour, I will grab her by the ears and smash her head against the granite work surface until it is a bloody pulp.

'Well, I just want you to know that if you need to talk, any time, you know who your friends are. You only have to ask.'

'That's really kind of you, Charlotte. At the moment I think I just need to rest.'

'Work, that's the thing,' said Charlotte. 'Think of all the time you'll have for your research now that . . . Well, I mean . . .'

'Yes, that's very true,' said Elizabeth, smiling despite the horrible pain, like a kitchen knife stabbing her in the heart. 'That's a great consolation.'

'Goodbye, then.' Charlotte turned abruptly and left.

'She has a point, I suppose,' said Elizabeth, after a long silence.

'Perhaps,' said the Prof.

'He wasn't . . .' No, even now she couldn't say it. It was too soon. 'I shall work, you know. I shall work very hard.'

'I'm glad to hear it.'

'I'll make you proud of me. And I'll make up for . . . all this mess.'

'I'm sure you will.' He didn't touch her.

Rachel was not dressed for dinner in a smart restaurant with a wealthy and influential man – in fact, she'd thrown on the first things that came to hand, a black sweater and a charcoal grey skirt that didn't match at all. She was wearing flat black ballet pumps, without even a hint of heel. Fortunately, however, she did have her trusty red lipstick in her bag, which she quickly applied in the loo, and so heads turned when she walked into the restaurant, and Gerald spent the whole evening staring at her mouth. By the time she was delivered to her door at two o'clock in the morning, with nothing more than a respectful kiss on the cheek, Rachel had learned that Gerald Partridge was not just 'in television' but was the producer/director of half a dozen of the most talked-about TV dramas of the last two years, that he had a track record for discovering new talent, and that he just happened to be casting for a six-part adaptation of a best-selling novel. And there might just be a part for a beautiful actress of about her age.

She had an audition on Monday.

This was not what Rachel had expected when she woke that morning in Nick's bed – Elizabeth's bed – full of misgivings and remorse. The crash had come, but she'd emerged not just unscathed but – what? Changed? Better? Worse? She took off her make-up and lay in bed, waiting for Natasha and Mark to return, thinking only of Monday.

She didn't check her phone to see if Nick had called.

Elizabeth woke from troubled dreams of missed flights and lost luggage, with a terrible feeling of nausea. She ran along the landing, her hand clamped over her mouth, and only just made it to the bathroom in time. She threw up until there was nothing left but bile. Tears streamed from her eyes, collecting at the end of her nose and dripping into the filthy water.

She has done this to me, she thought, looking at herself in the mirror, dabbing at her mouth with toilet paper. Rachel has done this to me.

And then she had a sudden, blinding flash of all that might have been – her life with Nick, fifty, perhaps sixty years together, bringing up children and grandchildren, travelling the world, sharing homes and memories, making love . . . Making love . . .

The one most precious thing in her life, that had come to her so easily, so unexpectedly, a gift from heaven after the death of her mother, and now it was gone. Nick was gone.

And Rachel had taken him.

And Rachel would pay.

She knew what people would say. Charlotte had already said it. He was no good for you, we never liked him, you're better off without him. He's done you a favour.

But it was too early to blame Nick, too early even to think of him. Each memory of his face, his body, was like a hammer blow on her bruised heart. She could not hate him – not yet. The time would come, perhaps, when she would see Nick as others saw him, she could admit that she'd had a lucky escape. But not now.

For now, all the misery and pain and hatred in Elizabeth's heart were focused on one person. One day, she thought, returning to her cold bed, Rachel Hope would curse the day she met Elizabeth Miller.

Two Years Later

Chapter 17

The rain was lashing down, drumming on the roof of the trailer, running down the steamed-up windows, turning the whole of the unit base into a quagmire. There was some concern that the catering wagon was actually sinking into the mud, and the supporting artists had been corralled into a marquee, hired at ruinous cost to the production, where they had to wait between scenes, under strict orders not to walk outside and soil their costumes. And so they sat, happily bitching about the director, the producer, the booking agency, the lead actors, the catering, their agents and the script. An urn had been set up on trestle tables at one end of the marquee, so they could have all the tea, coffee and biscuits they wanted. There was one chemical toilet to serve them all, and by two o'clock the only way to keep the disgusting smell at bay was to smoke heavily.

Rachel could watch this hive of discontent from her trailer window, if she chose to, but she did took no interest in any aspect of the production that did not directly involve her. She did not read the script all the way through, focusing her attention only on her scenes. But to these she brought an intense concentration, not only learning her lines but going over and over in her head the way she would move, the way she would look, every toss of the head, every lowering of the eyelids. Such attention to detail, which she could repeat times without number in front of the camera, was quickly gaining her the reputation of one of Britain's most employable young actresses. Yet another of Gerald Partridge's hunches had paid off, and since her TV debut eighteen months ago, she'd never been out of work. Now she was near the top of the second division, with a fighting chance at 'best supporting actress' awards. She wasn't yet a star; she didn't get interviewed much, she couldn't pick and choose her roles, and she certainly couldn't afford any tantrums or indiscretions, but she was getting noticed, and getting paid. And that, in a profession noted for its high rate of attrition, was good enough for Rachel Hope.

Being a television actress wasn't as glamorous as they had imagined at drama school. It involved a great deal of waiting around in rickety trailers, always located in indistinguishable car parks in dreary parts of Britain or, if you were lucky, Europe. As she rose from glorified extra to featured player, the catering improved; you didn't have to queue with everyone else at the chuck wagon, unless you particularly wanted to show that you had the common touch, and impress any journalists that might be around. You had to get up stupidly early every morning, which ruled out any chance of a social life, but you got driven everywhere, and you spent the first part of the day having your hair and make-up done by professionals, which went a long way to compensating for the hours. Being stroked and flattered and pampered by an army of women wielding brushes and sponges was worth sacrificing a couple of hours' sleep.

The money helped, too. After a year, she'd saved enough for a deposit on a small flat in Shepherd's Bush, leaving Natasha and Mark in the lurch (or so they would have it) in Camden Town. In her own home she could sleep and eat when she wanted to, she had peace and quiet in which to learn her lines and there was nobody listening on the landing if she had company. Which she did, four or five times a week. Always the same man.

Always Nick.

There had been an awkward, passionate reunion after a month of harrowing silence. Rachel cracked first, and texted Nick late one night when she couldn't sleep, plagued with anxieties about her first TV job and desperate for the kind of comfort that only he could give her. Across town, on a sofa in south London where he kipped when there were no better offers, Nick read the falsely jaunty text and thought . . . Let her wait.

He replied forty-eight hours later, by which time, he calculated, Rachel would be climbing the walls.

She welcomed him back with no questions and no discussion. At first it was the occasional night in Camden Town, very casual, very cool except when they were in bed. When she moved to Shepherd's Bush, the frequency of his visits increased. Soon he kept a toothbrush there, had his own drawer for socks and underwear, hanging space for shirts that Rachel washed.

It was getting to the point where he might as well move in. Nick was just waiting for her to ask.

Rachel wasn't exactly avoiding the issue, although being busy with work was a very good excuse for delay. She was not blind to Nick's faults: he was lazy and selfish, and although he'd picked up his camera again in the aftermath of his separation from Elizabeth, he was still a long way from earning a living. And it was hard to trust a man who had done what he had done – even if it was her with whom he'd done it.

Rachel was content with things as they were. Nick gave her what she needed, when she needed it, and then he was gone. Regular sex at home meant she could concentrate at work, and deal with the cocky actors or randy electricians who sometimes had a crack at her. She regarded Nick as other actresses regard a personal trainer or a nutritionist – expensive, but necessary.

And in a year? Two years? Five years? She didn't think it would last that long. Perhaps, if he became the big success he said he would, she might consider it. But time was running out, and as Rachel became more successful, she became more sought after. Her leading men were taking an interest – and a rising young actress had to be status-conscious.

There was another dimension to this strangely protracted affair, one which tied Rachel to Nick as surely as what he did to her in bed. She wanted to show the world that there was more to their relationship than just a casual affair – that they had not wrecked two marriages and broken up a family for nothing. Anna blamed her for her estrangement from the Prof, and Elizabeth had suffered some kind of breakdown, but as long as Rachel stayed with Nick, she could persuade herself that it had all happened for a reason.

Rachel's only connection with what might have been was Chris, who liked his stepsister enough, and resented the family's insinuation that 'this' was somehow all his fault, to remain in contact through the fallout from the cancelled wedding. It was a guilty, secret friendship at first, but the more Elizabeth suggested that Chris 'knew all along', the more the Prof froze him out as his own marriage collapsed, the more Chris confided in Rachel and enjoyed her company. They met for lunch when Rachel wasn't filming. Chris was at college now, doing a 'degree' (the Prof's punctuation) in media studies, and she got him bits of work experience in the studio. At first he didn't tell her about Alan, and she didn't tell him about Nick, and they barely mentioned Elizabeth, but as time went by, their reserve melted away, and they became like what they were originally meant to be – brother and sister.

When Rachel moved, Chris gratefully took her place in the flat in Camden Town, happy to escape at last from the chilly atmosphere of parental disapproval.

Today, Chris was picking her up from the unit base, a muddy, rain-soaked car park in Middlesex, for a quick bite before going on to a comedy club in Ealing, where Natasha and Mark were making one of their increasingly rare cabaret appearances. It was a small price to pay for a good catch-up.

'Look at you,' said Chris, stepping up into the trailer and carefully wiping his feet, 'with your name on the door and everything. Rachel Hope. I'm very impressed.'

'It's glamour all the way here, darling, as you can see.' She gestured around the mud, rubble and tarmac of the car park, towards the tent of squabbling, steaming supporting artists. 'Any minute now my private helicopter will arrive to whisk me off to Capri.'

'How about a taxi, and a curry in Ealing? It's handy for the club.'

'I suppose it'll have to do.' She threw down her script, put on a coat and walked through the mud holding up the hem. 'God, I hate location. Why can't it be like the good old days, when everything was filmed in a nice warm studio?'

'I'll swap you,' said Chris, holding the taxi door for her. 'Lectures all day, then going home to the madhouse in the evenings. Still, beggars can't be choosers. Anything's better than living at home.'

'How is the old man?'

'Alive. Doesn't speak to me. How's my wicked stepmother?'

'Still blames me for everything. Living in a flat in Putney, which your dad pays for, although you wouldn't know it from the way she complains. Making unwelcome noises about getting a place together, which I pretend not to hear.'

'Any talk of divorce?'

'Not from my end.'

'Nor mine,' said Chris. 'I wish they'd make their minds up. Still, none of my business, as the Prof always tells me. To be honest, I'm past caring. I'm better off without him and Elizabeth running me down all the time.'

Rachel looked out of the cab window. 'Families,' she said. 'Who need's 'em?' She rummaged in her bag. 'Except you, darling, of course. Look what I got for you!' She thrust a small package into his hand. 'It must be your birthday or something, isn't it?'

It was a watch – a very nice man's watch with a thick black leather strap. 'Good grief,' said Chris, 'have you been shoplifting?'

'No. But who else am I going to spend my money on? Do you like it?'

'I love it.' He put it on his wrist; it looked good against the gold hairs. 'But are you sure?'

'Of course. I like giving presents. Who else am I going to be nice to?'

They both knew.

'Don't say it.'

'You're still seeing him, then?'

'Yes. Can't seem to shake him off.' She laughed, then stopped.

'He's all right, is he?'

'Must we talk about this?'

'Not if you'd rather not.'

'I'd much rather not.'

'Okay.' They rode on in silence.

'And what about you, darling? Any nice boyfriends?'

'No one special.'

'What about a certain actor?'

'I'm not supposed to talk about that.'

'I'll take that as a yes, then.'

'Take it any way you like.'

'I hope he's looking after you.'

'I'm not that kind of boy,' said Chris, who wouldn't have said no if Alan Southgate offered to set him up in a nice flat or help him to a job on a film. 'Oh look, we're here.' They got out of the cab, and Rachel paid.

'You won't tell Natasha and Mark about a certain actor, will you?' said Chris.

'Are you mad? No, don't worry. His secret's safe with me.'

After stuffing their faces with the hottest possible curry and downing a couple of pints of lager each, Rachel and Chris hurried along the road to the bistro-come-nightclub where Natasha and Mark were booked for the evening. 'They'll be so pleased that you could make it,' said Chris. 'It's a big deal for them, apparently, and they're expecting loads of . . . Oh.' They opened the door, which jangled loudly in the almost-empty room. A few people were dotted around the tables, sipping drinks. Dismal music played quietly in the background.

'Is this the right place?' said Rachel.

'Yes. Look.' A handwritten poster stuck to a pillar confirmed that there was 'Kabaret Tonite!' Near the bottom of the bill was 'Destiny and Heartache', the name the Natasha had chosen for their act.

'What time are they on?'

'Mark said about nine.' It was ten to.

'Oh dear.'

They ordered a bottle of wine, and sat near the stage. 'This is going to be hideous,' said Rachel. 'Thank God for alcohol.'

The first act of the evening (Destiny and Heartache weren't *quite* the bottom of the bill) was a strange androgynous little creature with long black hair, bad skin and no discernible talent, who stood on stage wearing a belted mac and a bewildered expression, telling an interminable story about an encounter with a man in a butcher's shop, before singing 'Meat is Murder' in an off-key falsetto and producing a brace of pork chops from his underwear. During this, he removed the mac, slapped his bare body with the chops and, as a final gesture, flung them into the audience. They fell into empty space with an audible flop.

'Thank you, thank you, thank you, the Incredible Nigel,' said the compere, who was either ironically cheesy, or just plain cheesy. He rambled on for a bit, while Rachel and Chris finished one bottle and ordered another, before saying, 'The toast of the London cabaret scene, the one and only, the incredible, please put your hands together and give a big welcome to, ladies and gentlemen' – deep breath, swooping intonation – 'Destiny and Heartache.'

The opening bars of 'Wilkommen' blared over the PA. God, surely they weren't still ploughing the Fosse furrow, thought Rachel. But yes – here was Natasha in one of her old bugle-bead flapper dresses, many of the beads now shed in the dressing rooms of third-rate venues, her hair in a sleek bob that was certainly a wig, a black band around her forehead, a forlorn feather sticking up at a crazy angle. Mark followed, lugging his keyboard under his arm, his face made up like Valentino, a shiny dinner jacket over his naked torso, his legs in black footless tights. They both wore stilettos.

Mark plugged in the keyboard, Natasha took the microphone from the MC and they launched into their opening number, Natasha singing with a sort of insane conviction, Mark looking bored.

It seemed to go on for hours, but finally Natasha was screeching her way to the climax of 'Maybe this Time', positioning herself in front of the lights for that all-important silhouette effect. And then it was over.

Rachel and Chris applauded enthusiastically and drank deeply.

'Wasn't it amazing?' shrieked Natasha, coming straight from the dressing room (alias the disabled toilet) and joining them. 'Wow! It was so confrontational! I mean, that guy who heckled me – that really *worked*! It was really *inspiring*! It took me to a *whole different level*!'

Mark joined them, dressed in jeans and a T-shirt. He had more muscle and less body fat than before, thanks to a life-threatening regime of supplements and food avoidance.

'Hi darling.' He kissed Rachel coolly. 'Long time no see. Good of you to take time out of your busy schedule.'

Natasha was still fizzing. 'I just can't imagine how anyone can work without the buzz you get from a live audience. I mean, the energy in this room tonight! Incredible! An amazing sort of *negative energy* that I really feed off.'

'They hated us, Nat,' said Mark, tucking into a drink (he only took carbohydrates in liquid form). 'Face it.'

'Correction, darling. They hated *you*. I've been saying for months that I should go it alone,' she said, addressing Rachel. 'I mean, this whole cabaret schtick is all very well, but I'm not really a singer.'

Chris and Rachel glanced at each other, and looked away quickly.

'What I really am is a performer. I hesitate to say perform-ance artist, because that conjures up terrible images of people doing academic things with pork chops, but really I would say that I'm a performer in the great variety tradition, perhaps with a touch of burlesque . . .'

'She'll go on like this for hours,' said Mark in Rachel's ear. 'I'm sorry you have to hear it.'

'Why do you bother?' asked Rachel.

'Bugger all else to do. Crap, isn't it? Still dragging around with that old ruin.'

'But surely you . . .'

'Anyway, enough about me? How are you?'

'Oh, I'm . . .'

'How's that gorgeous Nick?'

'Fine, thank you.'

'You're so lucky. You've got a boyfriend and a career. I've got nothing.' He played with his glass. 'Just a crappy office job and a few gigs in lousy bars with *her*.' Natasha was still bending Chris's ear. 'I didn't think it would be like this when we left Alderman's.'

'You'll get your chance.'

'I don't think so, darling. I don't have any talent. No, please, don't contradict me, not that you were going to. I know my limitations. I only went to drama school because I thought I'd meet men. Fat lot of good that did me.'

'Come on, Mark. It's not that bad.'

'It's not fair. Everyone else is successful. Even Natasha's a star in her own mind, which is better than nothing. You're on telly. Chris is at college. Charlie Evans, who's got about as much talent as I have, is in Hollywood. And look at Alan Southgate. He's a bloody superstar.'

At the mention of Alan's name, a sudden silence fell; even Natasha stopped talking for a moment. 'Oh, Alan Bloody Southgate,' she said at length. 'Don't talk to me about him. He's completely sold out. The rest of us are trying to do something serious with our art and he's just swanning around Hollywood prostituting his talent.'

'Bloody closet case,' said Mark. 'I can't stand 'em. And Alan's the worst. He's so far in the closet, he's in Narnia.'

'That's not fair,' said Chris, and immediately regretted it.

Mark span round towards him. 'Oh, yes? And what do you know about it? You're his big buddy after all. Friend of the family. Come on, Chris, give us some inside information. How *is* Alan Southgate?'

'He's fine, as far as I know,' said Chris. 'You'd have to ask Elizabeth. I've not seen him for ages.'

'Days' would have been more honest; Alan was now doing very nicely in Hollywood, and dating a string of actresses and models, but he always found time to see Chris on his visits to London, and they did their catching up in bed. Alan trusted Chris; after two years, there had still not been a breath of scandal. Surely, he had other boys on other continents; Chris was not vain enough to think he was the only one.

Mark looked suspicious. 'Well, I'm convinced he's gay. I have it on very good authority.'

Rachel came to the rescue. 'What, a friend of a friend of your hairdresser's? I think that might just be wishful thinking. Anyway, Alan's dated some of the most beautiful women in the world.'

'And he hasn't married any of them,' said Mark.

'Please,' said Chris, 'can we change the subject? I'm sure you're dying to hear about Rachel's new job.'

Natasha and Mark wanted to hear about it very much, but pretended a blasé indifference. 'Oh, yes,' said Natasha, 'you're doing another telly, aren't you?'

'Yes,' said Rachel. 'I know it's an awful sell-out, but someone's got to do it.'

'What is it?' said Mark, who was less good at pretending than Natasha, and dined out on his friendship with Rachel.

'It's a contemporary drama about young urban people.'

'Sounds dull,' said Natasha.

'You're right,' said Rachel. 'It is dull. It won't get recommissioned. There isn't a story, just a lot of nice clothes and rainwashed streets. But it's good for me. I've got lots of scenes, and I'm the big love interest.'

'That makes a nice change for you, not,' said Mark. 'I suppose you float around looking fantastic while incredibly hot actors lust after you.'

'That's about right, yes.'

'Oh, you're so lucky.' Mark crossed his arms and pulled a sulky face. 'I wish I was on telly.'

'Well, darling you could be, if you weren't so committed to your art.'

'Oh, please.' He rolled his eyes. 'It's just something to do in the evenings.'

'If that's your attitude,' said Natasha, standing up and re-arranging her dress, 'I shall go and join people who appreciate me.' The Incredible Nigel and a few of his strange friends were grouped around a piano, massacring the work of Stephen Sondheim. Natasha joined them, her nose in the air, her step uncertain.

'She's a bloody liability,' said Mark.

'Why do you stick with her?' said Rachel.

'Misplaced sense of loyalty, I suppose.'

'Is that a rebuke?'

'God, no. I'm happy for you, really. When I'm old and fat, I'll be very proud to say that I used to share a flat with a big star like Rachel Hope.'

'I'm not quite there yet, darling,' said Rachel. 'But I'm working on it.'

'You'd better. Selling disgusting stories about you to the papers is my pension plan.'

Nick was already in bed when Rachel got home. He sounded grumpy, rubbing his eyes when she turned the lights on. 'Where you been?'

'Out with Chris.'

'Bloody hell.' Nick sat up and watched Rachel undress. 'I don't know why you bother.'

'I happen to like him.'

'You know he'll be reporting everything back to his sister.'

'I don't think so, Nick. Besides, what does it matter? It's all in the past. I'm sure she's moved on.'

'Think I'm that easy to forget?' He pulled the duvet back to let her into bed. It was good to feel his warmth, the smoothness of his skin.

'Of course not.' She kissed him. 'But it's two years. Elizabeth's not an unattractive woman. Chris says she's even been losing weight. She won't end up on the shelf.'

'I wouldn't bet on it.' Nick laughed, and turned out the light. 'Who's ever going to measure up to me?'

'Arrogant sod,' said Rachel, and kissed him again.

Chapter 18

It had been a long, hard afternoon in the Royal Albert Hall, watching rank upon rank of black-gowned graduates filing across the stage, making awkward bows and curtsies to the Royal Personage, listening to the little bursts of applause that greeted those who had brought supporters. First came the bachelors of arts, science, music, divinity, law and so on, followed some hours later by the masters. The doctors came towards the end, which seemed unfair to Elizabeth; surely those with higher honours should be given the privilege of getting out earlier. Still, she sat there in her maroon gown, waiting for her few seconds of glory, when she would affirm that the last three years of drudgery had been worthwhile, and that the world was a better place for her research on the influence of early feminist thought on the French realist novels of the nineteenth and early twentieth century, a hundred thousand words neatly bound in hard blue covers with gold lettering, copies deposited at the college and university libraries, and one for her own bookshelf, of course. Pride of place.

Her moment was approaching; the PhDs had begun, and there were not so very many of them, whatever the Prof said about the universities handing out doctorates like confetti these days. He was up there in the dress circle with the rest of her supporters, Kate, Charlotte and Chris, all of whom had taken time off work and college to be there. Elizabeth knew that they would not whoop, whistle or cheer when she crossed the stage, as others had; the Prof had strong views about such things, and did not think graduation ceremonies a proper place for behaviour more appropriate to football stadia. They would clap and, Elizabeth hoped, feel proud of her. She had done what she said she would do: she had dedicated her life to work, spending her days in libraries and her nights at her computer, sometimes seven days a week, skipping so many meals that the weight dropped off her. She gave up her social life; anything to avoid the pity in people's eyes. She didn't care how much she hurt people; she had been hurt, and she needed to heal. Work was a chrysalis into which she could retreat from the world. And now, in her maroon graduation gown, she was ready to emerge and spread her wings. As what? A twenty-five-year-old spinster with a broken heart who would never be able to trust another man again as long as she lived? A bitter ghost, haunting the review pages of academic journals, sniping at those happier and more successful than herself? Yes, she thought, as she shuffled out of her row to take her place at the side of the stage, among the potted plants, her rut was ready to receive her.

It might have been so different. She might have had children by now, be celebrating anniversaries . . .

'Elizabeth Miller.'

She stifled the thought, held her head up high and put her best foot forward, the maroon gown rustling as she stopped, turned and curtsied. The Royal Personage looked as if she was slipping into a coma.

She crossed the stage, walked down the steps, negotiated another phalanx of potted plants and resumed her seat. That was it, then. Her moment in the sun. The climax of three years of research. I am now a doctor, she thought. Doctor Elizabeth Miller. Not quite what I expected. I thought, by now, I would be Mrs Elizabeth Sharkey, also known as 'Mummy'.

She watched the rest of the newly minted doctors filing past, wondering how many of them had used their research to keep the screams at bay.

The Prof, who had been to many such ceremonies, both as spectator and graduate, knew all the best restaurants in the vicinity of the Royal Albert Hall, and it was to one of these that the Miller party repaired when the show was over. 'Let's get away from all these awful BAs,' he said. 'Far too many of them are one's own students.'

'Quite,' said Charlotte, with a shudder. She thought it was rather good to ape the Prof's contempt, little guessing the caustic things he said about her behind her back.

'Well, then, Doctor Miller,' said Kate, when the food was ordered and the wine poured, 'here's to the very successful completion of your academic career.'

'With respect,' said the Prof, 'we should toast the successful *commencement* of her academic career. A PhD is only a beginning, the "open sesame", you might say.'

'*You* might say,' said Kate. 'I say it's time Elizabeth moved on to something more tangible.'

'If you are going to suggest another foray into the gutter press,' said the Prof, 'please save your breath. That was weighed in the balance and found wanting.'

'Elizabeth was very good at it. Editors liked her. She got letters.'

The Prof sneered. 'The only letters that matter come after your name.'

'At least people were reading what she wrote,' said Kate, 'which is more than can be said for most academics.'

Charlotte sucked her teeth noisily, as if Kate had just announced that she'd joined the BNP. The Prof frowned, and was about to reel off a list of his recent publications, some of which had a readership that went into double figures, when

Elizabeth said, 'Do I have any say in this? Or am I simply here to be talked about?'

'Of course,' said the Prof. 'You must decide. And I can't imagine that you are going to throw everything away for a career in journalism.'

'What's wrong with journalism?' asked Chris. 'It pays well.'

'I can only imagine,' said the Prof, 'the sort of journalists that *you* would come across. I suppose that area does pay well. Muck-raking.'

'How would you know what sort of journalists I meet? You don't even know what I do at college.'

'Now,' said Kate, slipping into her customary role of peace-keeper, 'let's all enjoy a lovely lunch. I'm so proud of you, Liz.'

'Thanks.'

'And I know Susan would have been as well.'

'Ah,' said the Prof, staring into his glass. 'Yes.'

That shut him up, thought Kate, and moved the conversation on to more general observations about the ceremony, the graduates and the Royal Personage.

The starters arrived.

'And how's the family?' asked Elizabeth at length, realising it was rude to ask nothing at all about other people. 'Neil? The kids?'

'Lovely, thanks. Neil's doing very well at his new job . . .' She caught an unmistakable look in the Prof's eye. 'Yes, he's in charge of a very big IT department now. The children are growing up fast.'

'And your work?'

'Oh, you know. Turning them out.' Kate's thoroughly researched, lightly written historical novels were now guaranteed best-sellers, making a great deal more money than the Susan Barnard œuvre would ever generate. 'Writing the occasional review, when asked.

You know, Tony,' she said, 'journalism. No, don't look at me like that.'

'If only you would contribute to something worthwhile, like the *Times Literary Supplement*.'

'I wouldn't be sitting here in a Jasper Conran dress and Chloé shoes if I wrote for the *TLS*. I'd be down the second-hand bookshop trying to sell my review copies for cash.'

'But the quality of your writing,' said the Prof. 'Surely that means something to you? Sales are all very well, but what matters, is it not, is the literary value?'

'All right. Perhaps I'll write my next novel backwards. Would that do?'

'Sounds interesting,' said Charlotte, which made even the Prof laugh.

'Anyway, Daddy,' said Elizabeth, 'what about you? Been to any interesting conferences recently?'

'Let me see . . . Paris, of course. Berlin. Tokyo. That little shindig in Toronto. Next week it's Florence, then next month I'm off to Harvard, for my sins.'

'It's a tough life,' said Kate. 'I wonder how you find any time to do any teaching. I mean, that's what they pay you for, isn't it?'

'My teaching commitments are necessarily light.'

A nasty fight was brewing, and as the Millers still needed Kate's managerial services, Elizabeth was eager to calm things down.

'Ah, here comes the main course,' she said, and they spent the next five minutes talking about the food. The Prof was silent, with Charlotte sulking in sympathy. This left Elizabeth, Kate and Chris to chat.

It was all going quite nicely until Kate asked Chris about his course.

'It's great, thanks,' he said. 'I'm learning a lot. I should be able to apply for second AD jobs when I leave.'

'Are we supposed to be pleased?' asked the Prof, looking like the eagle on *The Muppet Show*. 'Is this cause for celebration?'

'I don't see why not,' said Chris. 'It's what I want to do.'

'Television,' said the Prof. 'This awful, unending stream of chat. Not saying anything, you understand. Just chatting. Not conveying *meaning*. Chatting. Filling a void.'

Chris sighed, shrugged, said, 'Whatever' and carried on eating. His father's contempt no longer hurt, at least not as much.

'And how is Anna?' asked Kate, provoked beyond endurance by the Prof's cruelty. It was either this or throwing a drink in his face. The question had the desired effect. His fork stopped halfway to his mouth, which hung open.

'I beg your pardon?'

'Yes, come on, Dad,' said Chris.

'How dare you?' said the Prof, glaring at his son.

'Don't blame him,' said Kate. 'I asked the question.'

'And it is none of your business.'

'It is *our* business, though,' said Elizabeth. 'We ought to discuss it.'

'There is nothing to discuss.'

'Yes, there is,' said Elizabeth. 'You're still married, aren't you?'

'We are.'

'And do you intend to stay married?'

'Perhaps you *should* consider a career in journalism,' said the Prof, 'as you take such a prurient interest in what does not concern you.'

'It does concern me. Us.'

'I don't see how.'

'Because you're our father,' said Chris.

'Very well,' said the Prof, 'I will tell you. Anna and I have agreed to live apart. We have not discussed a divorce. That is all you need to know.'

'So do you think you might get back together at some point?' asked Elizabeth. 'Do you still feel . . .'

The Prof held up the Hand, and silence fell.

'I have said what I have said. Let that be an end of it.'

'This is ridiculous, Dad. I mean, you can't just leave it like that . . .'

'That's enough!' His face was the colour of ivory, his lips thin. The whole restaurant fell silent.

Elizabeth wanted to raise the subject of her father's will but it couldn't in the face of his hostility. Post-honeymoon, he'd made it clear that the newlyweds had each made new wills making the other the benefactor.

'Well, then,' said Kate, in a voice that sounded to her ears insanely cheery, 'let's see, yes, I'm going on holiday soon, we're having a week in Greece.'

Four pairs of eyes looked at her imploringly.

'A few days in Athens to see the birthplace of western culture, and then we're off to Kefalonia to lie on the beach and eat kebabs. Heaven,' she said, wondering how long she could spin this out for. But Chris was quickly at her side.

'Oh, lovely,' he said. 'I went to Skiathos last year. Had a brilliant time.'

The Prof and Elizabeth both looked at him, puzzled. It was the first either of them had heard of Skiathos.

A week or so later, Elizabeth got a call at lunchtime, while she was sitting in the staffroom despairing over a huge pile of marking.

It was Kate. One of her children had been rushed into hospital with suspected meningitis. She was meant to be reviewing a play that night, and the *Beacon* had been unable to find cover. Could Elizabeth save the day?

Under the circumstances, she could hardly say no, but it was only after she'd said a definite yes that Kate told her what the play in question was.

A West End revival of Noël Coward's *Design for Living* – so far so good, she was familiar with the territory, could indeed write half the review without even seeing the show.

Starring, in his first London stage appearance in several years, Hollywood leading man Alan Southgate.

Had Elizabeth been in the habit of reading what her father called the gutter press, she'd have known about this production long ago; it had been in the showbiz columns for weeks. Alan was the main attraction, but the rest of the casting was enough to guarantee a good long run. In the role of Gilda was Meredith Chase, an American sitcom star recently separated from her actor husband, making her London debut and, more interestingly, rumoured to be Alan's latest flame. Completing the triangle was Johnny Khan, so-called wild child of British acting, who dressed, behaved and consumed drugs like a rock star, had starred in a number of hard-edged British films in which he showed off his tattoos and was bound for Hollywood and a career in action films. This *Design for Living*, according to advance publicity, was going to blow the genteel world of Noël Coward wide open, blah blah blah, which actually meant that people would take their clothes off and shout a lot in 'urban' accents.

As Elizabeth only read the quality press, however, she knew none of this, and approached her critical duties with an open mind. It would be interesting to see how Alan had changed in the years since she'd seen him. He moved away shortly after the wedding debacle, and there had been no contact since then – as if, thought Elizabeth, he were keen to dissociate himself from such a disaster. It was not the behaviour of a friend, and she resented him for it. Yes: it would be very interesting to review Alan Southgate for the Daily Beacon.

She took Chris as her date, her first move in a post-graduation bridge-building exercise. She couldn't turn her back on her family for the rest of her life; she didn't have enough friends to do that.

'Well,' she said, when they were settled in their seats and the lights were going down, 'let's see what they make of this.' She opened a notebook, and made ready her pencil. 'It's an interesting play, of course, historically speaking. Coward's one big attempt at honesty. But you could say . . .'

'Shhh,' said Chris, 'they're about to come on.'

The play was a disaster. Even those who had only come to see Alan Southgate in the flesh were looking at their watches halfway through the first act. More serious theatregoers were tutting and fidgeting; only the critics seemed to be enjoying themselves, scribbling furiously at every missed cue, every muffed bit of repartee. Alan was clinically proficient, but seemed to be on autopilot. Meredith Chase was constantly forgetting her lines, her accent veering wildly from the drawing rooms of Mayfair to the coffee shops of the East Village. As for Johnny Khan – was he actually on drugs? Was his stumbling and slurred performance deliberate – some peculiar whim of the director? Or was he simply untalented and stoned? Running around the stage in his underpants, he had charms that wouldn't have escaped Noël Coward, but in clothes he simply didn't project, and looked like he was waiting to appear in court on an ASBO infringement.

The second half was even worse than the first, with everyone shouting all the time, lots of emoting over even the most throwaway lines and a final curtain that looked more like the conclusion of one of Quentin Tarantino's films, there was so much blood.

'Oh my God,' said Elizabeth, rather too loudly, as they made their way to the post-show drinks, 'that was absolutely bloody awful.'

'Yes, all right,' said Chris, 'save your opinions for the paper.'

'Oh come on, you have to admit,' she said, taking a glass of sparkling wine from a tray, 'It was a mess.'

'I thought Alan was fantastic,' said Chris, who had never told his sister about their continued 'friendship'.

'He was so wooden!'

'Elizabeth, please,' said Chris. 'Not here.'

'Why not?'

'Apart from anything else, you're drinking the company's liquor.'

'So? It's a press night. I think I'm entitled to speak my mind.'

'There's a time and a place . . .'

'Oh. I see. It's all right for you and Kate to speak your mind on the morning of my wedding, but not all right for me to say that Alan Southgate is anything less than perfect. Thank you for pointing that out.'

Here we go again, thought Chris. He should have known it was about time she threw that in his face again. It happened, on average, once every six months.

'Look,' he said, 'there's Will Young.'

Elizabeth was not to be distracted by celeb-spotting. 'I'm sure you thought you were *acting for the best*,' she said, her voice low and hoarse. 'I'm sure you all *discussed it* and *thought it over* before you came bursting into my bedroom to give me the great news.'

'For God's sake, Elizabeth,' said Chris, downing his drink and deciding that, after all, the dressing room called, 'let it go. It's been two years.'

'Oh right, that's fine, I'll just put it all behind me and move on. Thanks for your input. No really, thanks for *sharing that*.' When did I become so bitter, she wondered, listening to her own voice sounding horribly like Charlotte's. But it was hard to stop, like picking at a scab. 'I suppose next you're going to say that time is a great healer and that there are plenty of other fish in the sea.'

'Something like that, yes,' said Chris, pecked her on the cheek and hurried away.

Elizabeth got the Tube home to her empty flat and poured her bile into five hundred words, which she read over twice and emailed to the Daily Beacon's arts desk.

It might have been better to sleep on it, but Elizabeth was inexperienced in the ways of journalism, and did not know that you should never file in anger.

Less than thirty-six hours later, she was thrilled to see her name in print under a review that was headlined 'Design for Disaster'. It had been moved to the top of the page, under a photograph of Alan looking stiff and awkward in his dinner jacket. A quote from her review had been pulled out as the caption. 'Alan Southgate: "all the charisma of an ironing board".' She had a momentary pang, but recovered quickly. For one thing, it was true. For another, Alan was at least partly to blame for what had happened. He was Nick's best man; he must also have known what was going on. She hated Chris for telling her, and she hated Alan for not telling her; even two years after the event, Elizabeth was no nearer processing her feelings about Nick and Rachel. She'd been in deep freeze for all that time – and now, as she thawed, the pain and confusion returned.

She read through the copy – not a comma had been changed. The concluding paragraph, in which she claimed that everyone involved in the production was a disgrace to the theatre and guilty of criminal damage to the reputation of Noël Coward, seemed quite justified.

It was shortly after lunch that the arts editor called to inform Elizabeth that Mr Southgate's lawyers had been in touch, with a view to an action for defamation.

'There's absolutely nothing for you to worry about,' he said. 'It won't come to court, and even if it does, it shouldn't be you individually that he sues. It's much more likely to be the paper.'

If this was meant to be reassuring, it failed. Court . . . sues . . . individually . . . Elizabeth's feeling of warm indignation was quickly drowned by a cold wash of fear.

'Oh dear,' she said. 'I didn't realise . . .'

'Making a splash, that's the thing,' said the arts editor. 'Going against the grain. Have you seen the rest of 'em?' She hadn't. 'Falling over themselves to say how great it was, just because it's got Hollywood stars in it. Bloody load of bollocks. That's not theatre, that's a glorified PA.'

'Did the others *like* it?'

'Loved it!' chuckled the editor. 'You're the only one who had the guts to say it was crap. Emperor's New Clothes, and all that. The boss is chuffed.'

'The boss?'

'Mike. Our glorious leader. Editor of the Year, don't you know. He loves a controversy. The *Beacon* sticking its neck out. Oh, yes. You're the golden girl around here this morning. A lawyer's letter is as good to him as an award. Any chance you might do some more for us? You'd be doing me a favour.'

'I don't know . . .'

'The money's not brilliant, but it's better than a poke in the eye with a sharp stick.'

'How much?'

'Ah, the true journalist appears at last. Two hundred per review. More for features.'

'But this defamation thing?'

'Don't worry about that. They haven't got a leg to stand on. It's a fair comment. They're just trying to bully us into printing a retraction.' He laughed. 'Little do they know, they're making it worse. Mike's told the press office to release it as a news story. You'll be quoted everywhere. Well done. Call you later.'

And so, by betraying one of her oldest friends – one who, unbeknown to Elizabeth, was screwing her own brother – Elizabeth became a journalist.

'And why not?' she asked her reflection in the mirror. 'Anything's better than this.' She thought of the untouched pile of marking on her desk, the endless trite variations on a minor theme, the spelling mistakes, the hopeless inadequacy of it all. Yes, she could ferret around in the margins of academia for the rest of her life, until her heart withered and she grew a moustache, sacrificing her mind on the altar of pointless research, her soul on generation after generation of uninterested students. Or she could get out in the world, use the talent that she'd been given, even if it was a talent to wound, to claw back some little scrap of territory, some vestige of status and self-respect. And love? Well, you can't have everything. If she couldn't be loved, she could at least be feared.

She read over her review. Yes, that final paragraph about criminal damage was harsh. She looked at it again, and thought of ways in which she could have made it harsher.

Chapter 19

Rachel was right about her latest TV drama: it didn't get recommissioned. But she did well out of it, and before the series was over she'd been called back into Gerald Partridge's office, not, this time, as a wide-eyed wannabe, but as an established actress with a string of TV credits on her CV. He was casting for an adaptation of Émile Zola's *Nana*, and he thought Rachel Hope might be the leading lady he was looking for.

The audition was a formality; he'd already decided to give her the job. But auditions served a purpose. They established right at the outset the relationship between producer/director and talent that, in a Partridge production, was along Hitchcockian lines. He was the despot, the dictator, the artist. She (and they nearly always were shes) was the medium. She was merely required to move and speak in a certain way, without discussion or inhibition. Nudity was a given. The words 'directed and produced by Gerald Partridge' guaranteed lashings of screen sex. Rachel was prepared to do almost anything short of full penetration if it would get her the job. But she, too, was aware that the audition was a crucial bargaining opportunity. Thus far she had resisted Gerald's suave charms, his tasteful suggestions that they might like to sleep together, well aware that the promise of sex was more powerful than the delivery. If she thought it was necessary, she'd let him have his way right here in the office; there was a sofa in one corner that just screamed 'casting couch'. But she'd much rather hold out until the ink was dry on the contract. And then? Well, Gerald Partridge was a very attractive man, despite his age and his reputation. He was the product of good breeding, good schools, Cambridge University and early success, those things that give polish and power – those things that Nick, for all his looks and his talent in the sack, so lacked. Gerald was handsome, too – in his youth, perhaps, as handsome as Nick, with dark hair, a strong jawline, blue eyes and big hands. Unlike most of his peers in the industry, he hadn't developed a pot belly. His shoulders were broad and his hips were narrow, his stomach flat and his legs strong, and he moved and talked and behaved like a man confident of getting what he wanted.

In short, Rachel was ready to upgrade. The time had come to leave Nick behind. She'd made her point; now she had to think about her future. She cherished no illusions of becoming the next Mrs Partridge; he would leave her, just as he was now leaving another. But while she had him, she intended to make the most of him.

'Are you familiar with the novel?'

'I haven't read it. But I've looked it up on Wikipedia.'

'Good,' said Gerald. 'Initiative and curiosity unburdened by intellectual zeal. That fits very nicely. Please, take a seat.'

They were in the west London headquarters of Channel Six, where Gerald had an office, all glass walls and venetian blinds, one huge window overlooking the Westway. He sat at his desk, the window behind him. She sat opposite. The sofa seemed to wink and leer from its corner.

'Thank you.' She ran her fingers through her hair and licked her lips. He was watching. She was dressed carefully – a tailored wool suit in a mottled slatey blue, nipped in at the waist, the skirt brushing the knees. A white silk blouse, open at the neck. Sheer tights, brown high heels.

'And what did Wikipedia tell you?'

'*Nana*, by Émile Zola, published in 1880, the story of a young prostitute who trades sex for money, power and position. And who eventually dies rather horribly.'

'Correct. Considered one of the most shocking books of its day for its frank treatment of sex, its social and political satire, and above all for its depiction of female sexuality as a form of currency.'

'Hot stuff.'

'As you say, Miss Hope, hot stuff.' He rubbed the back of his neck with the palm of his hand. 'Think you can handle it?'

'I'll give it a go.'

'It's not going to be easy. You will be naked in front of a bunch of cameramen and sparks and ADs.'

She recrossed her legs. 'Bring it on.'

'And it's going to be seen by all your friends and family. Are you ready for that?'

'They can't possibly think less of me than they already do.'

'I see.'

'Let's just say,' said Rachel, sitting up straight and thrusting her breasts forward, 'that my family has never approved of my life choices.'

'The ideal actress. No shame, and nothing to lose.'

'Oh, I wouldn't say that, exactly. I have a professional reputation to consider. I wouldn't want to do anything that would make me look . . . What shall I say? Cheap. Tacky. Ridiculous. There are plenty of girls in this business spend their lives getting their kit off for men's mags, and never see the business end of a TV camera again.'

'I don't think we need worry about that.'

'Is that so?'

'*Nana* is going to be,' said Gerald, leaning back in his chair and folding his hands behind his head, 'my masterpiece.' He pushed back from the desk, stretching his legs.

'Go on.'

'For one thing, I've updated it. It's not set in Second Empire Paris, it's set in twenty-first-century London. Nana is still a prostitute, but she doesn't hang around street corners – it's all done on the Internet. Her clients aren't merchants and aristocrats, but politicians, bankers, celebrities. She represents the greed and corruption of expense-account culture. What Zola called the golden fly on the dung heap of society.'

'I see.'

'And it's going to get you on the front page of every newspaper in the country.'

'Oh God,' said Rachel, 'you don't expect me to sleep with the Prime Minister, do you?'

'Certainly not. If you're going to sleep with anyone, it won't be the PM.'

'Although,' said Rachel, 'power is always an aphrodisiac.'

'Is it?'

'Oh, yes.'

The venetian blinds looked as if they were about to close themselves; the couch was begging to be romped on.

'Perhaps we could discuss it over dinner.'

'That would be lovely. Shall I invite my agent along, too? I know he'll want to discuss the finer points of the contract.'

Gerald sat up, pulled his chair into his desk. 'Of course. Here's one I prepared earlier.' He produced a document from underneath his blotter. 'I shall fax it to him straight away.'

'That's wonderful,' said Rachel. 'And when he gives me the green light, we can celebrate.'

'Canny girl,' said Gerald, confident that, after all, his instincts were one hundred per cent correct.

*　　*　　*

'Don't be alarmed. His bark's much worse than his bite.'

'Thanks,' said Elizabeth. 'My knees are shaking.'

'Come on.' The arts editor knocked on the door and held it open. 'You'll be fine. I promise.'

Elizabeth straightened her jacket, took a deep breath and walked into the editor's office.

He was seated at his desk, his feet on top of a filing cabinet, talking on the telephone. At first he did not seem to notice he had company, and she had time to examine him. A hard-faced, ugly little man in his forties with bristly black hair, hairy hands and a thick neck.

'Yeah, yeah, I know we promised them front page, but that's just tough luck. Something else has come up. No. No, I don't. Well just tell them they're not important enough. This is the *Daily Beacon* we're talking about here, Darren, not the *Pig Farmers' Gazette*.' He slammed the phone down. 'Right. This is . . .' He referred to notes on his desk. 'Elizabeth Miller, yes?'

'Yes,' said Elizabeth. 'Hello.'

'Mike Harris.' He looked at her over the top of his glasses. 'So you're the young woman who's been causing all the trouble.'

'Yes. Sorry about that.'

'Are you?'

'Well, yes . . .'

'Do you not stand by every word you wrote?'

'I suppose it was rather harshly phrased . . .'

'Hah! Tell that to the prosecuting counsel in court and we're fucked. You'd better sit down. You look a bit green.'

The arts editor placed a chair under Elizabeth's backside, and she dropped into it. So much for the editor's bark being worse than his bite.

'First rule of journalism,' said Mike. 'Never apologise, never explain. Well, unless the bastards have really got you in a corner, in which case, say any old crap that's going to get you out of it. I thought it was a good review. Haven't seen the play, and don't intend to, can't stand theatre most of the time, more my wife's sort of thing. But it's time these people were taken down a peg or two. Alan Southgate. Jumped-up posh kid who got where he is through family connections.'

'Oh, I don't think that's quite . . .'

'And this bloody woman, Meredith Chase, she's the one from that awful bloody American sitcom, isn't she? My daughters are mad about her. Pictures of her on their bedroom walls, believe it or not. Terrible role model for young girls. She looks anorexic. Hey, let's, do something about anorexic actresses. Have a go at her. She gets on my nerves. How bad was she?'

'She was pretty awful.'

'Did she remember her lines?'

'Some of them.'

'Very good. Some of them.'

'The accent kept hopping across the Atlantic.'

'I like it. Why didn't you say it?'

'I mentioned something about her accent . . .'

'So, what am I going to do about you?'

'I beg your pardon?'

'Am I going to tell Southgate's lawyer to fuck off, and put up a defence of fair comment, or am I going to offer you as a sacrificial lamb and say that you'll never work for this newspaper again?'

'I don't . . .' Hang on, Elizabeth. This is not a rhetorical question. 'I'd tell him to fuck off, if I were you.'

'Right you are.' He picked up the phone, stabbed a few buttons. 'Nicky? Yeah, that Alan Southgate business. We stand by our critic. Fair comment, blah blah blah. Right? Tell them in no uncertain terms to . . . What was it, Elizabeth?'

'Fuck off.'

'That's right. Tell them to get lost. You know the drill. Cheers.'

He stood up. 'Welcome to the team, Elizabeth Miller.' He stuck out a hand. 'I'll be watching out for your byline. I want more of this type of stuff.' He picked up a photocopy of Elizabeth's review; she saw Alan's mournful gaze looking out at her. 'Give it to 'em, kid, hot and strong. You've got what it takes. Don't let me down. That's all.'

The arts editor steered her carefully through the door.

'You just did yourself a very good turn,' he said, when she was sitting by the watercooler gathering her nerves. 'There are freelancers all over London who would kill for the opportunity you've been given. I hope you appreciate it.'

'I don't know how I feel about it,' said Elizabeth, 'but I suppose I shall soon find out. When's my next assignment?'

'Tonight, if you want it.'

'Oh, I can't . . .' Yes you can. 'Okay. What is it?'

Alan owned an apartment at the top of a thirty-storey building on the south bank of the Thames, a penthouse with windows at each end of the reception room looking upstream and down, a bedroom with glass brick walls and brown leather upholstery, a bathroom so sleekly and efficiently fitted, it belonged in a hospital. Like everything in Alan's life, the apartment was an investment, careful, conscientious, considered. Not permanent. Certainly not a home.

'Has she completely gone off her rocker?' he said, lying back in bed, running his fingers through Chris's golden curls. 'I mean, I know the wedding and everything knocked her for six, but come on, water under the bridge. Time to move on.'

'Don't ask me. I know as much about my sister as you do.'

'So what's this all about, then?' He reached over to the bedside table, picked up a letter from his solicitor. 'Is she just trading on the fact that we went to college together to lever herself into a job with the newspapers?'

'I've no idea.'

'Well it certainly bloody looks that way.' Alan frowned, tore the letter in two and chucked it away.

'Appearances can be deceptive,' said Chris, stroking Alan's naked stomach. 'Speaking of which, how is the lovely Meredith?'

'Very nice, thank you.'

'I'm so pleased.'

'Do I detect a hint of jealousy?'

'If anyone has cause for jealousy, it's Meredith, not me.'

'And what about your boyfriend?'

'I don't have a boyfriend.'

'Oh.' Alan removed his arm from around Chris's shoulders. 'I'm sorry to hear that.'

'Why? Hoping for a threesome?'

'Don't say things like that, Chris. It sounds so gay.'

'I am gay, in case you hadn't noticed.'

'Well, I'm not.'

'Don't I know it. I have to read about your many conquests, remember. I suppose you're going to tell me that's all a pack of lies made up for publicity.'

'No,' said Alan, 'it's not that. I do – how shall I put it? Follow through.'

'I see.' Chris swallowed hard.

'I hope you're not going to give me a lecture about being true to myself.'

'No . . .'

'Because I've had that up to here. People telling me I should come out. And why should I? I enjoy my life. I have the best of both worlds, and I have a career. You can imagine the roles I'd get if they knew about this.'

'Is it really that bad?'

'Be realistic. There are only so many movies with gay best friend characters in them, and Rupert Everett gets those jobs. What else am I going to do? Kindly wizard? Bitchy stylist?'

'Fair point.'

'I prefer to be the hero, thank you very much. And as long as I have you, I don't need other guys.'

'Pull the other one,' said Chris, trying to keep the delight out of his voice. 'You're not trying to tell me that all those gym bunnies in Hollywood don't tempt you.'

'I made that mistake once. Never again. It cost me a lot of money to keep that little slut's mouth shut.'

'Kiss and tell?'

'We did considerably more than kiss, but that was the general idea.'

'Hmmm. How much could I get, do you reckon?'

'Try it, and see where it gets you.'

'Is that a threat?'

'The question doesn't arise, because I trust you. Why do you think I keep coming back to you?'

'I thought it was because of my athletic young body, my charming personality and my amazing oral technique.'

'Don't forget your modesty.'

'I never forget that.' Chris's hand travelled south; something was moving north to meet it.

'But above all, dear boy,' said Alan, in a Noël Coward voice, 'I value your discretion.'

An hour or so later, Alan got up, showered, and started dressing to go to the theatre.

'Can you not do anything about it?'

'Hmmmm? What?'

'This bloody review your sister has written.'

'Oh come on, Alan. You're not still fretting about that.'

'It's upset me.'

'Too near the knuckle?'

'That's a hateful thing to say.'

'Sorry.'

'Can't you get her to retract it, or something?'

'You must be joking. She'd never do anything I asked her to do. Besides, we've only just really started speaking again for the first time in two years.'

'What? Surely she doesn't blame you.'

'She blames everyone. I just happen to be a very convenient whipping boy.'

He got out of bed, showing Alan his backside. 'Can't you see the marks?'

Alan fiddled with his tie. 'I suppose she blames me as well, then. Is that what this is all about?'

'She's not a happy woman, you know.'

'Right.' Alan adjusted the knot – not too tight, just a little loose at the throat, smart but not formal. 'So you wouldn't say, then, that she's missing me.'

'Not judging by that review.'

'I shouldn't be hoping for a rapprochement.'

'I wouldn't hold your breath.'

'Good.' He settled a jacket on his shoulders, shrugged it into place, surveyed the effect in the mirror. 'It won't make any difference, then.'

'What won't?'

'If I take this job I've been offered.'

'And what might that be?' asked Chris, with a horrible feeling that he knew already.

'The male lead in a new Channel Six drama series. Opposite Rachel Hope.'

Chapter 20

Nick wasn't happy.

'You're trying to get rid of me,' he said, which was true, but of course it would never do to admit something like that.

'Whatever gives you that idea?'

'I know what he's like, Gerald bloody Partridge.'

'You're being silly. Come on. This is what we've been dreaming of. Planning for. Working towards.' 'We' meant 'I'; Nick hadn't lifted a finger to help Rachel in her career, although keeping her satisfied in the sack certainly aided concentration. 'I'm not saying Gerald isn't an attractive man.'

'Oh, *Gerald* is it? I see.'

'Well, darling, that is his name.'

'Don't *darling* me. Bloody actresses.'

Rachel sighed; these outbursts of childish resentment were getting far too common. Even Nick's charms had their limits. 'He's twice my age.'

'So?'

'And, in case you'd forgotten, he's my employer.'

'Yeah, well you wouldn't be the first girl to shag her way to the top.'

Good God, thought Rachel, has he been reading the scripts? 'You have a very odd idea of what the acting profession is like. Girls don't shag their way to the top any more. We're lucky to get a hot drink and a lift to the studio. And for all Gerald's Casanova reputation . . .'

'Oh I see, he *has* got a bad reputation . . .'

She held up her hand. 'I said, for all his reputation, he is a married man with two children who are not very much younger than me.'

'And that makes it all right, then?'

'Makes what all right, Nick? The fact that I'm taking the kind of job I've always hoped for? The fact that I'm going to be earning more money in the next twelve weeks than you've earned in the last twelve years?'

Nick's face went pale. 'You little bitch.'

'I'm sorry, but you . . .'

'Throwing that in my face. Oh, yes. Now it comes out. You're the same as all the rest.'

'Well, darling, you haven't exactly . . .'

He screamed 'Don't *darling* me!', and Rachel thought for a moment he was going to hit her. She cowered, raising her arms to shield her face. She had make-up tests tomorrow, and bruises wouldn't create a good first impression.

'Fucking shit,' Nick said instead, and stormed out of the flat.

Rachel hadn't planned any of this but, she thought, as she got ready to go to the studio, things could have gone a lot worse.

Sunday lunch at the Prof's house carried on, unchanged by the shifting cast around the table. At present it was a two-hander, just Elizabeth and her father and a great big joint of meat that would last the Prof for the rest of the week. Chris didn't come very often nowadays: two hours of being harangued by the Prof was too high a price to pay for a bit of overcooked meat and a few vegetables. Anna was long gone, although not quite far enough gone for Elizabeth's liking, still the wife, still the next of kin and still set to inherit the bulk of the Miller/Barnard estate if the Prof didn't pull his finger out and change his will back in favour of his children. But he seemed as reluctant to do that as he was to get divorced. Perhaps, thought Elizabeth, he hoped for a reconciliation.

Conversation stayed on safe, easy paths. They talked about papers they were writing, lectures they were giving, books to which they were contributing. They could moan about the awfulness of undergraduates and, now that Elizabeth was safely doctored, the awfulness of PhD students. They could discuss the government's insane ideas about the funding of higher education, they could bitch about the governors of the University of London, they could tear to pieces some article in the *Times Higher Ed*. Thus occupied, neither of them need make any reference to their unexpected single status, to the disappointments and betrayals of those nearest to them or to the prospect of a lonely old age that both of them seemed to be facing.

Today, however, Elizabeth was nervous. She had something to tell her father, and he was not a man who reacted well to news. She was giving up teaching at the university – and that, in the Prof's eyes, was like a good Muslim girl turning up at the family home munching on a hot dog. The fact that she was leaving the hallowed groves of academia for a job on a news-paper – *a newspaper*! – was the salt in the wound.

'So, Daddy,' she said, when they had finished their lunch, for which she had no appetite. 'I've been offered a job.'

'Marvellous! At Queen's?'

'No.'

'Spreading your wings at last, eh?'

'Yes.'

'Where? Still London? Or are you headed to the provinces? Some of them aren't half bad, you know. Bristol. Exeter. Sheffield. You could do a lot worse.'

'No, it's not . . .'

'Not Oxford, surely.' He looked excited, his eyes shining.

'No, Daddy. It's not actually an academic job.'

'Not . . . an academic job? What do you mean?'

'Well, I think it's time I tried something else for a while.'

'Oh.' The twinkle had gone from his eyes. 'And what, exactly, did you have in mind?'

'I've been offered a job on a newspaper.' The word was out. The Prof arranged his knife and fork at the usual precise angle, then pushed the plate away as if the whole thing disgusted him. 'A newspaper.'

'Yes. You know I've been doing bits and pieces.'

'At Kate's instigation.'

'You make it sound like a crime.'

'Go on.'

'Well, they really like my stuff.'

'Your "stuff".'

'Yes. You know, my writing.'

'I see. And you don't see anything strange about debasing yourself to writing that sort of . . . "stuff", as you put it.'

'Oh, Daddy, come on, there's more to life than academia.'

'Perhaps you should have thought of that before you did a higher degree.'

'Well, I did, but I just got sort of carried along.'

'And now you're going to throw it all away.'

'Don't say that.'

'What should I say? Hmm? Please tell me. I merely seek information.'

'I've found something I'm good at. Something I can make decent money at. Meet people. Challenge myself. Get out into the world. I can't spend the rest of my life delivering the same old lectures and marking hundreds of bloody awful undergraduate essays.'

'I see.' He put the tips of his fingers together. 'And that's what the university world means to you, is it?'

'Let's face it, Daddy, there is a certain amount of drudgery.'

'I can't say it ever occurred to me,' said the Prof, 'but perhaps, after all, you are not so well suited to it as we thought.'

Elizabeth drew breath to swear at him, but thought better of it. 'No, perhaps I'm not.'

'Well, then.' He got up.

'Don't you want to know when I start? What I'm going to be doing?'

He looked at her as if she'd just asked the most ridiculous question in the world. 'Not particularly,' he said. 'No.'

Kate, however, was absolutely delighted, and had the fledgling journalist over for a celebration meal.

'My dear,' she said, 'I'm just so pleased for you. I think you'll be absolutely wonderful at it. Now tell me everything. What are you going to be doing, how many days a week, and how much are they paying you?' Kate had been self-employed for long enough to know that these were the questions that mattered.

'I'm going to be a television critic,' said Elizabeth. 'Me! Can you imagine? I've hardly switched a television on for God knows how long.'

'Well, then, you'll come to it nice and fresh.'

'Yes, that's what Mike said. He wants the same kind of unjaded critical eye that I brought to my theatre reviews. At least,' she said, realising she sounded hideously arrogant, 'that's what he said.'

'Mike? Mike Harris? The editor?'

'Yes. Do you know him?'

'Of course. He's one of the most powerful men in the business.'

'So I keep hearing. He's really quite sweet.'

'"Sweet" is not a word I would ever apply to a newspaper editor, but he is charmingly down to earth, in a rather ferocious way.'

'Yes,' said Elizabeth, 'and that's what I like about him. After all these years of working in the university, it's refreshing to have someone speak his mind.'

'He certainly does that.'

'Oh, yes,' said Elizabeth, sounding schoolgirlish, 'he's got quite a sharp tongue. I mean, when you first meet him he's actually rather terrifying, but . . . Well, he improves on further acquaintance.'

'I see. And how much further are you acquainted?'

'I know what you're getting at, Kate, and it won't wash. This isn't one of your novels, you know. I won't be swooning into his manly arms. Apart from anything else, he's very much married. And I, of all people, am not going to start anything with a married man.'

'I know that,' said Kate, and looked as if she might say more, but changed the subject. 'So, is it a permanent job? Don't tell me that you, of all people, has stuck in your thumb and pulled out the biggest plum on Fleet Street?'

'Well, I've got a contract.'

'You're kidding. Full time?'

'Part time to start with, but he's going to review it in six months.'

'Elizabeth Miller,' said Kate, filling their glasses, 'you never cease to surprise me.'

'That's the other thing. I'm not Elizabeth Miller any more. I'm Liz. Liz Miller. He said it made a better byline.'

'Oh, the *Beacon* is always trying to affirm its proletarian credentials. He probably thinks "Elizabeth" sounds poncey and middle class. Which, incidentally, is what his so-called book critic called my last novel.'

'Oh, Kate. I'm so sorry.'

'That's quite all right. I don't suppose you arranged it.' Oops, thought Kate, me and my big mouth; she did just that to Alan Southgate. 'Anyway, have I shown you the sales figures? A bad review in the *Beacon* is no bad thing. As long as middle-class ponces continue to buy my books, the *Beacon* can huff and puff to its proletarian heart's content.'

'Daddy's not pleased.'

'Of course he's not. What did you expect? He's threatened by the whole thing.'

'He thinks journalism is beneath contempt.'

'Don't you believe it, kid. If someone offered Tony a column in the Daily Beacon, he'd take it like a shot. He's just jealous. And, to be honest with you, he has a bit of a problem with successful women.'

'I don't think that's fair.'

'Don't you? Perhaps you're too young to remember the fuss he made when Susan started writing novels. Not to mention when her first book got all those wonderful reviews. And when it was made into a film – oh, my God, you should have heard the things he said about the film industry. Now, however, he joins in the chorus of praise, not least because the lovely royalties keep rolling in.'

'You make him sound like a hypocrite.'

'I'm very fond of Tony, but I don't believe everything he says. And neither should you, if you want to have a decent adult relationship with him. Let him sulk. He liked having you in the university, where you could never really compete with him. It's a terrible shock to have you breaking out like this. But just wait till you're enjoying the fruits of your labours and swanking around being a columnist in a national newspaper who gets quoted in the House of Commons, then he'll change his tune.'

'You make it sound so easy.'

'Do you doubt your ability?'

'Funny,' said Elizabeth, 'that's exactly what Mike asked me.'

'And what did you tell Mike?'

'I said I have every faith in myself.'

'Good. You'll go far. You have talent.' And no scruples, thought Kate.

'Thank you. I feel that this is right for me. Now, at this stage in my life. It's time for me to move on.'

'High time, too. Onwards and upwards.'

They toasted each other.

'So, Liz Miller, television critic, when do you start?'

'Soon. Next month. Just have to wind up my teaching commitments this term and that's it. Then I have to go into the *Beacon* photographer's studio to have my mugshot done. It's nerve-wracking. I've got to go to the hairdresser and buy some new clothes and everything. '

'Don't worry,' said Kate. 'I'll help. I'm looking forward to seeing what they make of you.' She pulled back Elizabeth's hair, which was falling over her face. 'You lost all that weight after Nick. I suspect that somewhere under there is a very beautiful young woman waiting to get out.'

'I'll believe it when I see it,' said Elizabeth, feeling a glow of pleasure. 'Anyway, it's the new start I've been looking for. I've been treading water for too long. I think I'll be good at it.'

'How wonderful. And what marvellous timing.'

'In what sense?'

'Oh, haven't you seen? It's all over today's papers. I assumed this must have been a factor in your decision. Hold on a second.' Kate rummaged around in a pile of newspapers on the kitchen work surface, and found the *Guardian*. 'Here you go.' She folded it open to page five, and put it down in front of Elizabeth. 'Recognise anyone?'

'Well well well,' said Elizabeth at length, after the shock of seeing Rachel's face printed next to Alan's. 'Fancy that.' She read for a while in silence. 'An adaptation of Zola's *Nana*. They can't be serious.'

'I'm sure they are,' said Kate.

'May I . . . ?'

'Of course. Take the whole paper. I've finished with it.'

'Now,' said Elizabeth, folding the paper and putting it in her bag, 'enough about me. How are you? How's Neil? How are the kids?'

'Fine,' said Kate, wondering, once again, if she'd done the right thing.

Chapter 21

The first thing Rachel noticed as the taxi bumped along the road from the airport to the centre of Bucharest was a dead dog lying on the verge, its belly bloated, flies clustering around its eyes. By the time they made it to the hotel, rattled half to death, she'd counted three more canine corpses. From the way the driver was driving, it seemed as if he was aiming at them, and at least one of those bumps may have been another stray pup going to meet its maker.

Once past the smoked glass doors of the hotel, however, they were in another world, a paradise of deep carpets, piped music and eager porters, the only dead animals adorning the backs of the red-haired Mafia molls that lurked around the lobby.

'Welcome to downtown Bucharest,' said Gerald, when they'd made it up to her room. There was one large window looking out over what appeared to be a bombsite, with a lot of chain-link fence, decayed tarmac and vigorous weeds, the sort of thing that would survive a nuclear attack.

'It's not very glamorous,' said Rachel, pouting.

'Wait till you see the location. It makes this look like Mayfair.'

'Christ. I hate Eastern Europe.'

'Now, my pet, don't be like that. Less money on the location budget means more money for the star. And let's face it, your pretty little feet will barely touch the ground.'

'No,' said Rachel, 'and we all know why that is. The script seems to consist almost entirely of sex scenes. Doesn't she *ever* just sit down and have a nice chat with someone? I'd like my face to be recognised, rather than my heels.'

'I wouldn't complain too much if I were you. You'll be occupying the thoughts of every red-blooded man from eight to eighty.'

'Will I indeed.'

'Yes,' he said, coming up behind her, putting his arms around her waist, 'if I do my job right, you will.' He rocked his pelvis from side to side, pressed his cheek against hers.

'And is this part of the job description?'

'It's an optional extra.'

'Hmm. Well if you don't mind, Gerald, I'd like to take a shower, assuming they have hot running water in this country, and put on some clean clothes.'

'The former, certainly. Don't bother about the latter.'

'Would you please bugger off to your room, and leave me in peace for half an hour?'

'Half an hour?' He stepped back, looked at his watch. 'It's a date.'

So, thought Rachel when she was alone, this is how it begins. No discussion, no grand seduction, just the easy assumption that we become lovers as soon as we're away from London. The cast and crew would figure it out, needless to say, but what happens on location, stays on location. They all have their secrets. Take Alan Southgate, for instance.

She pulled off her travelling clothes and threw them in a corner; maid service would take care of all that, no doubt. The bathroom was in the communist taste, wildly opulent, acres of marble, gold taps – this hotel had been built for the comrades, and although it was falling to pieces, it still looked pretty swanky. There was a huge mirror on one wall, a large bath – big enough for a friend, thought Rachel – and a shower cubicle with frosted glass walls. The frosting turned out, on closer inspection, to be a build-up of limescale. It was a bit like being at home.

She turned on the tap, and was instantly drenched with a boiling hot jet of water, which quickly turned icy cold.

While waiting for the temperature to settle down, she found her mobile phone, discovered to her surprise that she had network coverage, and composed a quick text to Nick. 'Got here safe & sound,' she said. 'Bucharest a dump. Just off 2 location. Miss u. x x x.' That would keep him quiet for now. Her shower was ready, and she stepped in, letting it wash away the dust and grime of travel.

When she was clean from the crown of her head to the tips of her rosy pink toes, Rachel stepped out of the shower, wrapped herself in a gigantic white towel and made a few final preparations. She did not want to look as if she was expecting anything, so make-up was out of the question. A little moisturiser here and there wouldn't go amiss, however, and so she smoothed a handful of Clarins over her legs, shoulders and arms. Not her breasts; she didn't want them to taste funny. She ran a comb through her hair, pushing it back from her forehead, letting it fall in dark snakes down the back of her neck; wet hair might add to the oh-my-goodness, I-wasn't-expecting-this vibe that she was going for. She dropped the towel, and had half a mind to be discovered naked, or wearing only a pair of knickers, but that looked too much like something out of the script, and so she plumped for the hotel's white towelling dressing gown. She adjusted it carefully, the front open below her sternum, the belt knotted quite loosely, to allow easy slippage.

Yes, she thought, seating herself at the dressing table, that looks sufficiently uncalculated. Perhaps just a little more open at the front? No. Too tarty. There. Perfect.

And then, right on cue, came the soft tap on the door.

'Just a minute!' she trilled, as if she thought it was room service. She opened the door a crack. 'Oh! It's you!'

Gerald had two champagne flutes in one hand, a bottle in the other. 'Who were you expecting?'

'Come in. Let me just make myself decent.'

He put the drinks down on the table. 'You look pretty decent to me. Come here.' He reached out, quick as lightning, and grabbed the towelling belt of the dressing gown.

'Oh, Gerald!' she said, 'I've just had a shower!'

'I couldn't help noticing that,' he said, burying his face in her neck, wet tresses falling against him. Ah, she thought. That had the desired effect.

'Oh!' she said, 'you mustn't . . .' and then, as if the pleasure of the kiss had overwhelmed her maidenly objections, 'aaaah . . . oooooh . . .'

He certainly knew what he was doing, and the stubble on his face was sending outrageous electrical impulses from her neck down to her breasts and her groin. Probably, she thought, he calculated that effect just as carefully as I calculated the wet hair. Then Gerald undid her dressing gown, and she stopped thinking anything much.

After about ten minutes of this, Rachel sat on the edge of the bed, completely naked, and leaned back on her elbows. Gerald stood before her, and stripped.

He had a remarkably good body for a man of his age. Powerful shoulders, a broad chest covered in thick dark hair with a pair of pointy pink nipples poking through, a slightly convex stomach, likewise hairy, and sturdy, shapely legs. He did not have the breathtaking, knee-weakening beauty of Nick, whose every contour, every move was enough to make a girl lose her sense of priorities. But Gerald was every inch a man – and at the final unveiling, there were plenty of inches.

He was also a gentlemen, and before launching himself full length on her reclining body, he dropped to his knees, placed one brown hand on each of her white thighs, pushed them gently apart and went down on her like a starving man falling upon a buffet . . .

When she opened her arms to welcome him on top of her, feeling the softness of his chest hair against her super-sensitized breasts, she was ready to give him the ride of his life.

And then, she thought – and this was her final thought, before he entered her – he will be so much easier to control.

A red pen swooped over a piece of paper, circling a word. 'What in God's name is "naturalism"?'

'It's . . . well, it's an artistic movement that, um, believes in the inclusion of every detail as a way of . . .'

'I don't like "isms",' said Mike. A line went through the circle. 'This is the Daily Beacon, Liz. The telly column. You're not writing your bloody PhD any more.'

'No, but surely . . .'

'If you can't say it in words that I understand, then what the bloody hell do you think the readers are going to make of it? They're thick as pig shit, most of them, and move their lips when they read.'

'You seem to have a very low opinion of the people who pay your wages.'

Mike looked up at Elizabeth over the top of this pretentious little half-moon glasses. There was a combative look in his eye. 'On the contrary, I have every respect for their stupidity. Stupid people are the backbone of this country.'

'Then perhaps you ought to get someone stupid to review television for you.' She folded her arms across her chest, pressing down her bosom. 'Seeing as I'm obviously far too intellectual.'

A hint of a smile, quickly suppressed, tugged at the corner of his mouth. He was scrutinising her, looking her up and down from the top of her newly sleek, expensively styled blonde hair to the tips of her super-chic Jil Sander high-heel pumps. It was hard to tell if Mike noticed such things as shoes and hairdos; Elizabeth was still getting used to her new self, made over (at great expense, and to great effect) for her new job. 'My dear girl, if I could find a stupid person who could string a sentence together and spell correctly, you'd be out of a job like that.' He snapped his fingers. 'As it is, however, I need a certain degree of literacy, and that, much to my regret, often goes hand in hand with *intelligence*.'

'I suppose that's a dirty word round here.'

'Abso-fucking-lutely,' said Mike. 'Now, apart from the odd lapse, you're doing a great job. You're funny, you're rude and you've got absolutely no respect for any of this crap.' He hit the TV listings page with the back of his hand.

'I told you right at the start, I don't know anything about television.'

'Which is why you're the right woman for the job. Do me a favour, and try not to learn anything. And for God's sake, don't socialise with these people. If you start going to launches and screenings, you'll get to know the publicists and producers and directors and even' – he made a face – 'the actors. Then you'll feel sorry for them and you won't be able to say what you really think. I'm sure they're all lovely, vulnerable, sensitive little souls who are deeply wounded by the horrible things that the *Beacon* says about them. Let's just keep it that way, though. Never let it get personal.'

'That shouldn't be difficult.'

'Right.' Mike looked her coolly up and down, as if appraising her clothes. He was a funny, tempestuous little man, with his bristly black hair, his ridiculously affected bow ties and spectacles, his penchant for loud, ill-fitting striped shirts, as if he was dressing the part of a newspaper editor. But there was something about him, a sort of repressed violence and barely contained mirth, that made his company bracing, if a little alarming. He opened his mouth to say something, then thought better of it.

'What?' said Elizabeth.

'Nothing. Go and watch some telly.' And then, when her hand was on the doorknob, he said, 'and thank you. You're doing a great job. There, now I've broken Harris's First Law, and actually praised a journalist. Run away before I take it back.'

Elizabeth ran away, and went to watch yet another documentary about extremely fat people.

Filming was going well. Once they were in the studio, a sprawling complex on the outskirts of Bucharest, formerly the pride and joy of the Romanian film industry, now being slowly reclaimed from dereliction by budget-conscious foreign producers, it was easy to forget the chill and squalor of their surroundings. Most of the scenes were interiors, and most of the interiors were the bedrooms, luxurious apartments and hotel rooms where Nana plied her trade. In some of them, Rachel was alone, preparing and pampering her body for her next tryst; a monologue would be added in voiceover. In others, she romped with a selection of men of various shapes and ages. But for the majority of her scenes, she was acting opposite Alan.

She had dreaded the moment of their first meeting, assuming that he would still hold a grudge for her part in Elizabeth's misfortune; it would be typical of Elizabeth to have spent the last two years poisoning his mind against her. She expected chilliness at best, open hostility at worst; what she didn't expect was the warm greeting that awaited her.

'You two know each other?' asked Gerald, when they finally met at the read through, a week before they'd flown to Bucharest.

'Oh, yes,' said Alan. 'We go way back.'

'Indeed?'

'We have . . . mutual friends,' said Alan, raising an eyebrow at Rachel. 'It's lovely to see you again, darling.'

'Lovely to see you, too,' said Rachel, reminding herself that she wasn't supposed to know about Alan and Chris.

Since then, there had been no time to catch up on the good old days, not least because Rachel was busy keeping Gerald satisfied, and Alan – well, Alan had other fish to fry. Mererdith Chase had seen him off at Gatwick, where there was a surprisingly large number of photographers for what was meant to be a private occasion, and Rachel had read all about their great love in the newspapers. He didn't seem to be pining, exactly; perhaps theirs was the kind of love that could withstand such separations. That's certainly what they told reporters.

At the end of the first week's shooting, when most of the studio stuff was done and they were about to move into town for restaurant and nightclub scenes, the two stars were summoned by Gerald for a meeting with the unit publicist.

'Guys,' said Gerald, 'this is Polly Hamlin. For the foreseeable future, she is your representative on earth. I place myself in her capable hands, and so should you.'

Polly was a voluptuous black woman of indeterminate age, with thick, wavy hair and an even thicker Birmingham accent. She wore gold lipstick, gold hoop earrings, a gold chain around her neck, gold sandals on her feet.

'Do your stuff, Pol,' said Gerald. 'I'm off to throttle the location manager.'

A few preliminary pleasantries were exchanged, during which Polly said the soothing words 'magazine covers', 'exclusive' and 'Rankin'. Then she said:

'So, Alan, Rachel. How do the two of you fancy having an affair?'

Alan crossed his legs. He was wearing, Rachel noticed, ironed jeans. 'I beg your pardon, Polly?'

'Well, you're both young, very attractive, up-and-coming.'

'Up and come, in my case, don't you think?' said Alan.

She ignored that. 'And you get on all right together, don't you? I mean, you could bear to be seen in public together.'

'Oh, yes,' said Rachel. 'We're old friends.'

'What's the deal?' asked Alan.

'I would like to place a story about how you found love on location in Romania.'

'Have we?' said Alan. 'I had no idea.'

'If I get it out tomorrow, it'll hit the papers on Friday. Good day for this kind of story.'

'I see. Well, you've certainly thought all of this through very carefully.'

'That's my job,' said Polly, laughing. 'Any objections?'

'Rachel? I always think it's nice to ask the lady, don't you?'

'I don't know what to say.'

'Never had an official affair before?'

'No.'

'Trust me,' said Alan, 'it's not nearly as painful as it sounds. You get used to it after a while. Actually, it's rather fun. Nice restaurants, first nights, premieres, all that sort of thing. I think it's a marvellous idea, Polly.'

'But you and Meredith?' said Rachel.

'Oh, yes,' said Alan. 'Good point. Are Meredith and I splitting up, Polly? Am I to blame, or is she? Am I seeking solace in the arms of co-star Rachel Hope, or am I a love rat? It does rather influence my choice of wardrobe, you see.' He turned to Rachel. 'One has to remain in character at all times.'

'Obviously I haven't spoken to Meredith's people yet,' said Polly. 'I wanted to make sure it was okay with you guys before I did that.'

'That's very decent of you, I must say,' said Alan.

'But I suggest that she's left you high and dry to return to America, and that you've rekindled a romance with . . .'

'Don't say childhood sweetheart,' said Alan.

'Okay. Let's see. Ever worked together before?'

'Not as such.'

'We need a back story.'

'Believe me,' said Rachel, 'you don't want this one.'

Polly put her hands over her ears. 'Please! No truth! We'll say that Rachel was a big fan, she got your autograph a few times, had your picture on her wall, never dreamed that one day she'd be starring with you and so on. Gives them hope.'

'Oh, that *is* romantic,' said Alan. 'This must be a big thrill for you, Rachel.'

'I'm beside myself,' said Rachel.

'So, we'll get some shots of you strolling around town together, I think,' said Polly. 'Long lens stuff.'

'Are you kidding?' said Alan. 'In this dump? Tripping over dead dogs and getting accosted by beggars? Not exactly aspirational.'

'I was going to suggest on the back lot here,' said Polly. 'They were shooting some costume drama last month. It's still dressed as a street in Victorian London. That'll do.'

'A make-believe setting for a make-believe love,' said Alan. 'How perfect. But could we get it over and done with before about seven? I've got a friend arriving at the airport, and I promised to pick him up.'

'Sure,' said Polly. 'It's your love affair.'

'Of course,' said Alan. 'Sometimes, one forgets. Come on, beloved. Let's have a little run-through.'

'I see your best friend is having another of his high-profile flings,' said Mike, dropping a celebrity magazine on Elizabeth's desk. 'He's a busy lad, that Alan Southgate.'

'Who's he . . . oh.' Something large and cold seemed to lodge in Elizabeth's throat. She dropped the paper in her lap, and put a hand to her heart. Alan and Rachel . . .

'Are you all right?'

'Hmm? Oh, quite. Sorry. Female trouble.'

'Right,' said Mike, backing away as if it were contagious. 'Don't let me interrupt you. Sorry. Just thought that might amuse . . .'

'Yes,' said Elizabeth weakly, picking up her handbag. 'I'll have a good look at that . . . Excuse me.' She made her way to the loo, taking the magazine with her.

So it was war, was it? Retaliating for a bad review by taking up with the one woman it would most hurt Elizabeth for him to be seen with? No: that was ridiculous. People don't do things like that, not even actors. This was fake, a publicity stunt, nothing more.

She scrutinised the photographs – grainy, a little soft focus, as if shot with a long lens, but it was easy to see what was going on. Two beautiful people, arm-in-arm in a picturesque old-world street, looking into a shop window, perhaps picking out something rather lovely to buy with all their wealth.

> *Little did Rachel Hope dream, as a star-struck teenager with pictures of Alan Southgate on her bedroom wall, that she would one day be starring alongside him. And is that all she's doing? From the look on Alan's face, we think this relationship might soon be more than just professional . . .*

Lies, all lies. She could blow it all sky high if she chose to. She knew the truth – and what she didn't know, she could guess. She just needed proof – something good enough to make the story lawyer-proof. And then she could hurt Rachel Hope, as she'd sworn to do on her wedding night. She could make her sorry.

Chapter 22

Rachel returned from Romania with a new official boyfriend in the beautifully proportioned shape of Alan Southgate. She stopped returning Nick's calls, was too busy to see him, seemed, in fact, to be avoiding him, which led Nick to conclude that she had a new actual boyfriend as well. And he didn't have to be Hercule Poirot to figure out who that might be. But the truth wouldn't be reported in the papers – they'd be given the much more saleable story of Rachel and Alan, a power couple if ever there was one, both beautiful, both successful and, amazingly, both British. Within a very few days of their arrival at Heathrow, they were being referred to in the gossip pages as 'Rach-Al'. They went everywhere together – wherever there were cameras, at least.

Nick was not happy. It should have been him on Rachel's arm, him in the beautifully tailored suits, him gaining access to the best clubs, the smartest parties. He was her boyfriend, not Alan Southgate. They'd been through hell and high water to be together, he'd thrown away a safe bet of a marriage, and he was not to be cast aside like this, just as Rachel was becoming rich and famous. Nick knew perfectly well that the affair was a smokescreen, not only for Rachel's relationship with a married man twice her age, but also, he suspected, for Alan's private preferences. He couldn't prove anything, but he had his eyes open that night when Alan plucked Chris Miller's cherry. But he had evidence of other things, and if he wanted Rachel back – wanted to remind her that Nick Sharkey was not someone to be lightly cast aside – now was the time to use it.

The Rachel Tapes, as he fondly called his little nest egg, were still just as clear and bright as the day they were recorded. Those four hours of video footage were the best four hours' work Nick had ever done. If Rachel continued to ignore him, he might have to let her into his little secret. It would not be in her interests for the footage to find its way on to the Internet. Okay, it hadn't done Paris Hilton any harm, but Rachel, unlike Paris, had to work for a living. If Nick released the Rachel Tapes, she would never work again – at least, not on terrestrial television. It would be the end of 'Rach-Al'. The end of everything.

It would not be enough, however, simply to release the footage. That would be playing all his aces in one go, leaving him with nothing. If he wanted to get anything out of Rachel – and if he couldn't get love, he might as well get money – he needed to play his hand carefully. Give her a taste of what he could do, and let her know that there was plenty more – and much worse – if she didn't co-operate.

But to do that, he needed access to the media. He needed someone in the press who could hold a gun to Rachel's head, someone with influence, someone with a grudge against Rachel and Alan.

Now, where was he going to find someone like that?

Mike Harris was short, and Elizabeth liked her men tall. He was far from fit, and she had been well and truly spoiled in that department. He dressed badly, he distrusted intellectuals, despised artiness and favoured in his editorials a straight-down-the-line, meat-and-two-veg prose style. He never used a word of three syllables where three words of one syllable would do.

He used adjectives sparingly, adverbs not at all, and might not even have been able to pick them out in a sentence.

That said, he was universally regarded as a good editor, even a great editor, and had a collection of ugly ornaments on his office windowsill to prove it. There was a tacky thing in the shape of a fountain-pen nib, with his name inscribed on a little plaque on the base. There was a piece of etched glass with a quill motif and his name in curly letters. There were framed certificates, the largest and most recent of which proclaimed him Editor of the Year. Of these Mike was openly, childishly proud. He arranged them for maximum prominence and played with them during meetings. He gave orders to the cleaners never, on pain of instant dismissal, to touch his trophies, and was sometimes to be seen, early in the morning or late at night, dusting them with a soft cloth. Elizabeth watched him once, a lonely figure in the largest office in the building, the light bouncing off his awards and his bald spot, gently lifting each object, caressing it with a duster, huffing on any grease marks, replacing it with a finicking exactitude.

This was the same Mike Harris who was capable of hauling a reporter over the coals for a shoddy piece of reporting, who could terrify hardened designers, lawyers and ad sales teams just by contracting his brows, who had driven one highly strung feature writer to take a grievance to Human Resources after what she claimed was a campaign of harassment. It took considerable charm, and a whole box of tissues, to talk her out of that one. She now languished in the safer, shallower waters of advertorials, and counted herself lucky.

His temper was quick and sulphurous. If you pleased him, he could be very appreciative: a juicy human interest story was his favourite, and the best reporters were lavishly rewarded. A good photograph made him skip with delight. And while he cared little about the arts, and still less for criticism, he liked his reviews team to have strong opinions, forcefully expressed. If you pissed people off and got loads of letters, all the better.

Elizabeth was no longer writing for some hazy Ideal Reader, as she had in her academic days, but for one very real reader, the irascible little man in the big office with the bald spot and the scary eyebrows, the Editor of the Year, Mike Harris. She figured out exactly what would please him, and what would not. She increased the one, and eliminated the other, and was soon billed as 'Liz Miller – the Bitch on the Box' for the harshness of her opinions. The derivative, the second-rate, she demolished with one stroke of her pen. She was quick to detect any whiff of moral irresponsibility, and to call the perpetrators to account. Woe betide the broadcaster who pumped violence into British homes: Liz Miller would be calling for the loss of the franchise the next morning, blaming them for every baby-battering or happy-slapping reported on the news pages. Reality TV was her particular hobby horse, and she rode that old nag into the ground, accusing the producers of exploiting the mentally ill, corrupting children, undermining the education system, causing unwanted pregnancies and spreading STIs. The readers lapped it up, debate raged on the letters page, and barely a morning went past without a threat from someone's lawyer landing on Mike's desk. These he read, noted with approval and passed straight on to the legal department, who checked every word of Liz Miller's copy before it went into print. Thus indemnified, Mike could tell potential litigants to do their worst.

One lunchtime, when Elizabeth had excelled herself by suggesting that the entire cast and crew of a viciously unpleasant crime drama should be collectively arrested on obscenity charges,

Mike summoned her into his office. She expected a stern warning and a period in the Siberia of Mike's affections. She had overstepped the mark, she realised, and she was going to be taught a lesson.

Mike was sitting at his desk, his forehead resting on his fingertips, apparently poring over some piece of copy. Elizabeth stood in the doorway, cleared her throat, shifted from foot to foot, coughed and said, 'Hello', all to no avail. After some minutes, Mike marked his place with a finger, looked up and said, 'Sit down'.

Here we go, thought Elizabeth. Payback time for the Bitch on the Box.

'That review,' she said, thinking a pre-emptive apology might improve matters. 'I realise I . . .'

He held up his hand to silence her. How like the Prof he could be sometimes, she thought. 'Do you like your job?' he asked.

'Er . . . yes. Yes, I do.'

'Do you like television?'

'I like writing about television.'

'A nice distinction. Do you mean that you despise the medium, but you like using it as a way of showing how clever you are?'

Elizabeth was about to protest, but something in Mike's eye changed her mind. 'You could say that, I suppose.'

'Yes, I suppose you could,' said Mike. 'And could you also say that you despise the people that work in the medium?'

'I would never bring personal feelings into my work.'

'Why ever not? What's wrong with personal feelings?'

'I don't think it would be very professional.'

'Liz,' said Mike, 'this is journalism.'

'So I gather,' said Elizabeth. As it seemed she was not going to get the bollocking of the century, she could afford to play it cool. The secretaries outside Mike's office had stopped eavesdropping, and plugged their earpieces back in. False alarm.

'Have you filed tomorrow's column?'

'Not yet. Should be done by about two.' Her deadline was four. 'That okay?'

'Don't bother. I'll get someone else to do it.'

Elizabeth swallowed. This was it, then. The sack. The elbow. The big heave-ho. Again. 'Oh,' she said, and 'right.'

When she'd stared at her feet for a while, breathing deeply and trying not to cry, she looked up to see his glasses pointing right at her, reflecting the light. It was hard to see his eyes, but she could feel them.

'You're wasted on the TV column. You should be doing something more worthwhile.'

I don't want to go back to academia . . .

'It's very nice of you to soften the blow,' said Elizabeth, 'but don't worry. I've dealt with worse.'

Mike frowned. 'Never mind that.' He obviously didn't want to hear the sob story, to know that this was a sensitive, vulnerable human being that he was sacking. This, as Mike would say, was journalism. 'I've got other uses for you.'

'And what's that? An exciting opportunity in advertorials?'

'Ah,' said Mike, rubbing his hands together, 'I knew I was right. You've got a sharp tongue, haven't you? You want to watch that.' He picked up a letter from his desk; she recognised the logo of a frighteningly famous city solicitor. 'Get you into trouble one day.' He transferred the letter to his out tray. 'So, Liz Miller. How do you fancy the showbiz desk?'

'I beg your pardon?'

'Showbiz. Show business.' He said it slowly, as if speaking to a foreigner. 'You know. Silly tarts and thick wankers with too much money and not enough clothes. Think you can handle it?'

'You want me . . . *me* . . .'

'Please tell me you're not offended.' He leaned back and laughed. 'Only you, of all the women I have ever worked with, could be offered the most desirable job on the paper and react as if I've just asked you to give me a blowjob.'

'Don't be ridiculous,' said Elizabeth, blushing. 'You can't seriously want me to contribute to the showbiz pages.'

'For now, yes. Eventually I want you to run 'em.'

'You mean . . .'

'I'm having a cabinet reshuffle. Think you can handle it?'

'I don't know what to say.'

'Then I suggest you say yes. We can discuss the finer points over dinner.'

'Dinner?'

'Tonight. You don't have any plans.'

'I have to watch . . .'

'No you don't. Remember? You're not doing that any more. Be ready at six. Dismissed.' He waved her away, flicking his fingers towards the door, but she could see that he was smiling.

A direct approach was never going to work. Elizabeth would hear Nick's voice, or see his name in her inbox, and that would be that. Visiting in person was out of the question, she'd throw him out. If Nick wanted a meeting with Elizabeth, he needed to bait the hook with something irresistible, and once she nibbled, he only had to reel her in. And he knew exactly what to use. He set up an email account in the name 'Starpix', wrote 'Rachel Hope: the Truth' in the subject field, and attached an unflattering of Rachel swigging from a bottle at a party. It was easy to find Elizabeth's email address: they printed it at the bottom of each of her columns, inviting comment. 'Want to know what's really going on between Rachel Hope and Alan Southgate?' read the message. 'If so, get in touch. I've got the story, I've got the photos, and I've got the sources to back it up.' He signed it, 'Starpix: candid celebrity photography', and hit the send button.

'Perfect timing,' thought Elizabeth when she opened the email, not stopping to wonder who Starpix was. Showbiz reporting was a scuzzy world – but she needed a good scoop to establish herself on the desk, and to let Mike know he'd made the right decision. He'd love this: it had all his favourite ingredients, the sleaze behind the public image, booze and immorality in high places. It had the added attraction of hitting Rachel and Alan where it hurt, but Mike didn't need to know about that.

'I'm interested,' she wrote back. 'Can we meet?'

They made a date for the next day.

Dinner with Mike was nothing like Elizabeth expected it to be. Outside the office, he seemed younger, cleverer, *nicer* than he did at work. He was never going to be a great beauty – his features were harsh, and didn't arrange themselves into those heart-stopping expressions that . . . But she'd had enough of beauty. Look where beauty had got her.

Mike liked to talk, and he had ideas to express – ideas that were so far removed from the intellectual hothouse in which Elizabeth grew up that she was frequently shocked, as if buffeted by a blast of cold, fresh air. And he could listen, not in the selective manner of the Prof, hearing only what accorded with his own views, but really listening to what she was saying, understanding it, sometimes agreeing, more often arguing. He was not a man given to ideals, and had little interest in the great notions of right and wrong that Elizabeth had always taken for granted – he seemed, in fact, to be the coldest, grimmest of pragmatists.

'Your problem,' he said at one point, 'is that you believe people are basically good. They're not. People are stupid, greedy and wicked.'

'What an awful . . .'

'And just because they happen to be poor, or foreign, or disabled, that doesn't make them any better. I feel just as sorry for them as you do. I give to charities. But it's a mistake to think that those little bastards who rob your house to pay for their crack habit, or those lazy fat bastards who defraud the benefit system while you and I graft in order to pay our income tax, or those illegal immigrants who come into the UK to sponge off the welfare state while plotting how to blow us all up, are anything other than scum.'

'You can't really believe that.'

'I do. What do you believe?'

'I believe everyone is a product of their environment.'

'Good. We're in agreement, then.'

'And I don't think we can assume that all illegal immigrants are evil terrorists.'

Mike scratched his chin. 'Not *all*, perhaps.' He could see that he was infuriating her, and was enjoying it. 'But surely it's worth sacrificing one or two good ones in order to keep the other ninety-eight per cent out.'

'That's ridiculous.'

'And that's the end of your argument, is it? All that education just led you up against a brick wall. Well, well, well, Doctor Miller. I expected more.'

'Doctor Miller? How do you know that?'

'I'm a journalist. I know how to investigate.'

'I see. And what else do you know about me?'

'Your father's a big noise in the university world. Your mother is a novelist.'

'Was a novelist. She's dead.'

'Quite so. She died in 2003, leaving you and a younger brother, Christopher, who is currently at college doing media studies.' He sneered in a way the Prof would approve of.

'You have been doing your homework.'

'It pays to know what you're investing in.'

'Is that what you're doing? Investing in me?'

'I've given you a promotion that's made you the most envied woman on Fleet Street.'

'And this?' She gestured around the table, the crisp white linen, the glinting silverware. 'Is this part of the investment?'

'He raised an eyebrow. 'Do you want it to be?'

'I've been doing some homework, too,' said Elizabeth. 'And I happen to know that you're married.'

'Full marks,' said Mike. 'Ten out of ten. Go to the top of the class. What else did you discover about my personal life?'

'That's all I need to know. I don't do married men.'

'Who's asking you to "do" anything?'

'Just thought I'd mention it. Wouldn't want you to think I'd been leading you on, or anything.'

Mike laughed. 'No, Doctor Miller,' he said, 'I certainly don't think that.'

Elizabeth was a bit hungover when she arrived at the *Beacon* office the next morning. She did not know what to expect. No more sitting in a darkened room watching TV, no more jotting down acidic little remarks in a notebook, later to be strung together into a column. Now, today, she was a showbiz reporter. She awaited instruction.

She looked at her diary, and saw a scribbled note that she had all but forgotten. '10:00: Starpix re RH.'

She just had time to make herself a super-strength coffee and swallow two paracetamol before her phone rang. There was a gentleman in reception to see her. He had not given a name. He said that she would know what it was about. She stepped out of the lift, hoping that the coffee and pills would do their stuff, and into the lobby.

And then she saw him.

Her first instinct was to run to the nearest toilet and lock herself in. But her shoes appeared to have been superglued to the floor, and she could no more run than she could fly.

Nick was leaning on the reception desk, a photographer's kit bag over one shoulder, wearing a black leather jacket, low-slung jeans and a blue shirt with an open collar. His hair, as dense and glossy as ever, was pushed back from his forehead, a few heavy strands falling forward. He had not gone bald, put on weight, aged or in any other way decayed.

'Surprised?'

'You could say that,' croaked Elizabeth.

'You look great, Elizabeth. Beautiful. You've lost weight.' He stepped closer.

Something in her lower intestines did a little roll. 'So you're Starpix, then.'

Nick held up his hands, as if in surrender. ''Fraid so.'

'Nice to see that you're working at last.'

'Okay,' said Nick. 'Let's keep this professional. I've got a story on Rachel Hope and Alan Southgate.' He said the names as if they meant nothing. 'I thought you might be interested.'

'And of all the journalists in London, you brought it to me.'

'Who else is going to be as interested as you?'

'This had better be good.'

'Oh, it is. Rachel and Alan are going out together, right?'

'If that's the best you can do, Nick, you'd better go back to riding motorcycles.'

He interrupted her. 'Alan is no more going out with Rachel than I am.'

There was a piece of news, but Elizabeth tried to take it in her stride. 'So it's a publicity stunt. Big deal.'

'Would it interest you to know who she's really going out with?'

'Maybe.'

'And what about him?'

'Do you know, or are you bluffing?'

'Oh, I know all right.' This wasn't true: Nick had his suspicions about Alan, but did not yet have hard evidence on who exactly was sharing his bed. 'I take it you're interested.'

'Maybe.'

'Okay,' said Nick, hefting his bag. 'While you're making your mind up, I'll pop round to the *Comet* and the *Mirror* and see if they want the story. Perhaps if they turn it down, I'll come back to you.' He turned to go.

'Wait.'

He carried on walking towards the revolving door, forcing Elizabeth to run after him.

'Nick! Stop!'

He stopped.

'I am interested.'

He turned. 'I thought you might be.'

'But not for the reasons you think.'

'Whatever.'

'You'd better come up to my office.'

'Nah,' he said, with a smile so bright it seemed to obliterate the past, 'we'll discuss it over dinner. My shout. Least I can do.'

'Okay,' said Elizabeth, 'that would be nice,' hating herself as she said it, as if one dinner could make up for the pain of betrayal.

He waved, and was gone.

Elizabeth stood in the lobby for a minute, then had to sit down rather suddenly, burying her face in her sweater, her breath coming too fast, panic rising in her chest. It took five minutes for her to recover. She returned to her office with a splitting headache.

And, perhaps, a front-page story.

Chapter 23

The affair with Gerald Partridge lasted into post-production, and fizzled out as he started work on his next project, and his next leading lady. Someone else was feeling his stubble on her neck, someone else was being told that she was the next Keira Knightley. It didn't hurt too much; Rachel never expected it to last, and had approached the relationship in the way that she'd approach any job. Gerald was a useful stepping stone; he'd also helped her to move on from Nick. Now she was back in London, alone in her flat, and although there were moments when she missed Nick's company, they were outweighed by the relief she felt at being rid of him. Nick was a distraction she could do without. It was time for Rachel to concentrate on her future, and to brace herself for the stardom that, Gerald assured her, *Nana* would bring.

She was still officially going out with Alan Southgate; they wouldn't split up until well after *Nana* was broadcast. For the time being, it was enough for them to be seen in public together once or twice a week, at an opening or a party, or walking in the park, every appearance carefully co-ordinated by Polly Hamlin, their personal publicist. What the photographers did not see was the chaste goodnight kiss as Rachel returned home to Shepherd's Bush and Alan went about his own business. He was seeing someone, of that Rachel was sure. Chris? Or someone new? She knew better than to pry.

While she was waiting for the next job to come along, Rachel had time to catch up with old friends. It was better to keep busy; too much time alone and she might be tempted to call Nick. So when Mark called up one morning and suggested a long liquid lunch, Rachel was very happy to accept.

'Well,' said Mark, as soon as they'd sat down in the dark, cosy little restaurant in Notting Hill Gate, 'your boyfriend's been busy, hasn't he?'

Rachel wondered which one he meant. 'Has he?'

'I'm so jealous I could stab his eyes out. Is it true?'

'Is what true?'

'Alan Southgate and Johnny Khan.'

So that was who he'd been seeing. Poor Chris. 'Where on earth do you pick up this stuff?'

'Well, I met this bloke last week, or was it the week before? I forget. Anyway, he was a publicist, or was it a PR? What's the difference?'

'I haven't a clue. Go on.'

'Anyway he was absolutely gorgeous and,' said Mark, lowering his voice and half-hiding behind the menu, 'well, I mean, he was really, you know.' He held his hands about a foot apart, and whistled. 'And I think he really liked me.'

'Good. I am pleased.'

'Anyway, what was I saying? Oh, yes. Alan Southgate. Well, he told me that he'd been working on this play that he was in, something in the West End, what was it?'

'*Design for Living*? Noël Coward?'

Mark waved the names away. 'And you know who was in that as well, don't you?'

'Of course. Meredith Chase.' She wouldn't give him satisfaction just yet.

'Oh, *her*,' said Mark, making a face. 'Couldn't act her way out of a paper bag. She's awful. No, not her, I mean him. Johnny Khan.'

'Yes, I believe he was in it as well.'

'Well, they were . . . You know.'

Rachel put a hand to her breast. 'What? My boyfriend, and . . . another man? Oh Mark, you wound me to the core. How could you break it to me like that?'

'Oh,' said Mark, with a sigh. 'You knew.'

'I'm saying nothing,' said Rachel. 'But go on. What else did your new friend tell you?'

'He said they were going at it hammer and tongs all through rehearsal, all through the West End run, and ever since.'

'Imagine that.'

'So you must have seen them together when you were in Romania.'

'Is that why you invited me out to lunch? To get it from the horse's mouth?'

'Yes.'

That was honest, at least, Rachel thought. 'I see. Obviously, Mark, I respect Alan's privacy.'

'Of course you do, but . . .'

'And if I did know anything, you'd be the last person I'd tell.'

'There's no smoke without fire,' said Mark. 'That's what I always say.'

'Shall we order?' said Rachel. 'I'm absolutely starving.'

Later that afternoon, Nick called round at the old Camden Town flat to pick up some of his belongings – that was the official story – and found Natasha and Mark, plastered, even though it was only six o'clock, singing along to a Kate Bush record.

'Well well well,' said Natasha, as she let him in. 'Look what the cat dragged in.'

'Pleased to see me?'

'Thrilled, darling. I knew you couldn't keep away forever.

Have you come round,' said Natasha, striking a vampish pose, 'to take advantage of me?'

'Taken a look at yourself in the mirror recently? You're in no danger.'

Natasha mustered what little dignity remained after four bottles of wine, and left the room.

'You'd better just pick up your things and leave,' said Mark, who was holding it together marginally better.

'Oh, come on,' said Nick, sprawling on the couch with his legs a yard apart. 'You weren't always so keen to get rid of me.'

'What do you want?'

'Don't know, mate. What do *you* want?' He let a hand dangle between his legs.

'I don't do straight men. I'm not that desperate.'

'Who says I'm straight?'

'Er, let me think. Rachel, maybe? Who I just happen to have had lunch with?'

'How is dear Rachel?'

'Never better, thanks.'

'Mention me, did she?'

'Funnily enough, no.'

'Anyway, I didn't come here to talk about Rachel.'

'And I don't imagine you came round here for a blowjob, either,' said Mark, to whom this degree of self-control did not come naturally. 'So best lay your cards on the table.'

'What do you know about Alan Southgate?'

Mark laughed, then checked himself.

'What's so funny?'

'Nothing. Rachel and I were just talking about him, that's all.'

'And what did she tell you?'

'You better ask her yourself.'

'I can't, and you know it. Come on, Mark. You can tell me. We were always good mates, weren't we?'

'Were we?' asked Mark, but he could feel himself being drawn in, like metal to a magnet.

'If you know something worth knowing about Alan Southgate, I'll make it worth your while.'

'I'm not going to spread gossip just because you . . . Oh.'

Nick stuck a hand into his pocket, and pulled out his wallet, which was not quite what Mark was expecting. 'Couple of hundred quid be of any use?'

'What sort of person do you take me for? Anything that Rachel might have told me – and I'm not saying she told me anything, mind you – is private. You can't just – '

'How about three hundred?'

'For God's sake, Nick.'

'Four. Final offer.'

Four hundred pounds would buy a lot at Abercrombie & Fitch. 'Well,' said Mark, 'you didn't hear it from me . . .'

The incumbent showbiz editor who was about to lose his job in Mike Harris's cabinet reshuffle was an ageing hotshot called Pete Goldman. In his heyday, he'd been a journalistic wunderkind; nobody could get closer to the stars than Pete Goldman. At one point, a couple of years ago, he'd been more famous than the people he was writing about, constantly on radio and television, analysed and fretted over in the broadsheets. But that was before cocaine got a grip. Now he was a loose cannon, missing deadlines, missing appointments, convinced that he was more important than the job. The fresh-faced, blue-eyed blond boy who'd charmed his way into the inner circles of showbiz was now a twitching, sweating liability, increasingly dependent on stringers and underlings to do his work for him, barely able to drag himself along to the parties that were his living. Mike had given him warning after warning, but how he had reached the end of the road. Pete Goldman had to go – but he would not go quietly. He regarded Elizabeth's arrival on the showbiz desk as a personal attack, but would not let this female upstart get the better of him. He'd been to Madonna's adopted children's birthday parties, for God's sake.

'Where do you think you're going?' he snarled, as Elizabeth got ready to go out for a working lunch.

'Just seeing a stringer.'

'Anything good, you bring straight to me, yeah?'

'Of course.'

'You'd better.' His eyes flickered to hers, then away.

'Actually,' said Elizabeth, trying to sound respectful, 'I could do with some advice. I mean, you've been in this business a lot longer than I have.'

'Too right.'

'Someone's brought me a very interesting story, and I want to know how I should handle it.' What she really wanted was a way of stitching up Rachel and Alan without it looking personal.

'Oh, yeah,' said Pete. 'Who's it about? Some fucking Z-lister, I suppose.'

'Rachel Hope and Alan Southgate, actually.' Pete looked like Gollum catching a glimpse of the Ring.

'What have you got?'

'Nothing definite,' said Elizabeth. 'I'm just trying to get an idea of the kind of thing you need.'

'If you have anything on Rachel Hope or Alan Southgate,' said Goldman, 'you bring it straight to me.'

'Of course,' said Elizabeth. 'You're the boss.'

*   *   *

Nick was wearing a suit. It looked like – could it possibly be? – the suit that she had bought him for their wedding.

'Thank you for agreeing to see me,' he said, getting her settled in her chair. He was never like this in the old days, she thought. 'I thought you might tell me to get lost.'

'I probably should have done,' said Elizabeth, unfolding her napkin, 'but this is business, isn't it? You've got something that I might be interested in. And I am authorised to . . .'

'What happened with Rachel,' said Nick, 'was the worst mistake of my life.'

Elizabeth felt the blood rush to her face. 'Please, can we not discuss the past.'

'I know it's too late to say sorry.'

'Well, you could give it a go. You never actually said it at the time.'

'I am sorry. Desperately sorry.' His eyes were wet, his forehead furrowed. 'It was madness. I don't know how it happened. Like a bad dream.'

'And now, I suppose, you've woken up.'

'Yes.' A hand reached towards hers. She withdrew.

'You mean she's left you. Don't look so surprised, Nick. I do read the newspapers, you know, as well as write for them. Rachel's love life is a matter of public interest. So now she's moved on, leaving you high and dry, and so you thought you might just look up an ex. Is that how it is? An ex who might, incidentally, be able to give you a bit of work.'

'I deserve that,' said Nick. 'I've been a bastard to you.'

'Yes.'

'Well, I'm going to try and make up for it now.'

'What have you got for me?'

He looked her directly in the eye. 'Whatever you want.'

Elizabeth's mouth filled with saliva. She swallowed hard. The waiter appeared, offering drinks. 'I'll have a martini,' she said. 'Plymouth gin. Very dry. With a twist.'

'Make that two,' said Nick. Things were going better, and faster, than he had dared to hope.

'Cheers,' he said, when the drinks came. 'You look very beautiful, Elizabeth. You've changed.'

She felt a surge of pleasure; he'd noticed. The makeover had worked. Money well spent. 'Flattery will get you nowhere,' she said, quickly reminding herself that she'd not done it for his benefit. 'Just tell me about this story.'

'Okay. So you know about Rachel and Alan, and you know that it's a pack of lies, right?'

'Right.'

'And you know who Rachel's really going out with?'

'Not you, obviously.'

'No, not me.' Nick grimaced. 'Gerald Partridge.'

'The director? Okay. Not bad. But not exactly front-page news. "Ambitious actress screws her way to the top." I don't think my editor's going to go for that.'

'But there's more.'

'There'd better be. I haven't come out with you just for the pleasure of your company, you know.'

'Sure about that?'

'Quite sure.' She was blushing, and he could see it. He could read her like a book, damn him.

He paid the bill. 'Come on,' he said, helping her into her coat. 'Lots more to discuss.'

'Nick . . .'

'Yes?'

'I don't think . . .' She had to swallow. 'I don't think this is a very good idea.'

'It probably isn't,' he said, steering her towards the door with a hand in the small of her back. 'But then, I'm always making mistakes.' He hailed a cab, and gave the driver Elizabeth's address.

Back at what should have been the marital home, but for the last two years had been Elizabeth's spinster flat, Nick went straight for the jugular. They were barely inside the door when he was kissing her. It was just like the old days, the feeling of his lips on her neck, his hands roving down her back. It felt so familiar, so right, as if nothing had happened – as if, as Nick said, it had all been a bad dream, from which they had both awakened.

Sex with the ex . . . the sort of stupid thing you read about in the agony columns. The sort of thing a woman like me would never do.

'I've missed you so much, Betty-Boo,' he said, unbuttoning her blouse. 'I'm so sorry.' He buried his face between her breasts.

'Nick . . .' This could not be happening. It was so wrong.

'Oh, baby,' he said, his voice muffled by her bra. 'I've waited so long . . .'

And in the morning, he told her all about Alan Southgate and Johnny Khan.

Chapter 24

Channel Six spared no expense in the promotion of *Nana*; it was not every day that they got a prestigious three-part drama, directed and produced by Gerald Partridge, starring the hottest power couple of the year. They arranged a preview screening at BAFTA on Piccadilly, invited anyone who was anyone, poured thousands into the catering budget and started churning out press releases at a rate of two or three a day. Polly arranged everything to the last detail, issuing Rachel and Alan with an itinerary of parties and events they would be attending in the week before the preview, giving them useful background information on key journalists and photographers so they could say things like, 'Oh, I read your husband's novel! It's fantastic!' or 'I was so sorry to hear about your mum'. Dresses for her and suits for him were couriered to the office, tried on, rejected or shortlisted. Little squibs of stories were placed in the evening papers, giving readers a steady drip-drip of Rach-Al. By the time *Nana* was finally broadcast in October, the entire nation would be brainwashed into watching it.

Polly was pleased with the talent. They never complained about interviews or photo shoots, they had answers for every question and they did not make stupid, unrealistic demands about magazine covers or copy approval. The campaign was going smoothly – almost too smoothly, Polly thought with a little trepidation. She wasn't used to this level of co-operation. Something was bound to go wrong.

She was right. The first tremor came when Rachel, for no apparent reason, refused at the last minute to do an interview for the Daily Beacon.

'But you said yes to this ages ago,' said Polly. 'It's an important one. The *Beacon* reaches an audience of – '

'I don't care,' said Rachel, quite politely. 'I won't do it.'

'Do you have some objection to the paper's politics?' asked Polly. 'I mean, you've done the *Mail*. What's so wrong with the *Beacon*?'

'I won't do it, that's all,' said Rachel. 'Next.'

Baffled, Polly moved on. About everything else – glamour shoots for lads' mags, intrusive interviews for the weekend supplements, banal Q&As for the Channel Six website – Rachel was as docile as a cow.

'What's the matter with the *Beacon*?' Polly asked Alan, when Rachel had gone into make-up for yet another photo shoot.

'Search me. Perhaps she's just trying to show temperament.'

'They'll slay us if we don't play ball.'

'They're not exactly my favourite paper, either,' said Alan. 'They gave me a terrible review in . . . Ah.' The penny dropped.

'What?'

'I think, perhaps, you'd better just steer clear of the *Beacon*,' said Alan. 'I know it's annoying for you, but under the circumstances, it might be better for all concerned.'

He would not be drawn any further. Polly wondered if the *Beacon* could be fobbed off with a story about the locations, or the costume design. In the very last resort, she could give them an exclusive on another client, whose facial surgery had gone disastrously wrong. 'I miss my nose.' That ought to do it.

'Christ no,' said Mike, 'I never go to those things. Can't stand 'em. All that kissing and posing and pretending to like stuff that you'd actually cross the road to avoid. I'd rather go home and get an early night. I'm sure you'll tell me all about it in the morning.'

'Actually,' said Elizabeth, 'I'd rather not go myself.'

'Any particular reason?'

She had not yet told Mike about her particular reason for hating Rachel Hope. 'I just can't bear to see them making a travesty of a great classic of French literature. Anyway, Pete was very keen to go.'

'Oh, God. The last time Pete Goldman went to anything at BAFTA, he was thrown out for attempting to steal a chair. I'd better read him the riot act.'

'Honestly, Mike, he was so keen . . .'

'I should think he was. He's on everyone's shit list these days. I'd be surprised if he even gets through the door.'

'He'll be fine,' said Elizabeth, who had given her invitation to Nick. 'Anyway, have a nice evening at home.'

'Thank you. I'm sure my wife will be pleased to see me. Not.'

'Unless . . .'

'Yes?'

It was not in Elizabeth's nature to ask a man on a date, especially a married man, but ever since Nick had blown the cobwebs away during their misguided reunion, she couldn't stop thinking about sex. 'Unless you fancied dinner.'

'Again, Miss Miller? People will talk.'

'Let 'em.'

'We'll make a hack of you yet, my girl. Half seven?'

'It's a date.'

The pavement outside the British Academy of Film and Television Arts on Piccadilly was crowded with famous people in expensive clothes. Taxis drew up, disgorged celebrities and chugged away. Journalists arrived on foot. Pete Goldman, who had just met his dealer in a pub in Soho, scuttled along with a guilty expression, already desperate to get inside the BAFTA's well-appointed lavatories to take his first line of the evening. That patronising bitch Liz Miller had better watch out; this was the night that Pete Goldman was going to reclaim the *Beacon* showbiz crown. All he needed was a little more energy . . .

Chris and Mark arrived together. Chris was wearing a suit, Mark was head to toe in brand new Abercrombie & Fitch.

Anna parked just off Pall Mall, where she would almost certainly be clamped, and was halfway up Regent Street when she realised that she had forgotten her invitation. Lesser women might have turned back, but not Anna. She had not seen her daughter for far too long, and she was damned if a little thing like an invitation was going to come between them, especially now that Rachel was doing so well.

Johnny Khan arrived in a white limousine, and was greeted with flashguns and wolf whistles and screams from the few dozen fans who were standing behind the security cordon. He posed, signed autographs and told reporters that his 'great mate' Alan Southgate had 'done a blinding job' in the new film, and that he was 'well made up' for him.

Finally, just a few minutes before the screening was scheduled to begin, Rach-Al arrived in a discreet black Daimler. Gerald Partridge handed them out of the car and ushered them on to the red carpet. She was wearing silver satin, Lanvin heels and not much else. He was in a black Armani suit, a white shirt and no tie. Cameras clicked, hands were clapped, questions were asked and ignored as the beautiful couple glided inside as if on casters. The doors closed, the crowds dispersed, while inside thousands of gallons of champagne were ingested by the great and the not-so-good. Canapés were pounced on by the hungry, avoided by the figure-conscious, scooped into handbags by one or two older journalists for whom these events were a convenient way of cutting down on food bills.

Rachel and Alan led the way into the auditorium, and the crowd followed. The lobby was silent but for the clink of glasses being collected, and the screening began.

Nick waited outside until everyone he knew was safely indoors, then slipped upstairs and found a dark corner in which to wait. He wanted Rachel to be surprised.

Pete Goldman was still locked in a toilet cubicle, where he'd passed out as soon as he arrived.

Rachel watched half an hour of the first episode, and then slipped out for a cigarette.

Mike was asking about Elizabeth's PhD. 'I appreciate the effort,' she said, 'but you really don't want to know.'

'Don't I? Wasn't it any good?'

'Of course it was good. You just won't be interested.'

'I'm interested in everything about you, in case you hadn't noticed.'

Elizabeth tried to remember if anyone else had ever felt this way about her. Nick? Her parents? 'Okay. Let's see if I can put this in *Daily Beacon* terms. The two most important heroines of French realist fiction are a sex-crazed housewife who commits suicide by eating arsenic and a money-grubbing prostitute who dies a horrible death from smallpox. How does that grab you?'

'Very sexy.'

'See? I knew it.'

'I'm sorry. I'd like to read it one day. No, don't laugh, I mean it. But right now, I've got other things on my mind.'

Oh God, this is where he tells me all about his wife . . . 'Really?' She tried to sound bright. 'What, exactly?'

'I was just wondering what you'd look like without your clothes on.'

'Ah.' She cleared her throat. 'I see.'

'I'm sorry,' he said.

'Don't be.'

Nick moved out of the shadows and into the lobby. 'Well, well, well,' he said. 'Look at you. Star.'

'Hi Nick.' Rachel kissed him lightly on both cheeks. Being polite seemed the easiest way of avoiding a scene. 'Fancy seeing you here!'

'Seems I have to get an invitation to see you these days.'

'You know what it's like,' said Rachel, her screen smile firmly in place. 'Busy busy busy.'

'Oh, yes. You were always a busy little bee, weren't you. I know that better than anyone.'

'You're not going to cause trouble, are you?' she whispered.

''Course not! I'm more professional than that. But how about a picture? Hmm? For old times' sake.'

'Of course.' She posed, he snapped.

'Lovely. Add it to my collection.'

'Right. Now, I really must . . .'

'I've got quite a big collection of photos of you now, you know.'

'I suppose so.'

'Stills and video.'

'Look, Nick . . .'

'Some you know about, and others you don't.'

'What?'

'Home movies. Not quite of the quality that we've just been watching, but, you know, same sort of subject matter.'

Rachel felt an unpleasant jarring sensation, akin to whiplash.

'Nick, what's this all about?'

Gerald appeared at her side. 'Everything all right here?'

'Fine,' said Rachel, with her too-wide smile. 'Gerald, this is Nick. An old friend.'

'Great to meet you.' They shook hands. 'Now, if you don't mind, Rachel, I've come to drag you back in. Doesn't look good to miss your own screening.'

'See you, Nick.'

'Just remember what I said.' He backed away, shooting photographs, and disappeared in the crowd.

'And what did he say?' asked Gerald.

'Oh, nothing,' said Rachel, trying to work out whether she had just been threatened with blackmail.

'Goodnight, then.'

They were in the cab, which had been idling outside Elizabeth's flat for some time, the meter still running.

'Goodnight.'

'See you in the morning.'

'Yes . . .'

He's waiting for me to ask him in, thought Elizabeth. He's too much of a gentleman to propose himself.

'Thanks for a lovely evening.'

'My pleasure.'

'Mike . . .'

She was just on the point of saying the fatal words (among them 'coffee'), when her phone beeped.

'You'd better get that,' said Mike. 'Could be work.'

'I very much doubt it.' She glanced at the phone, which was flashing up a text from Starpix. 'Oh. Wait a minute.' She opened it. 'Well, there you go.'

'Story?'

'Story.'

'Good story?'

'Potentially, very.'

'Good girl.' He rubbed his hands together, his wedding ring flashing in the orange glow of the streetlight.

'Mike,' she said, 'why don't you come up for a coffee?'

'I thought you'd never ask,' said Mike, handing twenty pounds to the driver. 'Receipt, please.'

He didn't pounce. They actually did have a cup of coffee. But within half an hour they were in bed, making love. Elizabeth did not feel that she had been whisked half out of this world, that she was soaring through the cosmos on the back of a dolphin or whatever other ridiculous images occurred to her when she was with Nick. There was none of the loneliness that followed when Nick rolled over and went straight to sleep, giving her only the breadth of his back. Mike let her rest on his chest, which was softer than Nick's and consequently much more comfortable as a pillow. They talked and talked until she, not he, drifted into unconsciousness. And when she woke up in the night, with a mild feeling of panic – she had fucked her boss! Her married boss! – he was still there, warm and reassuring. He put his arm across her chest, nestled closer to her and soothed her back to sleep again.

Pete Goldman woke from a dream of partying with Gwyneth Paltrow to a loud banging, and a voice shouting, 'Hey! Is there anyone in there?' He struggled to his feet, and brushed some vomit from his lapels.

'I'm all right,' he said, and looked at his watch. It was half past two in the morning.

Chapter 25

The TV listings page told one story. 'Channel Six, 9.00 p.m., *Nana*. First of a three-part adaptation of Émile Zola's nineteenth-century classic, updated to modern London. Stars Rachel Hope and Alan Southgate.'

Elizabeth was working on something very different.

For the last two weeks she'd been checking out every angle of the Rach-Al story, tracking the happy couple twenty-four hours a day, talking to anyone, drivers, make-up artists, hotel chambermaids, any one who might have a tale to tell. By the time the show was ready for broadcast, she had it all sewn up. Rachel and Alan were not lovers, and never had been. Rachel had been the mistress of Gerald Partridge, while Alan . . . Well, she kept that carefully under wraps until the morning editorial meeting.

'So,' said Mike, 'what's showbiz got for me today? Pete?'

'Yeah, right,' said Pete, who hadn't filed any copy for weeks. 'Bit quiet at the moment. Nice story about Prince William. He's got a new car.'

'Great,' said Mike. 'Who sent you that one? The car manu-facturer? Next.'

'There's a Coldplay greatest hits coming out. Could do some-thing on Chris and Gwynnie. They're sort of mates of mine.'

'Next.'

'Well, Jordan is . . .'

'No, Pete.' Mike slammed his hands on the desk, slopping coffee. 'Not good enough. Liz? For Christ's sake, make me happy.'

'Well,' said Elizabeth, flicking through the TV listings, 'there is this new adaptation of *Nana* starting on Sunday.'

'And?'

'I think there might be a story there.'

'You went to the preview, Pete,' said Mike. 'What did you get?'

'I . . . er . . .' Pete flicked through his notebook, which was basically a list of drug dealers' mobile numbers.

'Forget it, Pete. Liz, what have you got?'

'The truth about Rachel and Alan.'

'And what might that be?'

'They're not really together.'

Pete snorted.

'She's been sleeping with her producer.'

Pete feigned a big yawn.

'Go on, Liz. Anything else?'

She flicked through her notebook, as if trying to remember something. 'Oh, yes. Alan's screwing Johnny Khan.'

Pete stopped in mid-yawn. His watery blue eyes flickered around the office, looking for a way out.

'Indeed,' said Mike. 'I take it nobody else has the story.'

'Nobody else has the proof,' said Elizabeth.

'Photos?'

'Got 'em.' Starpix had been busy, lurking outside Alan's riverside penthouse, waiting until he got what he needed, a fuzzy photograph of the lovers coming out of the building together.

Mike picked up his phone and dialled the legal department. 'Nicky? Could you come to my office, please? I've got a story that needs to be one hundred per cent watertight.'

Elizabeth sat at her desk while Mike and the in-house lawyer picked over every detail of her feature. It was her first attempt at a big showbiz scoop, but she was confident that the material would stand up to scrutiny. It had all fallen into place so easily, after that night with Nick when he told her about Johnny Khan. From there it was a simple process of detection and deduction, following leads and working on hunches, the sort of thing she's spent three years of post-graduate research doing. The only real difference was that someone might actually read this.

With the story written and submitted, Elizabeth felt lighter. Cleaner. She'd hit back at Rachel and Alan, and that was enough. Two years ago, she might have given Clytemnestra a run for her money, but now the wounds were no longer fresh, and the desire for revenge had abated. She'd made a sort of peace with Nick, and she'd moved on.

And she had Mike.

She may have started out writing this story to hurt Rachel, but she finished it to please Mike.

They'd spent five of the last fourteen nights together, and although she knew it was wrong, that she was doing to another woman what Rachel had done to her, she could not stop. After such a long time, she finally had a taste of happiness, and mere scruples were not going to take it away from her.

If this story worked out, Mike would be pleased with her. He would almost certainly sack Pete Goldman and offer her the showbiz editor's job. And they might have a future.

'Happy, Nicky?'

'I'm a lawyer, Mike. I'm never happy.'

'Are we libel-proof?'

'I've been over it again and again and I can't see a single loop-hole. If Southgate or Khan starts an action for defamation, they know that every detail of their private lives will be dragged through the courts.'

'Which they can't afford, by the sound of it. Right, Liz?'

She'd been called in to hear the verdict. 'Right. There's much more that I haven't written.' She was thinking about Chris, another of the 'regular male visitors' to Alan's penthouse. 'There's this personal trainer in LA who says he was silenced with threats.'

'So, Nicky,' said Mike, 'what can they do?'

'There are two possible lines of attack,' said Nicky. 'First, they can say we're undermining their reputation by claiming they're gay. That's a non-starter. It's no longer considered defamatory to say someone's gay. No judge is going to uphold that.'

'Quite right, too,' said Mike. 'The *Beacon* is all for the gays.'

'Secondly, they might say we're calling them liars. Both men have had high-profile affairs with women. If our story suggests they're lying to their fans, that their public persona is a sham, that might be construed as libel. It's a long shot, but they might try it.'

'What's our defence?'

'Justification. If we're telling the truth, they don't have a leg to stand on, however much they dislike it. That's why the evidence is so important.'

'I've got recorded interviews with six people who have seen them together,' said Elizabeth. 'In bed, even. Room service.'

'Very indiscreet, even for two horny actors,' said Mike.

'I've got photos of them together at Alan's London home.'

'Photos can be faked,' said Nicky. 'Photoshop has pretty much destroyed their value as evidence.'

'Okay, okay,' said Mike. 'Let's not get carried away. The story's true: we know that, they know that. Now it's just a question of how badly they want it hushed up. Liz: who's handling publicity on the show?'

She gave him Polly Hamlin's number.

'Right. Now leave me in peace to do some editing.'

* * *

'You have to kill the story,' said Alan. 'It's as simple as that.'

'I'm afraid it's not that simple,' said Polly. 'It never is.'

'You don't seem to understand. This story cannot run. Period.' Alan's voice was calm, his hair in place, his shirt uncreased, but he was furious. Someone had talked, and someone was going to pay for their indiscretion. Who? Chris?

'They have proof, Alan.'

'It's a lie.'

'Photographs of you and Johnny.'

Alan's eyes flashed. 'I told you, I do not want his name dragged into this.'

'We have to face up to the possibility that the story is going to run. It's just a question of how we can turn it to our advantage.'

'No,' said Alan. 'If they run this story, I will sue. It's character assassination. That woman, that Liz Miller, has personal reasons for attacking me.'

'That's irrelevant, I'm afraid. If it's true . . .'

'I'm telling you it's a lie.' The colour was mounting in Alan's face, a vein standing out on his forehead. He didn't care on his own account – he'd earned enough money in the last few years to live comfortably – but Johnny Khan had made it quite clear that if anyone found out about them, he would never speak to Alan again. And Alan could not face that. For the first time in his life, he was in love.

'We have a chance to control the publicity,' said Polly.

'You mean if I roll over and confess everything.'

'If you give a little, you get a lot.'

'And the *Beacon* wants some snivelling coming-out story, about what a burden it's been to live a lie.'

'That's the sort of thing.'

'Forget it,' he said, putting on his jacket, making sure that the right amount of dazzling white cuff extended from the sleeves. 'If a story appears about Johnny and me, I will disown the show. Your choice.'

'The show will survive,' said Polly. 'Nobody is indispensible, Alan.'

'Fine. Good luck, then.' He closed the door quietly behind him.

Polly, who was never without a Plan B, shook her head and picked up the phone. Time for a bit of horse-trading.

Nick was very pleased with the way things were turning out. He'd handled Elizabeth beautifully, got back into her good books and talked his way into a promising gig as a celebrity photo-journalist. He'd hit back at Rachel, who would learn that deserting Nick Sharkey came at a price. Okay, he'd never get her back now – not once she found out who was behind the story, as she inevitably would – but he'd managed to exploit their affair, without even touching his capital. The Rachel Tapes were still stashed away, unseen by anyone but Nick. Their time would come. As Rachel climbed further up the celebrity ladder, their value increased.

For now, all that mattered was keeping Elizabeth sweet, ensuring that the work kept coming his way. And he knew exactly how to do that.

After two years without a love life, Elizabeth now found herself juggling her diary in order to accommodate two men. She didn't like lying, but it seemed a small price to pay. She was making up for lost time; didn't she deserve that? Her lovers could hardly complain: Mike was married, and Nick – well, she didn't have to worry about cheating on Nick. For once, she thought, I'm putting myself first. What does it matter if people get hurt? That's the way the world is. I tried being nice, and look where it got me. Now I've got the best job on Fleet Street, a huge scoop with my byline that's going to be the celebrity story of the year and two men vying for my attentions, one of whom just happens to be my boss. I've got money, I've got status and I've got . . . well, not love, perhaps, but the next best thing.

She kissed Nick goodbye and left him slumbering in bed; he'd be working late, covering parties, and needed to catch up on sleep. She, however, had good reason to get to the office early: the Rach-Al story was out today, and she wanted to be there to bask in Mike's approval.

She walked down the road towards the Tube station, and couldn't resist a peek in the newsagent's, where her story would be flashed on the front page. Her heart swelled with pride, and she switched her phone to camera mode to record the moment.

'Alan Southgate – my story EXCLUSIVE' ran the banner above the *Beacon* masthead, alongside a photo of Elizabeth's old friend looking as perfectly handsome as ever.

Strange choice of words, thought Elizabeth, trying to ignore the cold drip of misgiving. She picked up the newspaper, and turned to page twelve.

'British heart-throb Alan Southgate speaks exclusively to the Daily Beacon about his difficult childhood, his amazing Hollywood career – and the truth about that affair with Rachel Hope! First of a three-part exclusive by Pete Goldman, *Beacon* showbiz editor.'

She froze.

'Are you going to pay for that paper, love? This isn't a lending library, you know.'

She threw a pound coin on to the counter and ran towards the tube station, her eyes blurred by tears.

'What's this?' she said, bursting into Mike's office, where he was polishing his awards. 'Where's my story?'

His face gave nothing away. 'Spiked,' he said.

'*Spiked*? What do you mean, spiked? It's the biggest showbiz scoop of the year. You said so yourself.'

'This is better.'

'This,' she said, throwing the crumpled newspaper on his desk, 'is crap.'

'True. But it's very much in our interests.'

'It's a pack of lies.'

'Of course it is. His publicist wrote it.'

'Under Pete Goldman's byline.'

'I know. I'm soft-hearted. I wanted to give him one last cutting for his book before I sack him.'

'I don't understand.' She sat down, the tears welling up in her eyes. 'What happened?'

Mike sat beside her, and handed her a box of tissues. 'I don't expect you to understand, Liz. You're very new to all this, and I know this meant a lot to you. But I'm afraid shit happens.'

'You can say that again.' She blew her nose. 'But why? You said yourself the story was watertight. Why drop it for this piece of puff?'

'They made me an offer I couldn't refuse.'

Elizabeth remembered stories she'd heard of 'former friends' of Alan Southgate's who had met with mysterious accidents. 'They threatened you?'

Mike laughed. 'Threaten me? I'd like to see 'em try.'

'Then what?'

'Southgate's publicist phoned me up and asked me what it would take to make me drop the story. We did a bit of wheeling and dealing, and we came to a very generous arrangement.'

'A three-part interview with Alan? It's practically an advertorial for the show.'

'He's very popular with the ladies, you know. It'll sell a lot more copies than a nasty story about him being gay.'

'But that's the truth.'

'Nobody's disputing that, Liz. Not even Alan, apparently.'

'So you dropped the story just so you could sell more papers.'

'Precisely. Although I wouldn't have said "just". That's the business we're in.'

'Well it seems like a pretty shoddy deal to me.'

'And so it would be, if that's all we got out of it. Believe it or not, I fought hard for your piece. I told the publisher that we should run it. I told him you're a brilliant reporter and that it would be grossly unfair to spike the piece just for a short-term sales blip.'

'So why did you spike it?'

'Because Polly Hamlin is a very powerful woman. Channel Six is a very important TV station. We need them, and if we don't play ball with them, they'll take their stories to the *Comet*. And it just so happened that this was the bargaining opportunity I needed to get them onside.'

'Meaning what, exactly?'

'We get all their exclusives for the foreseeable future, starting with their Michael Bublé Christmas special.'

Elizabeth wiped her eyes. 'You sold me down the river for Michael Bublé?'

'Yes.'

'Right. Well, now I know where I stand.' She made for the door.

'No,' said Mike, 'you don't. Sit back down, please, Liz.'

'What?'

'I've let Pete Goldman go.'

'You've . . .'

'He's clearing his desk as we speak. You might want to give it a minute before you go round there. I don't think he's exactly your number-one fan just now.'

'I don't understand.'

'Liz Miller, showbiz editor. How does it sound?'

Ridiculous, she thought for a moment, then said, 'It sounds all right.'

'Doesn't it just?'

'Well,' she said, 'I'd better go and swot up on Michael Bublé.'

Nana was screened over three nights to massive viewing figures and unanimous critical acclaim. Elizabeth's replacement on the *Beacon* TV desk loved it, which was exactly what she'd been instructed to do.

Alan's three-part confession in the feature pages made him more famous than he'd ever been before, although it did very little for his relationship with his family. He'd been obliged to make up a turbulent, almost abused childhood, he'd invented a teenage drugs drama and he'd spilled the beans on every woman he'd ever slept with, and quite a few he hadn't. It was a wonderful work of fiction, and would have disgusted Alan but for one thing – there was absolutely no mention of Johnny Khan or the word 'gay'. The morning after the first episode was broadcast, Alan was on a plane back to Los Angeles for a reunion with his lover. He was photographed arriving at LAX with a gorgeous young woman on his arm, and he told reporters that film projects would keep him in Hollywood for the foreseeable future.

Elizabeth stepped up as the *Beacon*'s new showbiz editor with a fat salary, a company car and a picture byline that made her look like a severe, sexy schoolmistress. Mike took her for a gourmet weekend at the Manoir aux Quatre Saisons to celebrate.

Nick Sharkey, alias Starpix, was furious when the story was dropped. Elizabeth was authorised to pay him a kill fee, a fraction of what he would have received had the pictures been printed. She promised him any amount of work in the future, but suddenly stopped returning his calls. For the time being, he was forced to conclude that he'd been outmanoeuvred by Rachel Hope and Alan Southgate – and possibly, even, by Liz Miller.

But he still had an ace up his sleeve. He still had the Rachel Tapes.

Chapter 26

Rachel Hope was a household name after *Nana*, although it wasn't just her face that was famous. The cameras had scrutinised her from every angle, with very little between her and the lens than an artfully draped sheet, a bent leg or a convenient pot plant. Her body became the most admired, the most discussed, the most desired in the business. Websites sprang up, dedicated to her legs, her breasts, her backside. Outtakes from the filming were leaked on to the Internet (the mole was none other than Polly Hamlin) and were incorporated into the extras on the rushed-out DVD release.

Her agent advised Rachel to consider carefully before committing to any of the dozens of scripts that landed on her doormat every week; with a little strategy, she could use *Nana* to break into the big league, with a fighting chance at cracking Hollywood. For the time being she had only to sit tight, keep fit and count the money.

And there was very little else for Rachel to do. Between jobs and between boyfriends, she spent her days in the gym with a personal trainer, her evenings at launches and parties, refusing alcohol and canapés and her nights alone in bed in the flat in Shepherd's Bush. She would have to move soon: photographers were camping outside the building, much to the disgust (or delight) of her neighbours, and if she were to bring anyone home, it would be all over the papers in the morning. Fortunately, the only regular visitor to the flat was Anna, who had more or less moved in. Another good reason for leaving . . .

292 · *Rupert James*

She couldn't very well throw her own mother out: Anna was having a bad time, as she told her daughter at great length, and the hoped-for reconciliation with the Prof was a long time coming. She was running short of money, and resented the small, one-bedroom flat in which the Prof had installed her while they worked things out. 'He's forgotten about me!' she wailed. 'My life is slipping through my fingers. You can't wait to get rid of me.'

'Don't be ridiculous, Mum.'

'I'm a married woman. This is all wrong.'

Rachel knew what was coming; they'd had this conversation a thousand times before. 'Then sort things out. Call him. Ask him what's going on.'

'It's not as easy as that. He still blames me.'

'For what?' sighed Rachel, knowing all too well.

'For what you did to his daughter. As if it's anything to do with me. You've always gone your own way, you've never listened to a word I say, and just when I had a chance to make something of my life, you screw it up with your selfishness.'

With this conversation apparently stuck on repeat, Rachel was keen to get away from London for a while.

She called her agent and told her she would be interested in job offers that would take her out of the UK for a few months, and which would pay enough to buy a nice house somewhere in London, without having to sell the flat. Anna could have that. Surely that would stop her bitching.

She made the call on a Thursday. By the next Monday, she had an audition. She spent the weekend in the gym; it was the kind of film that required her to look good in a leather catsuit, and little else.

By Tuesday, she had a job.

*   *   *

Anna wasn't the only one who hadn't heard from the Prof in a while. Elizabeth was busy with her new job and love life, but even she noticed that the last few Sunday lunches had been cancelled. She didn't mind; she was sick of hearing her work described as a betrayal, a prostitution, etc. She was also increasingly bored by the Prof's lengthy accounts of the latest paper, the latest conference, the latest bit of academic gossip.

'What's up with the old man?' she asked Chris.

'Don't ask me. I've not heard from him in months, which suits both of us fine.'

'He is all right, isn't he? I mean, he's not lonely, or anything?'

'Frankly,' said Chris, who had started dating a nice young lawyer that he'd met at a dinner party and was far too happy to wonder, 'I don't care. He takes no interest in my life and I take no interest in his. If you're worried, go and see him.'

'I'm too busy at the moment,' said Elizabeth.

'And so am I. Goodbye.'

The family is falling to pieces, thought Elizabeth, with a mixture of concern and relief. She knew she would never have her father's blessing for what she was doing; at least this way, she could live without his disapproval.

In the good old days of Alderman's, when Rachel's only care was what to wear to the next party, the name on everyone's lips was Charlie Evans, he of the athletic torso, the opportunistic libido and the meteoric rise to fame. Now he was making the difficult transition from teen idol to adult artist, which, in effect, involved a good deal of time spent at pool parties in LA. A big fat advance for two solo albums meant he wasn't short of money, but things weren't quite going according to plan. He'd decamped to America to record with the hippest producers, at great expense. The much-hyped debut single was a gruesome din, attempting to position him as an 'urban' act; Charlie was about as urban as Dartmoor, and the song failed to chart. A hastily released ballad repaired some of the damage, but as a US tour got underway, and ticket sales fell massively short of expectations, there was a terrible whiff of Plan B about Charlie's career. Those who had been his biggest fans quickly abandoned him, those who had dined out on the flimsiest acquaintance now started remembering what a pushy, talentless stage-school brat Charlie Evans always was. Why, his name wasn't even Charlie. It was Toby. Toby Charles Montgomery-Evans. How urban was that?

And while Charlie bided his time in the US, his UK fanbase, distracted by a new generation of talent-show hopefuls, forgot all about him.

Two years, four record producers and several kilos of cocaine later, the second album was still not finished, and Charlie Evans had nothing to show for his Hollywood sojourn except a deep mahogany tan and a growing collection of tattoos. The body, once so taut and beautiful, began to sag; the tattoos obliterated the worst of the damage, but not all. Charlie started losing his hair, and after several disastrous attempts at twenty-first-century combovers, bowed to the inevitable and had a number-one crop. He spent weeks by the pool working on lyrics, most of which dealt with the fickleness of fame and the shallowness of former friends. For a while, the British press ran pictures of Charlie's sad decline, but even they lost interest in the end, and moved on to fresher meat.

At the age of twenty-four, Charlie Evans was all washed up. And then he re-met Rachel Hope.

They met, as people in Hollywood do, at a party. Someone's party for something, nobody seemed quite clear who or what, at a beautiful mansion in the Hollywood Hills. The catering was five star, the guest list was B-plus with a sprinkling of A-minus. Rachel, who was due to begin shooting an action thriller based on a popular video game entitled *Corpse Army* on Monday, went with her producer, a pushy New Yorker called Wayne, who insisted on the need to network. Beside him, she had no friends on the coast; Alan was filming in New York, and it just so happened that Johnny Khan was in a show on Broadway. But girls like Rachel don't need friends. Girls like Rachel just need to make an entrance, and this she did, by stepping out of the limo in a pair of Louboutins and a dark plum coloured dress by hot new designer Isabelle Cissé, gathered at the neckline, halter-topped, leaving her arms and shoulders bare. It was warm enough, just, to get away with it; if she got chilly later on, there would be plenty of men to lend a jacket.

She walked into the party like she was walking on to a catwalk, if not a yacht, conscious that heads were turning, eyes refocusing, breath drawn and comments prepared. She was pale while everyone else was tanned, her hair was dark while everyone else's was blond, and instead of slapping on so much make-up that she looked like one of the transsexual hookers who plied their trade just a few blocks away, she was working a natural look that involved only a minimum of concealer, eyeshadow and lip gloss. Rachel was dimly aware that this entrance mattered – just like another entrance, all those years ago, into a posh restaurant in north London, when she prepared to meet her new family . . .

Tanned blond non-entities materialised in her pathway, offering handshakes and smiles, and Rachel tried hard to make out individual words above the racket of the DJ who was playing records so loud that the guests could barely talk. They were outdoors, in a courtyard modelled on a Roman impluvium, with a small square pool in the middle, the water bright with underwater lights in yellow, red and green, tiny palms in faux antique pots at each corner and above them the stars, just visible through the brownish haze. There were statues and murals and a jumble of architectural features, there were waiters with drinks and canapés, there were faces that might be familiar from adverts or movies or adult websites. But Rachel saw none of this. Her eyes focused on a spot beyond the pool where a young man in aviator shades and a denim waistcoat reclined on a lounger, sipping a drink and attempting to entertain a bored young woman.

Well blow me, thought Rachel, that's Charlie Evans.

While Wayne whispered in one ear, and a woman who looked a bit like Donatella Versace chattered away in the other, Rachel took a long draught of wine and focused her attention on that lounger.

See me, she said in her head. See me now.

And he did. He raised his head to look around, stopped, did a double take in her direction and removed the shades.

Their eyes met, the music and the chat faded, and for a moment nothing mattered but the flash of recognition, the meeting of souls across a small square of over-chlorinated water at a B-list party in the Hollywood Hills.

'Sorry, Wayne. I've just seen someone I know from London.'

'I was just saying, honey, how great you were at your audition.'

The blonde attempted to look interested, insofar as one can with a completely paralysed face.

'Gosh, thanks,' said Rachel, who understood the value of British vernacular at times like this. 'Please do excuse me for a minute, I must go and say hello. Brits abroad, you know.'

'What-ho,' said Wayne. 'Pip-pip and all that.'

If Rachel could have walked on water, she would have taken the shortest route to Charlie's lounger, from which he was now getting up, revealing a pair of denim cut-offs that he could still just about get away with. She half-thought of diving into the pool, swimming the four strokes over and emerging, dripping, at his feet, but that would be a terrible waste of couture. Instead she took the clockwise route, hoping that he would do the decent thing and meet her halfway.

If he stays where he is, she thought, as she placed one Louboutin in front of the other, I will not go to bed with him. If he comes round to meet me, I might.

Charlie stepped on to the edge of the pool and then, using some Parkour moves that he'd once learned for a video, leaped across the water and landed safely by Rachel's side.

And that, thought Rachel, secured his berth for the night.

'Awright, love?' he said, in an almost-perfect cockney accent. Alderman's was famous for the quality of its regional accents.

'Hello,' she said, sending herself several notches up the class ladder. If he wants to be a bit of rough, she thought, I'm quite happy to be the posh bird.

'I know who you are. You're that Rachel.'

'Guilty as charged.'

'Yeah.' He stood there, shifting from foot to foot, beaming at her, waiting for her to acknowledge his greater fame.

She played it cool. 'We must know all sorts of people in common,' said Rachel. 'You went to Alderman's, didn't you?'

'Yeah,' he said, 'good old Alderman's.' He was less gor blimey than before. 'Still full of pompous twats?'

'Oh, I liked it,' said Rachel, unwilling to get drawn into his rebel fantasy. 'Gave me a very good education.'

'They kicked me out,' said Charlie. 'I suppose everyone knows that.'

'I thought you just left.'

'Got a job, didn't I?'

At least he didn't say 'innit', which would have snuffed out this fragile spark of romance. He was still an attractive man, for all the terrible loungewear and overtanning; at least he hadn't resorted to surgery yet. Rachel's eyes flickered down the furry chest and stomach between the flaps of the denim waistcoat. Needs to spend more in the gym, she thought, and less time on the Elvis diet, but that can be arranged.

'So,' she said, conscious that the eyes of the world were upon them – there were certainly photographers here, pictures possibly bouncing off the satellites even as they spoke – 'perhaps we could meet for lunch one day, talk about London. You must miss it.'

'Like a hole in the head.'

'Or you could visit me on set,' she said. Time to establish that one of them, at least, was working.

'Bollocks to that,' he said, and Rachel was just about to walk away when he continued 'I can't wait that long. Let's make a night of it. Just you and me. What do you say?'

'That sounds lovely,' she said. 'Where are you taking me?'

'If you give me five minutes, I'd love to take you for dinner.'

This was much more like it. 'Five minutes?' she said, looking around the party. 'Yes, I think I can just about stand it for five minutes.'

He kissed her on the cheek and ran into the house, giving Rachel a clear view of the bum that, in Charlie's teen idol heyday, had shifted an awful lot of units.

'Charlie Evans? Oh, come on, Liz. You can do better than that.'

'With Rachel Hope.'

'That's more like it.'

Elizabeth showed Mike a selection of images that had been coming in from LA over the last week or so. Charlie and Rachel at a pool party, Charlie and Rachel dining *à deux*, Charlie and

Rachel walking hand in hand along the beach, a cute black spaniel frolicking at their feet.

'Okay, nice, not bad, as far as it goes. It's a picture caption for now. Anyone else got it?'

'Probably.' Elizabeth sighed; the agencies would have sent the same photos to every picture desk in the world.

'Well, keep an eye on them. See what you can get. Sounds like he's just using her for publicity.'

'Leave it with me, Mike.'

He looked at her in silence for a while. 'Funny,' he said at length, 'how many Rachel Hope stories there are.'

'She's very famous,' said Elizabeth, not quite catching his eye.

'Indeed she is. They can't get enough of her, the readers. English girl makes good in Hollywood; well, there's a story that doesn't come along every day of the week.'

'Quite.'

'You do remember what I said, don't you, Liz? When you first came here?'

Elizabeth swallowed. 'What was that, Mike?'

'Never let it get personal.'

'Of course. Understood.' She looked towards the door of his office and made sure that none of the secretaries was looking. 'See you tonight,' she said, and kissed him on the lips. He pulled her closer, and squeezed her bum, prolonging the kiss.

Time seemed to go faster in Hollywood. Up at five, straight into make-up, on set all day, interviews and photo calls between scenes, barely time for lunch (prepared by the on-set nutritionist) and gym (supervised by the on-set trainer) before it was time to fall into bed, exhausted by the hard physical labour of running around and pouting in a leather catsuit in front of a green screen. The corpse army itself would be added in post-production.

Despite this punishing schedule, Rachel always found time for Charlie Evans, who managed to be in her dressing room when she needed him, turned up at her house when she was ready for bed, always sober, always tenderly considerate of the fact that she'd been working while he'd just been waiting. He was an excellent, efficient lover, not at all the self-obsessed narcissist that she'd expected, and when he'd finished he was quite happy to let her sleep. He told her he loved her after the fourth date, and within a month she began to think that she reciprocated.

And just about the same time as that, she realised that she'd missed her period.

It could be overwork. It could be diet, or exercise, or just being away from home. These things happened; periods could be a week late, ten days, even more.

But Rachel knew perfectly well that this was not the case. She was pregnant. She was carrying Charlie Evans' child.

She only hoped that the leather one-piece, cruellest of all garments, wouldn't reveal their joy to the world too soon.

'Me again.'

'What do you want this time?'

'I've got another little job for you.'

'Fuck that. Look what happened to the last one.'

'You got paid.'

'Not enough.'

Elizabeth sighed. 'Nick, it's never going to be enough for you, is it? Until you find a job that pays you a six-figure salary for sitting on your arse smoking dope.'

That shut him up. Perhaps if she'd treated him more like this back in the day, they might be married now. But that avenue of thought was sealed off.

'Want the job or not? There's plenty of other snappers out there with a lot more experience than you.'

''Course I bloody want it. There's no need to be so high and mighty.'

'That's more like it. What do you know about Charlie Evans?'

'Same as everyone else,' said Nick. 'He's a shagger and a coke-head who used to take it up the bum from his manager.'

'He's a pop star,' said Elizabeth, 'so all that goes without saying. I need something more damaging.'

'You won't let it rest, will you?'

'I don't know what you mean.'

'Rachel. Still hoping to get your own back, is that it? She's got a new boyfriend and you're looking for ways to put the boot in.'

'Not at all,' said Elizabeth. 'It just so happens that, like it or not, Rachel Hope's private life is my business now. Believe me, there's nothing personal about it.'

'Pull the other one,' said Nick. 'All right. I'll see what I can get. But this time I want a flat fee, whether it's published or not. I'm not being palmed off with another kill fee just because your editor doesn't want to stick his neck out.'

'Agreed.' Elizabeth had enough budget to be generous. 'But don't get pushy, Nick. Remember who's boss.'

'You're sexy when you're angry, you know.'

'You didn't always think so,' said Elizabeth.

'Yeah,' said Nick, 'but I was a twat back then, wasn't I?'

Mike was spending the night with his wife, and so, thought Elizabeth, it would do no harm to invest a little time in Starpix.

Rachel got back to London three months pregnant. There were still some additional dialogue recording to be done on *Corpse Army*, but the action scenes were in the can, and she could mothball the leather catsuit until it was time to get it out for the premiere. It was just as well; in the final weeks, the zips had become a bit of a struggle.

Charlie stayed in Los Angeles for a while, officially to work on his album, in reality to throw the British press off the scent. Rachel was not quite ready to be part of a celebrity couple again, even if this was the real thing.

Anna was still moping around the flat, but it wouldn't be Rachel's problem for much longer; the purchase of a four-bedroom house in a sought-after square in Kennington was currently going through, thanks to *Corpse Army*. Rachel didn't share her news with her mother – there would be plenty of time for that when things were a little more settled. But she had to talk so someone, and couldn't face Mark or Natasha, who would only say unkind things about Charlie Evans.

And so she had lunch with Chris, and told him all about it.

'Elizabeth.'

'Daddy!'

'You sound surprised.'

'Sorry. Just wasn't expecting to hear from you.'

'How are you?' He sounded worried, distant.

'I'm fine, thanks. You know. Working hard.' She bit her tongue; hadn't she learned not to mention work? It only set him off.

'Oh good,' he said, as if he didn't really mind, 'that's good. Yes.'

'Daddy, is something the matter?'

He paused before replying. The Prof never paused. 'Just wondering if I might see you for lunch tomorrow.'

'I can't, I'm afraid. I've got to go to a . . .'

'Please?'

There was something in his voice, some broken quality she had not detected before, something that made her plan to reschedule. 'Okay,' she said, trying to keep it light and bright. 'I'll fit you in.'

'Thanks, Lizzie.' He hadn't called her that since she was twelve years old. 'Usual time?'

'Of course. Daddy, are you . . .'

He'd already hung up.

Chapter 27

'You'll never guess who I saw yesterday,' said Chris, when he and Elizabeth met at the Prof's for the first Sunday lunch in months.

'I don't know,' said Elizabeth, kissing her brother on both cheeks. 'Some minor celebrity, I suppose.'

'You sound just like Dad sometimes.'

'Oh, shut up. Anyway, what's all this about? Why's the old man so keen to see us all of a sudden?'

Chris shrugged. 'Search me. I got the summons just like you did. He's not said a word since I arrived. He disappeared into the kitchen and shut the door in my face. Anyway, you haven't answered my question.'

'Oh God, Chris, I don't know. What is this? A guessing game?'

'Go on, then. I'll give you three guesses, who I saw and what they told me.'

'Alan Southgate.'

'No.' Chris blushed. 'Haven't seen him for ages. Guess again.'

'David Beckham.'

'I wish. No. Last guess.'

'Then I suppose you must mean Rachel.'

'Yes!'

'How lovely for you both. I'm sure you had a good chat about the old days.'

'No, we didn't, as a matter of fact,' said Chris. 'We were too busy discussing her big news.'

'Chris, everyone in the world knows about Rachel and Charlie Evans. We broke the story in the *Beacon* ages ago.'

'Yadda yadda yadda. I know something that you don't.' He was like a child again, picking a fight.

'Well, let me see. We know about her and Gerald Partridge, obviously. We know about her and Alan Southgate, which is the non-story of the year, by the way, and one day I will tell the truth about that one.'

Yes, thought Chris, Alan told me about your vicious little attempt to out him. 'Bo-ring! Old news. You'll have to do better than that, Liz Miller.'

'Go on, then. Whose marriage is she wrecking now?' A brief twinge of guilt twisted her stomach as she thought of Mike and his wife. 'As if it matters.'

'Nobody's. It's the most wonderful news in the world.' He felt like rubbing Elizabeth's nose in it. 'I'm going to be an uncle.'

'What?'

'That surprised you, didn't it? And don't pretend you knew already. I'm going to be a step-uncle, and you're going to be a step-aunt. How do you like that?'

'She's pregnant?'

'Well, that's usually how it happens, I believe, although I'm no expert. Yes, of course she's pregnant.'

'Who else knows?'

'Charlie, obviously. Her agent, I suppose. She hasn't told the producers. She's worried that they might sack her.'

'Right.' Elizabeth composed her face, trying to disguise any hint of glee. 'Well, that's great. Good luck to her.'

'So let's see if you can keep a secret,' said Chris, knowing perfectly well that she couldn't.

'I couldn't be less interested if I tried.'

The Prof appeared from the kitchen with a large glass of wine in his hand. 'Ah, Elizabeth,' he said. 'There you are.'

'Hello Daddy.' She kissed him; he smelled of alcohol and cigarettes. Since when had the Prof smoked? Cigars, occasionally – but fags?

'Good of you to come.' He sounded tired.

'I've been neglecting you shamefully,' said Elizabeth, deciding that attack was the best form of defence. 'But you see, in journalism we have these pesky things called *deadlines*. You academic types wouldn't understand.' A little raillery usually bucked the old man up. Instead, he grunted, and went back into the kitchen, leaving the door open. Chris pushed her. 'Go on,' he said. 'He'll talk to you.'

'Daddy,' said Elizabeth, 'what's the matter?' He was standing at the sink, his hands braced against the worktop as if to prevent himself from falling.

Elizabeth took a step towards him, and stopped. Even after her mother died, she'd found it hard to touch her father. He winced at physical contact, except the most conventional – a shake of the hand, a peck on the cheek. But an arm around the shoulders? A hug? It was unthinkable. And since Anna had gone, he had been in deep freeze.

'Elizabeth.' His voice was low, from somewhere deep in his abdomen.

'What is it?' She was frightened now. Something was wrong. He's found out. He knows about me, she thought.

Before she had time to figure out what exactly he'd found out – 'me and Mike' or 'me and Nick' – the Prof turned to face her. His face, she realised, looked terribly old. He cleared his throat. 'There is something we need to discuss.' He gestured towards the table. 'I think you'd better sit down.'

'Shall I ask Chris to come in?'

'No!' he said, too abruptly, and then, in a calmer voice, 'not yet. I need to talk to you alone first.'

It must be about the divorce. He's finally done it, and it hurts more than he expected. Or . . . God forbid, no. Don't tell me that they're getting back together again? Now that really would be an occasion for long faces. She braced herself for the worst.

The Prof waited until she was settled, then said, 'I have cancer.'

'What?'

'I have cancer.'

'You . . .'

'Have cancer. Yes. Of the prostate.'

'Of the prostate.'

'That's right.'

What could she say? 'Is that bad?'

'Yes, Elizabeth. That's bad.'

Are we going to sit here parroting each other until one of us screams or cries or drops dead? 'How long have you known?'

'About a year.'

'*A year*? Why didn't you tell us?'

'Because there was still some hope.'

Her face seemed to be frozen.

'But now,' said the Prof, his voice quite normal again, 'there is none. And so you should know.'

'No hope? Don't be ridiculous. Of course there is hope. Prostate cancer is common today,' said Elizabeth, without a clue whether this was true or not. 'They can do almost anything. What does the doctor say?'

'It is simply a question of when. Not if. The uncertainty was the worst thing. I think I can face the end with a degree of equanimity.'

He was smiling, damn him, actually smiling.

'And you haven't told Chris?'

'I wanted to tell you first. Somehow, I couldn't face him.' The Prof laughed. 'I know it's ridiculous, but I still think of him as a child.'

'Oh, for God's sake, Daddy . . .'

'And I never thought of you as a child. Even before Susan died. You were always like a grown-up.'

'I see.' It felt like a kick in the stomach.

'And so I'm going to ask you, if you don't mind, whether you might be able to handle that side of the business yourself.'

'The . . . business? What are you talking about?'

'Telling your brother.'

'Oh, Daddy, that's just not fair.'

The Prof shrugged, and wiped his eye. 'No, I suppose it's not. But it's what I want. I hope you will be able to oblige.' He selected a bottle of wine from the rack, looked carefully at the label as if considering its suitability to the occasion. What does one serve when one is dying? A robust little malbec?

'Help yourself to a drink,' he said. 'I'm going upstairs for a moment.' He grimaced. 'The medication I'm on has some rather unfortunate side effects.'

'How long?'

'I don't know, darling. I'm afraid I really don't know.'

'Who have you told?'

'Nobody. Just a couple of close friends. It's personal, Polly. You seem to be treating it as some kind of marketing opportunity.'

'It is,' said Polly, whom Rachel had retained after the success of *Nana* as her personal publicist. She could afford such things now. 'However you look at it, having a child at this stage in your career is going to get massive amounts of coverage.'

'I don't want all that.'

'You should have thought of that when you had unprotected sex, love. Not to mention sexually transmitted infections.'

'Don't think that hadn't crossed my mind. I've been tested.'

'I'm glad to hear it. Anyway, that's none of my business. My business is controlling how the press deals with it. And if nobody knows, then we have all the cards in our hand.'

'I didn't say nobody knows.'

'Who?'

'An old friend of mine.' Rachel suddenly realised that she'd made a bad mistake. 'A guy called Chris.'

'And who, exactly, is Chris?'

'He's . . . Oh dear. He's Liz Miller's brother.'

'Rachel, I think it's time you told me what exactly the problem is with you and Liz Miller.'

And so Rachel did.

'Right,' said Polly, reaching for her phone and spooling through the address book, 'we need to move fast.'

The Prof's illness was cruelly fast. Within a fortnight of telling Elizabeth about the cancer, he was admitted to hospital with rectal bleeding. He was discharged after two nights, and re-admitted the following week. This time, the doctors were not talking about a probable release date, but of palliative care. He was transferred to a hospice in a quiet residential street in Belsize Park, where birds sang in the trees outside the windows and squirrels capered from branch to branch. He had a private room, where Elizabeth and Chris could visit him at any time, for as long as they liked.

Elizabeth's visits were frequent but short; she hated the hospice, felt sick every time she walked down the street and saw the falling autumn leaves, the glossy conkers littering the ground as so many harbingers of death. Deadlines ruled her life – and although Mike would have been quite content to give her time off, she chose not to tell him. At least work offered some semblance of normality. If she kept going to parties and launches and lunches, she could forget that her father was dying, forget the skull that was showing through his face, the smell of antiseptic, the hushed kindness of the nurses.

Chris visited the Prof every morning for at least an hour, and again in the evening. Two or three times a week, he slept on a couch at the side of the bed. They didn't have much to talk about, and for much of the time the Prof was sleeping or stoned on morphine, but at least, thought Chris, he is not dying alone. The idea gave him some peace of mind. Elizabeth may be frantic, playing the drama queen, but Chris didn't really blame her. It was harder for Elizabeth. She actually loved her father, after all. Chris did not.

As luck would have it, neither of the children was by the Prof's bedside when Anna chose to visit.

'I most certainly can,' she said to the nurse who told her that she couldn't go into the Prof's room. 'I'm his wife.'

'Nobody said anything about a wife.'

'No,' said Anna, narrowing her eyes, which were already half-closed by mascara, 'I don't suppose they did. But the fact remains, and here I am.' She flounced into the room with a jangle of jewellery and a waft of perfume, and closed the door behind her.

'Well this is nice,' said Anna, glancing at the bed long enough to register something that resembled a skeleton with a sheet over it. 'Good heavens, it's stuffy in here. Doesn't anybody open any windows?' She looked out at the horse chestnuts, and fiddled with the lock. A magpie stared crossly at her, and flew away, complaining. She gave up on the window.

'I must say,' she said, taking a seat beside the bed but not looking at it, 'it's rotten of you not to tell me that you were ill. I had to find out for myself.'

The Prof wasn't saying much, in fact Anna was far from sure that he was even conscious. His eyes were open, but cloudy, and his mouth was making vague shapes.

'It was only because your secretary called me to find out when you were coming back that I had any idea that anything was wrong. I suppose you must have given them my number, which is sweet of you. I know we've not seen eye to eye over the last couple of years, but we're still man and wife, aren't we, and where there's life, there's hope.'

The Prof made a groaning sound.

'Darling, you look terrible,' said Anna, casting a quick, scared glance at his face. 'They're not feeding you properly. You need looking after. Thank God I came. What are those children of yours thinking? I suppose they're both too busy to visit. It's a good job you've got me.'

The door opened a crack, and the nurse looked in.

'Mrs . . . er, Anna Bates?'

'Mrs Miller will do, thank you. What?'

'I've just been speaking to Professor Miller's daughter.'

Anna made a face. 'Oh, yes. Was there a message?'

The nurse frowned. 'No message. She says she'll be here in an hour or so.'

Anna looked at her watch. 'An hour? Oh, I couldn't possibly stay that long. I'm afraid I'm going to miss her this time round. But just tell her when she gets here that I'll be back. Would you be sure to tell her that? I'll be back.'

Elizabeth and Chris had an emergency bedside meeting at eight o'clock that night.

'What the hell does she want?'

'What's hers, I suppose,' said Chris. 'They are still married.'

'She's got a bloody nerve, showing up like this.'

'There must be some reason why they never got divorced.'

'Yes,' said Elizabeth, lowering her voice, although there was no need – the Prof was far, far away. 'Because he never got round to seeing a solicitor.'

'Perhaps he didn't want to get divorced. Did you ever think of that?'

'Don't be ridiculous. He couldn't stand the woman.'

'No, Elizabeth. You couldn't stand the woman. He loved her. Enough to marry her, at any rate.'

'They've barely spoken in the last two years.'

'And why was that, do you imagine?'

'If you're trying to suggest that I somehow broke up their marriage . . .'

'Shh! For God's sake, this is hardly the time and place.'

Elizabeth felt sick. She wanted to run away, to see Mike, Nick, anybody. 'You do realise what this means, don't you?'

Chris scowled at her. 'I presume you're talking about the will.'

'Of course I am.'

Chris stood up. 'You amaze me sometimes, you know that? He's lying here dying, and all you can think about is who's going to get the money after he's gone.'

'Well? These things matter.'

'For Christ's sake, Liz Miller, you make me sick some-times.' He walked out of the room, out into the street. She watched him for a while, pacing up and down, in and out of the pool of light from a streetlamp. He was right, damn him. She'd gone too far. She followed him outside and tried to apologise.

And while they were gone, the Professor died. They knew, as soon as they came back in and saw the nurse's face.

* * *

The next morning, the *Beacon*'s arch rival, the *Daily Comet*, published a double-page spread in which Rachel Hope revealed to an enthralled readership that she was not only carrying Charlie Evans' child, but also that they planned to make it legal as soon as their schedules allowed. Polly Hamlin had acted quickly, and sold the feature to the exact place where it would damage Liz Miller the most. 'I'm a great believer in marriage,' said Rachel in the interview, 'and I know that Charlie wants to be part of our baby's life. It's time for me to put my career on hold and concentrate on the most exciting role I've ever had – being a mum.'

Elizabeth, who was going through the Prof's address books looking for people that she needed to inform of the death, read the feature with a feeling of dread. The *Comet* shouldn't have got the story, she thought. I should have got it. The *Beacon* should have got it. Mike will be angry. We'll need to hit back with an exclusive of our own.

She called Nick.

'What have you got on Charlie Evans for me?' She had not yet told him about the Prof.

'Plenty, babe. Plenty. Want to discuss it over dinner?'

'No,' she said. 'You'd better come to the office. I'm . . . I'm rather too busy for dinner.'

And so, without having seen each other in the flesh for over two years, Rachel Hope and Elizabeth Miller found themselves locked in a struggle that was rapidly spiralling out of control. This time, it wasn't just a question of who would get the man; now there were big budgets at stake, professional reputations, people's livelihoods. Polly Hamlin was delighted; now that the gloves were off, it was so much easier to deal with the likes of Liz Miller. Rachel sat back and waited, wondering what Elizabeth's next move would be. And Elizabeth, disorientated by grief and terrified of losing her job and her lover, made the first of a series of very bad judgement calls.

'I'll take anything you've got,' she told Nick when he came to her office. 'No holds barred.'

'And you'll pay?'

'Oh, yes. I'll pay.'

Chapter 28

The Prof's funeral took place ten days after his death, the earliest they could fit him in at the cemetery. Elizabeth and Chris spent the days in an administrative whirlwind, choosing coffins and forms of service, agonising over whom to invite, arguing over how much input the widow should be allowed to have. Elizabeth was barely sleeping, and got through the working day on autopilot. Chris took time off from his studies, did most of the donkey work and, at night, slept soundly in the arms of his lawyer boyfriend, Dev.

Rachel and Charlie's wedding was rushed into production as soon as the *Comet* feature had appeared, and they capitalised on the sudden surge of public interest by selling the exclusive photo rights to *Super!* magazine, the *Comet*'s celebrity stable-mate. The happy day was scheduled just three days after the funeral.

'If you need time off,' Mike told Elizabeth, 'you must take it. The *Beacon* will survive without you.'

'Work's the only thing that's keeping me together.'

'You're making mistakes, Liz. The subs and the lawyers are very worried.'

'I'll do better.'

'And you slipped up badly over that Rachel Hope business. She shouldn't have gone with the *Comet*. You told me you had it covered.'

'It's not my fault.'

'You're starting to sound like Pete Goldman.'

'Please, Mike. Don't be like this.'

He pushed a box of tissues across the desk. 'Now, then, there's no need to get upset. I know what it's like. I've lost parents myself, you know. Work's a great comfort, but not if you're fucking up. I'd rather you took a few weeks off and came back fresh.'

'I'm fine.' She sat up straight and tried to look it. 'I can handle it.'

'Then prove it. Get me the real story about Rachel Hope and Charlie Evans, and make it snappy. We need it in time for the wedding.'

'Consider it done,' said Elizabeth.

Nick set about his new commission with an energy that he had never before brought to his working life. The money was good, and he had a lavish expenses account – but rather than blowing it all on drugs as he would once have done, Nick shepherded his resources and focused on the job. If he could exploit the animosity between Elizabeth and Rachel to his own ends, he'd come out of this with a fistful of money and a career as a press photographer. He could not afford to blow it. This might well be his last chance.

He needed a strategy. It wouldn't be enough to print off a few stills from the Rachel Tapes and hand them over to Elizabeth; she'd get the credit, and after the last disaster he wasn't about to hand over his trump card. He'd use the Rachel Tapes when he was ready, or desperate; for now, their value as a threat was still high. First of all, he'd attack where his opponents were most vulnerable. Charlie Evans had a past, and Nick knew exactly which cupboards to search for skeletons.

'I knew you couldn't keep away for ever,' said Natasha, opening the flat door. It was noon, but she was still dressed in last night's finery, a loud floral print cocktail dress that she'd obviously slept in. Her eyes were black with make-up, and a cigarette was stuck to her lower lip.

'You're looking well,' said Nick, 'but then you always did.'

'Liar.' She coughed long and hard. 'What do you want? I assume you haven't come here to sweep me off my feet.'

'Information.'

'On your bike, sleazeball.'

'I'll pay.' Nick produced his wallet.

'Where are you taking me?'

He took her for cocktails at a bar in Camden Town where it was Happy Hour twenty-four hours a day. 'They know me here,' said Natasha, waving at the bar staff who whispered to each other. 'We'll have my usual table.' Nick took her coat, got her settled and started pouring martinis down her throat.

'So, what can I tell you? I've known everyone. Worked with some of the best in the business.'

'It's about Rachel.'

'*Quelle surprise.*'

'And Charlie Evans.'

'I had a vague hunch it might be. Call me psychic. Well? Fire away.'

'How well did you know Charlie at college?'

'Quite well enough, thank you.'

'Meaning?'

'He was the star of his year, and I was the star of mine. I'm a year younger than him, of course, but we went to the same parties. Went about with the same people.'

'And what was he like?'

'I assume you don't want me to tell you that he was a warm and talented boy with a heart of gold.'

'Was he?'

'No.'

'Good girl. Go on.'

Natasha dived into a fresh martini. 'Well, the thing you need to know about Charlie Evans is that he was always broke. He was posher than the rest of us put together, but either his parents didn't give him any pocket money or he spent it all. He used to cadge drinks and fags off everyone, then he started borrowing, and he got a terrible reputation for not paying it back. Of course, *I* never lent him anything. I was far too smart for that. I used to tell people, "You'll never see that money again, you know, you're a fool to trust him".'

'So he got into debt?'

'Terrible debt, darling. He was so charming, you see. He could wheedle money out of anyone – students, lecturers, you name it. By the end of his second year, he owed thousands.'

'And he had to find a way of paying it off, I suppose.'

'Exactly. At first he did what anyone would do under the circumstances, and started dealing drugs.'

'Sure about that?'

'Oh, yes,' said Natasha, placing her empty glass where Nick could not fail to see it. 'Alderman's was absolutely awash with the stuff in those days, and guess where most of it came from? Charlie by name, Charlie by nature, if you know what I mean. If he wasn't dealing it, he was taking it. Cocaine Charlie we used to call him,' said Natasha, warming to her theme. 'A party simply wasn't a party without Charlie. But the trouble was he ended up sampling his own wares, and got into even worse debt than before. He was desperate. And then he had his big idea.'

'And what was that?'

'Oh, another martini? Are you sure? I shall get quite tipsy. Well, here's how.' She half-emptied the glass and toyed with her olive. 'I don't know whether I ought to be telling you this.

I mean, the drugs were common knowledge, you can ask anyone who was at Alderman's if you don't believe me.'

'I believe you.'

'But the other thing . . . Well, I mean, Charlie was a *friend* . . .'

Nick pulled a few fifty pound notes from his wallet and put them under Natasha's martini glass.

'Prostitution! There. I've said it.' She drank deeply, and put the cash in her handbag. 'Well, it made sense. I mean, he was notorious for shagging half the faculty to get into the student shows, and it was just a question of making them pay for it. That's how it began, but he turned out to be rather good at it. He started advertising on the Internet.'

'My God.'

'What do you expect him to do? Hang around Piccadilly Circus? Anyway, he was very successful. Suddenly, he had all this money, and a lot of new friends who picked him up from college in flashy cars.'

'Men or women?'

'Men, of course. Women don't pay for sex, darling. We don't need to.' She swallowed her olive and choked a bit, tears making rivers of mascara run down her face. 'He was quite shameless, you know. Used to brag about it. Some of his clients were quite famous, apparently. Politicians, pop stars, that sort of thing. I'm not one to gossip so don't ask me for any names.' She blew her nose, and glanced towards Nick's jacket pocket, where the wallet nestled. 'All that was forgotten when he got his big break in music and became the nation's sweetheart. But ask yourself – how did he get that big break, do you imagine? On the strength of his talent alone? I don't think so.'

'Thanks, Nat,' said Nick, settling the bill. 'You're a good girl.'

'There's plenty more where that came from.'

'I'm sure there is.' He slid a fat envelope across the table. 'This'll do for starters.'

'Don't you want to hear about me?'

'Another time, love. Another time.'

He left her sitting at the bar, spending her earnings.

Chris was spending most of his nights at Dev's, but had not yet completely moved out of the old Camden Town flat. On one of his rare visits, he found Mark sitting at the kitchen table, looking worried.

'What's the matter?'

'I've just had a rather peculiar conversation with someone.'

'You're always having peculiar conversations with people. Who was he?'

'An old friend of yours, as a matter of fact. Nick Sharkey.'

'What did he want?'

'Information.'

Chris had a sinking feeling. 'About what?'

'Rachel and Charlie.'

'What did you tell him?'

'To fuck off.'

'Well done.'

'Although he did mention rather a large sum of money. Which, I must say, would come in rather handy just at the moment.'

'Not like you to turn down cash.'

'How dare you,' said Mark, thinking guiltily of his spending spree in Abercrombie & Fitch. 'Anyway, I think someone ought to tell Rachel.'

'Why? What kind of questions was he asking?'

'Intimate things. Damaging things. Just before they get married. It's fishy.'

'You're telling me,' said Chris, who immediately called his sister.

'Is this anything to do with you?'

'Of course not.'

'I see. Just a coincidence that Nick's sniffing around offering large amounts of money to Rachel's old friends just a few days before their wedding.'

'And you think I told him to? Honesty, Chris, if this is the sort of thing they teach you on a media studies course . . .'

'Yes, that's just what I think. Are you going to tell me I'm wrong?'

'Think what you like.'

'Can't you let it lie? It was years ago, Elizabeth.'

'It's got nothing to do with that.'

'You know something about it, then.'

'Look, Chris, I'm a journalist. I have to do things that I don't necessarily like.'

'Using your position for personal revenge? Very professional.'

'That's not what this is about. My editor wants a story and it's up to me to get it.'

'So you use Nick, of all people?'

'Why not? He's good at his job.'

'He's got you wrapped round his finger again, hasn't he? Just like before. You were always blind when it came to him.'

'Look, Chris . . .'

'Why do you think he's doing this for you?'

'For the money, I imagine.'

'Well, at least you don't think it's for old times' sake, that's one thing. You're mad if you trust that snake. He's bitten you before.'

'I don't trust him,' said Elizabeth, hoping that Chris had not somehow found out about her sex with the ex. 'I just use him.'

'To hurt Rachel.'

'It's not about bloody Rachel!'

'You've changed, Elizabeth. I used to look up to you. Now you're just like all the others. Looking after number one.'

'If you think I'm going to listen to this . . .'

'But guess what, Liz Miller? Not everyone's like you. Mark wouldn't play ball. Told Nick to get lost.'

'He's a fool, then.'

'He was tempted all right. Nick offered him a huge sum of money. Two thousand pounds, apparently. That's a fortune to someone in Mark's position.'

'And what is Mark's position, exactly? Flat on his back as usual, I assume.'

'He's got a job in telecommunications, actually.'

'Big deal.'

'And he didn't want to have anything to do with your pathetic little plot against Rachel.'

'For God's sake, can we just drop the subject? My head is splitting.'

'All right. Let's talk about the funeral. I'm sure there's a thousand and one things to discuss. But if I discover, Elizabeth, that you've done something to sabotage Rachel's marriage, I will never speak to you again.'

'Why are you on her side? Just because she's the famous bloody actress?'

'Look, Elizabeth, you may want to live in the past, but I don't. Mum's dead, Dad's dead, what's done is done. I want to think about the future.'

'Well, bloody good luck to you,' said Elizabeth, and put the phone down.

The funeral was well attended; Professor Anthony Miller was highly regarded by his peers, colleagues and students, who turned out in force to see him buried in Hampstead Cemetery. It was a cold, clear morning as the mourners gathered at the cemetery gates, chatting about their latest papers and conferences, offering their condolences to 'the children'. Elizabeth and Chris put on a united front, and managed a smile and a few polite words with every well-wisher. Dev was at Chris's side, both of them dapper in dark suits. Elizabeth came alone.

It looked for a while as if Anna was going to do the decent thing, thought Elizabeth, and stay away from the funeral, but she was only late. As was the Prof's old friend, Uncle John, who had flown over to promote a book as well as to bury his lamented colleague and delivered an abstruse eulogy over the grave. Anna came striding across the cemetery wearing a bright red coat, a bright blue hat and huge black sunglasses, her only concession to mourning. She muscled her way to the front ranks and ostentatiously blew her nose. When it was time for the earth to be sprinkled, she produced a large bunch of lilies, which she hurled on to her late husband's coffin before swaying slightly on the grave's edge. Chris took her arm and rescued her. As the party moved away, she held on to him, leaving Dev and Elizabeth to follow awkwardly behind.

At the wake, a buffet lunch for fifty in Jack Straw's Castle, Anna stuck to the spotlight, playing the grieving widow to the hilt. 'He was taken too soon,' she told anyone who would listen. 'My Tony had so much left to give.'

Nobody dared mention the fact that her Tony had chosen not to share a bed, nor even a roof, with her for most of their married life. The question of whether or not they were still married was discreetly debated over glasses of wine and delicious canapés, to which Anna helped herself freely. After an hour or so, she was drunk.

Elizabeth kept as far away from her as possible, not trusting herself to risk a conversation.

'She's making a fool of herself,' she said to Kate, who had brought her husband and children. 'I don't know how she's got the nerve to turn up in the first place.'

'Funerals are always difficult,' said Kate, hoping to avoid any unpleasantness. 'You're doing very well.'

'Please don't tell me I'm bearing up wonderfully, like that old fart with the half-moon glasses did.'

'Now, then. He's a very famous philosopher.'

'Then you'd think he'd have something more original to say on the subject of death.'

'I'm sure he meant well.'

'Oh, Christ, look at her now.' Anna had latched herself on to Uncle John, leaning heavily on his arm. 'I hope she's not come here to find a new husband. I wouldn't put it past her.'

'That's a rotten thing to say. What have you got to be so angry about?'

'I'll tell you when the will's read.'

'Not still harping on about that.'

'If it turns out that Daddy didn't change it after all, then she gets everything.'

'This isn't the time or the place to be discussing that.'

'Oh, please,' said Elizabeth, who'd had more than enough to drink herself, 'you're as bad as Chris, always telling me what I shouldn't be doing. Someone's got to think about these things.'

'Let's cross that bridge when we come to it, shall we?'

'Shit,' said Elizabeth, rather too loud; people looked round. 'She's coming over. Please don't let her talk to me.'

'Hello, Anna,' said Kate, holding out a hand, which was grasped and tightly wrung. 'I'm so sorry.'

Anna pressed Kate's hand to her lips. 'Thank you, my darling. This isn't easy for me, you know.'

'I'm sure it's not. You're doing very well.'

Elizabeth snorted.

'Elizabeth.'

'Anna.'

'I wasn't sure that you'd be here.'

'Why ever not? I am his daughter.'

'You didn't exactly part on the best of terms, did you?'

'Meaning what, exactly, Anna?'

'Tony told me that you'd had your differences.'

'That's none of your business.'

'Excuse me, Elizabeth, but I think it's very much my business. He was my husband, you know.'

'Only because he never got round to divorcing you.'

'Elizabeth, please,' said Kate. 'People can hear.'

'I don't care. She's got a bloody nerve coming here at all, but to tell me that I didn't get on with my father is too much. For God's sake, Anna, you've hardly spoken to the man for two years.'

'That's all you know, Elizabeth. And if we had our ups and downs, whose fault is that?'

'Certainly not mine, if that's what you're implying.'

Chris and Dev were making their way across the room, responding to Kate's discreet semaphore. 'Anna,' said Dev, putting a light hand on her shoulder, 'can I get you a drink?'

She shrugged him off. 'Oh, listen to her!' said Anna. 'Miss Bloody Perfect. You've never put a foot wrong, have you? No. It's always someone else's fault. It's Rachel's fault that you couldn't keep your boyfriend. It's my fault that you didn't get on with your father, I suppose. It's your father's fault that you were an academic failure and it's your mother's fault that you're such a bloody rotten writer.'

'How dare you bring my mother into this?'

Just before things descended to the drinks-throwing,

hair-pulling stage, Chris and Dev executed a deft scissor manoeuvre that separated the two combatants, and steered them safely to opposite corners of the room, where they were plied with cakes and cups of tea and kept apart.

'Congratulations,' said Chris, when the party was over and there was no further need to be charming. 'You just couldn't get through it without making a scene.'

'I didn't do anything. It was her.'

'Have it your way, Liz Miller.'

'Don't call me that.'

'Why? That's who you are now, isn't it?'

Elizabeth went home, sobered up and called Nick. Over the course of the evening, and well into the night, he told her everything he'd discovered in the course of his research. Charlie was a coke dealer, Charlie was a rent boy, Charlie had screwed his way to the top and now, when his career was in trouble, he'd latched on to Rachel Hope in one last desperate grasp at fame.

Elizabeth started writing.

Chapter 29

Rachel and Charlie were packing up a few last boxes. It was the day before the wedding, and when they came back from their honeymoon – two weeks in Umbria paid for by *Super!* magazine in return for exclusive photo rights – they would take up residence in the four-bedroom house in Kennington, which was currently being done up by decorators. One of the bedrooms was being prepared as a nursery.

Polly joined them for coffee, as she normally did. She had become, in recent weeks, a cross between a publicist and a wedding planner.

Today, however, she did not look happy. She threw the Daily Beacon on to the breakfast table, amid half-eaten croissants and puddles of orange juice. 'They didn't even bloody warn us,' she said. 'They're not playing the game.'

'Charlie's wild years' ran the coverline, directing readers to a double-page spread on 'drugs and massage shame of Rachel's man'. In the course of 1,800 words, 'our reporters' detailed just how Toby Charles Montgomery-Evans transformed himself from a middle-class drama student into a pop idol, omitting no detail, sparing no blushes. There were photos of Charlie with various 'friends', most of them older men who had 'helped him in his career'. There were photographs of Rachel at 'theatrical parties' (snapshots from drama school knees-ups that Natasha had sold) looking a bit the worse for wear, suggesting that she, too, was part of Charlie's 'drugs ring'. In a four hundred-word sidebar, showbiz editor Liz Miller wondered whether this was the sort of man who ought to be marrying in a church, as planned, and whether he was fit to be a father. She mentioned the fact that a 'celebrity magazine' (the *Beacon* never named its rivals) was paying for the celebration, and suggested that Charlie 'still knows a good deal when he sees one'.

'They can't do that!' screamed Charlie, tearing the paper in pieces.

'How much of it's true?' asked Polly.

'Okay, I sold drugs.'

'And the other thing?'

'Look, I might have let the occasional old man have a fiddle for money . . .'

'Oh, God,' said Rachel. 'What have you done?'

'They're making out I was some kind of high-class prostitute.'

'Not so high-class, I'd say,' said Rachel. 'You bloody idiot!'

'What am I supposed to say? You're not perfect yourself.'

Before this could escalate into a deal-jeopardising row, Polly intervened. 'We've got to fight back.'

'Sue the bastards,' said Charlie.

'We can't if it's true.'

'Then what?' said Rachel. 'We can't let her get away with this. My God, I know she's a bitter old spinster, but this is taking it too far.' She picked up a scrap of paper with Liz Miller's photo staring smugly from the byline. 'My mum said she was on the warpath, but I never thought she'd do something as shitty as this.'

'What did your mum say?'

'Oh, they had a barney at the Prof's funeral. Ugly scenes at graveside, that sort of thing.'

'Right,' said Polly, already dialling. 'Leave it with me.'

* * *

Elizabeth, Chris, Anna and Kate were summoned to the solicitor's office for the reading of the will. Anna and Elizabeth were both hungover and remorseful, and kept their distance.

It was quite simple, said the solicitor. The Prof had left twenty thousand pounds to each of his children, and the residue of the estate to his wife, Anna. The will was dated shortly after their wedding.

'That's impossible,' said Elizabeth, as Chris shot daggers at her across the table. 'There must be another will.'

'No, Miss Miller,' said the solicitor, 'there is not.'

'But he was going to revise it.'

'He gave me no such instructions.'

'This is insanity. They weren't even married any more. Not really.'

'Yes we were,' said Anna, in a threatening whisper. 'Like it or not.'

'It's not his money to leave.' Elizabeth's voice was getting higher. 'Most of that money was earned by my mother. It was meant to come to us. That's what she would have wanted.'

'Your mother left her entire estate to your father,' said the solicitor, 'and we have just learned of your father's intentions.'

'This isn't over,' said Elizabeth, running from the room before she burst into tears. Chris and Kate stared at their hands while Anna blew her nose on a dainty little handkerchief, hiding a smile that she could not suppress.

'Liz.'

Mike Harris was standing at the door of his office, his face dark, his eyes flashing. 'In here, please.'

Elizabeth's eyes and nose were red, her voice hoarse; she'd been wandering around the park crying and swearing for the last hour. 'Oh, Mike, I'm sorry I'm late. The will was read this morning. It was awful.'

'Sit down, please.' He shut the door behind her without asking how she was, and stood with his back to the window. He did not look at her, but played with his trophies. 'I've had a call from Rachel Hope's publicist.'

'I thought you might. I don't suppose they're very happy.'

'Liz, who is Starpix?'

'He's . . . well, he's a stringer that I've been using.'

'He's your former fiancé, isn't he?'

'That's got nothing to do with . . . with anything.'

'Who is Anna Bates? Or should I call her Anna Miller?'

'She's my stepmother. Look, what's this about?' She knew perfectly well, but could think of no other defence but feigned ignorance.

'What was the first thing I told you when I gave you a job?'

'I know, but this is . . .'

'What was it, Liz?'

'Never let it get personal.'

'Correct. Never let it get personal. And what have you done? You've squandered *Beacon* resources, time and budget on a personal vendetta.'

'That's not true.'

He spun towards her, the fluorescent lights making his glasses flash. 'Let me finish. It made a pretty story. Almost worthy of a Liz Miller exclusive. The two old people who found love late in life and got married. Their two daughters who became such good friends – real sisters. So far, so Brady Bunch. But then it all went wrong.'

'Mike, please . . .'

He held up a hand. 'The younger sister stole her older step-sister's fiancé. Ran off with him on the eve of the wedding, then dumped him as soon as she got successful. And the older sister never forgave her. For two years she brooded on the injustice of it all. She put herself in a position where she could get revenge, and from the moment she had access to the media she began a campaign of harassment. First of all she attacked her stepsister's relationship with another actor by saying he was gay.'

'Alan Southgate *is* gay.'

'But when that didn't work, she waited until her stepsister was about to be married, and expecting a baby. And what do you know? Enter the old fiancé, also with an axe to grind. And between them, they cook up this nasty little story.' He tapped a copy of the paper, open on his desk. 'They make sure there's just enough fact in there to prevent anyone from suing. They time it to inflict maximum damage, knowing that the editor of the *Beacon* will swallow it because she's keeping him sweet in bed. And then they run off sniggering into the sunset together. Is that how the story ends, Liz? You're the big literature expert. You tell me.'

'No,' she said. 'That's not how it is at all.'

'You deny that you and this Starpix – what's his name?' He referred to his notepad. 'Nick Sharkey. You and this Sharkey have been engaged in a personal vendetta against Rachel Hope?'

'You asked me for the story. I gave you what you wanted.'

'Very clever, Miss Miller. Blame the boss. Yes, I asked you for it. Of course I did. The little bitch went and blabbed to the *Comet* when, if you'd been a proper showbiz editor, she would have come to us. I was angry. I wanted to hit back.'

'So did I.'

'But she's not my fucking stepsister.'

Elizabeth could think of nothing to say.

'I spoke to your friend Sharkey this morning,' said Mike. 'He was good enough to call me – hoping for congratulations. This was before I knew who he was. Did you know he'd been in touch?'

'No.'

'Right. I did wonder. And do you know what he offered me?'

'No.'

'Seeing as we'd done such a great number on Charlie Evans, as he put it, he wondered if I might like a bit of an exclusive on Rachel, for tomorrow's paper. For the morning of the wedding. Good timing, he said it would be.'

'What was it? Kiss and tell?'

'Oh, it was a bit more than that, Liz.' Mike clicked on his computer, and pushed the screen round. There were four photographs – grainy black and white, but instantly recognisable – of Rachel Hope taking it from every conceivable angle from a man on a bed. The man's head was cropped off, but Elizabeth had no difficulty in recognising the body.

And she had no difficulty in recognising the bed. Her bed. What should have been the marital bed.

'Oh, God.'

'Seen these before?'

'No. I swear I haven't.'

Mike frowned. 'You'd better get out, Liz, before I say something I might regret. Take the rest of the week off. You look like you need it.' He took off his glasses and rubbed his eyes. There was a look of regret, of compassion even, in those tired eyes. Then he put his glasses back on.

'I'm sorry,' said Elizabeth, leaving the office, but Mike was already talking on the telephone.

The next morning, the *Daily Comet* printed a small story, near the bottom of the showbiz pages, mentioning the fact that Rachel Hope and Charlie Evans were tying the knot today at a village church in Suffolk. Nothing was said about Charlie's interesting past – nor was there any mention of the fact that *Super!*

magazine would carry the exclusive wedding photos later in the week. *Super!* was suddenly having second thoughts.

Meanwhile in the *Daily Reporter*, a newspaper that wasn't shy about nipples and was largely funded by ads for sex chat lines, the front page promised 'Sizzling Sex Pics of Rachel's Raunchy Romp!', guiding eager readers to a hastily assembled page of photographs of the actress working her way through every position in *The Joy of Sex*. The accompanying copy had a jaunty tone, saying that 'Charlie Evans is a lucky lad' and mentioning 'uncensored footage' that might yet see the light of day. It didn't actually claim that Rachel had appeared in porn films. It didn't need to. The readers of this particular paper paid much more attention to pictures than to words.

Nick pocketed the money – it wasn't as much as he'd hoped to get from the *Beacon*, but it was better than nothing – and told the *Reporter*'s editor that there was plenty more where that came from. He mentioned a few famous names that he'd met during his years with Rachel, and said he could deliver photos and stories pretty much to order. The editor said yes, please, and talked about putting Starpix on a retainer.

Knowing that Elizabeth would probably not want to speak to him, he did not bother trying to call her.

Rachel and Charlie's wedding, in that pretty little village church in rural Suffolk, turned out to be a much quieter affair than expected. The *Comet* group duly sent a photographer – just one – in order to fulfil their side of the contract. Rachel and Charlie turned up, posed and smiled, got married, posed and smiled some more, to fulfil theirs. Nobody wanted to be sued. A few reporters hung around, hoping for fights and tears, and attempted to ask impertinent questions as the happy couple came in and out of the church, but Rachel and Charlie carried on smiling, and said nothing.

Instead of returning to the new house in Kennington, which was already surrounded by reporters on the scent of a showbiz scandal, they were driven to a large house just off the Finchley Road. Anna had moved into the Prof's old house the minute the will was read, and was more than happy to offer them refuge.

A week later, Elizabeth visited the old family home to collect a few of her belongings. On Kate's advice, she was in a conciliatory mood; nothing was to be gained by another row.

Anna, however, felt differently.

'You've got a bloody nerve coming here after what you've done to my daughter.' She stood on the doorstep, her arms crossed, her feet planted firmly apart.

'Please can I come in, Anna? I just want to pick a few things up.'

'Why should I let you?' Anna did not budge. 'There's nothing for you here.'

'There are things that belong to me.' Elizabeth stepped to one side, Anna mirrored her.

'Perhaps you should have thought of that before you screwed up my daughter's marriage, you cold-hearted bitch.'

'Look, Anna,' said Elizabeth, trying to keep her voice even. 'I just want what's mine.' There were personal things – family photograph albums, diaries, mementos of her mother and her childhood.

'Take it up with you solicitor.'

'Anna, please . . .'

'Tony said you were a selfish cow, but I never thought you'd stoop as low as this.'

Elizabeth felt desperately tired. 'What do you mean?'

'The rest of your family may pretend it never happened. You're very good at that, you Millers. But I know your game. You've never forgiven Rachel. Well, I won't have it. This is my house now, not yours. And you may have been able to pull the wool over your father's eyes, but you can't fool me.'

'I want my things, Anna. Please don't try and stop me.' Elizabeth put a foot over the threshold, and Anna pushed her back.

'Don't you dare.'

'I didn't come here for a fight.'

'Tough luck. You got one. Now leave us alone.'

'You haven't heard the last of this, Anna. I shall get my solicitor on to you.'

'Go ahead! Contest the will! Tony said you'd do something like that. I didn't believe him. More fool me.'

'That's not true. I'll take you to court.'

'I bet you will. That's just your style, isn't it? Solicitors letters and nasty little pieces in your filthy rag of a newspaper. But that's not how I do things. Now get away from my house before I kick your scrawny arse halfway down the street.'

'Your house?' shouted Elizabeth, backing away. 'It's not your house, and it never will be.' Anna slammed the door. 'Probate hasn't been granted yet! You won't get away with this!'

She ran to the street, tears blurring her vision, and looked back at the house – her house, her father's house, her mother's house. In an upstairs window – the room where Susan Barnard had written her novels – she saw a curtain moving, and the silhouette of a face.

It was the first time Elizabeth had laid eyes on Rachel for over two years. She turned and ran to the tube station, empty-handed.

Chapter 30

Things moved fast after the wedding.

Elizabeth learned that a really exciting opportunity had arisen on the *Beacon*'s 'special projects' team, developing a free celebrity magazine that had long been on the publisher's wish-list, and they wanted her to edit the dummy. Mike pitched it to her as kindly as he could, softening the blow with all sorts of stuff about how the publisher had asked for her specially, how it was a great chance to move into new areas and develop her editorial portfolio. He also made it quite clear that she wasn't being offered a choice in the matter. He was 'taking the showbiz pages in a new direction' and putting them in the care of the features editor, a 'safe pair of hands' who would steer them through these 'difficult economic times'. And if she didn't take the special projects job? Well, he would have to talk to human resources, but off the top of his head, he didn't think she'd been working for the paper long enough to qualify for any sort of redundancy payment.

Take it, or leave.

For once, Elizabeth did not answer right away. She asked for twenty-four hours in which to think things over, and Mike agreed. He couldn't give her longer than that. The publisher, she must understand, was very keen to get the special project underway.

Meanwhile, Rachel called up the *Corpse Army* producers in Los Angeles for some legal advice. She had been, she said, the victim of a gross invasion of privacy by the *Daily Reporter*, and had every intention of suing them. The *Corpse Army* lawyers, far from sharing her righteous indignation, informed her that pre-release sales of the DVD had spiked massively in the UK, and they were seeing a similar pattern in other territories as the nude photos were syndicated around the world. The movie's theatrical release, which was originally going to be a modest hors d'oeuvres to the DVD main course, had now been extended to national circuits. They reckoned that they might recoup from cinemas alone; anything else would be profit.

This was some comfort, but Rachel was far from happy about her sudden, unwanted career as a porn star, particularly when the photographs in question were taken without her knowledge or consent. She consulted a lawyer in London, who advised her that while she might make an application under article 8 of the European Convention on Human Rights, which guarantees a right to respect for privacy and family life, she probably didn't have a leg to stand on given that her entire career was based on romping in front of the cameras wearing little more than a pair of high heels or a leather catsuit. He was, however, perfectly willing to give it a go. And then he gave her an idea of how much it might cost.

Corpse Army would have to sell an awful lot of DVDs to make that worthwhile – and, with a baby on the way and a husband whose earning capacity seemed to be diminishing with every passing month, Rachel decided to put the whole ghastly episode behind her and face her new-found fame with all the equanimity she could muster.

Nick made a tidy sum out of those pictures. Starpix retained the rights, and sold them all over the world, charging more with every sale. With the movie on the way, editors in America were starting to take an interest, and he made one last deal with a glossy glamour magazine for a substantial six-figure sum. This enabled him to buy a flat, set himself up with some decent photographic equipment and start promoting Starpix as a legitimate photographic business. He charmed picture editors and PRs, and soon found himself on every guest list. Six months after Mike Harris turned down his kind offer of exclusive nude Rachel Hope photos, Nick Sharkey had become the thing he always wanted to be – a celebrity photographer. Money rolled in, as did women, and for a long time he forgot about Elizabeth and Rachel, the two people who had made it all possible.

For the first time in her life, Elizabeth had nobody to think of but herself. She was single: Mike had made it quite clear that she was out of his bed, as well as out of a job, and once she discovered that Nick had tried to go above her head with the Rachel Hope shots, and had brought the whole house of cards down in the process, she was determined never to speak to him again. She was an orphan, and no longer had to wonder whether her mother or father would approve of what she was doing. She had left the university behind long ago, and so her academic standing and the opinion of colleagues like Charlotte were matters of complete indifference. Chris wasn't speaking to her. She barely even had any friends. Kate was just a phone call away, if she needed her – but Kate had told her exactly what she thought of Elizabeth's behaviour over the will, and that kind of disapproval was something Elizabeth could do without.

So she found herself making the biggest decision of her adult life absolutely alone. She had twenty-four hours in which to come up with an answer. Swallow her medicine like a good girl, serve out her time in special projects with quiet dignity and then, if she was lucky, start again at the bottom of the *Beacon*'s editorial ladder, while her replacement got the picture byline and the party invitations? Or tell Mike Harris to shove his special project where the sun don't shine, scrape together the most impressive CV she could and sell herself to the highest bidder?

Her parents, if they'd deigned to consider such a grubby question at all, would have counselled caution. Nick would have told her to do whatever guaranteed a good level of income. Kate would say that she should learn by her mistakes, work hard and concentrate on her writing. Mike – well, Mike was the only one who might have told her what she wanted to hear, and he was the very last person who was in a position to say it.

Elizabeth was sick of being sensible and good. She was bored of being the responsible provider. She had twenty thousand pounds coming from her father's will – not exactly the fortune she'd been hoping for, but enough to live on for a little while, if push came to shove. And she still hoped to get more: in the fallout from the funeral, and her unpleasant doorstep confrontation with Anna, she had engaged a lawyer to contest the will on the grounds that it was no longer a true expression of the Prof's intentions, that he had been 'persuaded' by Anna not to make a new will. The bulk of the estate came from her mother – and her mother's will had specifically stated that, if the Prof died, everything would be divided between the children. The lawyer warned Elizabeth that the chances of cancelling the Prof's will were slim, but as far as Elizabeth was concerned, it was a chance worth taking.

But with her money fast being eaten up by legal fees, Elizabeth needed a job. She weighed her desire to storm out of the *Beacon* against her need to contest her father's will, and spent a sleepless night tossing and turning between the two.

And then, to her astonishment, she received a phone call from the editor of the *Daily Comet*, the *Beacon*'s number-one rival, the paper that had stolen the Rachel-and-Charlie scoop from under her nose and led to her current precarious position. They had heard on the grapevine, said the editor, that Mike Harris was putting her out to pasture. Taking her off the paper. Could that possibly be true?

This was no time for prevarication. Elizabeth said yes, it was true.

And what was she going to do?

That rather depended, said Elizabeth, on what came up in the meantime.

The editor rather hoped she might say that, because his showbiz editor was going on maternity leave. He asked Elizabeth out for lunch.

Later that afternoon, after a couple of bottles of very expensive Vouvray, Elizabeth took a cab back to the Daily Beacon, walked into Mike's office, where he was in conference with the head of HR, and told them both that she had made her decision.

She started at the *Comet* on the following Monday.

Six months into their marriage, Rachel and Charlie were sitting in the living room of the four-bedroom house in Kennington, into which they had finally moved when interest in Rachel's naked past had waned and photographers were no longing camping on the pavement. They had eaten some grilled chicken, which Charlie had cooked; he had also done the washing-up. Now they were sprawled out on the sofa watching a DVD of *The Family Guy*, laughing hysterically, wondering if they dared call their firstborn Stewie if it was a boy, while Charlie massaged Rachel's sore feet. She was within a few weeks of her due date, but the baby's head was engaged and, according to the midwife, 'it could happen any time'.

Things, thought Rachel, were really not too bad. Elizabeth and Nick had done their worst, and she'd survived. If anything, they'd done her a favour. She was much more famous now than *Corpse Army* alone could ever have made her, and offers were pouring in. For now, her agent had put everything on hold until the baby was born, but then she'd have her pick of the crop. First up was a sequel to *Corpse Army*, just as soon as she'd got her body back into shape, and this time round she'd be paid a great deal more to leap around in that leather catsuit delivering knockout kickboxing blows to flesh-eating zombies. This was just as well, as Charlie still had not cracked it; the 'mature' second album was stalled after an army of producers and remixers had failed to come up with something that the record company was prepared to release, and while he still made a bit of money from gigs, it looked as if he was in line for the househusband role. He seemed quite happy with this. He loved children, he said, and would be perfectly happy changing nappies while Rachel went out to work.

Perhaps, after all, the affair that started at a pool party some-where in the Hollywood Hills – they could still not figure out exactly whose party it had been, or for what – had survived, despite the best efforts of the press, the treachery of former friends who had sold their stories for a handful of coins and the cold, implacable hatred of Elizabeth Miller who would have hounded them into the divorce courts given half a chance. They had Polly Hamlin to thank for rescuing them from that bitch's clutches: Polly had gone straight to Mike Harris, told him that Elizabeth was using his paper to pursue her own personal revenge and had offered to drop any talk of a libel action provided Elizabeth was taken off the showbiz pages and put somewhere she could do no harm.

Fair play to Elizabeth: she hadn't taken it lying down, she'd defected to the *Comet* and was now spreading her poisonous views on everything from drugs to gay marriage in a regular column that was somewhere to the right of the Vatican. But, Rachel noticed with some satisfaction, she was very careful never to mention the names Rachel Hope and Charlie Evans. Perhaps she'd learned her lesson.

They were so grateful to Polly Hamlin that they'd asked her to be a godparent. She'd accepted with great pleasure, as had their other first choice, Chris Miller – who would, after all, be the baby's uncle.

Rachel was finding it hard to get comfortable, and Charlie's massage was starting to get on her nerves. Her stomach was painful, her back was aching and she was feeling rather sick. At first she wondered if there had been something wrong with the chicken – Charlie tended to have a heavy hand on the chilli – but then her waters broke, and her contractions began.

Charlie called the midwife, called the hospital, fetched a ready-packed bag and got his wife to the car.

'Kate, it's Elizabeth.'

'Oh, hi. Just a minute.' Elizabeth could hear children's voices squealing and gabbling in the background, Kate telling them to pipe down while Mummy was on the phone. 'Sorry about that, darling. How are you?'

'Fine, thanks. Well, not so great, really. I've had some news.'

'Oh dear.' Kate went through a quick mental checklist of all the things that could possibly have gone wrong. 'What is it?' She stopped herself from saying 'this time'.

'They've granted probate. The will has gone through.'

'Ah.' I told you so. 'Well, that's that, then.'

'It's wrong, Kate. It's all wrong.'

'I'm sorry, Elizabeth, but that's what Tony wanted. I know it's hard to accept, but he made his will and you have to respect that.'

'It's not what my mother wanted.'

'I'm afraid that's got nothing to do with it.'

'How can you say that? You were her friend. Her literary executor.'

'I still am.'

'And can you honestly tell me that you'll continue to manage the estate if the money is going to . . . that woman?'

'If you'd rather I didn't . . .'

'I'd much rather you didn't.'

'We can place it entirely in the hands of the agent. They're perfectly competent.'

'That won't change anything.'

'What would you suggest, Elizabeth?'

'We must do something.'

'You've done everything you can. You've spent a fortune on legal fees, against everyone's advice, trying to contest a will that you knew was absolutely watertight. If I had the time and the money, I'd sue that bloody lawyer for taking a case he knew he couldn't win. He's the only person who's making any money out of this.'

'Apart from Anna.'

'She was his wife, darling.'

'For about a week. My God. What was he thinking, changing his will like that?'

'He loved her.'

'But they didn't live together! They barely spoke!'

'We don't know how he felt, do we? But the fact that he never changed his will suggests that . . . well . . .'

'What?'

'That he wanted her to have the money.'

'Her, and not his own children?'

'Yes, if you must put it like that.'

'I will never accept it, Kate.'

'No,' said Kate. 'I don't suppose you will. But you must make your peace with it. It's high time you let go of the past and thought about your future. You're not . . .' The children were fighting in the background. 'Hang on. Will you give that back immediately! No! I don't care! Right now! Thank you. Sorry, Liz. It's mayhem here.'

'I'll let you get on. I can hear that you're busy.'

'No, it's okay. I think we need to talk this through.'

'Don't worry,' said Elizabeth. 'I'll work it out for myself.' She put down the phone.

Kate worried about Elizabeth: she's unhappy and unloved, she's going to end up lonely and bitter by the time she's thirty. But then the children demanded her attention, and she quickly forgot all about it.

Labour was long and excruciatingly painful, but after thirty-six hours of unmitigated hell, Rachel gave birth to a little girl, whom she named Sasha.

When Chris went to see his new goddaughter, he found mother, baby, father and grandmother all doing very well indeed. Anna was a little frosty at first, but even she melted in the heat of love surrounding the hospital bed.

'When are you going home?'

'As soon as the doctor's happy with me. I'm stitched up like a kipper down there,' said Rachel, pointing along the bed. Chris and Charlie winced.

'Oh, you men,' said Anna, 'you're so squeamish. When Rachel was born, I was . . .'

'Thank you, Mum,' said Rachel. 'We don't want anyone fainting. How are you, Chris? It's sweet of you to come.'

'I'm fine. Leaving college soon.'

'Of course. And what will you be doing then?'

'Looking for a job in TV, I suppose.'

Rachel grimaced. 'Rather you than me, darling.'

'Something will come up. In the meantime, Dev has an awful lot of shirts that need ironing.'

'Have you moved in?'

'Yes. Finally. I took the last few bits of my stuff out of the old flat last month.'

'Were they sorry to see you go?'

'Hard to tell. Mark's out every night. I don't think Natasha knows who I am most of the time.'

Rachel shuddered. 'You're well out of it, Chris. Would you like to hold her?'

She placed the tiny child in Chris's arms, and lay back on the pillow.

'She's beautiful, Rachel,' said Chris, his voice choked.

Neither of them mentioned Elizabeth.

Now that probate was granted, and there was nothing that Elizabeth could do short of burglary, Anna allowed Chris to arrange the collection of a few personal items from the Miller house. Elizabeth sat in the car while Chris rang the doorbell.

'You've got three hours,' said Anna, handing him the keys and pulling on her gloves. 'I'll be back about six. Please make sure you're gone by then.'

'Don't worry,' said Chris, 'we will be.'

'And by the way,' said Anna, walking down the drive, in a voice loud enough to reach Elizabeth's ears, 'the solicitors have a full inventory of everything that's in the house.'

'Fucking bitch,' said Elizabeth, once Anna was safely out of earshot. 'Does she think we mean to steal from her? I only want what's mine.'

But Chris wasn't listening. He was already halfway up the stairs. The room that had once been his was tidy and empty, the bed stripped, a few cardboard boxes neatly stacked in the middle of the floor. Anna had wasted very little time. There wasn't much that he really cared about – a few books and records, some clothes, some old letters. Most of it would go to charity shops, and the rest of it would be burned. He had no particular desire to remember this childhood. He carried the boxes downstairs, and loaded them into the car.

Elizabeth walked around the house, her hands trailing along familiar surfaces, her eyes searching for objects – a clock, a painting, a bookshelf – that had been there all her life, now missing. This would be her last time in the house. How could she simply leave – tear herself up by the roots – shake off the past and forget?

The Prof's study was at the back of the house on the ground floor, three windows on to the garden that made it freezing in winter, boiling in summer, the desk always covered in papers yellowed by the sun and cockled by the damp. It was here that she would find the diaries and photograph albums that documented their childhood.

The room was empty, the books and papers gone, just the desk remaining, the surface bare, dusty, nothing left but a few dead flies and flakes of paint.

Elizabeth ran from room to room, opening cupboards and drawers, ransacking shelves, looking for the traces of a childhood, a family, that seemed as insubstantial as the cobwebs that hung from the ceilings.

She thundered up the stairs to her bedroom, where she had cried her heart out for the death of her hopes, years ago when Nick and Rachel had stolen love and happiness and a future from her, and left her with ice in her heart.

Again, a few cardboard boxes, her personal possessions stacked neatly for collection.

They had stolen her future, and now they had destroyed her past.

She ran out of the house as if pursued. Chris was waiting in the car. They barely spoke as they drove away.

Mark spent very little time at the old flat these days. When he wasn't at work, he preferred to sleep with one of his several boyfriends. It was easier than coming home. For one thing, you were not likely to be woken up by a drunken flatmate in the small hours of the morning, crawling home from God knows where, rambling about a fight she'd got into with God knows who, sometimes bruised or even bleeding if she'd got a bit too handy with her fists.

He went back every few days to pick up clothes and records; bit by bit, he was moving house.

He turned up one day to find a police officer standing outside the door.

'Have we been burgled?' he asked. He hoped to God it wasn't a drug bust.

It was neither. Natasha had used the last of the money she'd got for selling Charlie and Rachel to the Daily Beacon to go out shopping, which in her case meant taking a trolley round a supermarket and stocking up on premium brand spirits. She'd spent two days inventing new cocktails, dancing ever more wildly to her beloved Bob Fosse musical soundtracks, before succumbing to acute alcohol poisoning and choking to death on her own vomit.

It was twenty-four hours before a neighbour realised that 'All that Jazz' was still stuck on repeat, and called the cops.

This Year

Chapter 31

'Alan Southgate? You have to be joking.'

'No, I'm not. His people are talking to your people.'

'In other words, you.'

'Yes.' Chris put down the clipboard on Elizabeth's desk and folded his arms. 'Well? Are you going to say anything? Why are you smiling like that?'

'I was just thinking what a difference success makes,' said Elizabeth. 'Now that he's desperate for publicity, he's forgiven me.'

'I don't think Alan's the sort to bear grudges.'

Elizabeth snorted. 'Rubbish. He wouldn't have anything to do with me if I didn't just happen to have my own extremely successful chat show.'

'So what shall I say?' Being an assistant director on the Liz Miller Show was a good gig, and Chris was grateful, but he had to put up with an awful lot of attitude.

'Tell them we're thinking about it. Let him stew a bit. His latest effort is flopping badly in America, and he's hoping to get a following in the UK. Let's see him beg.'

Elizabeth picked up a hand mirror and surveyed her face. She was looking good: thinner, more beautiful and much better groomed than she had ever been before. Her face, which at best would have been called 'pleasant' in her early twenties, had matured into something strong and commanding – and the camera loved her. Her hair was now cut and coloured by the best stylists money could buy, and her make-up was done by experts. Her wardrobe, which at the age of twenty-three had looked mumsy, was carefully chosen these days from designers who could accentuate her narrow waist, her long legs and her large bust. The academic ugly duckling had metamorphosed into a TV chat show swan – and all because she'd walked out of a dead-end job at the Daily Beacon. It was worth getting up at the crack of dawn, spending all day in meetings before doing the show at 5 p.m., then spending the evening at parties and functions. It was worth fitting in pilates classes three times a week. It was worth watching every mouthful she ate, every glass of wine she drank. People talk about how hard it is raising children, thought Elizabeth; they should try a career in television.

'How do I look?'

'Honestly?'

'Depends.'

'You look fine.'

'Liar. I look exhausted.' She put the mirror down and rubbed her eyes. She didn't sleep well, and needed all the skills of the make-up department to get her looking fresh and fragrant on screen. The mornings could be tough. If they put me in front of a camera now, she thought, the viewers would switch off in terror. Strange, given that Liz Miller's stock in trade was the tough question, the stern moral line, that she still had to look flawless. It would be so much easier if she could just go on looking like a hag. But no: even mean people had to be gorgeous, however much effort it took. After two years, the strain was starting to tell – but when Elizabeth looked at her end-of-year accounts, it all seemed worthwhile. She earned more in a week than she could have done in a year of journalism or a decade in academia.

'Well, now,' she said. 'What are we giving them tonight?'

'The mother who rescued her daughter from Facebook paedophiles.'

'Is she going to behave?'

'She'll be fine. Then there's the guy off *The X Factor*.'

'Oh, the one who . . .'

'Yes. That should be fun.'

'And the headliner?'

'John Barrowman promoting his new record.'

'Another one?'

'Be nice. He always gets good ratings.'

'Business as usual. What's in the diary for tonight?'

'I'm an assistant director, Liz, not your PA.'

'All right. Keep your hair on. What's left of it.'

Chris ran a hand over his number-two crop; the luxuriant blond curls of his teens were long gone, and after a few years of post-modern combovers, he'd finally succumbed to the inevitable, and gone to a proper barber. Oh, well; Dev liked it, and that was all that really mattered. Dev couldn't keep his hands off it.

'I think you're doing something for Children in Need. Don't make that face.'

'Charity. I bloody hate charity. No wonder I don't have a love life. I never get a minute to myself.'

'And whose fault is that? You say yes to everything.'

'Well, I might as well be busy. There's no point in sitting at home with a microwave meal for one, watching television.' She wrinkled her nose. 'I hate television as well, actually.'

'Have it your way,' said Chris, who had been around this circular track more times than he cared to remember. 'Perhaps you'll meet someone nice at the event tonight.'

'Men never come near me. They're frightened of me.'

Chris held his tongue; after all, she paid his wages.

'Oh, well,' she said. 'That's the price of success, I suppose.'

'In your book, you said it was worth it,' said Chris. 'You said a woman didn't need a man if she loved her job.'

'Quite right, too. Thank you so much for reminding me. Well, those books have made us a great deal of money.' She stressed *us*. 'If people want to buy that sort of reassurance, then I'm perfectly happy to dish it out.'

'Even if you don't believe it yourself?'

'That'll be all, Chris. Give me the half-hour call.' She dismissed him, like she would dismiss any other employee. Nepotism may have got Chris the job, but the favours stopped right there.

Elizabeth leaned back in her chair, folded her hands on her stomach and closed her eyes. She needed these quiet moments more and more, ten or twenty minutes when nobody was speaking, no phones were ringing, no cameras running. She told people that she was meditating, and they believed her; her agent had already suggested a book about the power of meditation, if she could get someone else to do the research. In fact, all she really craved was silence and solitude. Not the roaring silence, the marked solitude of her bed at night, when she appreciated neither of those things, but a little oasis of peace in the daytime. At night, thoughts crowded into her head, like solicitous colleagues and fans, all wanting something from her. Now, if she concentrated, she could clear her mind completely.

But not today.

Alan Southgate, indeed. What a bloody nerve. After all these years, thinking he can just show up and promote some under-performing TV hospital drama – a *hospital drama*, really, in this day and age! – and tout for work in the UK. He'd been eager enough to shake the dust of England from his shoes when Hollywood wanted him. But now he was no longer the suave young Brit in town, now the crags and bags could no longer just be passed off as 'ruggedness', he came crawling back to good old Elizabeth, thinking, no doubt, that he'd be doing her a favour by appearing on *The Liz Miller Show*. Well, she thought, if anyone is doing favours, it ain't Alan Southgate.

She had never said out loud, 'I'm bigger than the stars that come on the show', but it was getting that way. A lot had happened in the last three years. Maternity cover on the showbiz desk of the *Daily Comet* led to work on the features pages where, in a series of breathtakingly indiscreet but legally water-tight celebrity profiles, she put the name Liz Miller back at the top of the page where it belonged. From the *Comet* she moved to the *Express*, and from the *Express* to the *Mail*, where Liz Miller became one of the most feared writers in the business. Celebrities queued up to be excoriated in public, knowing that Liz Miller would only do them if they were willing to confess to some humiliating weakness. It quickly became apparent that readers were interested in Liz Miller, the star around which these lesser satellites orbited. Her opinion became the voice of 'the people'. And so it was only a matter of time before television executives came sniffing around.

A late-night pilot, in which she reduced a notoriously philandering actor to tears of contrition, became the channel's most-viewed online clip; Liz's new agent quickly got her a gig on terrestrial teatime. And there, five times a week for the last two years, *The Liz Miller Show* had flourished. Viewers applauded her as a lone voice of decency and reason in an increasingly immoral showbiz world. As peers crashed and burned, victims of ill-advised on-air pranks, tasteless jokes or drug hells, Liz Miller never put a foot wrong. Broadcasters and viewers trusted her. When the broadsheets derided her as a neo-Thatcherite, Middle-England authority figure, she knew that her future was secure.

Since then there had been advertising offers (which she turned down), charity work (which she accepted) and book deals. She liked the book deals. They connected her, in some way, to the distant past, when she lived through literature. Okay, titles such as *Single Success* and *Work Comes First!* were not exactly what she'd done her PhD for, but they sold like hot cakes. There was talk of a novel. Her agent was keen, and had offered the services of a ghost, which Elizabeth furiously declined. If she were going to do it, she'd do it herself. She'd find the time. She was already working sixteen-hour days – but what the hell, there had to be some advantages to chronic insomnia. She'd write it at night. It might be therapeutic. At the very least, it might be soporific.

She'd sketched out a rough plot about a young woman who's set a course for marriage, domestic bliss and motherhood only to discover that her fiancé is a faithless bastard, her best friend a treacherous bitch, that she can only rely on herself and, by doing so, be rewarded by a fabulous career. This wouldn't be a delicate psychological study. Gorgeous women would triumph over loathsome men, and the heroine would reduce her repentant fiancé to a snivelling wreck. I pity you, she would say, but I can never love you. Goodbye.

It would be better than life.

There was a tap at the door. 'Half-hour, Liz,' said Chris.

She sighed. 'I wish you wouldn't call me that.' If only he would be a brother for once, rather than an employee. But this was work, and work was what she paid him for.

'They're ready for you in make-up. Do you want me to go over the schedule again?'

'I think I can probably manage, thanks very much,' she said, sounding more bitter than she meant to. Chris just shrugged; he was well past being hurt by her now. He'd unload it all on to Dev tonight – Dev, who listened to everything, sympathised and soothed it all away. Dev, who had talked him out of resigning a dozen times. Dev, who was not only a great lover, but also a great cook, a great host, a great handyman, and had his own well-paid job, mercifully nothing to do with television. If Chris really couldn't stand it any more, Dev would provide.

'Jan's waiting to see you.'

'Oh, Christ.' Jan was her agent, the person responsible for the last two or three noughts on the end of Elizabeth's end-of-year accounts. 'What does she want?'

'To make you more money, probably,' said Chris. 'It must be a terrible burden to you.'

She sat in the make-up chair, the small, cool sponges running over her face, smoothing away the shadows, soothing the fatigue, editing her for public consumption.

'Close your eyes, please, Liz.' Dab, dab, dab went the sponge around the eyelids, the browbone.

'I need a title for this novel,' said Jan, a ferocious little brunette with no discernible waistline. 'At least give me that.'

'How can I give you the title before I've written a word of the bloody book?'

'Liz,' said Jan, as if she was talking to a slow child, 'we could print anything on the pages as long as it's got a snappy title and your name on the cover. So please, just give me something. Anything.'

'Like what?'

'I don't know. What's your favourite novel of all time?'

Once, thought Elizabeth, I would have said *Madame Bovary*. 'I don't have time to read novels.'

'Well I hope you have time to write them,' said Jan. 'Just give me a clue, darling. Come on. What's it about? Anything?'

It's about me, thought Elizabeth, and the bastards who have done me wrong. 'Basically,' she said, 'it's about personal integrity and the survival of the human spirit.'

'Christ,' said Jan. 'You'll have to do better than that.'

'Okay,' said Elizabeth, thinking about Rachel and Nick and Alan and everyone else she'd leapfrogged. 'It's about how success is the best revenge.'

Jan tapped her pen against her teeth. 'Right,' she said, and made a note. '*The Best Revenge*. That will do nicely.'

Elizabeth pressed her lips against a piece of tissue paper, threw it in the bin and got out of the chair. 'Can I go now?' she said. 'Show to do, you know.'

She submitted herself to the sound people, who threaded the microphone lead through her suit.

'Ready?' asked Chris. 'Ready.'

'Don't suppose you've had time to think about Alan Southgate?'

The floor manager was counting down; a minute till they were on air.

'No, I haven't. Why are you so keen, anyway? Hoping for a reunion?'

'He's an old friend.'

'Let's just keep it that way for now, shall we?' said Elizabeth. 'Remember: he needs us more than we need him.'

'Thirty seconds,' said the floor manager.

Elizabeth closed her eyes. Chris watched her face, the subtle, familiar transformation from Elizabeth to Liz.

'Ten, nine, eight . . .'

She opened her eyes; the pupils were large and dark. 'I'm ready.' The brows came down in her trademark frown.

They were on air.

Chapter 32

The phone rang, waking Rachel from a sleep far deeper than she ever got at night, a sleep without dreams, a sleep like death. She woke with a jolt, her heart racing, her face crumpled from the cushions she'd been leaning against, now damp with saliva. What time was it? She looked at the clock. Three fifteen. Thank God, she hadn't missed picking Sasha up from playgroup. The phone was still ringing, louder and louder. Where the hell was it? She picked her way across the carpet, a minefield of hard, brightly coloured plastic toys, towards the ringtone. On the TV stand? No, not there. On the windowsill? Not there, either. Where was the bloody thing? She swept a pile of cuddly toys off a beanbag and there was her phone, where Ella, who was now crawling, had hidden it. Just as Rachel reached out her hand, it stopped ringing.

Shit, she thought, and then said it out loud, because it made her feel better. It might have been her agent. It might have been some work, and God knows she couldn't afford to miss calls like that.

'Come on, come on, come on,' she said, waiting for the beeps that would tell her if someone had left a message. They finally came, and she pounced on the buttons.

It was not her agent. It was only Charlie, telling her – again – that he wouldn't be home for dinner, might not even be home tonight, the gig was going on later than they'd expected. 'Surprise surprise,' she said, throwing the phone back down on the bean-bag, where it collided with a grubby green plush frog. Charlie's gigs these days tended to be in-store appearances, or PAs at exhibitions – anywhere that a bit of noughties nostalgia was in demand. Charlie didn't see it like that, of course; as far as he was concerned, he was just making ends meet while he planned his big comeback. But Rachel knew all too well that Charlie's only remaining audience were no-longer-young women who escaped from the drudgery of family life by remembering their carefree youth. Okay, Charlie wasn't quite the bright-eyed, priapic boy-next-door he'd once been, but he brought back memories of a happier time for women whose waistlines were now bigger than their busts.

Rachel bent down and started picking up toys, throwing them into a bin bag. She pushed her hair out of her eyes, and tied it back with a scrunchy. Her hair was dirty, and needed washing, but there was no time; she had to wake Ella from her nap, get her into her coat and into the car and be at playgroup in ten minutes, ready to collect Sasha with all the other mothers. She'd been late too many times, finding Sasha alone, peering through the security fence, anxious teachers hovering. They made allowances for Rachel Hope, of course, and admired her for giving up her career to look after her kids. But that was no excuse for being late.

That was the official line: she'd stopped working so she could concentrate on the 'best job in the world', being a full-time mother. Nobody could argue with that. But the strange thing was that it was the truth. Oh, the phone may have stopped ringing before Ella was born. And she'd turned down so many jobs that, finally, her agent stopped putting her up for things. But the sequel to *Corpse Army* was duly made. Only when Rachel got pregnant for the second time shortly after filming was completed, she discovered she didn't have the heart to sit in trailers and dressing rooms struggling with morning sickness, worrying about her waistline and, worst of all, missing Sasha. Charlie was a perfectly good father – but what was the point of having children if she wasn't going to be there to see them grow up? She managed one low-budget TV drama shot largely on location in the Home Counties, and then decided, to her agent's dismay, to retire. Money was still trickling in from *Corpse Army* and its associated merchandise, and if things got tight they could always sell a bit of their family life to *Now!* or *OK!* But until Sasha and Ella were both in full-time education, Rachel was staying at home and being a mother.

But that was three or four years away. How long could they make the money last? They'd already given up the gym member-ships, beauty salons, designer clothes and expensive holidays. They had two cars – as long as Charlie was running around the country doing gigs, doing his best to be the breadwinner, they could not manage with one. But even if the money didn't run out, what would she do? In four years she'd be knocking on thirty – not a good time for an actress to be starting again. People's memories were short, and her triumphs in *Nana* and *Corpse Army* – even her unlooked-for fame as a glamour model – would be forgotten. She might hope for a role in a soap, or something in the costume drama line, but she had no illusions that she was going to return as a star.

Things could be worse. Charlie was convinced that his come-back was only an audition away, and put himself up for every single celebrity reality show that he could find. Anna was waiting in the wings, eager to be 'more of a grandmother' to the girls, offering childcare and financial support in return for a bigger investment of time, something that Rachel found herself reluc-tant to give. Anna had never been much of a mother, and now that she was a rich widow, she'd returned to her old ways, taking up with a string of unpleasant boyfriends that Rachel didn't want anywhere near her babies. At least they'd never be out on the streets – but for now, at least, Rachel preferred to swallow her pride, tighten her belt and concentrate on being a full-time mother. And, if she was honest with herself, that was all she wanted to do.

Motherhood had taken her by surprise; it wasn't planned, and when she first got pregnant, she saw it only as a spanner in the works of her career, or a good publicity angle. But when Sasha was born, and Rachel had recovered from the shock and pain of childbirth, when she got the baby home and could hide from the prying lenses of the press, she discovered something quite unexpected. She loved that little squalling red-faced thing more than she had loved anything in her life. She felt a physical connection from the child straight to her heart, as if an invisible cord still joined them. She loved Sasha completely, and without qualification. It was not like the love she sometimes felt for her mother, 'despite everything'. It was not like the love she'd felt for Nick – a hectic, guilty need, coming and going in hot waves. It was not like the love she'd felt for Gerald, a flattering reflection of herself. And it wasn't even like the love she felt for Charlie, which had grown, over the years, into a happy, reassuring companionship. This was a love that obliterated any sense of self, but which also seemed to complete her. And when Ella came along, the love doubled, quadrupled, squared. The thought of going back to an acting career seemed silly and shallow in comparison. There was only one reason to put herself out there again, and that was to provide for her daughters.

She took a quick look in the mirror – hair tied back in a ponytail, no make-up, the lack of sleep easy to see under the eyes – and picked up her car keys. Just as she was about to leave, the phone rang again.

* * *

When Charlie got home the next day – the after-show party had gone on longer than expected, and he'd crashed in a fan's spare room – he found his wife in a smart suit, her hair shiny and swept up, her face flawless, ready for business . . .

'Ah, there you are,' she said, dropping her phone and diary into her green leather Marc Jacobs bag, a relic of more prosperous times. She didn't greet him with recriminations or a sarcastic remark. She didn't sniff him for unfamiliar perfume, or tell him to have a shower. She trusted him, after all, wherever he'd been. She just closed her bag, kissed him lightly on the cheek and said, 'Right, you're picking Sasha up from school. Ella's lunch is ready, she has it at about twelve. I'll be back later.' She buttoned her jacket.

'Where are you going?'

'Oh!' she said, as if surprised that he would take an interest. 'I've got a casting. Didn't I tell you? No, I suppose I didn't, I only got the call yesterday. I won't be late. You can feed them and bathe them and get them to bed, can't you?'

'No can do.'

'What?'

'I've got meetings this arvo.'

'You'll have to cancel them.' She picked up the car keys. ''Bye.'

'No, wait a minute.' Charlie put a hand on her arm. 'You can't just run out like this.'

'I must.' She looked at her watch. 'I'll be late as it is.'

'But the kids . . .'

'You're their father,' said Rachel. 'You take care of them.'

She shook his hand off, walked out and, at the last moment, refrained from slamming the door. There was no point in taking her anxiety out on him.

It wasn't exactly a casting, but that was a white lie; if things worked out, this would make more money than the Hope-Evans's had seen in the last two years. She'd been approached out of the blue by *Bloke* magazine to do a swimsuit shoot, and if it came off, they wouldn't have to worry about Christmas any more. Sasha could have all the pink spangly rubbish her heart desired, Ella could have a year's worth of new clothes and shoes, and they might even manage to take them to Disneyland. Okay, it meant baring parts of her body that had not seen the light of a studio for over three years – BC, before childbirth, when she 'romped nude', as the newspapers had it, without a second thought. The breasts weren't quite as gravity-defying as they once were, the abdomen less firm – but much could be achieved with underwiring and Photoshop. She'd said more than once that she would never pose for lads' mags, but that was then. This was the all-too-real now of household budgets and bank charges, of soaring food bills and plunging income. Charlie's earning capacity was, on an annual basis, about the same as a supermarket checkout worker. He did too much for too little, or nothing at all, always believing that this was the break he'd been waiting for. It never was.

And so – tits out for the lads, or at least as much tit as they ever showed in these things. It wasn't what she'd imagined doing, but it wasn't so bad. And after all, everyone had seen those blurry black-and-whites. Such images were not easily forgotten. Why shouldn't she make some money out of her body, as well as everybody else?

Charlie would cope, wouldn't he? She started the car, fighting back a sudden impulse to cancel the meeting, turn around and give Ella her lunch as she normally did. But, no – he was their father, and he could manage. Rachel fought back images of Ella with her fingers in live sockets, Ella wandering out of an unlocked front door, Ella pulling a pan of boiling water on to her head. Charlie is not stupid, she said. He's perfectly capable. He can cope for a day. Half a day. Five hours, six at the most. It's the most he can do after the days and nights that I've coped on my own. And if anything goes wrong, he can always call Anna. As a very last resort.

Bloke magazine was produced in a small office north of Oxford Street, up two narrow flights of stairs above a seedy-looking wholesale fabric shop. It was not exactly glamorous, but then again, neither was sitting in a trailer in a muddy car park, or hanging around in a smelly dressing room in Shepperton. The glamour was up on screen, or at the parties – or, in this case, on glossy paper in a few months' time.

'Hi, yeah, thanks for coming in, er, Rachel, yeah, brilliant,' said the editor, a sweaty little man with shifty blue eyes and wispy blond hair. He held out a hand; it was clammy. 'Pete Goldman. Come and meet the team.'

The team looked like bored schoolchildren, none of them over seventeen, at least on first glance. As Rachel's eyes adjusted, she realised that most of them were older than her, just dressed inappropriately. It was like walking into a sixth-form common room struck by some dreadful ageing disease. 'Yeah,' said Pete, 'Rach, this is Gary, Josh, Wilf, Harry, Zack. Guys, this is Rachel Hope.' He said her name in a fake showbiz voice, as if he were introducing her on American television. But I've been on American television, she thought, then quickly brushed the thought away. This was no time to be grand. This was a time to think of the eight thousand pounds that had been mentioned, and all it could buy for Sasha and Ella.

'Hi everyone,' she said, shaking hands and trying to ignore the snide looks. 'It's great to meet you all. Looking forward to working with you.' This must be how an escort feels when she turns up at a conference, she thought.

'Right, yeah,' said Pete Goldman, who was the most obvious cocaine addict Rachel had ever met in her life, 'this is the basic concept, yeah?' He said 'yeah' like other people breathe. 'Harry. The basic concept, yeah?'

'Okay,' said Harry, who was wearing a pre-distressed denim jacket with – surely it couldn't be? – safety pins in the lapels. 'It's, like, a portfolio type of thing.' He started drawing squares on a piece of paper. 'Headline up here.' He scribbled across the top. 'Then the babes like here, here, here.' He scribbled some roughly humanoid shapes. It looked like something Sasha might bring home from school and insist be stuck to the fridge door. 'It's, like, going over eight pages, I think we said, PG? Right?'

'Yeah, dependent on ad sales,' said Pete, looking pleased with himself.

'Babes?' said Rachel. 'I take it there are other models involved.'

'Yeah, right, well that's pretty much UFD at the moment,' said Pete. 'Sorry. Magazine-speak. Up for discussion.' The men sniggered. 'But we can definitely say that you're the star, yeah? You're the big name. The cover name, yeah? Rachel Hope.' He gestured with his hands as if putting boxes on a shelf. 'Sounds good, yeah?'

'Mother's Day special, right?' said the one introduced as Zack, a peculiar shrunken little man with thick, greasy glasses.

'No, yeah, I mean that's just what we were calling it in the office, yeah? I mean, that's not written in stone, or anything,' babbled Pete. 'Typical sub-editor, yeah? Always having to give things a *label*.'

'Mother's Day?' asked Rachel.

'Just an idea, Rach, just a crazy idea, yeah? You know, mothers are sexy. Mothers are hot. Your best friend's mum. Bored house-wives, yeah?'

Think of the money . . .

'MILFs,' said one of the others, either Josh, Wilf or Gary, she could no longer remember which. They were staring at her in a way she didn't quite like. One of them licked his lips.

'Is that magazine-speak, too?' said Rachel, trying to sound innocent.

'Yeah, kind of,' said Pete. 'But moving swiftly on. You're basically up for it, right? I mean, we have a deal, Rach?'

'We haven't really discussed the kind of pictures that . . .'

'Gary will be doing that end of the business, yeah? Gary's our top smudger.'

'I see. But I think we need a bit more discussion of . . .'

'We could do it now, yeah? I mean, the studio's free.'

'Which studio?' In her heyday, Rachel had posed in some of the most luxurious photographers' studios in London.

'Just through there,' said Pete, pointing to a door that Rachel had assumed led to the lavatory. 'We can have it set up in no time, yeah? Gary? Yeah? Art department? Yeah?'

'I'm sorry,' said Rachel, clutching the Marc Jacobs to her bosom – anything to shield it from those hungry eyes and mouths – 'I think I've changed my mind.'

Pete's pupils had diminished to pin pricks. 'No, yeah? It's fine. We'll just, you know, we'll just do it, yeah? Just do it.' He was almost shouting now. The others were half-raised from their chairs. Any second now, thought Rachel, they will lurch towards me, hands oustretched, drool hanging from their lips.

She turned and fled.

It took two hours of weeping in Debenhams' toilets, thinking of how she was going to explain to Sasha about the shortage of Christmas presents, before Rachel was ready to repair her face and make the journey home. At least she didn't have to see the other mothers at the school gates. The hot mums, the sexy mums, the MILFs . . . At least Charlie would have spared her that.

The house was quiet. There was a note stuck to the fridge door by a magnet in the shape of an ice-cream cone with a cherry on top.

'Couldn't wait. Taken girls to your mum's. Later, Charlie.'

She got back in the car.

The Miller house had changed. It lacked the grandeur of the old days. The gravel drive was full of weeds, the ivy was out of control on the walls and the exterior paintwork was in desperate need of renewal. Where once there were carefully clipped conifers now stood wild, shaggy trees, half dead, the branches tangled with old carrier bags that had blown in from the street. The facade of the house, which used to look stern but kindly, now looked like the face of a stroke victim, one of the windows boarded up, the remaining glass dirty.

Rachel rang the doorbell. She could hear raised voices inside – Anna having another row with Rick, her man of the moment, the one who was helping her get through what was left of the Miller estate with unbelievable efficiency.

She rang again, and the voices stopped. They probably think it's the bailiffs, or the cops, thought Rachel.

'Who is it?' Anna's voice; she sounded drunk.

'It's me, Mum. I've come for the girls.'

The door flew open. She *was* drunk. Her hair, which currently boasted a good inch and a half of grey roots, hung round her face in hanks. Her eye make-up looked as if it had been on for well over twenty-four hours. 'Well ,you've got a bloody nerve, I must say.'

'I'll just take the girls and say goodbye.' She walked into the hall; it smelled stale and smoky, and there was the reason at the foot of the stairs. 'Hello, Rick.' He went to kiss her, but she recoiled from the stink of tobacco. 'Sasha! Ella! Come on, get your coats. Time to go home!'

'He said you'd walked out on him,' said Anna.

'What?'

'Charlie. Your husband.' Oh, the poison she put into that word! 'Turned up here unannounced, informed me that I was having the girls for the afternoon because he had to go to a meeting and then just buggered off.'

'Well,' said Rachel, squeezing past Rick, who made no effort to get out of her way, 'you're always saying that you don't see enough of them.'

'It's not fair,' said Anna. 'You just use me as a free child-minder when it suits you. I never have a chance to do anything nice with them.'

Sasha and Ella bounded out of the living room and threw themselves at their mother's legs. There were no obvious injuries or signs of neglect.

'Come on, girls. Time to say goodbye.'

They raced to the front door.

'Haven't you got a kiss for Nana Anna?' She held out her hands towards the girls, who looked to Rachel for guidance.

'Come on. Give Grandma a kiss.'

'I told you, Rachel, not Grandma. It makes me sound ancient.'

'I don't want to,' said Ella, who was not quite three but already alarmingly articulate. 'She smells funny.'

Anna's hands dropped to her sides, her chin retreated into her neck like a tortoise withdrawing into its shell.

'Another time, Nana Anna,' said Rachel, pushing the children out into the fresh air. 'Thanks for looking after them.'

They were getting into the car when Anna came storming out of the house, her towelling slippers crunching on the drive.

'Why don't you sort yourself out, Rachel?' she shouted. 'Why don't you get a bloody job and make me proud? Look at your stepsister. On television every afternoon, one of the richest and most influential women in the country . . .'

Rachel fastened the children's safety belts, got into the driver's seat and shut the door.

'You don't care about me!' shouted Anna, audible even above the sound of the engine, the wheels on the gravel, the children gabbling happily in the back. 'You've only ever cared about yourself!'

Rachel drove away at speed.

Chapter 33

'I've got some good news for you,' said Jan, after they'd ordered lunch at Soho House. Elizabeth was having a Caesar salad, no dressing. Jan, who was married and well past caring, went for bangers and mash.

'Go on.'

'We've had a very firm expression of interest in *The Best Revenge*.'

'What?'

'Your novel.'

'I haven't written a novel.'

'Not yet. But you're going to. Remember?'

'I'm going to have to, if someone wants to publish it. I assume the money is good.'

'Oh, that,' said Jan, waving her hand to dismiss this minor detail. 'I'm not talking about publishing. It goes without saying that you'll get a good publishing deal. I was talking about something else.'

'What, then?'

'Television.'

'Sorry?'

'Six-part prime-time adaptation. Very good independent producer. Probably for Sky.'

'Jan,' said Elizabeth, sipping the fizzy water that the waiter had just poured for her, 'don't you think you're rather jumping the gun here?'

'If someone wants to option your novel for the kind of money we're talking about here, I rather think we should let them.' Jan drank half of her large glass of red wine. 'Don't you?'

'You are seriously telling me that someone is willing to pay thousands of pounds . . .'

'Hundreds of thousands of pounds.'

'Ah. Right. Someone is willing to pay hundreds of thousands of pounds for the rights to a book that doesn't exist yet?'

'They're not buying the book. They're buying your name.'

'But a six-part series, Jan. Come on. You could be setting me up for the biggest disaster in television history.'

'I don't see why. I have every faith in you, and so does the producer.'

'What are they expecting?'

'Something sexy and starry, with just a hint of autobiography. People are fascinated by you, Liz. How did she get to be where she is? What happens behind closed doors? That sort of thing.'

'What happens behind closed doors is that I take off my make-up, wonder whether or not to take a sleeping pill and then lie in bed worrying about production schedules. Not very sexy.'

'It is fiction, darling.'

'Well, I suppose I could invent a couple of imaginary lovers.'

'That's my girl.'

'And a juicy bit of rivalry.'

'You've got it.'

'Actually,' said Elizabeth, seeing an opportunity to rewrite history to her liking, 'it could be rather good.'

'The producer certainly hopes so,' said Jan. 'You haven't asked me who it is yet, by the way.'

'Until I've written the bloody thing, it hardly matters. It could be Steven Spielberg for all I care.'

'Close, but no cigar.'

'And how much control will this mysterious producer have over the content?'

'Some,' said Jan. 'They're going to invest a great deal of money in this project. So the least you can do is deliver the kind of thing they want, don't you think?'

'If I'm going to write fiction, Jan, I'm going to do it properly. I have a PhD, you know. Not to mention the fact that I'm Susan Barnard's daughter. I'd like to be taken seriously.'

'Perhaps,' said Jan, signalling to the waiter for another glass of wine, 'when I tell you how much they're offering, you'll change your mind.'

Mark's showbiz ambitions, never strong, had died with Natasha. Now he was working nine to five at a job he despised – in telecommunications – and gave up his wild ways when he gave up drugs. Being clean and sober meant he wouldn't end up in an early grave, but it also meant he'd put on a great deal of weight, which limited his pulling power. Now he was quite content with one boyfriend at a time, and was never happier than when he got together with Rachel to talk about the good old days. Mark was the one person, it seemed, who still truly believed that Rachel Hope was a major celebrity, and for this reason she called him up whenever she needed a bit of an ego boost.

'Bloody cheek,' said Mark, helping himself to another dollop of tiramisu while Rachel cleared up after lunch. 'You were right to walk out. You're a big star.'

'Not any more, darling.'

'Just you wait,' said Mark. 'When Ella's at school, and you've got more time, the offers will come pouring in.'

'I wish I had your certainty.'

'You just have to remind people. You were famous once, and that means you can be famous again.'

'Sometimes I wish everyone would forget.'

'No, you don't. You're saying that now because you're tired. You won't say that when you get a big role on TV.'

'That's never going to happen again, Mark. You know it, I know it.'

'I know nothing of the sort. If I was your agent, I'd be putting you up for reality shows.'

'Oh God, not you as well. Charlie's up for every reality show going. I'm a Has-Been, Take Pity on Me. No thanks. I'll do celebrity mags when we're really desperate, but I hate even doing that. I'm not living in a jungle for two weeks with maggots crawling around my fanny for anyone.'

'Not even for them?' said Mark, nodding towards the living room, where Sasha and Ella were sprawled in front of *Dora the Explorer*.

'They're doing all right.'

'They could do a lot better.'

'Says the man who knows so much about children.'

'All right!' Mark put up his hands. 'I only want what's best for you.'

Rachel threw a tea towel at him. 'Then help me dry this lot up,' she said.

They worked for a while in silence, but Rachel could tell, from the occasional intakes of breath, the sidelong glances, that Mark was itching to say something. Eventually, she made coffee, and they joined the girls.

'Out with it, then.'

'It's just that I think you should be doing more with yourself. If I had what you had . . .'

'You'd have three men every night. I know. You've told me before.'

'I don't mean that,' said Mark, 'although God knows I would.'

'Then, what?'

'You've got so much inside information. You should be making it work for you.'

'Kiss and tell?'

'Why not? You've had affairs with some of the most famous men in the world. You're the stepsister of one of the most famous women on British television.'

'Don't remind me.'

'Someone needs to remind you, love. Because you seem to have forgotten.'

'Go on then, Max Clifford. Tell me what I should be doing.'

'You could start off by spilling the beans on Alan Southgate and Johnny Khan. That was going on under your nose.'

'And get myself kneecapped? No, thank you.'

'What do you mean?'

'Alan is very powerful these days. He has what are politely known in entertainment circles as 'people'. Bad things happen to those who cross Alan Southgate, and that's why nobody does. There must be dozens of shallow graves in West Hollywood containing the battered remains of waiters and personal trainers who thought they'd make a quick buck out of him. Maybe a couple of years ago we could have got away with it, before Alan became so powerful and so paranoid. But now, if a newspaper tried running a story about his personal life, they'd be putting themselves in real danger.'

'Okay, then. Gerald Partridge.'

'Nothing to say. Married film producer shags actresses. That's about as exciting as dog bites man.'

'Nick Sharkey, then.'

'Scraping the barrel, aren't we?'

'My Three-Way Heartbreak with Liz Miller's Fiancé,' suggested Mark. 'Why not? He's got a certain amount of profile these days. And she . . . Well, they'd love to get their teeth into her, wouldn't they? Miss High and Mighty Miller, the conscience of the nation.'

'Nick Sharkey is ancient history.'

'Please don't say you've forgiven him,' said Mark. 'After what he did to you . . .'

'Darling, I appreciate your efforts,' said Rachel, 'but no thanks. I'm quite happy the way I am. When the girls are at school, I might stick my head above the parapet again, see if anyone wants to give an old woman a job. But for now, I'm doing fine.'

'Really?' said Mark, who didn't believe a word of it.

Ella chose that moment to launch herself off her beanbag, hitting her forehead quite hard on the corner of the TV stand. Her screams made any further discussion impossible.

Mark was right about one thing: Nick Sharkey did have a certain amount of profile these days. Starpix went from candid nudie screengrabs to red carpet shots and after-party exclusives, then graduated from the *Daily Reporter* and started freelancing, getting as far as magazine shoots and production stills. Nick would never be famous in his own right, but he was on first-name terms with a lot of famous people, and had slept with quite a number of them, which was almost as good. It was the lifestyle he had always wanted, and he lived it to the full.

Freelance photography, however, did not a player make, and Nick was always on the lookout for additional revenue streams. And so, while declaring his photographic earnings to the taxman, the main bulk of his income came from drug dealing. The two things went hand in hand. Nick got jobs because everyone, from picture editors through models to stylists, knew that he had the best gear, and enough for everyone. While assistants set up lights, Nick was to be found in the studio lavatory supplying small packages to an orderly queue of discreet clients, who paid him in cash that would never be declared to HM Revenue and Customs.

Nick wasn't entirely happy with this state of affairs – he saw himself as an artist rather than a dealer – but he was not in a position to argue. If he didn't have drugs, the commissions would dry up; he was a competent photographer, but that was all, and dealing gave him the edge over the competition. And without access to the models, designers, actors and musicians who posed for his camera, Nick would be elbowed out of the lucrative drugs trade that kept him in fast cars and first-class flights. He worried, sometimes, that the law would catch up with him – but if the anxiety ever got too much, Nick could always take something to help.

It was all going well until, as occasionally happens, a dodgy batch of methamphetamine hit the market. This particular consignment was drastically purer than usual; someone along the way had forgotten to cut it with laxatives. But nobody twigged until, in the space of thirty-six hours, three of Nick's regular clients – one young actor, one Mercury Prize-winning singer and one ageing supermodel – all overdosed. Unfortunately for Nick, the Mercury Prize-winning singer had also downed a bottle of bourbon in the two hours before her final, fatal line of crystal meth. She passed out at a party in her own house, which was not unusual, but this time she didn't wake up. Her death was front-page news for the next week.

Nick's main supplier, a Mr Big who drove a BMW and owned a large portfolio of slum properties in Essex, had no desire to attract attention and so, until the fuss had died down, decided it would be better to sever his connections with the entertainment industry. Nobody had put two and two together yet – the actor and the supermodel had both recovered, and were selling their rehab stories – but, Mr Big explained to Nick, he couldn't afford any unnecessary risks. Yes, of course they'd get back in business again – some time. Just not now.

And so Nick lost half of his income – three-quarters, even. Bookings dried up as soon as word got round that Nick was no longer good for supplies. Party invitations stopped coming – and, worst of all, he was obliged to spend his own money to service the nice little habit that he'd developed during his years as a dealer. Picture editors who had once been his best clients, his 'mates', even, blamed the lack of work on the 'current economic situation'.

Nick was spending too much time at home, drinking too much, smoking too much – and it was taking a toll on his looks. His features coarsened. His hair, once so obligingly, effortlessly beautiful, was duller and sparser. Patches of scalp became visible. He caught sight of his rear view on a CCTV monitor, and was just forming the thought 'who's that baldy twat?' before he realised it was him. Hair dye and careful combing could only do so much. He was getting old.

There was only one solution. If Mr Big wouldn't do business with him, then he would set up in competition. He knew where the drugs came from. He'd been to all the major warehouses on the south coast. Why not just pay them a call as a private individual, and propose a little bit of extra business? In the current economic climate, they would welcome him with open arms.

And at first, they did.

But when Nick got back to his flat one night, he discovered the fire brigade in attendance. Petrol-soaked rags had been put through his letter box and started a blaze, which destroyed most of his living room.

His cameras, fortunately for Nick, were in the bedroom at the back of the building, and were undamaged.

So, too, was a small plastic storage crate that contained his few valuable personal possessions. He checked: yes, they were all there. The few pieces of jewellery that he owned, most of them gifts from admirers. The signed CDs given to him by grateful clients.

The small brown padded envelope that contained two DVDs, each bearing the legend, in black marker, 'Rachel Hope'. For the time being, its value was questionable. Rachel's career was over, and the market was not interested in yet more stills. But supposing she made a comeback? Supposing, suddenly, there was a demand? He had never released the video footage. It might yet be the goose that laid the golden egg.

'You have to be joking.'

'No,' said Jan. 'I'm absolutely serious.'

'But why on earth would Gerald Partridge want to adapt a book that hasn't been written yet? He's Hollywood. He's got Oscars, for God's sake.'

'The kind of films that Gerald Partridge wants to make just aren't being commissioned any more. They're too expensive, and the returns aren't guaranteed. He's too arty for Hollywood. They want sure-fire family favourites, the sort that recoup in the first weekend. Gerald's last couple of films have struggled.'

'But all those awards . . .'

'Awards are meaningless, Liz. It's the bottom line or nothing.'

'So he comes back to England to shoot a six-part TV series based on a book by a first-time novelist who might have no talent at all. Of course. Perfect. Why didn't I think of it?'

'Save your sarcasm for the show, darling,' said Jan. 'Gerald Partridge knows exactly what he's doing. He thinks this could be the biggest drama of the year – and he's right.'

'Why? What's so special about this?'

'Ah,' said Jan, narrowing her eyes. 'That's the clever bit.'

Charlie turned up at seven, very much the worse for wear. His eyes were bloodshot, and he stank of liquor, but he was carrying a huge bunch of flowers, all autumn reds and oranges, which he presented to his wife with a woozy flourish.

Mark went to read the girls their bedtime story.

'Darling wife,' slurred Charlie, 'I want to apologise.'

'What for?' Rachel buried her face in the bouquet; the roses did not smell.

'For everything. For being a rubbish husband. For being a crap father. For being a shit pop star and an even worse actor.' He went down on one knee.

'Get up, Charlie,' said Rachel, who had witnessed these bouts of drunken remorse before. 'You look silly.'

'But I want you to know that from now on, things are gonna be different.'

Rachel busied herself with a vase. 'Good,' she said, not really listening.

'Because I'm going to change. I'm going to make you proud of me.'

'Yes, yes . . .' She could hear the girls giggling upstairs at Mark's overdramatic reading of *The Gruffalo*.

' . . . going to be rich.'

That caught her attention. 'What?'

'I said we're going to be rich. I've got a job.'

That caught Mark's attention as well; he had very good hearing for things like this, and stopped reading.

'What sort of job?'

'Ah,' said Charlie, getting to his feet. 'Interested now, aren't you? Knew you would be. Well, guess.'

'If you want to play guessing games, try it with the children. I don't have the time or the energy.'

'Humour me.' He had the mischievous twinkle in his blue eyes that once made teenage girls, and middle-aged men in the music business, weak at the knees.

'Okay. You've got that club residency.'

'No. Guess again.'

'You're doing the Ideal Homes show again.'

'No. One more go.'

'I don't know, Charlie. Come on, for God's sake . . .'

'One more go.'

'You're going back to prostitution. I don't bloody know.'

Charlie winced, rubbed the side of his chin. 'Ouch, Rachel Hope. That was a mean punch. But I suppose I deserved it.'

'If you don't stop this, I'll bloody thump you for real.'

'Okay, okay!' He stepped back, as if frightened. 'Your husband, Mrs Evans, is going to be a star all over again.'

'What do you mean?'

'I went to that audition . . .'

A faint bell began to ring. Weeks ago, Charlie had mentioned another of his endless round of auditions for reality shows.

'You're not telling me . . .'

'I am.' He threw his arms open. 'I fucking got it.'

Footsteps thundered down the stairs. Mark appeared in the door, breathless and wide-eyed.

'That's fantastic, darling,' said Rachel, hugging her husband. 'Now, just remind me. Was it the snooker one?'

'*Strictly Pot Black*? No, they turned me down for that.'

'What about *I'm in Therapy*?' asked Mark, who would have given his right arm to be on a show in which a bunch of famous names had to enter a very public group therapy and tell the nation about their troubled inner lives. (The more troubles they revealed, the better chance they stood of staying in.)

'No,' said Charlie, 'guess again.'

Rachel had run out of ideas; fortunately, Mark took more notice of these things. 'Oh my God, Charlie,' he said, 'don't tell me you're going to be on *Stars Under Fire*?'

Charlie whooped, and punched the air. 'This is it,' he said, his face flushed, his eyes shining. 'I'm back!'

'Enlighten me. What is Gerald Partridge's brilliant idea?'

'The casting.'

'Oh, yes. Go on.' Elizabeth had a feeling she knew what was coming.

Rachel, Charlie and Mark were still celebrating at ten o'clock. They didn't even mind that the girls had got out of bed to join them. When Charlie mentioned the amount of money that he was being paid just to appear on *Stars Under Fire*, little details like bedtime didn't seem to matter. For the next six weeks, he'd be in basic training at an army camp, an ordeal that would get him fit enough to appear on the show itself – and there would be cameras recording every press-up, every drop of sweat. And then, he and his fellow contestants would be dropped into 'real combat situations' in a hot, sandy part of southern Spain that would look a bit like Iraq, Afghanistan or any other distant war zone. They would face 'insurgents', suicide bombers and friendly fire. Each week, one contestant would be sent home in the light entertainment version of a body bag, after a debrief by the presenter, a former actor who had once played a soldier in a soap.

For signing up, Charlie would get a six-figure sum. And with every week he stayed in the show, his fee got higher and higher. If he got to the finals, the sky was the limit.

At midnight, while Charlie was attempting to do press-ups with Sasha sitting on his back, Mark was speculating about who the other contestants might be, and Rachel was changing Ella's nappy. She was feeling, above all, relieved. If Charlie could be a breadwinner, she might never have to go to another audition.

'No. Absolutely not. No way. Are you mad, Jan?'

'Think about it, Liz. It would be the biggest showbiz story of the year. Of the decade. It's never come out that you and Rachel are sort of related and this could be the biggest publicity angle ever.'

'I am not having that woman in a drama based on one of my books. That's final.'

'Why not?'

'Why not?' Elizabeth was almost screaming; heads were turning in Soho House. 'Why not?' she repeated, in more moderate tones. 'Do you have any idea what Rachel Hope has done to me?'

'You've told me some,' said Jan. 'The rest I've guessed.'

'Okay. Take notes. First, she stole my fiancé. Second, her mother drove my father to the grave. Third, she is living off my mother's estate. Is that enough?'

'You're being ridiculous.'

'If you really think that, maybe I should get another agent.'

'He's offering an awful lot of money.'

'I have money.'

'For the right casting.'

'I told you, Jan. I don't want to discuss it . . .'

'For the right casting,' repeated Jan firmly, and then named a figure.

That shut her up, thought Jan. It always did.

* * *

The *Stars Under Fire* publicists wasted no time, and announced the line-up for the new series in the Monday morning papers.

Nick Sharkey, like everyone else, was delighted to see that Charlie Evans had made the final cut. But while most people were delighted because Charlie made them feel rather warm and fuzzy about the not-so-distant past, Nick was delighted because he knew to the nearset hundred pounds just how much contestants were paid. And if Charlie was rich, then Rachel was rich.

It was time, he thought, to look up an old flame.

Chapter 34

Rachel was feeling good about life before the call came.

She'd just heard that Charlie had definitely, one hundred per cent, got *Stars Under Fire*, and he'd been spending so much time in the gym that he was bound to get through to the quarter finals, or even the semis – so that was Christmas taken care of, a trip to Disney, new furniture for the girls' bedrooms. She'd also had a call from her agent offering her an advertising campaign; not great work, but she could do it while the girls were at school and playgroup, and it definitely did not involve nudity. True, it was a rather jokey campaign for anti-ageing face cream, playing on the fact that Rachel was not as young as she once was, and that by her age all women basically need to grout their faces in order to be seen in public – but she didn't mind. It was easy money, and her agent was so pleased at the thought of the commission that she didn't have the heart to turn it down.

The cherry on the cake was the news that Anna had had one 'final' almighty row with Rick and was throwing him out of the house, having caught him stealing from her handbag. Rachel was familiar with her mother's fluid concept of 'final', but this sounded promising. With Rick out of the way, there was some chance that Anna might settle into a dignified – and more sober – middle age and actually be of some use as a grandmother.

So she was whistling and singing as she cleaned the kitchen that morning, having seen Charlie off with a kiss and a cuddle that made Ella giggle and squirm and insist on joining in.

The phone rang when she was getting Sasha ready for play-group, wiping her nose and combing her hair and trying to wrangle her into her shoes.

'Rachel Hope.' It could always be a business call, and it was as well to sound businesslike.

'Hi.' A man's voice, followed by a long pause. 'It's me.'

She recognised Nick immediately, but thought it better to say, 'Sorry, who is this?'

'You know.' A low chuckle.

The warm feeling in her stomach was replaced by a trickle of ice. 'This is Rachel Hope. Who's speaking, please.'

Another laugh – mocking, she thought. 'It's Nick, Rachel. You know that.'

'Nick . . . ?' As if trying to place *which* Nick. 'Oh!' Feigned delight at hearing from an old acquaintance. 'Nick! Well! How are you?'

'Oh, I'm just fine, Rachel. Just fine.' Another long pause.

'Well,' she said at last, still sounding bright and busy, 'it's lovely to hear your voice. I'm just getting my little girl off to playgroup . . .'

'That's nice,' he said, in a tone that meant anything but. 'Bet you're wondering why I've called like this, after all these years.'

'What? Sasha, come here. Come on, darling.'

'I've got a business proposition for you.'

'Hmm? What?'

'Something that you might be interested in.'

'Oh, really? It's best if that sort of thing goes through my agent, Nick.'

'Not this.' There was no mistaking the menace in his voice. 'This is something we want to keep on the downlow.'

'I'm sorry, Nick, I don't really have time for this.'

'Yes,' he said. 'You do.'

She smoothed Sasha's hair – still blonde, just as hers had been at that age, fine and shiny – and sent her off into the living room. 'Just let Mummy talk on the phone for a minute, darling.' Sasha ran away, happy for the reprieve. 'What do you want, Nick?' She no longer sounded bright and breezy.

'That's more like the old Rachel that I knew. Straight down to business, eh? That's my girl.'

'Look, Nick, I don't . . .'

'What are you doing for work these days?'

'I beg your pardon?'

'You know. Apart from being in magazines for a living.'

'I've just got a cosmetics campaign, actually.'

'Really? Good. Great. What sort of cosmetics?'

'Face cream.'

'Ah!' He barked with laughter. 'Wonder if they'd like to see what I've got.'

'Nick, if you're trying to blackmail me . . .'

'Like I said, Rachel, it's a business proposition. I've got something you want, and you've got the money to pay for it.'

'If it's more of those sordid photos, forget it.'

'Respectable now, aren't you? Married lady. Mother of two. The perfect little family.'

'Are you threatening me, Nick?'

'That's your call.'

'What do you mean?'

'If you can afford to buy what I've got to sell . . .'

'I don't know what you're talking about.'

'Or, more to the point, if your husband can afford it. Done well, hasn't he? After all these years. You must have been giving up hope.'

'I see. You've heard that Charlie's got a job on TV, and suddenly you think there's some money in it for you. Are you a full-time blackmailer these days, Nick, or is it just a hobby?'

'Shut up and listen,' said Nick. 'I've got stuff that will screw up Charlie's deal, screw up your deal, mess you up so bad that those two precious children of yours will be taken into care.'

'Oh, piss off, Nick. I'm not listening to this.'

'Have it your way. Just tell Charlie to check out XTube in a couple of days. I'm sure he's familiar with the site. Homemade porn. It'll be easy to find. Just search on a couple of keywords. Try "Rachel Hope" and "doggy position" for starters, and you'll see some of my little home movies. But don't worry if he can't find it. It'll be in every newspaper by the weekend. News travels fast these days.'

'And I'm supposed to believe that a few thousand quid will buy your silence?'

'I was thinking more of a few hundred thousand quid, love, but that's the general idea.'

Sasha came running back into the kitchen, clutching her favourite cuddly owl, singing a maddening little song she'd learned at playgroup.

'Nick,' said Rachel, 'you are barking up the wrong tree.' She mustered a laugh. 'If you think I give a . . . that I give two hoots about your nasty little video, then you're very much mistaken.'

'You don't fool me, Rachel.'

'How did you do it, by the way? I'm curious. Hidden camera in the wardrobe, was it? That would be about your level.'

'Something like that, yeah. It's good, you know. Close-ups. The lot. Your fans will love it.'

'Well, sweetheart,' said Rachel, using her free arm to cuddle Sasha to her in the hope she didn't hear her next words, 'happy wanking. Because that's all you're going to get out of me. Now do me a favour and fuck off.'

She put the phone down, kissed her daughter and joined in with Mr Owl's little ditty, her heart beating so hard that it made her voice shake.

'You'll have to talk to her.'

'Why me?'

'I can just imagine the kind of welcome I'd get if I turned up on her doorstep.'

'If you don't mind my saying, Elizabeth, that's your problem, not mine.'

'My problems *are* your problems. That's what I pay you for.'

'You pay me to direct the show.'

'I thought perhaps you might like to have a go at prime-time.'

'I see,' said Chris. 'So that's the carrot on the end of the stick, is it? I sweet talk Rachel into considering a role in your super-duper new drama, and you pat me on the head and say that Gerald Partridge might just give me a job as a runner. Gosh, Liz Miller, you're so generous. No, really. Giving a break like that to a humble little nobody like me.'

'If you don't want it, fine. I'll get Jan to talk to her.'

'You do that.'

'Perhaps you'd better start looking for a new job, Chris. The show's getting a bit stale. Several people have commented on it.'

'Isn't it just?'

Elizabeth waved him away with one manicured hand. It would be so easy, thought Chris, to walk out right now, to tell her that he didn't need the job, didn't need her, would be quite content to be kept by Dev until he found a job where he could keep his self-respect. But curiosity got the better of him. 'Why are you so keen on this project, anyway? You don't need the money.'

'Don't I?'

'You don't spend a quarter of what you earn as it is.'

'Maybe I'm saving up for something.'

'What? A small African nation? Your own private island?'

'If you must know, Chris, I want to buy back Mum's estate.'

'You're kidding.'

'No, I'm not, and if you had any interest in her reputation, you'd understand why.'

'Tell me this isn't about getting back at Anna.'

'It's nothing to do with her. I just hate the idea that someone else owns what is rightfully ours.'

'You can't stand the idea of Anna getting the money, you mean.'

'Not everything is about money, Chris.'

'Easy for you to say, Miss Millionaire Miller.'

'Look, if Gerald Partridge makes a TV series out of my book, it puts me in a very powerful position. I can concentrate on writing novels, I can give up all of this' – she gestured around the office, a chaos of whiteboards and piles of paper – 'and I can spend the rest of my working life doing what I want, rather than what other people expect of me.'

'Gosh,' said Chris, 'I had no idea you suffered so much.'

'You have no idea about anything,' said Elizabeth. 'You think I'm just a spoiled, lonely, bitter old woman . . .'

Chris put his fingers in his ears.

'Well, you asked. And, as usual, when I try to say what I really feel, nobody's interested.'

'Oh, Elizabeth, you're such a martyr. Very well. I'll talk to Rachel. Perhaps I won't mention that you want the money so that you can force her mother to sell one of her most valuable assets, thus depriving Rachel and her children of a very substantial chunk of their inheritance.'

'Oh, shut up.'

'Or hadn't that occurred to you? No, of course, why would it? I'm sure you're blind to the delicious irony of the whole situation.'

'If Rachel does this job, she'll get her career back. She won't be forced to sell her baby photos to celebrity magazines any more. She'll earn enough from this to soften the blow of losing the Susan Barnard estate, don't you think? And I don't imagine she's interested in its literary value.'

'Unlike you.'

'Go and see her, tell her this is an olive branch and see what she says.'

'Is it? Are you sure this olive branch doesn't have a few concealed thorns?'

'I'm sure. It's time we put the past behind us.'

I think Rachel did that quite some time ago, thought Chris, but kept his opinions to himself. He wasn't paid to have opinions.

The line-up for *Stars Under Fire* pressed all the right buttons. There was a black one, a brown one, an old one, a fat one. There were three sexy girls, and three sexy boys, one of them gay, one of them a homophobic rapper, to ensure conflict. There was a Welsh one – for some reason, the Welsh vote was considered important – and an American one, just in case of interest from US broadcasters. The potential for off-screen romance and onscreen punch-ups was enormous. Whether or not any of the contestants actually learned how to survive in a modern warfare situation was secondary to the human interest that would arise from the mix.

Charlie Evans, former boy babe, brought low by saucy scandal and now famously a) desperate and b) married to Rachel Hope, had been set up in planning meetings with Shania

Tennyson, briefly a singer in a girl group, now more famous for her ever-expanding bust measurement. She'd spilled her guts to the celeb mags so often (sexual abuse as a child, substance abuse as an adult, bullying, bulimia, proudly presenting her new boob job) that there was nothing left to spill; at the age of twenty-six, this was her last throw of the dice. She'd been booked largely on the basis that she'd look good in a tight camouflage vest and combat boots, toting a gun, thrusting the chest that had been paid for by so many magazine spreads.

What the producers really hoped for was a sweet, redeeming love story in which they'd wash away their sordid pasts in the cleansing waters of romance, but failing that a squalid bunk-up would suffice.

Charlie entered the boot camp with the best of intentions – to earn money, to be a good provider for his children and a better husband to his wife. Then he met Shania Tennyson, and his good intentions evaporated in the blazing heat of her desperation. She aimed her bosoms at him, and they found their target.

Before the show even went on air, a rumour spread that Charlie Evans and Shania Tennyson were putting in a bit of extra training in each other's barracks. The producers were delighted. It was the kind of pre-season publicity that money could not buy.

Dev's long, strong fingers worked firmly at the knots in Chris's shoulders.

'Bad day?'

'The usual. She threatened to fire me. She tried to get me to do her dirty work. Just another day in paradise.'

'It's okay,' said Dev, putting his arms around him. 'You can forget all about it till tomorrow.'

'I won't sleep.'

'When I've finished with you, you'll sleep.'

'I think it's time to move on, Dev.'

'Whenever you want. You don't have to worry about the money.'

'I don't want to be a housewife.'

'No one's suggesting you would be,' said Dev, although he quite liked the idea.

'You'll never guess what she wants me to do now.'

Dev sighed, disentangled himself and lay back on the pillow, arms behind his head. 'Come on, then. Get it off your chest.'

'She wants me to go and see Rachel.'

'You like Rachel. She loves you. So do the girls. What's the problem?'

'I don't mean in that way. She wants me to sweet talk her into doing a job.'

'What kind of job?'

'An acting job.'

'So? She's an actress.'

'I haven't told you about the project yet,' said Chris. 'They're making a series out of some novel Elizabeth's written. Can you guess what it's about?'

'I have a horrible feeling that I can.'

'It's about two young women . . .'

'Who become linked through the marriage of their parents, huh? Am I warm?'

'Boiling hot.'

'One of them a sensitive, misunderstood career girl who's unlucky in love?'

'And the other a gold-plated bitch. Correct.'

'Hmm,' said Dev. 'I wonder which part she wants Rachel for?'

'And here's the punchline. It's a Gerald Partridge production. And if I'm a very good boy and drop Rachel at my mistress's feet, she might just have a word in Gerald's ear.'

'So? What are you waiting for?'

'I'm not sure this is what I went into television for.'

'It's going to be hysterical.'

'If I do this for Elizabeth, it's the last thing I do for her. After that, I'm quitting. Right?'

'Right,' said Dev, stroking Chris's head. 'Now, have we finished? Because there's something much more important that's just come up.'

'We've finished,' said Chris.

Charlie insisted that the stories about him and Shania were just made up for publicity purposes, that yes, she was trying every trick in the book to get him, but no, he was having none of it, that he 'didn't like the taste of plastic' and that there was 'no point eating hamburgers when you've got steak at home'. Rachel tried to find this reassuring, but Charlie was away from home, easily led, and Shania did have very large breasts. The producers would be doing everything they could to throw them together, guaranteeing coverage in the press, building up viewing figures for the first show as people tuned in just to see if the rumours were true. It might start out as a publicity stunt, thought Rachel, but it could all too easily become real. Charlie wasn't the celibate type, and if he was cooped up in an army camp for six weeks he was surely getting it from somewhere. She tried to trust him, but it was hard, faced with a daily diet of photos of a topless Charlie helping a top-heavy Shania over a climbing wall not to have her doubts. A full-scale romance with Shania Tennyson would do wonders for the show, and would almost certainly propel Charlie to the final, and the kind of money that meant Rachel would never have to work again – but on the other hand, it might just wreck their marriage. And she would be left as a single mother, chasing after alimony, forced to put the girls into daycare while she did the glamour mags. It was not an appetising prospect. Rachel suddenly felt very vulnerable. The foundations of her happy little world were suddenly shifting. She'd been a fool to rely on a man. She needed independence.

To make matters worse, Nick Sharkey was still circling. He had yet to make good on his threat to post his home movies on the Internet, but every time he called the price went up, the scale of the damage increased. Divorced and disgraced, a single mother with a porno past, she might even lose the children.

And so when Chris Miller came to see her with vague hints of an interesting job in the pipeline, Rachel was all ears.

The girls loved Chris. They climbed all over him, both determined to monopolise his lap. They stroked the stubble at the back of his neck, played with his ears, his nose, stared at him with the kind of adoration that only small children can give to an adult. After half an hour of small talk while the girls had their love-in, Rachel sent them packing.

'I take it this isn't just a social call,' she said.

'Sadly, no. I come bearing an olive branch.'

'What does she want?'

'You.'

'Don't tell me this is the great reconciliation I've dreamed of night and day for the last five years?'

Chris winced at the sarcasm in her voice. 'That's not really Liz's style. Everything's for a reason.'

'Go on, then. Hit me.'

He hit her. It took about five minutes.

'I see,' said Rachel. 'So, basically, she wants me to play myself.'

'She wants you to play her version of yourself. There's a difference.'

'Well, I wasn't expecting to be the heroine.'

'So what shall I tell her?'

'Chris . . . I'm not sure if I can do this. Old times. Bad times. I'd rather forget about it.'

'That's what I told her.'

'I suppose she'll be very angry if I turn her down, won't she?'

'Very.'

'And she'll say horrible things on air about me and Charlie and Titticaca, whatever her name is.'

'Oh, Shania. Yes. Probably.'

'So either way, she gets her revenge. With my co-operation, or without it. I must have hurt her very badly.'

'You did.'

'Well, I've paid for it, God knows,' said Rachel, but thought better of telling Chris about the Rachel Tapes and Nick's escalating demands. 'Look, I can't give you an answer right now. I've got to think about it. Can you ask her to wait?'

'I can ask her.'

'All right. Forty-eight hours, that's all I need. I just have to . . .' Her voice wobbled, but she fought back the tears. Oh, it was so tempting to cry on Chris's shoulder, to tell him everything – Nick, Charlie and Shania, Nana Anna, *Bloke* magazine, the indignity of promoting an anti-ageing cream – but it would get back to Elizabeth. And Elizabeth must never know. 'I just need to think things over. Discuss it,' she said, 'with my husband.'

'I understand.'

'I'll call you.'

They kissed. 'I'm sorry, Rachel. I really am.'

'Sweet,' she said, 'but there's no need. Send Elizabeth . . .' Not *my love*. Not yet. 'Tell her thanks for thinking of me.'

She thinks of little else, thought Chris, squeezing Rachel's hands as the little girls queued up for their goodbye kisses.

Chapter 35

The only trouble with having a book deal, as far as Elizabeth could see, was that it meant you actually had to write a book. *The Best Revenge* was all very well as an idea, but the business of putting it on paper took up what little spare time she had. Elizabeth's life, which was lonely enough already, became a sort of retreat from the world, her only human contact with guests on the show. She declined evening invitations, and went home alone to write. She got up early in the morning to write. When she couldn't sleep, which was frequently, she wrote. At weekends, if she wasn't absolutely required to turn up to some public function, she wrote. Pages were filled with the heartbreak, disappointment and yearning of the last few years. Words flew from her fingertips on to the screen. Her laptop went everywhere with her, even to the lavatory.

Jan tore the completed chapters from her as soon as the save button was pressed, and emailed them directly to Partridge Pictures, where they were seized on by writers, script editors and designers. Everyone assured Elizabeth that there would be time to go back and revise, to change any details she wasn't happy with – but she didn't need to. The book came out of her whole and complete. She could no more revise it than she could revise the past.

She was on the verge of exhaustion, and allowed Chris to persuade her to take a holiday. To Elizabeth, the idea of a holiday was alarming – but she could, at least, keep writing, maybe even finish the book. *The Liz Miller Show* was due for its annual break, flights were booked for her, a villa in Umbria rented and ready. Chris saw her off at Gatwick, and promised to call her the minute he had an answer from Rachel about the TV series.

The flight was fine, but once she was through Fiumicino airport, watching the traffic on the autostrada through the smoked glass of the limousine, she began to feel a sense of panic. She was alone. Not just here, now, in the car with a driver whose command of English extended to 'pliss' and 'okay', not just for the two weeks of the holiday, rattling around in an over-luxurious villa in a picture-postcard medieval walled town – but generally, infinitely alone. '*Sola*,' she murmured, as stand after stand of cypress trees whipped past, and the congestion of the A1 gave way to the prettier, slower roads that led into the *cuore verde* of Umbria. The views should have made her heart leap for joy – but all Elizabeth could see was despair.

'I am a hugely successful woman,' she said in firmer tones. The driver glanced in his rear-view mirror, so she pretended to be talking on her phone. 'I am a household name, a television personality, a respected journalist and I am about to become a best-selling author. I have achieved more in the last ten years than anyone I know. I am so rich that I could give it all up tomorrow, I could live to ninety and want for nothing. I could buy the villa I'm staying in, and this car and this chauffeur, and not feel it. I have everything I want . . .'

Her voice went wrong on that last word, and she had to rummage for a tissue.

Chris, her brother, nothing more than a colleague.

Kate, her best friend, her mother's disciple, the strongest remaining link to the past, estranged and distant, communicating only on matters of money.

Her father – dead.

Her mother – dead.

Her stepmother destroying whatever was left of the estate, letting the house fall into ruin, spending the money faster than she could get her hands on it.

Her stepsister . . . A voice came into her head, so clear that she had to check that her phone really was switched off.

We're celebrating . . . The fact that we like each other. Not because we have to. Not just to please our parents. But because we really do. Don't we?

She turned on her phone; perhaps Chris had left a message. Perhaps Rachel had said yes. Hope surged in Elizabeth's heart; she wasn't quite sure why.

As the car made the steep, awkward ascent through the cobbled streets of Todi, the tiny jewel of a city that made most visitors gasp with delight, Elizabeth saw nothing but the screen of her mobile phone.

Nobody had called.

'Charlie and Shania – The Real Life Story of That Kiss', said the coverline of *Super!* magazine, with a picture of TV's latest celebrity couple wearing enough make-up between them to paint the Forth Bridge, walking hand in hand along a Spanish beach during a break from filming *Stars Under Fire*. Down the page was a grainy shot of 'Lonely Rachel' taking Sasha and Ella for a walk in the park and getting used to 'Life as a Single Mum'.

And that was just the tip of the iceberg. The Internet was alive with stories of Charlie and Shania, Charlie and various other women and men, Rachel and Gerald, Rachel and 'celebrity photographer' Nick Sharkey, even 'Rachel's tragic drug pal' Natasha.

Rachel did her best to keep things on an even keel for the girls, but was obliged to place them in Anna's care more often than she would have liked. Rick, far from being out in the cold, seemed more comfortably ensconced in the house than ever, and Rachel was far from happy about having him around her daughters, but she didn't have much choice in the matter. With her marriage in meltdown, she had to work. Flogging anti-ageing cream took up a certain amount of time, and didn't pay nearly enough money.

She needed a proper job, some kind of security for the future.

She'd told Chris that she'd talk over Elizabeth's offer with her husband – but Charlie was not around, and after what she'd read in *Super!* it seemed quite possible that he might never be around again.

If Elizabeth can put the past behind her, thought Rachel, then so can I. Okay, it's only for the money – I don't imagine for one moment that she wants us to be sisters again. But if we can smile for the cameras and do the Jackie-and-Joan routine in public, it doesn't matter what we think about each other in private, does it? It's been five years – time to pick up the pieces. I can forgive Elizabeth for what she's done to me, if the price is right. I'm sure she can do the same.

The thought of meeting Elizabeth again made Rachel sweat with anxiety; just seeing her from an upstairs window had been bad enough. If it were up to her, she might still forget the whole thing. But it wasn't just about her. It was about Sasha and Ella, too.

She called her agent first, and then Chris.

Rachel arranged to meet her agent in the bar of the Century Club on Shaftesbury Avenue, one of the few places she could be sure that nobody would have the bad taste to mention her current not-so-private problems. There was a lot to talk about, her fee being top of the list, and it took two hours, and several bottles of fizzy water, before they allowed themselves a celebratory cocktail. The agent downed his quickly, and rushed off to another meeting, leaving Rachel to finish her drink in peace.

There was no hurry; Anna was taking care of the girls. Rachel sat back in her armchair, and tried to picture her life as a wealthy single mother.

She wasn't alone for long. Nick had been waiting and watching.

'If I didn't know you better, I'd think you were avoiding me,' he said, slipping into the seat beside her.

Rachel took a sip of martini. 'What makes you think I'm not?'

'Because you're not stupid.'

'You say the sweetest things.' It seemed a shame to waste such a good cocktail, but she started putting on her coat.

'The price goes up every time, you know,' said Nick, laying a hand on her arm.

'Goodbye, Nick.' He looked ill, ugly, sweaty. How could she ever have desired him?

'Not so fast.' His grip was tight. She sat down. 'That's better. You think I'm bluffing, don't you?'

'Oh, no. I'm sure you're capable of sinking to any depths.'

'You'd better believe it. It's all ready to go. All I have to do is press the send button and there it is. Your arse for the world to see.'

'Go ahead.'

'Very brave, Rachel. Very noble. What is it? Publish and be damned?'

'Something like that.'

'What do you think Sky will make of it?'

'You seem to know an awful lot about my life. Nice of you to take such an interest.'

'I know exactly how much you can afford, and I know how much you've got to lose. That's why the price keeps going up.'

'You're full of shit.'

'With every week that Charlie stays in the show, you can afford to pay me just a little bit more.'

'This is sick. Let me go.'

'And now you've got this job . . .'

'What job?'

'Come on, Rach. Everyone in this club knows that you're going to work for Gerald Partridge again. They might not know exactly why you're quite so perfect for the role.'

'Okay, Nick. Here's the deal.' She knocked back her drink. 'If you come anywhere near me or my family again, I am going straight to the police. This is blackmail, pure and simple. And that's a crime.'

'Fine,' said Nick. 'Do what you think best. And when your divorce comes through, and they're deciding who gets custody of the kids, don't be surprised if the judge decides you're not fit to be a mother. Did I mention the close-ups?'

'You did.'

'They're very good, you know. Very clear. Obviously you. Considering the circumstances, the low lighting. Digital video wasn't so brilliant in those days. But, you know, it scrubs up surprisingly well. Not quite high definition, but good enough. DVD sales should be pretty healthy. And, hey, if you play nicely, I'll give you a cut. Only fair, isn't it? Mention that to your agent.'

He walked out, nodding to acquaintances as he left.

The villa was a strange, higgledy-piggledy construction that seemed to pour down over three terraced levels, looking out from the steep side of the city over the great Umbrian plain beyond. The interiors were dark and cool, the walls covered in William Morris wallpaper – willow in the kitchen, acanthus in the dining room, golden lily in the bedroom – the furniture black with age. Elizabeth spent a happy afternoon getting lost in the maze of rooms, and then, in the cool of the evening, set up her laptop in the shade of a large persimmon tree, looking over the garden wall at the endless misty view. She wrote until it was dark and cold, poured herself a large whisky and went to bed. It took a while to get to sleep; strange bed, strange house, strange country. And she had the most unsettling dreams – not of this house, but of a substantial four-bedroom house in north London, with leaded lights, a smart gravel drive, clipped conifers and neat lawns. She had been dreaming of the house a lot recently, like the second Mrs de Winter returning to Manderley. Sometimes she dreamed that they had never left, that Susan and the Prof were still alive, and she and Chris, although grown up, were still their children. Sometimes she dreamed that Anna allowed her to stay, and she drifted from room to room noting with sadness the decay of things, but happy despite it all just to be back within those walls.

If I go on like this, she thought, sipping coffee under the persimmon tree the next morning, I will go mad.

She put on scarf and shades and climbed the steep cobbled street to the Piazza del Popolo, the perfectly proportioned square that led the eye and the feet straight to the cathedral steps. It was tempting, thought Elizabeth, to seek out the nearest priest and make confession. To be welcomed into the religious life, take holy orders, live out the rest of her days in silent contemplation. Chastity, poverty and obedience . . . Well, the chastity bit wouldn't be too difficult. She hadn't had any action in that department for so long, she could hardly remember what all the fuss was about. All that effort and discomfort, all the ridiculous positions that people get themselves into . . .

God, she thought with a horrified jolt, I've turned into Charlotte. The bitter bluestocking, the thin-lipped critic of those who are really living.

She walked towards the cathedral and mounted the first few steps. The tourist coaches must have arrived; she could see the crowds forging up the hill from the lower part of town. Soon the piazza would be teeming with families, children screaming, cameras clicking, teenagers texting, another day's litter piling up on the cathedral steps, empty tins rolling through the square.

Time, then, for a few moments' silent contemplation in the church, a breath of incense and then back to the shade of the persimmon tree. She pushed open the heavy old door, and turned her back on the advancing crowds.

She had still not switched on her phone.

'Chris, darling, it's Rachel.'

'Hi. What's up?'

'Any word from Elizabeth?'

'Not yet.'

'You did call, didn't you?'

'I left a message. She might not be able to pick it up. I don't even know if she gets network coverage where she is.'

'Will you try again?'

'Okay, if you want. But I'm sure she'll –'

'The thing is, Chris, I really need this job.'

Chris grimaced at Dev; they, like everyone else, had read about Charlie and Shania's hot new love affair. 'I'll let you know as soon as I hear anything.'

'She's not changed her mind, has she?'

'Of course not,' said Chris, assuming that even Elizabeth

wouldn't do something so perverse. 'I'm sure she'll call, and I'll let you know just as soon as she does.'

'Promise?'

'I promise.'

The sunshine dazzled her when she left the cathedral, the sea of humanity rushing in where she, battling against the tide, was trying to get out. She could see only silhouettes, hear only a babble of voices.

'Liz? Liz Miller?'

Shit, she thought. Someone's recognised me. She clamped the sunglasses to her face, put her head down and headed for the steps.

'Wait! Liz! It's me!'

It's always 'me' – someone she met at a party, or a guest she'd had on the show, where they'd pretended to be great friends while the cameras were rolling. These people never knew when it was over.

'Liz! It's me! It's Mike!'

Mike? Not . . . Mike?

She turned, so the sun was behind her, his face in front of her. It was, unmistakably, Mike Harris, former editor of the Daily Beacon, former boss and former lover. He was balder and uglier than ever.

'Good God,' she said. 'What are you doing here?'

'I'm on holiday.'

'What a coincidence,' she said. 'So am I.' She looked around for his wife. 'Well, enjoy the cathedral. It's really wonderful.'

'Wait,' he said. 'I've seen plenty of cathedrals in the last week. They're starting to look the same. I don't suppose it would matter too much if I gave this one a miss.'

'Oh, that would be a shame. There's some very fine glass.' She gestured upwards. 'The rose window, for instance . . .'

'Can I take you for lunch? I mean, if you have time.'

'Lunch? But surely . . . I mean, aren't you . . .'

'I'm alone, if that's what you're asking. Both on this trip, and in general. My wife and I are separated.'

'I see.' This was news; how come she hadn't heard? 'Well, why not?' Let the writing wait for once. 'There's a very nice little place on the corner of the square.' A clock started to strike the hour. They looked up; it was only eleven.

'Is it too early for an *aperitivo*?'

Elizabeth considered for a moment. A life of chastity, poverty and obedience, or a glass of something cold with a man who had once made her feel desired?

'It's never too early for an *aperitivo*,' she said, and took his arm as they walked down the cathedral steps.

Rachel walked around the living room, trying to calm Ella, who had a temperature, and had been fretful and nauseous all day. She wasn't feeling too good herself; a cold was the last thing she needed right now, as the photographers started circling again, vying for that one candid snap that would show Rachel was cracking under the strain.

There was still no word from Elizabeth. Perhaps, after all, it had just been some kind of joke. She wouldn't get the job, and she wouldn't get the money, and she'd end up with no husband, two children and a blackmailer around her neck.

She texted Chris again, knowing that it would achieve nothing, but unable to stop herself. If she simply did nothing, she might panic.

Elizabeth lay in bed, her eyes scanning the intricate tracery of the golden lily wallpaper, Mike Harris sleeping beside her.

This kind of thing doesn't happen in real life, she thought – the two old lovers meeting by chance in a romantic setting, letting bygones be bygones, falling into bed after the best Italian food and wine that money can buy. Good things like that certainly don't happen to me. God, she thought, if things go on like this, maybe my life is about to change . . .

She suddenly remembered Chris, and the unanswered question of Rachel's participation in *The Best Revenge*.

She reached for her handbag, and found her phone. Almost as soon as she switched it on, it started beeping.

Mike stirred, turned towards her, put an arm across her waist. 'Work?' he said.

'Yes, work.' Voicemails and texts, all from Chris.

'Good news?'

She opened one. 'Yes,' she said. 'Very good news.'

Chapter 36

Planning the great rapprochement between two women who had not spoken to each other for five years, but who had affected each other as the moon affects the sea, stretched Chris's organisational skills to breaking point. Neutral ground, of course, but some grounds were more neutral than others. Chris suggested a restaurant; Elizabeth vetoed it because it was an 'actors' hang-out'. Chris suggested a club; Rachel turned her nose up, because they'd once refused Charlie's application for membership. A picnic in the park? Too cold (Rachel) and too public (Elizabeth). His house? No: both women thought he would side with the other. Exasperated, Chris said, 'What do you want? A private capsule on the London Eye?', thinking this was ridiculously over-the-top and James Bond, but the suggestion was accepted and the capsule duly booked. And so, as dusk fell over the city one chilly November evening, Rachel Hope and Elizabeth Miller approached County Hall from opposite directions, both dressed to kill, both determined to keep cool and businesslike. If *she* wants to start something, then it won't be *my* fault. *I* am a professional – but I don't know about *her*.

Elizabeth left her driver on Westminster Bridge.

Rachel got off the Tube at Waterloo.

Chris was waiting at the London Eye ticket office, expecting at any moment to hear the theme music from *High Noon*, to see tumbleweed blowing along the riverfront. If it came to a bloodbath, he'd be well out of it. He's usher them into their capsule, let the doors shut and wave them on their merry way.

For half an hour, they'd be sealed in a glass bubble high above the water. They could scream themselves hoarse, and no one would hear. If the pod walls were running with blood and clumps of hair when it touched down, he would simply dial 999 and wash his hands of the whole affair.

Rachel turned up first, wearing a long, soft camel coat, the collar turned up, her dark hair twisted in a knot on the back of her head. She was carrying the Marc Jacobs handbag. 'Well,' she said, blowing on her hands, her breath smoking, 'I'm here. Do you think she's going to . . .' And then, in a long, soft black coat, the collar turned up, her blonde hair sleek in shoulder-length layers, Elizabeth arrived from the west. Both women were wearing Remembrance Day poppies. They looked, thought Chris, like each other's negatives.

'Hello Chris,' said Elizabeth, and kissed her brother lightly on the cheek.

'Hi.'

Neither woman acknowledged the other except through side-long glances. Damn, they both thought. She's looking good.

'Right,' said Chris, 'I've got your tickets.' He handed them one each.

'Aren't you coming with us?' said Rachel, sounding slightly panicked.

'Two's company,' said Chris, offering each an arm. Neither took it. They walked towards the Eye two or three yards apart; either could have bolted into the crowd and disappeared. Somehow he herded them successfully across the few yards of pavement and on to the boarding ramp. The queue moved slowly. Chris made a few observations, which were not picked up by his sisters. Discouraged, he fell silent.

'Right,' he said, when they got to the pod door. 'This is as far as I go. Ladies, your carriage awaits.'

The attendant ushered them in as the empty pod glided by. The doors closed softly behind them, and the ascent began.

'Well,' said Rachel, with that big, screen-melting, too-wide smile, all brilliant teeth and rosy-pink gums, 'this is exciting. I've never been on it before.'

'Nor me,' said Elizabeth, going to the glass and looking out towards the City. 'One of those things one always meant to do, but never got round to.'

'The girls would love it.'

'Ah, yes. The girls. How old are they now?'

'Sasha's three. Ella is eighteen months.'

'Wow. How did that happen?'

'Time flies by,' said Rachel.

'It certainly does.'

They fell silent as they started to climb. Suddenly, they saw the downstream view, a wide ribbon of black water bordered with lights, the sky rising huge and dark above them.

'Five years,' said Elizabeth at last. 'It's a long time.'

'Elizabeth, I've never had a chance to say sorry.'

That was good, thought Elizabeth, glancing at her watch. We've been in here less than two minutes, and she's already apologised. She's either sincere, or she's very clever. I've never really been sure which.

'Well, I . . .' said Elizabeth, and suddenly realised she didn't know what to say. Should it be 'that's all ancient history, we both made mistakes, let's start again'? Or should it be 'you hurt me very badly indeed, you screwed up my whole life and turned me into the hard, bitter obsessive you see before you'? Neither was satisfactory. Where was the middle ground? Where was Chris when she needed him?

'I suppose you know why I wanted to see you,' she said finally, sounding even to her own ears unnecessarily businesslike.

'Yes,' said Rachel. 'Your kind job offer.'

'I don't know about kind.'

'All right, then,' said Rachel. 'Not kind.'

The gloves were inching off.

'Well? What do you think?'

'The money's very good, and I'm not in a position to turn it down at the moment.' They watched the dome of St Paul's appear above the scrum of buildings on the waterfront. 'I have two children to support, and as you're well aware, my marriage isn't exactly a bed of roses. I have to take whatever work I'm offered.'

'I was sorry to hear about you and Charlie,' said Elizabeth.

Like hell, thought Rachel, but said, 'thank you.'

'So,' said Elizabeth, 'Chris says you might be persuaded to say yes to the job.'

'I made my mind up when my agent got the details of the fee.'

'And what do you think of the role?'

'I don't care about the role. I'll play Rosemary West if it puts bread on the table.'

'You realise, of course, that this is a work of fiction?'

'Oh *yes*, Elizabeth,' said Rachel, with undue emphasis. 'Of *course* I understand that. I'm sure there will be one of those little disclaimers about "any resemblance to persons living or dead". I mean, why on earth would anyone jump to the silly conclusion that the total bitch of a stepsister is in any way based on little old me? It's just one of those crazy showbiz coincidences that you *happened* to want me to play it when we *happen* to be related by marriage. I understand that perfectly.'

'It was Gerald Partridge's idea, not mine.'

'He always had balls, I'll say that for him.'

'It makes sound commercial sense.'

'Oh, yes. And I'll promote the hell out of it. I'm not proud.

I'll flog our story to anyone who wants it, if it ensures high viewing figures and repeats and overseas sales. My agent's very hot on all that stuff.'

'Of course,' said Elizabeth. 'These things are important.'

'A matter of life or death,' said Rachel.

They were approaching the ten o'clock position, a third of the way round their ride.

'My God,' said Elizabeth, looking down through the glass sides, 'how high we are.'

'We've got a way to go yet,' said Rachel, looking up.

Back at ground level, Chris watched the capsule ascending until it was beyond the range of the lights and he could no longer see its occupants. At least there had been no hair-pulling or face-slapping so far. He had enough time to repair to the bar of the Royal Festival Hall, order a large whisky and text Dev an update.

In a scorching patch of desert punctuated by giant aloes somewhere in the eastern reaches of Andalucia, Charlie Evans and Shania Tennyson were posing for press photographers along with the remaining contestants in *Stars Under Fire*. Charlie was doing well; he'd dropped several kilos and got his body back into shape, and after a few weeks in the Spanish sun he was getting a good suntan. He knew his way round a wide range of weapons, he had excelled at the assault course and, in real-life, make-believe battles behind enemy lines, had managed to wipe out several of his opponents. He was confident of a place in the finals. So was Shania, not because of any particular aptitude for warfare, but because she found it necessary to take regular showers. They stood with their arms round each other's waists, their heads touching. Their affair had gone down very well with the viewing public.

Once the photographers had gone, she turned on him.

'Well?' she said. 'Have you seen a lawyer or haven't you?'

'Stop pressuring me,' said Charlie. 'I told you, I'll do it when I'm ready and not a minute before.'

'I don't believe you, Charlie Evans. I don't think you want a divorce.'

'I do, babe, I do,' he lied, because the more he got to know Shania, the more he seemed to appreciate his wife. 'You've got to give me time.'

'I'll give you a week,' she said, and stomped off to the make-up tent to have her face touched up. They were on air in an hour.

Up in north London, Anna was staring into the bathroom mirror. The lights were bright, but even so you could barely make out the bruising. She squeezed a tiny spot more concealer out of the tube, and dabbed it around her right eye. Standing back to survey the effect, she realised that she looked lopsided. The concealer had taken out not only the bruising, but also the dark shadows from too many sleepless nights, too many years on this bloody planet.

She balanced herself up with more concealer under the left eye.

The skin was not so tender there. Her right eye was still sore from where Rick had fetched her a stinging backhander as he stormed out of the house – hopefully, for the last time.

Well, thought Anna, a black eye is a small price to pay for getting rid of Rick. Good riddance to bad rubbish. Time for me to be an independent woman, to cultivate interests other than bad men, to sort out my financial affairs and look to the future.

She said this every time she bust up with a boyfriend.

She did not yet know that Rick, who was rather more computer-savvy than her previous boyfriends, had emptied several hundred thousand pounds from her online savings account, using her username and password, which she had a very bad habit of writing on a Post-it note attached to the side of the computer.

In his flat in west London, Nick Sharkey was composing a text message to Rachel Hope.

Time is running out, it read. If u do not pay me the agreed sum by Friday, then u r going live on xtube. Don't say I didn't warn u.

Just as they passed their zenith, Rachel's phone beeped.

'Shit,' she said, 'sorry. I thought I'd turned that off.'

'It's probably Chris making sure we haven't killed each other.'

'What shall I tell him? The bitch has her hands round my throat. Can't breathe . . .'

Elizabeth laughed. 'No, give him a real shock. Tell him that we've kissed and made up.'

Rachel returned the laugh, but it died on her lips when she saw who the text was from. 'Oh, shit,' she said.

'Is it the girls? Are they okay?'

'What? Oh, the girls are fine. It's . . . something else. A work thing.'

'Oh.' Elizabeth waited for more, 'Anyway, as you say, the money's good. With the kind of money they're talking about, I could give up TV. I could actually concentrate on writing some proper books. Not just rubbish like this, but . . . Rachel? Are you okay?'

'I'm fine,' said Rachel, running a hand over her brow, which was as pale as ivory. 'I think it's just the height. It's made me feel a bit . . .' She sat down hard. 'Oh dear. Sorry.' She closed her eyes and breathed deeply.

Elizabeth fought an impulse to put an arm around her. Rachel was trying to delete the message, but her eyes were clouded and her fingers too clumsy for the tiny buttons. 'Shit,' she said, attempting to throw the phone into her bag but chucking it on the floor instead. It spun and skidded to Elizabeth's feet.

It was impossible not to see the name in the inbox.

Nick Sharkey.

'Oh,' said Elizabeth. 'I see.'

The wheel was definitely going down now, a slightly queasy sensation.

'It's not what you think.'

'I don't think anything in particular,' said Elizabeth. 'But I'm guessing it wasn't a purely social call.'

'There's nothing pure about Nick Sharkey,' said Rachel, then took a sharp intake of breath. There. The name was out of her mouth, hovering in the air between them, a third party in the pod.

'No,' said Elizabeth. 'I would never have described Nick as pure.'

They looked into each other's eyes, both remembering a time long ago when the future had looked so different.

'What does he want?'

'Money,' said Rachel with a shrug. 'What else?'

'How much?'

'About as much as I'm being offered to do this job.'

'He always did have an uncanny sense of how much to ask for.'

'It goes up every week.'

'Rachel,' said Elizabeth, trying to keep her voice even, 'is Nick blackmailing you?'

'Of course he is.'

'More photos?'

'Photos? Oh, they're old news. No, darling, this is the full-length triple-X-rated motion picture version. Quite the film-maker, our Nick, even then. Very clever use of hidden cameras, available light and so on. He says it's pin-sharp.'

'We have a problem.'

'You can say that again.'

'And what,' said Elizabeth, as the pod glided past the three-quarter point of their journey, 'are we going to do about it?'

'*We?*'

'Yes, we. It's my problem, too, now. I need this deal just as much as you do, and if Nick screws it up like this, the whole thing will be cancelled. '

'You can get another actress. The world is full of girls who would kill for this part.'

'Gerald Partridge doesn't want them. He wants you.'

Rachel wiped her eyes, blew her nose, surveyed her face in a little round compact. 'Well,' she said, 'it's nice to be wanted. So.' She snapped the compact shut, dropped it in her bag. 'Any suggestions?'

'I'll talk to my lawyers.'

'If this goes to court, it'll be just as bad. It'll be all over the press. Nick knows I daren't do that.'

'So what's the alternative?'

Rachel sighed. 'I just wish I could press a button and make Nick Sharkey disappear.'

Elizabeth thought for a while, as the capsule came back down towards the river. 'You know,' she said, 'I think we might be able to do just that.'

Chapter 37

Having a common enemy did more to heal the rift between Elizabeth and Rachel than any amount of forgiveness and diplomacy. The fact that they both stood to lose a great deal of money if Nick Sharkey carried out his threats wiped out any remaining grudges, at least for the time being. Hating Nick allowed them to like each other – and it was easy to believe that he was responsible for all that had happened in the past. He was the villain of the piece. By the time they stepped off the London Eye, he'd practically sprouted horns and hooves. They took a taxi to the Groucho Club, found a quiet table and assessed the threat.

'What exactly does he have on you, Rachel?'

'You don't want to know.'

'I think I need to.'

'Okay.' Rachel took a deep breath. 'He filmed us having sex one night in your flat.'

'I see.' Elizabeth's head swam for a second, but she took a deep breath and got herself under control. 'Just before the wedding?'

'I'm afraid so.'

'And all that time,' said Elizabeth, 'I thought his plans to become a photographer were bullshit. Just goes to show, doesn't it? You never can tell.'

'He's been holding it over me ever since, either to keep me in line or, after I'd finished with him for good, to get money out of me. First of all, there were the photos.'

'For which I must take some of the blame,' said Elizabeth, staring into her glass. 'I gave him access to the press.'

Rachel waved a hand. 'No real harm done. My producers say they won me a whole new fanbase. But now he's threatening to post the video footage on the Internet.'

'And I suppose it's . . . explicit?'

'Yes, I think we can safely assume that.'

'Do you think he's bluffing? I mean, if people can see you in the film, they can also see him.'

'He might be. But what's he got to lose? People will just think he's a bit of a lad. Whereas I will be branded as a complete slut. My marriage is in enough trouble as it is, and this will be the final nail in the coffin. You can just imagine what the judge would say if it comes to a custody battle.'

'You don't know that. Being in a sex tape doesn't necessarily mean you're a bad mother. Look at Pamela Anderson.'

'That's Hollywood. They do things differently there. Besides, I'd like to have a career in which my shady past isn't mentioned in every single interview.'

Elizabeth was thoughtful, picking at the label on the wine bottle. 'We could just take it on the chin and turn the publicity to our advantage, of course.'

'Easy for you to say.'

'You said yourself that the photos didn't do you any harm.'

'This is different.'

'It's only a question of scale.'

'No. I'm sorry. I have to think about my children. Besides which, there's the little matter of the contract. What do you think Sky would say? Not to mention foreign broadcasters? We want this to go out on network prime-time, not at three in the morning on subscription channels.'

'Fair point.' After all her years castigating the moral short-comings of the television industry, Elizabeth could hardly start arguing for the publicity value of sex tapes. 'So, how can we stop him? I presume money would do it.'

'More money than I've got,' said Rachel. 'And anyway, I don't trust him. If we shut him up now, he'll just be back in a year or so. As long as we're successful, he won't rest.'

'What about threats?'

'Short of holding a gun to his head, I can't think of anything we could threaten him with.'

'Then I don't see what our options are,' said Elizabeth. 'You won't go to the police, you can't afford to pay him and you're not prepared to let him do his worst. It seems like Nick has got us exactly where he wants us. Yet again.'

'Me,' said Rachel. 'He's got me. You can just bail out. He's got nothing on you.'

'What do you mean, bail out?'

'Sack me. Get another girl.'

'It's not quite that simple,' said Elizabeth. 'Without you, the series won't get made. Gerald Partridge made that quite clear. You must have made a very big impression on him.'

'There's only one thing that makes a big impression on Gerald Partridge,' said Rachel, 'and that's the bottom line. If he wants me in this show, it's because he thinks it'll make more money.'

'And he's probably right. If I was him, I'd do the same. It's irresistible, isn't it? Two famous women with a spicy back story, the man that came between them, the tears and tantrums, nobody really knowing where the truth ends and the fiction begins. Guaranteed monster hit. Genius. Sends my book to the top of the best-seller list on both sides of the Atlantic, and keeps it there. Magazine profiles, *Vanity Fair*, Annie Liebovitz, the whole works. But only if you're on side. Without you, it looks like the carpings of a bitter old spinster.'

'So? Just ditch the whole project. You don't need it.'

'Yes, I do.'

'Why? You've got more money than you know what to do with. You're famous. You're a celebrity. Your books will sell.'

'Oh, they'll sell a bit, but only as long as I have a TV show on which to promote them. I don't have any particular illusions about myself, Rachel. I don't think I'm a great writer. I'm not the next Jilly Cooper, and I'm certainly not the next Susan Barnard. If I keep doing the show, I can crank out the odd novel that will sell on the strength of my TV profile. But I want more than that. I want to get out of the TV business and write full time. I'm not much good now because I can only do it in the evenings when I'm exhausted. I'm twenty-eight now. If I start right away, I might write a decent book by the time I'm forty.'

'What's stopping you? You could give up your job tomorrow and have enough to live on for a year or two.'

'True. And I'd be back to square one. But if we make *The Best Revenge*, I'll be starting at the top. My books will be snapped up by publishers, they'll be optioned for film, and I'll have a career.'

'Okay. You've convinced me. We both want this job, we both need to stop Nick from releasing his film and neither of us has a clue what to do next.'

'But I know a man who might,' said Elizabeth. 'Leave it with me.'

Elizabeth had been looking for an excuse to see Mike Harris since they got back from Italy. What happened in Umbria could have been a holiday romance, nothing more, two old lovers reuniting in the irresistibly romantic atmosphere of blue skies and cypress trees, parting again in the chilly reality of London, picking up their real lives. But it didn't have to be that way. Mike was no longer married, for one thing, and no longer her boss, for another.

He'd taken a generous redundancy package from the Daily Beacon as the paper hurtled towards closure, and used the money to set himself up as a freelance media consultant, currently numbering a handful of large city firms among his clients. If anyone could give useful advice, it was Mike.

He answered his phone on the first ring, and said, 'Liz! At last!', and invited her out for dinner without even asking what she wanted. If nothing else, thought Elizabeth, she might get a lover out of all this, if not a sister.

They flirted over the starters and the main course. When Mike's dessert arrived, and Elizabeth sipped a decaffeinated coffee, she laid her cards on the table.

'It seems,' said Mike, when Elizabeth had outlined the facts of the case, 'that Sharkey holds all the aces.'

'That's the conclusion we came to.'

'And you're absolutely committed to the idea of making this film, are you? I mean, this isn't just some complicated way of getting your own back.'

'No,' sighed Elizabeth. 'Believe me, I'm tempted to call the whole thing off, tell Gerald Partridge I've changed my mind and just carry on as if nothing had ever happened.'

'Then why don't you?'

'Because this is the chance of a lifetime. I can get out of all that celebrity stuff, and have a real life.'

'Sure that's what you want? Could you let it go? You're very good at it. I'm proud of you.'

'Mike,' said Elizabeth, 'I hate it. I hate every show I do. I hate the audiences, I hate the guests and, most of all, I hate myself. I don't want to be Liz Miller – the Bitch on the Box any more. I want to start again.'

'And you think that making this show is the way to do that?'

'It's a means to an end.'

'Spoken like a pro. So,' said Mike, 'what are you going to do?'

'I was rather hoping you'd tell me. I've thought of everything.'

'I very much doubt that,' said Mike, grinning and rubbing his hands, just as he did when a juicy human interest story landed on the *Beacon*'s front page.

'Well, genius, what would you suggest?'

'Play him at his own game. Find his weak spot, and attack.'

'He doesn't have a weak spot. He's got nothing to lose. He's a blackmailer and a pornographer.'

'Everyone has a weak spot, Liz. It's just a question of finding it.'

'And if we find this Holy Grail, what then?'

'You make sure that your threat is equal to his. Mutually Assured Destruction. A very good starting point for diplomacy.'

'It sounds so simple. But I don't know where to start.'

'Come on, Liz. You're a journalist. You just have to start digging.'

'I'm a very busy journalist.'

'Do you want this, or don't you?'

'I want it.'

'Then,' said Mike, licking the last bit of ice cream off his spoon, 'get digging.'

Elizabeth held a Conference of War-come-Sunday lunch at her flat. Sitting at the table were the four people who, she thought, might between them come up with the final solution to the Nick Sharkey problem.

She was at the head of the table. Opposite her was Rachel. On her left was Chris, and on her right, Mark.

If these people didn't know something that would spike Nick's guns, then they might as well send the contracts back to Gerald Partridge and tell Jan to take *The Best Revenge* off the market. But after two hours, a large roast chicken, a whole bowl of roast potatoes and several bottles of wine, they were no nearer a solution.

'Oh, this is hopeless,' wailed Rachel, close to tears of frustration. 'Why are we wasting our time talking? He's already asking for more than this bloody job's going to earn me. I'm ruined either way.'

'There's no point in getting hysterical,' said Chris. 'We just have to be methodical. That's what Dev said.'

'I'm sure I could get a list of everyone Nick's had sex with,' said Mark. 'That would be a start.'

'And what good's that going to do us?' said Elizabeth. 'Everyone knows that Nick can't keep it in his pants. We need something much more incriminating.'

'Well, you've known him longer than any of us,' said Chris. 'Isn't there something shady in his past?'

'He used to deal a bit of dope to his friends. He didn't always pay his council tax. What else? He might have got a few parking tickets. It's not the collateral we're looking for.'

'He dealt more than dope, darling,' said Mark. 'A friend of mine worked as a hairdresser's assistant on a shoot that he was doing a couple of years ago . . .'

'Oh Christ, Mark,' said Rachel, 'we're not going to get another of your interminable stories of what the hairdresser's assistant told the woman who held the brushes for the deputy make-up artist, are we?'

'All right, then, fuck off,' said Mark, folding his arms across this chest. 'What do I know? Nothing, apparently.'

'We need hard facts,' said Elizabeth.

'Well, I heard that he was running around with that model, what's her name? The lesbian one. Well, she used to be a lesbian. A has-bian.'

'Converting a lesbian is something most men would boast about. We need something he'd be ashamed of. Something he wants to hide.'

'I'm just trying to say . . .'

'Look,' said Rachel, 'I really appreciate what everyone's trying to do. But it's not going to work. I think I just have to bite the bullet and pay up.'

'That's a thoroughly defeatist attitude,' said Chris.

'But what choice do we have? It's not you who's facing disaster. Even if I don't lose my girls, every single person in the world is going to see me on the Internet. Do you know what that's like? To walk into a room and have everyone think you're a slut?'

'It's not that bad,' said Mark.

'Okay,' said Chris. 'Let's assume that there really is something that Nick wants to hide. Each of us knows a little bit about Nick. We just have to fit the pieces together. It's like a jigsaw. The picture will emerge.'

'I'll start, then,' said Elizabeth. 'He had these friends in Dalston, I think it was, where he used to get his dope.'

'Tabitha Mensah, that was her name,' said Mark.

'Who?'

'The model Nick was going out with.'

'Oh God, her,' said Chris. 'Didn't she die, or something?'

'No, she's still alive, because a friend of mine saw her in a club the other day.

'The one you're thinking of is that singer. You know, her girl-friend. Libby Whatsername. She's the one that died.'

'Libby Wallace?' said Chris. 'Wow, did she really have an affair with Tabitha Mensah? I never knew that.'

'Oh, everyone was talking about it at the time. Always snogging in public. I don't think Libby was really a dyke, she just did it for the publicity, Anyway . . .'

'Could we give the gay gossip a rest!' said Rachel, her hands buried in her hair. 'We're not talking about Libby Wallace or Tabitha Mensah! We're talking about me, here. Me!'

Mark tutted and rolled his eyes. 'Typical actress,' he said. 'Me me me.'

'Please,' said Elizabeth, 'let's have some order. As I was saying, he had these friends in Dalston, where he used to get his dope.'

'Oh, this is a waste of time,' said Mark, standing up. 'I'm off.'

'Go on, then,' said Rachel. 'Don't bother calling me again.'

'I won't, darling. See you on XTube.' He emptied his glass, and left the room.

'And then there were three,' said Chris. 'Go on, Liz. Dalston, dope. What else have we got?'

'Rachel. Can you think of anything?'

Rachel rested her head on her forearms and said nothing.

'Okay,' said Chris, catching Elizabeth's eye, 'let's assume he's still dealing drugs. It started with a bit of dope to his mates, then he got greedy. Cocaine. Ecstasy. Crystal meth.'

'We don't have any proof of that, though,' said Elizabeth.

'Admit it!' wailed Rachel, 'this is hopeless. I give up.' For the first time that either of them could remember, Rachel looked ugly. 'I might as well just kill myself.'

Mark popped his head round the door. 'Just like Libby Wallace,' he said.

'I thought you'd left.'

'Well, if you're going to kill yourself, I'd better say goodbye properly. Goodbye, Rachel. Thanks for the memories. Oh, and if you see Natasha in heaven, or hell, or wherever it is that girls like you end up, say hi from me.'

Rachel pouted, and said nothing.

'What was it that Libby Wallace took?' said Chris. 'What killed her?'

'Crystal meth, as far as I know.'

Three pairs of eyes looked up at him.

'Funny, isn't it,' said Mark, 'that you can search and search for something and it turns out it was staring you in the face all along?'

'What do you mean?' asked Chris.

'Who, me?' Mark pressed a hand to his chest. 'Little me? What could I possibly say that was of any interest to you lot? Just silly gay gossip.' He flapped his wrist. 'No, you don't want to listen to me.'

'Mark, for God's sake,' said Elizabeth. 'If you know something, please tell us.'

'Well,' said Mark, 'it might be something, or it might be nothing. A friend of mine was styling on this shoot with Libby Wallace, although "styling" might be stretching it a bit, because she refused to wear anything he'd brought for her, and insisted on wearing the skanky stuff that she came in. Apparently, it was absolutely minging.'

'Go on,' said Chris.

'So, she's staggering around, in and out of the loo all the time, God knows what she was taking. A bit of everything, I should imagine. And then, apparently, she disappeared for half an hour with the photographer. Kept everyone just standing around waiting.'

'Who was the photographer?' asked Elizabeth, upon whom a faint light was dawning.

'Oh, silly me,' said Mark. 'Didn't I say? Now let me see. What was his name. No, don't tell me. I'll get there. Ah!' He raised his finger, and beamed at the company. 'That's it! His name was Nick Sharkey.'

Chapter 38

Mark chased rumours with the tenacity of a terrier, talking to a hairdresser here, a stylist there, buying endless drinks for over-groomed, over-tanned hangers-on who just happened to know a thing or two, yes, but their lips were sealed, at least until alcohol unsealed them. It didn't take long to put the pieces of the jigsaw together. Mutually Assured Destruction? Oh, yes, they thought, rubbing their hands in glee as the picture emerged. Who would have thought that Nick Sharkey had so much to hide?

It didn't take much to work out that Nick was a drug dealer – not just supplying a line or two to friends, but buying directly from major importers and manufacturers, and selling to a large clientele that included several household names. That was a useful, powerful piece of information that might be of interest to the police. But it quickly became apparent that Nick's dealing days were over, that he'd shut up shop and, as one informant put it with a sour expression, 'cleaned up his act'. Shopping someone retrospectively was never going to work; the police would think, rightly, that Rachel and Elizabeth were just two ex-girlfriends with a grudge.

Then there was the Libby Wallace story. Everyone seemed to know part of the truth, and made up the rest, but some details were consistent. Libby falling out of clubs at six in the morning, Libby's dramatic weight loss, Libby's regular trips to rehab, Libby's notorious all-night parties at her home in Primrose Hill. Others knew more, having actually been to these legendary parties, and they confirmed that Libby had a ravening appetite for cocaine, crack and crystal meth.

Those who were really in the know confirmed that Nick Sharkey was Libby's dealer of choice, that he supplied her personally, went to her parties and had pretty much set up shop in her house. The jury was out on whether or not they were lovers; some said yes, of course they were, others said that both Libby and Nick were so terminally drug-addled that neither of them could actually manage a sex life. It didn't really matter. Nick's intimacy with that circle, and his role within it, was unambiguous.

And then there was the matter of Libby Wallace's death.

There were plenty of theories. Some said it was suicide. Some claimed it was murder, with various crackpot ideas about motive (Libby was a spy, Libby was a working-class woman whose voice must be silenced, Libby was carrying the love child of the heir to the throne). Libby's family blamed the dealers who had got Libby hooked – and they were out for revenge. Her father, a notorious Essex criminal by the name of James 'Diamond Jim' Wallace, let it be known that there was a price on the head of the 'bastard what killed my little princess'.

The coroner said that Libby Wallace died as a result of a crystal meth overdose, and that there were underlying heart problems brought on by her massive consumption of drugs and alcohol. Some pointed out the fact – or coincidence – that several of Libby's inner circle, including her bosom buddy, model Tabitha Mensah, had similar health problems at the same time. Nobody had publicly stated that the one factor that linked Libby's death to the various blackouts, comas and near misses was the fact that they all shared a dealer – Nick Sharkey. But the fact had not gone unnoticed by Libby and Tabitha's friends. The two women had been at the studio together, and had both gone into the loo with Nick. One of them ended the day in hospital, one of them ended the day in the morgue.

And then Nick Sharkey shut up shop.

It didn't take a genius to work out that Nick was responsible for Libby's death, that he had somehow supplied her, perhaps inadvertently, with a fatal dose. But to give up dealing out of remorse? That didn't make sense. Nick was not the remorseful type, and he wouldn't surrender that kind of income unless he had no other choice. He must have been frightened, or coerced – and that kind of coercion could only come from someone of whom he was afraid. And who could that be?

A bigger dealer than him, of course. Someone higher up the food chain, who wanted to cover their tracks by putting Nick out of business. And if Nick was still not dealing, if he was desperate enough to be hounding Rachel for money, risking her going to the police, he must be very scared indeed.

The facts were starting to stack up. Nick was a dealer. Nick had caused Libby's death. Nick was terrified of Libby's family finding out, and kneecapping him – or worse. Nick was under pressure from his supplier to keep out of the business, unless he provided a trail that led the police straight to the source. As the number and power of his enemies increased, the net began to close around Nick Sharkey. Mutually Assured Destruction, Mike had said: find a threat that's equal to his, and you're in a position to bargain.

The council of war was smaller this time: Chris had opted out on Dev's advice, knowing that whatever happened now was likely to be illegal. So Elizabeth and Mark came to Rachel's house when the girls were tucked up in bed, Charlie still playing soldiers with Shania Tennyson in southern Spain.

Afterwards, there would be much debate over just whose brilliant idea it was to lure Nick Sharkey to an empty studio, slip a couple of Rohypnols in his drink and then, when he was under the influence of the drugs, extract a confession from him. Their video against his. If he posts the Rachel Tapes on the Internet, we release the confession to the police, the press and the grieving Wallace Family. Mutually Assured Destruction.

But at the time they were delighted with their plan. Elizabeth would book the studio and get hold of the camera; with her connections, what could be easier?

Rachel would send the invitation, make the arrangements, lure Nick in with a promise not just of money but of sex.

Mark would get the drugs. He thought he might have something like the appropriate dose knocking around the flat. Not that he was into date rape, of course, but it helped some people to relax.

And with Nick unable to resist, all they had to do was handcuff him to a chair and get him to spill the beans. What could possibly go wrong?

The date was set, the studio booked, and Nana Anna agreed to babysit. And so, as dusk fell one cold, wet evening in Earls Court, the three conspirators arrived at the studio with cameras, drugs and lingerie at the ready. Mark helped them set the stage, wished them luck and left.

'Hi.' A voice from the darkness. 'I'm over here.'

'Where?' Nick groped forward, feeling with his hands; dark studios were booby-trapped with cables and stands. 'I can't see a bloody thing. Turn on a light.'

A tap-tap-tap of high heels on a wooden floor. The voice again, nearer this time.

'Who needs light?' Rachel's voice, unmistakably. Low, husky, intimate – a tone Nick remembered well. 'We can do what we need to do in the dark.'

'Come on, love. I don't want to brain myself.' Nick was uneasy, sweating slightly. For all his threats and bravado, he'd downed a bottle of red wine and a couple of Valium in order to go through with the business. He felt superficially calm, but something was wrong. This darkness, he thought. That's what it is. It's freaking me out a bit, nothing more. I need light.

'All right, Nick.' Her voice was soothing now, almost motherly. 'I didn't realise you were such a baby.' She tutted. 'Honestly. A big boy like you afraid of the dark. And you always were a big boy, Nick. A very big boy.'

This was going to be easier than he thought. She never could resist him, even at a time like this. But if she thought all she had to do was drop her drawers in order for him to drop his price, she was very much mistaken.

There was a click, and a light went on – a small light on a stand, pointing downwards, almost directly into Nick's eyes. Between him and the lamp there was a silhouette.

Nick drew breath and bit his lip.

Her hair was loose, falling around her perfect shoulders. Her torso curved in from the width of the bust to the narrowness of the waist, impossibly narrow . . . Was she wearing a corset? And out again to the fullness of the hips. Then down, down, the thighs, the calves, the feet, the shoes, the heels.

She was carrying something, playing with it between her hands. Something long and soft. What was it?

She stepped forward, only a couple of yards from where Nick stood rooted to the spot. He could see her a little more clearly, fill in some of the details.

It was a glove. A long, black, satin glove that she was pulling through her hands. She was wearing the other one.

'You're dressed to kill,' he said, then cleared his throat. Damn! He sounded nervous. 'Expecting company?'

'Only you.'

'You always did know how to get a man's attention.' She was closer now, and he could see what she was wearing: a corset that pushed her breasts up almost to her chin, cut high on the legs. A suspender belt. Stockings, stilettos. Nothing else. Hair loose, face made up, nails painted.

'Not too shabby,' she said, running the gloved hand down the side of her ribcage till it rested on her hip. 'Of course, we're all older now. And wiser, I hope.'

'I hope so, too,' said Nick, thinking it was time he took control of the situation. 'So you've seen the wisdom of doing what I ask.'

'Oh, Nicky . . .' She slipped the glove round the back of his neck, and pulled him close. She smelled intoxicating. 'You don't really want to do this to me, do you? After all we've meant to each other?'

'Business is business, love.'

'When did you become so . . . hard?' She breathed the word, letting her thighs brush against his.

'You know me, Rachel,' he said. 'I'm always hard.'

'So I seem to recall. But surely some things should be kept private? Just between us? Hmm? What do you say?'

Their faces were close now, close enough to kiss. They had moved around so the light was on her, and he could see the wetness of her lips, the brilliance of her eyes.

'I've told you, Rachel. Play the game my way, and we can be friends again.'

She stepped back. 'Are you sure I can't change your mind?'

'It's too late for that.'

'Oh, well,' she said, running her hands through her hair in that well-remembered gesture, baring one perfectly shaved armpit. 'You can't blame a girl for trying.' The tone of her voice was businesslike now. 'At least let's have a drink on it.'

'Where's my money?'

'All I have to do is press a button and it goes straight into your account. Just like you said. There's the laptop, all charged up and ready to go. I just have to log on, enter the amount and whoosh!'

'Do it,' said Nick.

She was opening a bottle of champagne. Nick was thirsty, his mouth dry. A drink was just what he needed. The cork popped, a little smoke curled from the mouth, caught in the light, and she poured two glasses.

'What should we toast?' she said, handing him one. 'Old acquaintance? Absent friends?'

He didn't like the look on her face, the slight raising of the eyebrow. 'How about a toast to the future?' he said. 'That's good enough for me.'

'Very well, then.' She raised her glass. 'The future. A bright and prosperous future for all of us. Cheers.'

'Cheers.'

They drank.

'I'm cold,' she said. 'Seeing as you're immune to my charms, I might as well slip into something warmer.' She picked up a fleece that was tossed over a chair and pulled it over her head. It looked off with the stockings and heels. 'So much for my *femme fatale* act. Well, drink up.' She refilled his glass. 'No point in wasting good champagne. Now,' she said, tapping the computer keyboard, 'let's see if I can remember my password. Oh, I'm hopeless at all this stuff. Help me, Nick.'

Nick moved towards a chair, stumbling slightly, sitting heavily. The champagne must have pushed him over the top, he thought. Well, he'd have no more.

'It's Sasha's name, and then her date of birth. Oh, blast, I've done it wrong again. Are you all right? You look terrible.'

'Can you put some more lights on? This is giving me a headache.'

'Oh, sorry darling. Move round this way. You'll see better.' The shuffled round so the light was behind him. 'Now, let's try again.'

Nick's eyelids were drooping. The drugs were working faster than Rachel had expected. 'S, a, s, h, a,' she said, tapping in the letters, looking sideways at Nick. 'And then the birthday. Eighteenth of April.'

'I can't see the screen. It's the light . . .'

'There's nothing wrong with the light.'

'I can't see proper . . . properly . . . I feel . . .'

His head fell forward again. 'Nick, what's the matter?'

'Dunno.' He ran a hand over his forehead. It came away wet with sweat.

'Dear me. You'd better just sit quietly for minute.'

'Lie down,' he said, slumping sideways a little. 'Wanna lie down.'

Tap, tap, tap came another pair of heels across the floor. 'Whoozaire?'

A shadow extended against the wall in front of Nick. It looked familiar.

'Hello, Nick.'

He whipped his head round, and almost threw himself off the chair by doing so. 'What the fuck . . . Eliz'beth?'

'Aren't you going to say it's good to see me?'

Nick's eyes were closing, his mouth hanging open. 'Hewwo . . .' he managed to say. 'Hewwo, Liz'beth . . .'

They took one wrist each, and handcuffed him to the metal legs of the chair.

'Now the ankles,' said Elizabeth. 'Gently does it. He might kick.'

He didn't. He sat there, stupefied, while they bound his ankles with rope.

'There,' said Rachel. 'That's better. Now we can have a proper chat.'

They pushed the chair around so the light was shining directly into Nick's face. Elizabeth switched on the camera. 'And action!'

'Smile, Nicky,' said Rachel. 'You're on telly.'

His head was still hanging.

'How long did Mark say this bit lasts?' whispered Elizabeth.

'Only a few minutes. He should come round soon.'

'Nick. Can you hear me, Nick?'

The head rocked a bit, then came up. Nick's neck seemed to have turned to rubber, but he was conscious.

'There we are,' said Rachel. 'Now, Nick, we're going to ask you a few questions, and you're going to answer as honestly as you can. All right?'

'Fuck off.'

'That's not a very good way to start. Let's try again.'

'What do you want?'

'I want you to tell me all about Libby Wallace.'

'Libby . . .' His mouth hung open.

'Yes. You remember. What happened to Libby, Nick? What do you know about that?'

"S'an accident.'

'An accident? What was?'

'Jus'an ass'dent.'

'Nick, listen to me,' said Rachel, putting a hand on his shoulder. He fell forward, like a rag doll. 'I don't like this, Elizabeth.'

'He'll be fine.' But Elizabeth's voice was tense.

'Nick, tell me about the accident. Nick?' His head was on his chest again, saliva dripping from the corner of his mouth. 'Oh God, this isn't right. He shouldn't be like this.'

Elizabeth stepped out from behind the camera, and squatted

down in front of Nick's chair. 'Nick,' she said, in her most school-marmish voice. 'Now, Nick, listen to me. It's Elizabeth.'

His eyelids flickered, and his lips worked a little, but that was all.

'Is he all right?'

'I don't know. He doesn't seem to be –'

Nick's shoulders shrugged forward, and a stream of vomit flowed down his chest, pooled in his lap and splattered on to the floor.

'Oh, Jesus. What are we supposed to do?'

'I don't know. I'd better call Mark.'

Elizabeth fumbled with her mobile, and was already dialling when Nick started convulsing. It was gentle at first, just a slight tremor, increasing until he was shaking all over, making the chair jump across the floor.

'What the fuck is happening, Rachel?'

'I don't know.'

'Untie him, for God's sake.'

They plucked at the knots, fumbled with the handcuffs. It wasn't easy with him shaking like that.

'Get him on the floor. On his side.'

They rolled him into the recovery position, but it was too late. Nick was falling into a coma from which he would never wake.

Chapter 39

Rachel and Elizabeth stood at opposite sides of the studio, cowering against the walls. Between them, lying on the floor in an awkward foetal position, was the vomit-stained corpse of the man they had both once loved.

Rachel was shivering, despite the heat of the lights and the fleece she'd put on. It had nothing to do with the temperature. She was going into shock.

Elizabeth was clutching her phone in one hand, the tape from the video camera in the other. This was one home movie that would never be shown.

Much to her surprise, her brain seemed to be working quite calmly, and were it not for the fact that she was digging her nails so far into her palms that she was almost bleeding, you might never have known that she'd just committed manslaughter. Well, she thought – that certainly solves one of our problems. Nick will never release the Rachel Tapes now.

It did, however, leave them with the rather more urgent problem of what to do with the body.

She needed advice, but even the most hypothetical question would incriminate them. Besides, who could they trust? Mark? They might as well turn themselves in at the nearest police station; Mark would never be able to keep their secret. Mike? For all his pragmatism, Mike would never condone this kind of cover-up. Chris was out of the question (lawyer boyfriend), Charlie was in Spain with another woman, Kate would tell them to hand themselves in and Anna would panic and start screaming blue murder.

Elizabeth could only think of one other person. Someone who might just know the kind of people who could help. Someone who, moreover, was looking for a favour.

'What have we done?' said Rachel, her voice coming out in staccato bursts. 'What the hell have we done?'

Elizabeth marched across the floor, skirting the body of the man she nearly married. 'Get up, Rachel. Pull yourself together.'

'He's dead, isn't he?'

'Of course he's dead. Now change your clothes.'

'What?'

'Change. Put everything you're wearing in a bag and destroy it.'

'What are you talking about?'

'We've got to keep our heads. I'm going to call someone.'

'Who?'

'I'd better not tell you.'

'Okay.' Rachel was docile. She kicked off her shoes and wriggled out of her tights. 'I can't go to prison,' she said. 'I can't leave my girls.'

'Nobody's going to prison,' said Elizabeth, 'as long as we're sensible. I'll take care of everything.'

'Will you?'

'Yes. Now get dressed, and get away from here as inconspicuously as possible. Go somewhere where there are lots of people who know you. Make sure they all see you. Hurry.'

'What are you going to do?'

'I'm going to clean up this mess,' said Elizabeth.

Rachel changed into the clothes she'd arrived in, a plain black dress and a heavy winter coat. 'What now?'

'Go to a club. Get photographed, if possible. Establish your whereabouts.'

'And what about you?'

'Don't worry about me. You didn't see me tonight. Remember, as far as most people know we're barely on speaking terms.'

Rachel was crying. 'Oh, God, Elizabeth. What have we done?'

'Stop snivelling and get out of here.' Elizabeth's voice was harsh; if she relaxed for a moment, she'd crumble. Someone had to take control. 'Call me tomorrow morning.'

'I can't go home . . . Knowing . . .'

'You must. Things must be normal. Where are the girls?'

'At home. Mum's with them.'

'What time's she expecting you home?'

'Late.'

'Good. Now go.'

Elizabeth watched Rachel hurrying down the street. As soon as she was safely away from the building and out of sight, she clicked into her address book and found the number she was looking for. Alan Southgate's publicist.

'Hi, is that Jerry? It's Liz Miller here. Yes. In person. Look, Jerry, I know it's late, but I've just come out of a very long meeting and we've been discussing . . . Yes, I know, but we've been talking about it, and we've decided that we'd love to have Alan on the show. Yes. As soon as possible . . . Sure, sure. There's just one thing, Jerry. Something I want to ask Alan in person, if I may. Could you possibly – I know this is a big favour, but could you possibly give me his personal number? We're old friends, I'm sure he won't mind. But I absolutely must ask him something in the strictest confidence . . . Oh, I see. Well, that's a shame, Jerry. Perhaps we'd better go back to the drawing board on this one . . . What? Oh, thank you. No, don't text it to me. I'll write it down. That's it. Thanks. Got it. Goodbye, Jerry.'

If anyone would know how to cover their tracks, it was Alan Southgate. If the stories Elizabeth had heard were true,

Alan had friends in low places who could clean up any mess, if the price was right. He might refuse to speak to her, of course. He might still hold a grudge for things that happened in the past. But on the other hand, his career was in trouble and he was desperate for the kind of exposure *The Liz Miller Show* could give him. And he had things to hide – things that Elizabeth knew.

'Alan? It's Elizabeth Miller . . . I know, it's been ages. I'm sorry. Well, yes, we're both busy people . . . Yes, that's exactly what I wanted to talk to you about. But first, I just wondered if I could ask you a favour. I have a bit of a problem on my hands, and I need some advice . . . Personal? Yes, you could say it's personal . . . In London, yes . . . Right now. As soon as possible . . . Yes, I'm sure it will, but I've got money, don't worry about that. Yes. Yes, please. Get him to call me right away, if you would. Thanks, Alan. I owe you.'

An hour later, Elizabeth left the studio in the capable hands of two of Alan's London-based personal assistants, nicely turned-out young men who could have been bank managers. No introductions were made, and a minimum of questions asked. They named their price, to which Elizabeth readily agreed. It was almost as much as Nick had been asking for. Even when she'd asked Rachel for her share, it would leave a big hole in her bank account – but this, thought Elizabeth, was no time for haggling. And it was instructive, Elizabeth thought, that disposing of the body of a dead blackmailer cost slightly less than paying him off.

But there were more pressing concerns. She needed an alibi, and scanned her diary for inspiration. Of course! Charlotte had been pestering her to come to an illustrated talk she was giving at the Institut Français entitled 'The Silenced Scream: Intimations of Feminism in Fifteenth-Century French Monasticism'. She walked up to Kensington High Street, got a bus to Knightsbridge and arrived just in time to hear Charlotte's concluding remarks. The rest of her audience, all eight of them, seemed to have been reduced to a state of trance, but Charlotte's eyes were shining, her cheeks flushed, her upper lip sweaty. Elizabeth slipped in unobserved, and took a seat near the back.

'Brava!' said Elizabeth, when it was all over. 'That was wonderful!'

'I didn't see you arrive.'

'I got here just after you started, darling. Sorry about that. Better late than never. I wouldn't have missed it for the world. Now, introduce me to some people. Who's that, for instance?'

'Oh,' said Charlotte, blushing slightly, 'that's one of my PhD students. He's terribly bright. Vernon!' she called, and they were joined by a thin, stooping man of about thirty, who looked as if he had been involved in post-graduate studies for almost as long as his supervisor. 'I'd like to introduce you to an old colleague of mine.'

Vernon stuck out one long, fishlike hand. 'I know who this is,' he said, peering through greasy glasses, 'even though I don't actually watch television myself.'

'Pleased to meet you,' said Elizabeth, shaking firmly, and she meant it.

Rachel walked from Earls Court to a nightclub in Chelsea, where she was sure to meet several hundred of her closest personal friends. It was a tacky joint, the sort of place favoured by the up-and-coming and the down-and-going. The truly famous steered clear for the one reason that Rachel was now heading there: it was always surrounded by photographers.

'Hi boys,' she said, whipping off her shades. She posed, turned this way and that, smiled, answered questions about Charlie and Shania. 'I'm a single lady tonight,' she said, flashing a hand devoid of a wedding ring. That would give them something to write about. Brave Rachel, out on the town, smiling through her tears, blah blah blah. If she could be seen leaving with someone vaguely famous, even a former *Big Brother* housemate, that would be even better.

She strutted into the club, checked her bag in the cloakroom and hoped that it did not smell of vomit.

Once inside she loaded up on brandy and Cokes, talked to everyone, and flirted heavily with a young soap actor whose chat-up line was 'I used to have your poster on my bedroom wall.' They were photographed leaving the club together at 2 a.m. Rachel kissed him goodnight and walked down to Battersea Bridge. She stopped halfway across, and threw her bag into the river.

The evening papers did a very effective job of establishing Rachel's alibi; she was pictured going into the club alone, and leaving the club, somewhat the worse for wear, with the famous teenager.

In the same edition, they reported former top model Tabitha Mensah arriving at a party with 'fashion photographer Nick Sharkey', alongside fifty words of copy focusing on Tabitha's see-saw sexuality. Nick looked, if not well, at least alive, and the report claimed that they'd 'partied till dawn'.

Elizabeth saw the photograph, and felt as if someone had just walked over her grave. Was it really that easy to lie about death? An old picture, some money in the right hands, a photographer and a newspaper editor bribed or blackmailed to run the story, the price of silence and secrecy – and the dead will walk and talk and go to parties.

Alan Southgate had earned his place on *The Liz Miller Show*. As far as Elizabeth was concerned, they could turn the whole week's programmes into an advert for Alan's latest project. Nothing was too much for her dear old friend.

'So, how did it go?'

'Like a dream,' said Rachel, 'just like you said it would.'

'The drugs *do* work,' trilled Mark. 'See? You can always rely on me.'

'Darling, I always have done and I always will. You're my rock.'

Mark beamed. 'I've always wanted to be someone's rock. We won't be hearing from Nasty Nick in a hurry, then?'

'No,' said Rachel. 'I don't think we will.'

'Are you okay, Liz?'

'I'm fine. Why?'

'Well,' said Mike, putting a hand on hers, 'you've been rather distant the last few days. I just wondered if there was anything wrong.'

'No,' said Elizabeth, brightly. 'Nothing at all.'

'You're not having second thoughts about this, are you? About us?'

'Good lord, no.' She forced a laugh. 'I've never been more certain about anything in my life.' She picked up a menu. 'Are you ready to order?'

'Because if we're really serious,' said Mike, 'there needs to be complete honesty between us. Right? I've done too much lying in my life. I want to start again with a clean slate.'

'Me, too,' said Elizabeth. 'Tabula rasa.'

'So,' said Mike, squeezing her hand, 'if there is anything troubling you, anything at all, you must tell me.' He looked into her eyes – too hard, too deep.

'Honestly,' she said, returning the squeeze and the gaze, 'there's nothing. I'm happy. Working too hard, but happy. You'll get used to my little ways.'

'I hope so. Because . . . well . . .' Mike cleared his throat, and straightened his glasses. 'I love you, Elizabeth Miller. There. What do you say to that?'

'Oh, Mike.' She felt the blood rush to her head, and for a moment the lights in the restaurant seemed to blur and multiply. She took a deep breath. 'That's the most wonderful thing I could possibly hear.'

She wanted to say, 'I love you, too,' to seal the pact, but at that moment the waiter arrived to take their order.

Elizabeth and Rachel did not see each other for six weeks.

The Liz Miller Show went on, with the usual mixture of guests, among them Alan Southgate, who was very charming, and flirted with his hostess so much that there was some speculation in the newspapers. Rachel stayed at home, waiting for the 'scandal' of her affair with her soap toyboy to die down (he seemed to think it was real, and kept texting her), following Charlie's progress towards the *Stars Under Fire* final. Where he would go after that – and with whom – she did not know.

It was up to Chris, as usual, to get his two sisters around the same table. There were contracts to be signed, scripts to be discussed, publicity to be planned. *The Best Revenge* was in pre-production and, true to her word, Elizabeth had got her brother a job on Gerald Partridge's team.

They met in Partridge's office: Elizabeth, Rachel, Chris, Gerald and Elizabeth's agent, Jan. 'So,' said Gerald, beaming in an avuncular way, 'the gang's all here. Great to see you ladies getting on so well.'

Elizabeth took Rachel's hand. 'The past is the past. We're looking forward to the future now.'

'Yes,' said Rachel, playing her part. 'A lot of water has flowed under the bridge. And we've both grown up a lot, haven't we?'

'We certainly have,' said Elizabeth. 'I'm just glad to have my sister back.'

'What do you think of the scripts, Rachel?' asked Gerald.

'Fantastic.'

'Have you actually read them? I mean, they're pretty harsh.'

'Oh, I love all that,' said Rachel. 'The bitchier, the better. Shoulder pads and pulling hair. Very *Dynasty*.'

'Rachel knows perfectly well that this is fiction,' said Elizabeth. 'We've talked it over at great length.'

Jan dived in with questions about production schedules, a TV tie-in edition, foreign rights. With every word she said, the potential profit seemed to multiply.

Chris said very little until the end of the meeting.

'There's just one thing that I think we need to address.'

All eyes turned on him.

'It may seem like a niggling point, but it's an important one. It's about Nick.'

Elizabeth and Rachel both stared directly ahead, smiles on their faces.

'Go on,' said Gerald.

'Well, don't you think that he might object to the way he's portrayed in the script? I mean, anyone who knows your history – and when this comes out, everyone will – will realise that the character of Rico is based on him.'

'So?'

'You've portrayed him as a violent, abusive drug dealer. A conman. There's even a suggestion that he's a rapist.'

'Well?' said Rachel, that fixed, Stepford Wife look still on her face.

'Supposing he sues.'

'I suppose Dev put you up to this,' said Elizabeth. 'Rest assured, Chris, Nick won't sue.'

Gerald was scowling. 'Are you sure of that, Elizabeth? I don't want any trouble. We could change a few things.'

'I'm sure,' said Elizabeth. 'Absolutely sure.'

In a landfill site at a former beauty spot in Cumbria, buried beneath several tons of household waste, circled by seagulls and hazy with flies, the body of Nick Sharkey was rotting rapidly inside its black plastic sack. The hair, once so shiny and sleek, had formed dull, matted clumps that stuck to the head like dirty brillo pads. The nose, up which so much cocaine had flown, was rotted away, giving the maggots easy access to his brain. The eyes, those beautiful, hooded eyes, were closed for ever. His teeth had been broken post-mortem. And his fingers – long, brown fingers that had given so much pleasure, that had switched on the cameras that recorded the Rachel Tapes, that had composed the blackmailing texts and emails that led Nick Sharkey to his final resting place – the fingers were burned and blackened. The fingerprints had been carefully removed with acid.

Chapter 40

Chris could not sleep. Even after a long day of revising production schedules, co-ordinating location and studio time and haggling with agents, even after dinner and drinks and sex with Dev, he lay awake, his brain racing, his heart pounding. He couldn't get comfortable. He was too hot, then too cold. He lay on one side, then on the other, then on his back. He was either getting flu, or cracking up.

'Okay,' said Dev, after this had gone on for an hour, and he'd been woken up for the fifth time. 'What's wrong?' He put on the light and rubbed his eyes.

'Nothing. Go back to sleep.'

'Fat chance with you bouncing around like that. Come on. Let's talk.'

'It's Nick.'

'Oh God, not that again. I told you to keep well clear.'

'I did.'

'So? What's he done now?'

'Nothing. That's just it. He's disappeared.'

'Good. So they paid him off. I've no doubt he'll be back when he needs more money.'

'I suppose so.'

'Then why are you so worried?'

'They were climbing the walls with worry, and now, suddenly, everything's great. It doesn't make sense.'

'He'll turn up, mark my words.'

'I guess so.'

'Now please, can we get some sleep? I've got to be in court at nine o'clock in the morning.' Dev put his arms around Chris. 'Stop worrying. Everything's going to be fine. It's not your problem.'

Warmed and reassured, Chris slept. But with every week that passed without word of Nick, with no ripple disturbing the calm surface of *The Best Revenge*, he got more and more worried.

Rachel lay awake, her husband breathing softly beside her. The house was quiet. The girls had long since gone to bed. A distant siren blared for a while, then faded. The pipes clicked, a bird sang, Charlie grunted and turned over.

He'd come back.

He made it to the final of *Stars Under Fire*, when his supposed mistress Shania Tennyson turned on him, 'killed' him with a sniper's bullet and snatched a victory that, the public felt, was rightly Charlie's. He squeezed out a few on-screen tears – that good old Alderman's training! – and came home more popular than ever. He went straight from Heathrow into a meeting with a record company, then to a central London hotel to meet the press.

All they wanted to know about was Shania and Rachel, and who he would choose.

'Shania and I were just good friends,' said Charlie. 'I can't wait to get back to my wife and children.'

Rachel saw the interview along with the rest of the viewing public, and was greatly relieved to learn that Chris was coming home. She welcomed him home with open arms, and accepted the story that the whole 'thing with Shania' was cooked up for the cameras. She was desperate for a return to normality.

And, for now at least, everything was normal. Her husband was back, her children were sleeping, there was more money in the bank than they had ever had before and she was working again. Anna was a headache – she was broke, spending too much time hanging around the house hinting that she needed to borrow money – but that was a minor headache. The nightmares of the last few months had gone away. She didn't know exactly how; Elizabeth had volunteered no information, simply asked for some money 'to cover costs', and Rachel had paid up. It was a very large sum, and if Charlie hadn't been earning so much, it would have ruined her. But, under the circumstances, Rachel felt it was money well spent.

The filming was going well. Everyone who saw the rushes said that Rachel Hope was giving the performance of a lifetime. She had Elizabeth to thank for that, of course – Elizabeth and Gerald, who, between them, had given her another chance.

She had a husband, a family and a career. She even had a sister.

But at what price?

Every time she closed her eyes, she saw Nick's face, saw the weird hunching of his back as he went into convulsions, the vomit dripping from his lap on to the floor. It was red and foaming, and smelled of wine.

When the cameras were on her, she was fine. She felt alive. She poured herself into the role, savouring every bitchy line, every shocking love scene. She hit her mark in every take, word-perfect. She never missed an early call; she was often the first to arrive. She gossiped and laughed with the make-up artists, the hairdressers, the carpenters, the sparks. In short, she was the life and soul of *The Best Revenge*. Anything was better than being alone. When she was alone, she had to think.

Charlie might have noticed that something was wrong, but Charlie had other things to occupy his mind. Perhaps she was a little distant when they made love – perhaps, he thought, she'd believed all that crap about Shania Tennyson, and was jealous. True, he'd slept with Shania, and yes, he'd made promises in the heat of the moment that he had no intention of keeping – but that was ancient history now. What mattered to Charlie was his career, his children and his wife. This was their big chance to establish themselves as the hottest celebrity couple of the decade. Minor details, like his wife's odd moods, just didn't matter.

Night after night Rachel lay in bed waiting for the phone to ring, for the hammering of fists on the front door. 'Miss Hope. We need to talk to you about the disappearance of Nick Sharkey . . .' But the call never came, the nights went by undisturbed, the days turned into weeks and then months. Nick Sharkey had slipped out of her life just as easily as he had slipped into it. There were no headlines, no questions asked, no missing person's case. There were rumours, dutifully reported by Mark: Nick was making porn in Thailand; Nick was living on a movie star's yacht in the south of France; Nick was dying in a hospital in New York City. Mark believed them all, and spread them all, and thus kept Nick alive. Rachel wondered who was starting these rumours – but that avenue of speculation was closed to her. Elizabeth had never told her what, exactly, had happened in the studio after she left. Someone had come along, waved a magic wand and made the whole horrible mess simply disappear.

Rachel was too grateful to ask for details.

As time went by, the horror faded. She started to think of 'the night that Nick overdosed' rather than 'the night we killed him'. The image of his face receded from her conscious mind and into her dreams. Sometimes she woke from a nightmare, shivering with cold, the smell of sour wine in her nostrils and then she would get up, creep quietly into the girls' bedroom and watch them sleeping. When she saw Sasha and Ella so calm, so happy and so innocent, it all seemed worthwhile.

Elizabeth was spending every possible night with Mike; the alternatives were too horrible to contemplate. When she was with him, she could pretend that nothing unusual had happened. Hadn't he insisted on absolute honesty between them? If she couldn't give him that, she'd give him the next best thing – the illusion of it. When they were together, she let herself believe that Nick had simply vanished.

Tell a lie often enough, and it starts to overtake the truth. It was so easy to reinvent things: she'd done it before. Five years ago she was crushed, squirming like an insect that someone had stamped on. And now? Now she was the one on whom everyone depended. It was her book that was making them all this money, her book on which Gerald, Rachel, Chris, Jan, everyone depended for their livelihood. It was her TV show that gave them the kind of profile that would ensure the biggest viewing figures of the year. And it was her cool-headedness that had managed Nick Sharkey without betraying them into the hands of the law.

'A friend of ours has overdosed,' was all she'd told Alan the night Nick died. He seemed to understand. The men in suits had asked no questions, simply told her that everything would be taken care of.

Nobody knew the whole picture. Only Elizabeth – and even she didn't know where the body was buried. It was better that way.

Thanks to her, it was all holding together. And as long as she kept her cool, nothing would go wrong.

But there were times when Elizabeth's cool deserted her, when the nightmares became too awful to bear, when it seemed as if the whole house of cards was tumbling about her ears. All it would take was one tiny mistake – someone saying the wrong thing, raising suspicions that turned into doubts that turned into questions that turned into an investigation . . . There were too many loose ends. Mark would talk, or Chris would talk, or Rachel, or Alan, or the men in suits. Nick's parents, whom he hadn't spoken to in years, would suddenly get curious. Former friends would start asking questions. Their faces passed before her in review, their voices chattered in her head.

What did you do to Nick, Elizabeth?

Where is the body?

How much did you pay?

And one night, when the voices got too much, when Mike was not with her, Elizabeth started to panic. Her breathing was shallow, her heart racing, sweat breaking out on her forehead. If she didn't talk to someone, she would go mad.

There was only one person she could turn to.

'I'm sorry to wake you.'

'I wasn't asleep.'

'It's just . . .'

'What, Elizabeth?'

'I've got to talk to someone.'

'Do you want me to come over?'

'What, now?'

'Mum and Charlie can look after the kids. I'm guessing this isn't the kind of conversation we can have in front of them.'

'Thank you, Rachel.'

'I'm on my way.'

Rachel watched the streetlights speeding past the cab window, saw a few late drinkers staggering home, counted the lighted windows where other people were unable to sleep.

Elizabeth was wearing a pink towelling dressing gown. Her hair was scraped back off her face, which was shiny with cleansers and moisturisers. In a couple of hours she'd be on her way to the studio, to be turned into Liz Miller for the day. Rachel had never seen her like this before – out of her shell, exposed.

The light in the hallway deepened the shadows under her eyes.

'Don't look at me,' she said, shading her face with a hand. 'I look like death.'

'You look like I feel.'

'Are you sleeping?'

'Not a lot.'

'Nightmares?'

'All the time. You?'

'Yes. Awful.'

They went into the living room, where the lights were low.

'Want a drink?'

'Better not. Filming tomorrow.'

'I suppose you're right.' Elizabeth put the cork back in the whisky bottle. 'Can't even drink ourselves into oblivion any more. Talk about the price of success.'

They looked at each other, saw the fear reflected in their eyes.

'I can't stop thinking about it, Rachel. I think I'm going mad.'

'What are we going to do?'

'There's nothing we can do, is there . . . Just wait.'

'Wait for what?'

'Until we forget, I suppose,' said Elizabeth. 'Or until something happens.'

Rachel shuddered. 'Don't say that.'

'We have to face the possibility.'

'No.' Rachel put her hands over her ears. 'Don't say it.'

They sat for a while. Was this it, then? The silent sharing of a secret they could not even mention to each other? A secret that would bind them together for the rest of their lives?

'I see his face all the time,' said Rachel at last, and promptly burst into tears. Elizabeth put an arm around her shoulder.

'I know.'

'We killed him, Elizabeth.'

'No,' said Elizabeth. 'It was an accident. It wasn't our fault.'

'I'm not sure if I can believe that.'

'You must.'

'But how can we go on doing what we're doing? Turning up in the studio, smiling, appearing in public together? How can I raise my children to be decent human beings? How can I make love to my husband when I have Nick's blood on my hands?'

'You must. If you don't, it was all in vain.'

'How?'

'We'll get through it together.'

'Do you really think we can?'

'Let's try.'

The Best Revenge came in on schedule and under budget, the buzz was building and already there was talk of a commissioning a sequel. Chris spent his days booking ADR studios, organising screenings, talking to foreign broadcasters. Gerald had given him a six-month contract, and there was talk of a permanent position in Partridge Pictures. Dev had just become a partner at his firm, and they had booked a fortnight in Goa to celebrate. Chris should have been happy.

But the worm of suspicion was still gnawing at him.

Everything looked perfect. Elizabeth and Rachel were friends again, even to the extent of visiting each other's homes. Rachel had a happy family life, and Elizabeth had a boyfriend who seemed to be devoted to her. She'd just signed the contracts for a new series of *The Liz Miller Show*, with a greatly increased fee, and was finalising a deal for the sequel to *The Best Revenge* that would make her one of the highest-paid writers in the country. They were rich and happy and successful.

So what was wrong with the picture?

A piece was missing, that was all. And without it, nothing made sense.

'Liz,' he said one afternoon, as they rode into town to watch a rough cut of the first episode. 'Do you ever hear anything from Nick?'

'God, no,' she said. 'Whatever made you think about him?' Her face was flawless, her voice betrayed nothing.

'I don't know,' said Chris. 'I just can't help wondering where he went. One minute he was here, and the next minute he wasn't. It's weird.'

'I'll tell you what happened, Chris.' She pulled a compact out of her bag, flipped it open and checked her make-up. 'I paid him an absolutely enormous amount of money to make him clear off.'

'You paid him? Why? Why not Rachel?'

'She contributed.'

'You said he was asking too much.'

'He was. But it came down to a choice. And between us, we managed.'

'And that's it? He's vanished into thin air, and you'll never hear from him again?'

'Nick's cast a shadow over my life for far too long, Chris. For now, I'm happy to let sleeping dogs lie.'

'That's what Dev says I should do.'

'Then why don't you listen?'

Because I don't trust you, thought Chris, but they had arrived at the edit suite, and Elizabeth was whisked away.

'Blimey. This is an honour.'

'Hello, Mark. How are you?'

'Fine. Going to buy me a drink?'

'Of course,' said Chris. 'What'll it be?'

'Large vodka and Coke, please.'

Chris returned with the drinks. Mark was sitting alone.

'Don't often see you in places like this any more. Not now you've got a boyfriend and everything.'

'Mark,' said Chris, 'do you ever hear from Nick Sharkey?'

'That scum?' Mark pretended to spit. 'Certainly not. Good riddance to bad rubbish, I say.'

'Any idea what happened to him?'

Mark sucked his drink through a straw. 'Well, one hears things.'

'Like what?'

'At the last count, he was in Mexico.'

'Mexico? What the hell is he doing there?'

'Same as he always did, I should think, taking drugs and screwing around.'

'Who told you that?'

'Oh, this travel rep that I know. Used to work for Libby Wallace back in the day. He ran into him out there.'

'Really?'

'Yes, really. Why does everyone think I make these things up?'

'And did your friend find out why Nick left the UK?'

'Scared of what would happen to him if he came back, I should think. Dangerous place for people like him. Everyone knows what he did to Libby. He caused that poor woman's death.'

'Is that what they're saying?'

'That's the truth, Chris. Believe me. I *knew* Libby.'

'Chris! Mate! Good to see you.'

'Hi, Charlie. Is Rachel here?'

'Yeah, hang on a sec.' He yelled up the stairs. Sasha came charging down the hall and launched herself at Chris's knees.

'I brought these for you,' said Chris, kissing Rachel and giving her tulips. 'And these,' he said, producing large bags of chocolate buttons, 'are for the girls.'

Sasha cheered, grabbed the sweets and skipped off to the playroom.

'You know the way to a girl's heart,' said Rachel. 'Can't think when my husband last bought me flowers.'

Charlie kissed her on the cheek. 'Point taken,' he said, and went back into the living room, where he was practising dance moves for a new video.

'How are things?'

'Fine, as you can see them. Girls growing up fast. Charlie behaving himself. He's working hard, I'm working hard.'

'Must cost a fortune in childcare.'

'Mum looks after the girls,' said Rachel, frowning.

'And how's that working out?'

'Badly,' said Rachel. 'I need to sort something out more permanently I know, but she insists. And I don't have the heart to turn her out. The old house is falling around her ears. She can't afford to have it done up. I'm afraid she worked her way through your father's estate rather quickly.'

'Good luck to her.'

Rachel sighed. 'Anyway, you didn't come here to talk about my domestic problems.'

'Not really, no.'

'Then what? Trouble at the mill?'

'In a manner of speaking.'

'You and Dev?'

'What? Oh, no, Dev's fine. Dev's great.'

'I see.' They went into the kitchen, and shut the door. 'Elizabeth, I presume.'

'Well . . .'

'What's she done now?'

'It's not what she's done. It's something she said. Something that's been worrying me.'

'Go on.'

'Rachel, this is probably none of my business, but what happened to Nick?'

'Nick?' Rachel didn't miss a beat. 'What did Elizabeth tell you?'

'That you paid him off.'

'It wasn't quite as simple as that.'

'I didn't think so.'

'Nick was . . . well, I don't like to say this, even now, about someone I once had feelings for.' She lowered her voice. 'But Nick was greedy. We knew that however much we paid him, he'd keep coming back for more.'

'That's what I thought.'

'So we had to come up with a way of making him keep his promise.'

'Oh, yes?'

Rachel sat quietly for a while, her hands clasped between her knees. 'Chris,' she said at last, 'can you keep a secret?'

'Of course.'

'I mean a real secret. A deep secret that you will never tell anyone.'

'All right.'

'Swear.'

'I swear. On Dev's life.'

'Okay. That'll do.' She took a deep breath. 'I know where he is.'

'I thought you might.'

'In fact, I've seen him quite recently.'

'What, here? In London?'

'Yes.'

'But I thought he'd left the country.'

'He has, officially speaking. And if anyone knew he'd been back, he'd be in terrible trouble.'

'The police?'

'Oh, them,' said Rachel. 'No, it's not the police Nick's scared of.'

'Then who?'

'When Nick was blackmailing me, we had to find a way of silencing him. And the only thing we could think of was by blackmailing him back. So we got hold of Libby Wallace's father, and we told him exactly who was responsible for his daughter's death.'

Chris whistled. 'And he's not someone you'd want to mess with, from what I've heard.'

'Exactly.' Rachel rubbed her forehead, as if in pain. 'I hated doing it, but it had to be done. And now he's terrified for his life.'

'Then what on earth possessed him to come back to London?'

'He's desperate. He's trying to pick up where he left off, as a drug dealer.'

'That doesn't surprise me,' said Chris. 'And he had the nerve to get in touch? What did he want?'

Rachel laughed. 'Money, of course. What do you think?'

'Tell me you didn't.'

'I always loved him, Chris. Even at the worst times.'

'You must be bloody mad.'

'I probably am. You won't tell Elizabeth, will you? If she knew he'd been back, she'd shop him straight away. She's so much tougher than I am.'

'I won't tell her. But you be careful.'

'I will,' said Rachel. 'I just can't bear to think of him out there' – she waved a hand to indicate the big, wide world – 'so alone, and so frightened. Whatever he may have done.'

Chris could think of nothing to say, and squeezed her hand. He believed her completely and felt, at last, that he understood.

It was this kind of performance that was gaining Rachel such great reviews.

They went into the playroom, and spent the rest of the afternoon with the girls.

'You're in a better mood, I'm glad to say,' said Dev, when Chris came home in time for dinner.

'Seeing Sasha and Ella always cheers me up.'

'And how's Rachel?'

'Great. They're all great.'

'Good.' Dev scanned Chris's face, looking for some clue. 'So have you solved the Mystery of the Missing Blackmailer?'

'Yes,' said Chris. 'I think so.'

'Thank God.' Dev kissed him. 'Maybe now you can start concentrating on something else.'

'What did you have in mind?'

Dev fumbled in his pocket, and went down on one knee on the kitchen floor. A pan of rice was boiling on the hob, and he was wearing an apron. 'Chris Miller,' he said, producing a small black box, 'will you marry me?'

And in the excitement of planning their civil partnership, Chris forgot all about Nick Sharkey.

Chapter 41

Elizabeth and Rachel sat side by side in large leather chairs, both wearing identical nylon capes, their faces framed by hairbands. Two make-up artists, two hairstylists and three assistants bustled around them. In the studio, the photographer was setting up lights and backdrops. A journalist from the *Times* magazine, who was providing the words to go with the pictures, had already been waiting for two hours to get his interview. Polly Hamlin kept him out of the way until 'the girls' were camera-ready.

Little by little, the faces transformed. Shadows and blemishes were concealed, shine was eradicated, features defined and enhanced, bone structure accentuated.

'Steady on,' said Rachel, as the eyeshadow got bigger and darker, 'I don't want to look like a drag queen.'

'It's Hollywood glam,' said the make-up artist.

'Looks more like Hollywood Boulevard,' said Rachel, but closed her eyes and leaned her head back. If they want to make me look like a whore, she thought, let them. They know what they're doing. It's the cover of the *Times* magazine. Rachel Hope and Liz Miller telling the extraordinary true story behind their screen blockbuster. Animal prints, big hair, cleavage. Jackie and Joan for the digital generation.

'Where's Polly?' said Elizabeth.

'Don't know.'

'Could someone get her?'

'I'll go,' said an eager young assistant, whose job so far had been to hold brushes.

'Right,' said Elizabeth, when Polly had been delivered. 'Has he been briefed?'

'Yes. I've passed on all your requests.'

'And has he agreed?'

'He's noted them.'

'I want a signed letter of agreement,' said Elizabeth. 'If I pick up the magazine and find that he's written about certain things, I will not be happy.'

'Liz,' said Polly, 'this is the *Times*. It's not a crappy celeb mag. We don't get copy approval.'

'Do they want the interview or not?'

'Oh, Elizabeth,' said Rachel, 'calm down. If he asks a question you don't like, just talk about something else. It's easy.'

'I don't want any personal stuff.'

'Then he'll think you've got something to hide,' said Polly. 'Just give him enough to think he's got an in-depth profile. He wants to like you. There's no point in pissing him off.'

'Ask him to come in, Polly,' said Rachel. 'Let's get this show on the road.'

'No! I'm not ready!' said Elizabeth. 'I look awful.'

'Then he'll think he's getting exclusive access, darling,' said Rachel. 'Bound to make him more sympathetic.'

The journalist was ushered in, switched on his digital recorder and began.

'So,' he said, 'how close to the truth is the version of events that we see in *The Best Revenge*?'

Elizabeth drew breath to claim that it was all fiction, a huge exaggeration, but Rachel cut her off. 'Oh,' she said, 'you don't know the half of it, Jack. There was so much we had to leave out.

Some very famous names . . . Well, you understand.' She winked in the mirror. 'Perhaps when you've got that thing turned off, we can tell you some tales. Can't we, Liz?'

The journalist was beaming, his bright eyes going from face to face.

'Absolutely,' said Elizabeth. 'Things to make your hair stand on end.'

'The character of Rico, for instance,' said the journalist. 'Did you really fall out over a man like that?'

'Rico is a lot of different men rolled into one,' said Elizabeth. 'If I'd written the truth about all the men we fought over, we'd come across like a couple of sluts.'

Rachel laughed. 'The truth is far, far stranger than the fiction, darling,' she said, as the make-up artist applied more shading under her jawline. 'But that's entertainment.'

'Are you sure it's not some elaborate form of revenge?' said Kate, as she and Chris sat in the lawyer's office waiting for Elizabeth. 'I mean, it doesn't seem healthy to me.'

'I don't know. She asked for my opinion and I told her to do whatever made her happy. It's none of my business, is it?'

'It's your mother's literary estate she's buying back. That must mean something to you.'

'I'm glad it's back in the family. That's about all.'

'I wish your sister was as sensible as you.'

'She's got to do something with her money. It might as well be this.'

'I get the feeling she's trying to erase the past. She's making Anna sell the estate . . .'

'Hardly! Anna's desperate for the money.'

'Even so, she's edging her out.'

'And why not? She didn't do us any favours.'

'I know.' Kate sighed. 'Well, I suppose I should be pleased. I'd hate Susan's work to be forgotten.'

Elizabeth arrived, salon-fresh, power-dressed. 'Sorry I'm late. Let's get down to business. Chris, just need you to sign the agreements.'

'Okay.'

'You're sure about this, aren't you?' said Kate.

'Absolutely.' He signed. 'Ten per cent is very generous.'

'And you, Kate.' The solicitor pushed a document across the desk towards Kate. 'Just to confirm that you waive any previous claim you have on the estate.'

'I was only ever the executor.'

'Quite so.'

'There.' Kate signed. 'Happy now?'

'Thank you both very much,' said Elizabeth. 'I don't suppose it's going to make me a fortune, but it's good to have it back.'

'And now,' said Kate, 'I hope you can leave the poor woman alone.'

'Absolutely,' said Elizabeth. 'I don't imagine any of us are going to see her again in a hurry.'

'What do you mean?' said Chris.

'Oh, didn't Rachel tell you? Anna's moving to France for a while. Lovely little place down in Languedoc. She's going to paint, apparently.'

'That's nice,' said Kate, 'but whatever is she going to live on? Fresh air? You didn't pay her that much for the estate.'

'Good lord, no,' said Elizabeth. 'The estate was just the icing on the cake. I bought the house.'

'You did what?'

'She was happy to sell, Kate. I gave her a good price. A very good price, actually.'

'Tell me you're not . . .'

'What?'

'Going to live there.'

'Of course I am! I'm squashed to death in that old flat. It's high time I moved. I've just never found anywhere I liked before.'

'And of all the houses in London, you had to choose that one?'

'All right,' said Elizabeth. 'There's an ulterior motive.'

'I knew it,' said Kate.

'I did it for Rachel.'

'You did it for . . . Rachel?'

'Well, it takes Anna off her hands, doesn't it? I mean, she was becoming a liability.'

'My God,' said Kate, 'is that what money can do? You just get rid of people who are in the way. Ship them off to France. Pretend they never existed.'

'If you want to put it like that, Kate, you're quite welcome. It doesn't really bother me.'

'Chris,' said Kate, 'what do you think of this?'

Chris shrugged. 'Fine by me. Money talks.'

'If your parents could hear you . . .'

Chris looked at Elizabeth. 'But they can't,' he said. 'We're adults now, Kate. We're responsible for our own destinies. And if Elizabeth wants to live in the old house, then I don't have a problem with it.'

'I'm glad to hear it,' said Elizabeth, 'because when you and Dev get married, I'm going to throw the biggest party that house has ever seen.'

The Best Revenge was a smash. The critics were cautious at first, but as audiences built week after week they jumped on the bandwagon. It was 'a super-glamorous bitch-fest', 'an ironic spin on the classic bonkbuster', 'a celebration of post-feminist sexual empowerment'. For the penultimate episode, in which love-rat Rico crashed his MG while fleeing from his gangster enemies along a French coastal road, viewing figures went through the roof. Rico survived long enough to tell Julia, the long-suffering heroine who rushed to his hospital bed, that he had always loved her. The final image of the episode was Jasmine, Julia's faithless sister who had betrayed Rico to the mob, smashing up her apartment while swigging from a champagne bottle and wearing fur.

Contracts for the second series were signed before the final episode was shown. 'Of course, we're delighted,' said Elizabeth in a small piece in *Broadcast* magazine. 'What could be nicer than working with your own family?'

The fees were astronomical.

The guests were arriving thick and fast, cars crunching on the newly gravelled drive. Chris and Dev stood at the front door in their suits. The trees were neatly clipped into shape, the windows repaired and gleaming, the front of the house freshly painted. The ceremony – just Dev and Chris and a few close family members – had been quick and painless. Now it was time for the main event.

'Chris.' Alan kissed him on both cheeks, and squeezed his upper arm. 'Good to see you again. It's been far too long.'

'Thanks for coming, Alan. This is Dev. Dev, this is Alan Southgate.'

'You're a very lucky man, Dev. Congratulations.'

'Thanks. And this is . . . ?'

'Sorry,' said Alan, turning towards the flawless blonde at his side. 'I'm forgetting my manners. This is Jacqueline.' He pronounced it the French way. 'We're going to be making a film together.'

'Pleased to meet you,' said Chris, thinking what excellent casting it was. They looked good together: Alan the epitome of the handsome, upper-class Englishman, Jacqueline fresh from the Paris catwalks.

Alan looked around the entrance hall. The walls were freshly painted in a warm, clean oyster colour, the parquet sanded and waxed. From the banisters hung garlands of fresh flowers. 'She's done wonders with the old place, hasn't she? I'd hardly recognise it.'

'I don't recognise it, either, and I grew up in it.'

'That's what money can do,' said Alan, gliding into the party with Jacqueline on his arm. 'We'll talk later. Ah! Elizabeth!' They kissed. 'Wonderful to see you, darling. Just saying to your brother what a wonderful job you've done.'

'Thank you, Alan. You, too.'

'It looks absolutely perfect.'

'Well, I do believe in keeping up appearances,' said Elizabeth, as Jacqueline drifted off to find a drink. 'I'd like you to meet Mike Harris.'

'Mr Harris,' said Alan. 'We meet at last. Last time we spoke you were splashing me all over your newspaper.'

'Relax,' said Mike. 'I'm not a journalist any more.'

'Good. Can't stand them,' said Alan. 'Present company excepted, of course.'

'Once a hack, always a hack,' said Elizabeth. 'But give me time. The novel's selling well.'

'Having your own TV show does have its advantages,' said Alan. 'Must save a fortune in advertising.'

'It does. And how's your show going? I heard there was some question of it being cancelled.'

'Oh, you don't want to believe everything you hear. Anyway, I'm bored of television. I'm much more interested in directing now.'

'And making art movies with beautiful French models.'

'Exquisite, isn't she?'

'Absolutely.'

'It's going to be a marvellous film.'

'I'm sure.'

'And, of course, we'd love to come on to the show to promote it.'

'Always glad to have you, Alan. Any time. You know that.'

'You're a pal.' Jacqueline materialised at his side, with two glasses of champagne and a frosty expression. 'Well, Elizabeth, I mustn't monopolise you.'

Sasha and Ella dragged Chris through the hall and out into the garden, shrieking with delight. Alan and Elizabeth watched him pass. 'No regrets, Alan?' asked Elizabeth.

'None whatsoever. You?'

'What do I have to regret?'

Alan looked as if he was about to say something, but thought better of it. 'Nothing, of course. Not that I know of, anyway.' He winked, and moved off with Jacqueline.

'Poor bastard,' said Mike. 'Can't be much fun, living a lie.'

'I don't think he suffers too much,' said Elizabeth. 'I suppose, after a while, you get used to it. Look. Here's Rachel.'

There were photographers outside the house – Polly Hamlin made sure of that – and when Rachel arrived with Charlie and the girls, they had detained them for nearly ten minutes. The Hot Celebrity Couple happily posed and chatted, made sure everyone had what they wanted.

'Gary, hi. Good to see you. How's the leg?'

'Dan, mate. All right? See you at the O2 on Friday?'

'Oh, absolutely. We're absolutely thrilled. Chris is more than just a brother to me. We're all one big happy family.'

Finally, they were allowed to leave, with much back-slapping and air-kissing. It paid to be nice to the press. There was talk of a book, and maybe an Armani campaign.

'I'm afraid your daughters have already kidnapped my husband,' said Dev. 'You'll find him in the garden playing horsey, I imagine.'

They walked into the hall. 'Elizabeth.'

'Darling.' The women kissed. The photographer from *Super!* magazine, who had exclusive rights to the party proper, got them to do it again, better lit, against a backdrop of floral garlands.

'Who are you wearing, Rachel?'

'Armani, of course.' Now that the money was rolling in, she could afford it. 'The shoes are by Patrick Cox, whom I adore.'

'And Liz?'

'Chanel.'

'You look gorgeous, sis.'

'Thanks.'

They held hands. The camera clicked, and moved on.

'Show me round.'

They climbed the stairs, went into the bedrooms, the bathrooms, everything restored and freshly painted, the ghosts of the past exorcised. There were vases of flowers everywhere, their perfumes mingling – rose, lily, hyacinth, freesia.

'It's beautiful.'

'It is.'

'And are you happy?'

'Mike's asked me to marry him.'

'That's wonderful. Have you told people?'

'Not yet. This is Chris's day.'

'I won't steal this one from you.'

'Please don't. I can't afford to go through all that again. It's too expensive.'

They looked over the banisters, on to the heads of the guests, most of them moving out into the garden, where the voices of children were raised in play. The hall was empty.

'Is it over?' said Rachel, at last.

'I suppose so.'

'Do you still . . . have dreams?'

'Yes. Fewer, but still . . .'

'I've never told anyone,' said Rachel. 'Not Charlie. Nobody.'

'And you never will.'

'Elizabeth . . . Does anyone know?'

'I suppose so.' She was thinking of the two men in suits, the eerie efficiency with which Nick's disappearance was managed, and the price of Alan Southgate's silence. He'd said nothing. Perhaps he knew nothing, she would never be sure. For the rest of her life, she would live in doubt, in fear of a secret that she could only share with one person. Lying to the man she was going to marry, to her brother, even to her children, if she ever had any. Only Rachel knew the truth. Nick's death had tied them together for ever.

'I suppose we should go down and join the merry throng,' said Elizabeth.

'Yes.' Rachel blew her nose; Elizabeth hadn't noticed that she'd been crying.

'Come on,' said Elizabeth, taking her arm. 'Together.'

They descended the stairs like showgirls making an entrance, and went out to the garden to face their audience.

Turn the page to read an extract from

Silk

by

RUPERT JAMES

Getting Ready

Christine stood in front of the mirror, composing her face into a suitably serious expression, what her ex-husband called her 'legal look'. She wasn't too displeased with what she saw. Her hair was still almost entirely brown, apart from the odd grey strand, dead straight, well conditioned and cut in a long bob; so many of her fellow female barristers were strangers to the salon, and looked as if they'd been dragged through a hedge backwards. Her skin no longer had the elasticity of youth – she was forty-seven, after all, and the only way to have tight skin at her age was the have the slack chopped off. But she didn't sag or pouch, there were no double chins, no scrawny chicken neck either, just a softness and slight crinkliness that could be controlled and concealed with lotions, potions and powders. She took care with her make-up, as with every other aspect of her life. She wanted to appear subtle, high class, worth-the-money – not like some of the painted skulls that she saw rattling around the robing rooms.

Satisfied that she still looked the business, Christine put on her black legal gown – grasping it by the yoke, swinging it behind her shoulders and letting it settle – a move she'd perfected over twenty-plus years at the bar. She stepped back and surveyed the effect. It hung perfectly, accentuating her slim waist, her full bust, drawing the eye down to her legs, still her best feature, long legs encased in dark tights, disappearing up into the skirt of her well-tailored suit. It was always to her legs that men looked first – from clients to solicitors to counsel to judges. It didn't do any harm for a woman in this profession to look sexy – discreetly sexy, of course, one didn't want the clerks to gossip. But if there was one thing Christine had learnt since she graduated from law school and was called to the bar, it was that looks count. Many the promising career that had stalled, unaccountably, ten years after the call. It was easy to blame the men at the top, keeping the women in their place – but, Christine thought, bad grooming was just as much at fault.

Her career had certainly not stalled. After the children were born, she'd returned to work with one goal in mind – to ascend through the ranks of the legal profession, case by case, step by step, from knockabout work in the magistrate's court to being briefed in her own right in the county court, then up to the high court, building on her reputation to attract the lucrative private cases that now made up the bulk of her practice. And then, the final step, the ultimate goal: to become a Queen's Counsel – to 'take silk' – by the time she was fifty.

That was young for anyone, particularly a woman, but Christine was confident it was within her reach. One more big juicy divorce case, one more victory, another round of press cuttings, more credit reflected on her chambers, and she would make her application. They couldn't, in all conscience, turn her down. Her name had been associated with some of the most high-profile divorces of the last ten years. She'd freed celebrity husbands from gold-digging wives, sending the ex away with a modest settlement and a flea in her ear. She'd championed the downtrodden spouses of playboy company directors, taking those love rats so comprehensively to the cleaners that they'd be lucky if they could afford to keep the Docklands *pied-à-terre*. Crushed husbands licked their wounds with disappointed mistresses, who suddenly found that lover boy was less of a catch without endless credit. Ousted wives made a last few thousand spilling their guts to the celebrity press before returning to the hunt, a little less ambitious, a little more desperate this time. It could be an ugly business, divorce. It brought out the very worst in people: greed, spite, anger, malice.

Christine caught herself smiling in the mirror. It was true: the messier the case, the more she liked it. Crime may be more glamorous, with its robberies and shoot-outs, its murders and abductions, but family law showed human nature in all its disgusting glory. It was like having the best gossip in the world laid out in forensic detail for your own private delectation. What other people guessed between the lines of newspaper reports, she knew for a fact, had evidence, sworn testimony, photographs of the soiled sheets, the guilty holiday hideaway, the indiscreet gifts. She knew of the cabinet ministers with the second families concealed in the country, visited at weekends, the children employed as 'researchers'. She knew of the Premier League footballers who visited male escorts for a bit of discreet – in their dreams! – slap and tickle. Secrets attracted secrets. She'd heard stories in conference with her clients that would keep the libel lawyers busy for the rest of the century. It was one of the perks of the job, stories to be savoured privately, hinted at over dinner, noted and filed away for future reference. After twenty years at the family bar, Christine Fairbrother knew more secrets than anyone else in London. She could no longer look at a man in a well-cut suit, a woman in an expensive car, without guessing the worst. She was seldom wrong.

Only once had her radar let her badly down – and that was in the case of *Cissé v Cissé*. Her own divorce. Her own husband, not only having an affair under her very nose, but playing away throughout their marriage, even when the children were small, even when Christine, who always used her maiden name for practice, returned to full-time work in order to support Andy in his fledgling architectural practice. Yes, even then, when she came home exhausted from the magistrates and the county courts in far-flung corners of England to face grizzly babies, dirty nappies and sulky nannies, when Andy was allegedly burning the midnight oil over some new project that was bound to make his name, he was entertaining his girlfriends in restaurants and clubs and half-built flats all over town. Christine had been the last to know – in the time-honoured fashion. It was the gossip of the robing rooms that Christine Fairbrother could handle the hottest divorces in the world but couldn't manage her own marriage.

Well, that was all behind her now. They'd settled out of court – 'amicably' – as the euphemism has it, for Andy was far too smart to risk it all in a messy trial. They'd divided the assets, she'd held on to the family home in Highgate, and Andy moved in with his mistress. Oh, it was all such a cliché, so vulgar, so predictable. Christine would grow old alone, abandoned, wondering where it all went wrong. He'd get through one mistress after another, until his capital and his business were run into the ground and he ended up lonely and bitter in rented accommodation, scratching around for work, calling in favours, an embarrassment to his friends. She'd seen it a thousand times before. If this wasn't her and Andy, the love of her life, the father of her two children, she'd laugh.

What had gone wrong? It was easy enough, in retrospect, to blame her career. Maybe she hadn't been around enough, never had the time to be a good wife to Andy, pushed him into the arms of other women – but there was always a good reason. Mortgages had to be paid, children fed, clothed, cared for and schooled, holidays booked, bigger houses bought, cars upgraded and multiplied. She, Christine, had provided it all – at least in the early years. And when Andy's architectural practice took off, they'd been able to give the kids the best of everything. Isabelle had clothes, riding lessons, ballet lessons, skiing holidays with her friends, the best education, from nursery school right through to a fashion degree at Central St Martins. Benedict, music mad from the moment he could clap his hands and sing, had every instrument, gadget and gizmo that money could buy. He had a home studio in his bedroom. When he went to university in September, he'd be taking a small orchestra with him.

And with Ben gone, and Isabelle visiting only to ask for money and to blame her mother for the divorce, what was left for Christine? What had it all been for, this life of hard work and sacrifice? A husband who had never been faithful, children who no longer needed her, and in her daughter's case actively resented her? Well, thought Christine, standing in front of mirror, lowering the heavy horse-hair wig on to her head, there is always work. And in a couple of years' time, I'll be a QC – able to pick and choose my briefs, raking in the cash, at the top of my profession, envied, admired and feared. Loved? Well, perhaps not, but we can't have everything, can we? Work has never let me down. And if I concentrate, if I focus all my energies on this one goal, then the gown I wear will no longer be wool, but silk – the silk that's reserved for QCs, the ultimate symbol of success.

Christine adjusted her wig, shook out the folds of her gown, and turned away from the mirror, ready to deliver the *coup de grâce* to another dying marriage.

Victoria stepped out of the shower and reached for a towel. She loved this time of day – late afternoon, early evening, her skin still warm and tingling from the sun, a gentle buzz from a good lunch and a couple of cocktails, the promise of a party to come. She dabbed the water from her face, patted her hair and wrapped it up in a towel turban, then set about the long, sensuous process of 'getting ready'. Ever since she was a teenager, Victoria had loved getting ready – the anticipation, the self-indulgence, the pampering, awakening her body and mind to the possibilities of the evening. So many evenings, so many possibilities, so much pleasure to be enjoyed and given . . . And tonight, here at Le Mûrier, Massimo's 'hideaway' villa in Sainte-Maxime, she would step into her rightful place by his side, playing hostess to his friends and colleagues, more than just the mistress. Here, in France, she could be what she really wanted to be, at least for a few days: his wife.

She unscrewed the lid from a jar of subtly fragranced white cream, scooped out a good handful, rubbed it between her palms and made a start. Arms first, feeling the firmness in the muscle that she'd maintained from all those Pilates classes. Then the shoulders, still as smooth and rounded as a marble statue, up around the neck, where a few damp tresses of dark blonde hair escaped from the towel and clung to her nape, then swooping down to her breasts. Ah, her breasts, her best friends, her weapons, her nest-eggs – they deserved extra special care. She dabbed a little blob of cream on to each nipple, shuddering slightly as she worked it outwards, finally taking a breast in each hand and working the moisturiser in until they shone. Then down the gentle curve of her stomach, her thighs, calves and feet, good enough to eat.

Still naked, Victoria stepped into her slippers – all of her shoes had a heel, even these – and trotted into the bedroom. The windows were wide open, letting in a soft, pine-scented breeze, the buzz of insects, the occasional whirr of a passing bird. She could see right across the bay to Saint-Tropez – 'that vulgar resort', as Massimo called it, where they sometimes went at night to laugh at the excesses of the *nouveaux riches*. She stepped out on to the balcony and felt the heat from the last rays of the evening sun before it dipped down behind the hills. There was perhaps half an hour to go before sunset and that sudden drop still surprised and delighted her.

Massimo was down by the pool, stretched out on a lounger, naked but for a towel wrapped round his waist. The garden was shielded from the road by a thick stand of conifers, and was cleverly oriented to avoid being overlooked by the other villas that studded the hillside – and so, when there was no company, they could swim and sunbathe naked, even make love by the pool, in the pool, the sun beating down on their tanned skin, the smell of chlorine and pine resin and rosemary mingling with the animal scents of sex. Massimo loved that pool. Whenever they arrived at Le Mûrier, the first thing he did was strip off his clothes and dive straight in. It was more to him than just a swimming pool – it was a symbol of his success, the first real luxury he indulged himself in when he hit the big time. 'When I built that pool,' he told Victoria, 'I knew that nothing could stand in my way.'

It was hard to tell if he was awake or asleep. One arm was crooked behind his head, the other hanging limp over the edge of the lounger, a book barely held in his fingers. His eyes were concealed by sunglasses. His chest and stomach – firm and solid and hairy, not bad for a man in his fifties – not bad for a man of any age – rose and fell gently. A few drops of water clung to his tanned, oiled skin; Massimo laughed at Victoria's arsenal of high-factor sunblock, and used only olive oil, tanning to a shockingly deep brown, shrugging off any concerns about skin cancer with his usual bravado. 'If that bullet's got my name on it, then no overpriced crap in a bottle is going to make a difference,' he'd say, before handing Victoria the olive oil to 'do my back', which usually ended up with her straddling him and slipping and sliding her way to glory.

'Yoo-hoo!' she trilled from the balcony. Massimo stirred, scratched his stomach, looked up. She leaned forward, letting her breasts swing like bells over the railing. '*Ciao, bello*,' she said. 'Isn't it time you started getting ready?'

'Maybe I cancel everyone,' he said, his hand going down to his groin, where something was stirring under the towel.

'But darling, all the catering! All the booze!'

'We can have a party, just the two of us.' He parted the towel, giving her a bird's-eye view of his rapidly lengthening cock. She loved it like that, when it was stirring, not yet fully hard. Anticipation, for Christine, was often nine tenths of the pleasure – of a party, of a lover. 'Look,' he said, making it jump. 'There's plenty to eat. Come and get it.'

'Oh, Massimo, I just had a shower. I don't want to get all sweaty and oily again.' She knew this would drive him wild; he liked it when she played the proper English Miss. In truth, she could feel herself getting wet between the legs, and was tempted to take a flying jump from the balcony and land straight on his now-upstanding prick – if she didn't break her neck instead.

She turned around, making sure he got a good view of her white, creamy arse, and went back into the bedroom, threw the towel into a damp pile in the corner of the room – the maid would pick it up later – and started drying her hair.

'Ten.'

She knew in her head exactly how long it would take Massimo to get from the side of the pool up the stairs and into the bedroom. He was a fast mover, especially when his dick was leading the way.

'Nine.'

He was still eager, even after banging her for all these years. She was little more than a girl when he first met her – fresh out of university, struggling to make her mark as a journalist, full of ambition and dreams, with a taste for the high life that her meagre earnings could never satisfy. And then along came Massimo Rivelli, the up-and-coming name in the Italian garment industry, now the head of one of the most prestigious manufacturing companies in Milan, powerful, rich, respected – and married. That sad fact had not changed, despite her promptings. But Victoria was still there, still desired as much in her mid thirties as she was in her twenties, still – she hoped – loved.

'Eight.'

And she'd done well out of him. She had the lifestyle she'd dreamed of, the money and the leisure, the beautiful clothes, the holidays when his wife thought Massimo was on a business trip, here at Le Mûrier, or skiing in Aspen, or in the beautiful seaside cottage in the Highlands of Scotland – but never yet in Italy, which Massimo still regarded as home, for all that he'd married an English wife and settled her and his son in Surrey.

'Seven.'

Victoria had a home of her own, a gorgeous penthouse in Kensington, two floors at the top of a perfect stucco-fronted townhouse, with views across London and a key to the private gardens in the middle of the square. She had friends – good friends, she believed, however much they bitched about each other – and even, when Massimo was out of town, lovers of her own.

'Six.'

She had a job that allowed her to indulge her passion for fashion, combing the couture houses, her wardrobes bursting with samples and freebies. As an ambassador for Rivelli Srl – a cross between a talent scout and a PA – Victoria had an *entrée* to every show in London, Paris and New York. But never Milan . . .

'Five.'

He would be here any minute; she could hear his footsteps on the stairs. Her hand went to her pussy and started gently stroking. He liked her to be wet and ready for him.

'Four.'

And the job that gave her a salary and a company credit card was anything but full time. She had leisure to develop her creative and cultural interests – to write the book she'd always meant to write, to practise her painting – all those things that you dream of doing when you don't have time to do them, and never get around to when you do.

'Three.'

Pound pound pound went his feet on the stairs. He must be taking them two or three at a time. She closed her eyes and imagined his huge, thick, upcurved cock bouncing between his thick, hairy thighs, slapping up on his belly, his balls swinging . . .

'Two.'

And yet, for all that he had provided, what did she really have? What could she put her hand on and say 'This is mine, I earned it, I paid for it, I deserve it'? The flat? The job? The wardrobe? The jewellery? It could all disappear tomorrow, like a feast in a fairy tale . . .

'One.'

She felt her stomach turning over, half in fear, half in antici-pation. She had this strange, falling sensation more and more now – as if everything she tried to hold on to was slipping through her fingers, greasy with olive oil and expensive moisturiser and sweat and her own juices . . .

'Baby . . .'

He stood framed in the doorway, his cock harder than ever. Victoria moaned, as he liked her to, and opened her legs to let him in. Well, if that's what stood between her and penury, she'd better make it a good one – every time.

Afterwards, when she came back from the loo, there was a box on the bed that had not been there before. She squealed, rushed to open it, and from the rustling tissue paper inside pulled a brand new evening dress by Alexander McQueen, the lightest blue silk with a subtle feather print, the whole thing weighing just a few ounces.

She stepped into it, felt the silk against her breasts and hips, where it skimmed and clung. She would need no bra, perhaps not even underwear. She knew how much Massimo liked that . . .

She fixed her hair in a knot at the back of her head, and clipped in an eighteen-inch extension that cascaded down her back. A few deft touches around the eyes and lips, a quick spritz of her favourite summer scent – Gucci's *Envy* – and she was ready for whatever the night might bring.

'Isabelle!'

'What?'

'Where the fuck is she?'

'How should I know?'

'Well if she doesn't turn up . . .'

'I know. I KNOW! We're fucked.'

'So where is she?'

'Stop asking me questions I can't answer and hand me that scarf.'

Isabelle grabbed a huge silk square from Will's hand, twisted it round the model's head, tied it in a loose bow. 'Right, you'll do. Next!'

The model joined four others in a corner of the cramped backstage area. The air was thick with hairspray, deodorant and steam from the iron. Isabelle could barely make herself heard above the unnecessarily loud pre-show DJ set. She had ten models to prep, ten gowns to show, only one assistant in the shape of Will, an audience of tutors, friends, fellow students, journalists, graduates and designers waiting to judge her – and her number one model, her star attraction, who had promised promised *promised* to take her graduate collection off the catwalk and into the headlines, had not turned up.

'You'll have to go on.'

'What?'

'You . . . Oh for Christ's sake, what's this?' Will held up a dress that had a huge, dark brown cigarette burn on the front. 'Who's been smoking?'

The models shrugged and looked gormless. They had come as a job lot from one of the lesser agencies; it was all Isabelle could afford. At least they were professionals – most of her peers were relying on their thin friends, but Isabelle had managed, after several heated conversations with her parents, to scrape together the budget for a proper show.

'It's fucking ruined.' Will threw the dress on to a chair.

'Give it here. Get that lot moving, please.' She pointed towards the remaining models, who were variously texting, gossiping or staring vacantly into space.

Isabelle picked up the ruined dress, and held it up to the light. The burn was big, about the size of a five-pence piece, right at the front, an inch above the hem.

'You.' She pointed at one of the models, a petite Oriental girl.

'It wasn't me. I don't . . .'

'Shut up and come here. Strip.'

The model pulled off her T-shirt and stepped out of her sweatpants. She was naked underneath.

'Right. Stand still.'

Isabelle put her hands up inside the dress and dropped it over the model's head. Thank God – it fitted around the shoulders. It was a little loose around the waist, and the drop was too long.

'Scissors.'

Will handed her a huge pair of fabric shears. They whooshed through the fabric – one, two, three, and a hoop of purple satin fell around the model's ankles.

'Walk up and down. Hmmmm. You'll do. Bulldog clip.'

Will handed her a clip, and she cinched in the waist. The offcuts she fashioned into a belt, tied in a bow at the back. From the front, at least, the dress looked as if it had been modelled specifically to the girl's body – and, if it wasn't hemmed at the bottom, that could be put down to a stylistic innovation.

'Now for Christ's sake don't breathe out. You understand?'

The model nodded, giggled, and was sent off to join the 'readies'. The rest were all changed now; Will was making the final adjustments.

One dress remained – the jewel of Isabelle's collection, a violet chiffon gown split to the hip, scooped low at the bust and tightly tailored at the waist, designed specifically for Amelie Watts, the up-and-coming catwalk star who was supposed to have been Isabelle's passport to glory.

But Amelie was not there, and the gown was.

'Where the fuck is she,' moaned Isabelle, choking down a scream.

'Oh, I saw her,' said one of the models, a porcelain-skinned blonde with an unexpected Geordie accent. 'She was hanging out with Maya Rodean.'

'Shit!' The word exploded simultaneously from Isabelle's and Will's lips.

Maya Rodean – the bane of their lives, their *bête noire*, the daughter of superwealthy rock star Rocky Rodean, who had sailed through Central St Martins with little talent and a big name. Maya Rodean, who hogged the press attention for the graduate shows, who was putting her second-rate designs on the back of some of the biggest names in the modelling world, who could afford show producers who were more at home with Versace, McQueen, McCartney. Maya Rodean, who was already rumoured to be signing a deal with one of the big Paris houses before she'd shown a stitch, whose clumsiness on the cutting table had earned her the nickname The Shredder.

Well, if Amelie Watts had defected to Maya Rodean, so be it. The show was fucked. Weeks of careful planning had all gone to ratshit. Yes, she could change the dresses around, stick one of the other models in the violet chiffon, brief the tech team to change the lighting script, the music . . . And look forward to a lifetime of fashion obscurity, picking up crumbs from the great woman's cutting table, her only claim to fame being that she went to St Martin's with Maya Rodean. The Shredder.

'The bitch.'

'Well,' said Will, the violet chiffon in one hand, a hairdryer in the other. 'What are you waiting for?'

'Wha . . . Oh, come on. You can't be serious.'

'You've done it a thousand times in rehearsals.'

'I'm not a model. I'm a . . .'

'Designer. I know. And you're the best designer of our year. And this is your best piece. This little scrap of stuff is the thing that's going to get you noticed. And there's only one person who can wear it. You.'

'But I'm the wrong colour. It was designed for Amelie. She's white. She's whiter than white. I, in case you hadn't noticed it, am black.'

'It had come to my attention.' Will held the dress up against Isabelle's face. 'But you know what? I prefer it on you. Look in the mirror.'

He pushed her up to the dressing table, turned a light on her.

'See what I mean? Brown and purple. Beautiful.'

'I look like a bar of chocolate.'

'And that's a problem? Half the bitches in that audience would sell their souls for a taste of Dairy Milk.'

'Oh, Christ . . .'

'Come on, Is. You've got ten minutes.'

'But my hair! My make-up!'

'Leave it to me. Girls? You ready?'

There was a vague affirmative mumble.

'Right, then. Take your clothes off. Sit down. Let Will work his magic.'

He attacked her hair, loosening it from its rough braids, working on it with a comb and a hairdryer until it stood out from Isabelle's head in a huge, spherical halo. He put two huge crescents of black above her eyes, coloured her lips in deep plum, and dusted her with gold glitter – her forehead, her cheekbones, her neck, her chest.

'Stand up.'

She stood, and he surveyed. 'You'll do. Here.' He handed her the gown, kicked over a pair of jewelled stilettos. 'Two minutes to go. Not bad. Now get dressed.'

She stepped into the gown, the pride of her collection, felt the chiffon landing on her like cobwebs. Will zipped her up and she slipped on the shoes.

'Jesus.'

She stood before the mirror, her hands clasped in front of her legs, her shoulders high with tension.

'We're on.'

The music changed, the announcer's voice boomed over the PA, she heard the words 'Isabelle Cissé', and the first of the models strode into the glare of the lights.

'Hear them?'

There was applause, whistling even, as each new model went out.

'You're going out there a nobody, kid, and coming back a star.'

The last two models were waiting to go, bracing themselves, standing tall, smoothing their gowns. Will put his arms around Isabelle's waist, his hands on her backside, pulling her towards him, kissing her on the neck.

'For luck,' he said, but she could feel he was hard inside his pants.

'Hang on a second,' she said, breaking away. 'I thought you were gay.'

'So did I.'

She was on. She stepped on to the catwalk, blinded by light, deafened by music, puzzled by the fact that her best friend and fellow student, her assistant, her biggest supporter and, hope-fully, business-partner-to-be – had just grabbed her arse, kissed her and pressed his erection against her leg.

All of this must have shown in her face. As she reached the end of the catwalk, stopped and slipped one brown, toned leg through the slit in the violet chiffon, letting the lights play on the crystal encrustations on her shoes, the applause reached a crescendo.

They like me, she thought. They really like me.

For a few seconds, she held the pose, scanning the front row for friends and family.

The seats that she'd reserved for her mother and her father were empty.

Red Hot Erotic Romance

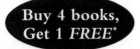

Obsessed
Erotic Romance for Women
Edited by Rachel Kramer Bussel

These stories sizzle with the kind of obsession that is fueled by our deepest desires, the ones that hold couples together, the ones that haunt us and don't let go. Whether just-blooming passions, rekindled sparks or reinvented relationships, these lovers put the object of their obsession first.
ISBN 978-1-57344-718-8 $14.95

Passion
Erotic Romance for Women
Edited by Rachel Kramer Bussel

Love and sex have always been intimately intertwined—and *Passion* shows just how delicious the possibilities are when they mingle in this sensual collection edited by award-winning author Rachel Kramer Bussel.
ISBN 978-1-57344-415-6 $14.95

Girls Who Bite
Lesbian Vampire Erotica
Edited by Delilah Devlin

Bestselling romance writer Delilah Devlin and her contributors add fresh girl-on-girl blood to the pantheon of the paranormal. The stories in *Girls Who Bite* are varied, unexpected, and soul-scorching.
ISBN 978-1-57344-715-7 $14.95

Irresistible
Erotic Romance for Couples
Edited by Rachel Kramer Bussel

This prolific editor has gathered the most popular fantasies and created a sizzling, no-holds-barred collection of explicit encounters in which couples turn their deepest desires into reality.
978-1-57344-762-1 $14.95

Heat Wave
Hot, Hot, Hot Erotica
Edited by Alison Tyler

What could be sexier or more seductive than bare, sun-warmed skin? Bestselling erotica author Alison Tyler gathers explicit stories of summer sex bursting with the sweet eroticism of swimsuits, sprinklers, and ripe strawberries.
ISBN 978-1-57344-710-2 $15.95

Out of This World Romance

Steamlust
Steampunk Erotic Romance
Edited by Kristina Wright

Shiny brass and crushed velvet; mechanical inventions and romantic conventions; sexual fantasy and kinky fetish: this is a lush and fantastical world of women-centered stories and romantic scenarios, a first for steampunk fiction.
ISBN 978-1-57344-721-8 $14.95

The Sweetest Kiss
Ravishing Vampire Erotica
Edited by D.L. King

These sanguine tales give new meaning to the term "dead sexy" and feature beautiful bloodsuckers whose desires go far beyond blood.
ISBN 978-1-57344-371-5 $15.95

Dream Lover
Paranormal Tales of Erotic Romance
Edited by Kristina Wright

A potent potion of fun and sexy tales filled with male fairies and clairvoyant scientists, as well as darkly erotic tales of ghosts, shapeshifters and possession.
ISBN 978-1-57344-655-6 $14.95

Fairy Tale Lust
Erotic Fantasies for Women
Edited by Kristina Wright

Award-winning novelist and erotica writer Kristina Wright goes over the river and through the woods to find the sexiest fairy tales ever written.
ISBN 978-1-57344-397-5 $14.95

In Sleeping Beauty's Bed
Erotic Fairy Tales
By Mitzi Szereto

"Who can resist the erotic origins of fairy tales from Little Red to Rapunzel's long braid? Szereto knows her way around the mythic scholarship and the most outrageous sexual deviations in Pandora's Box." —Susie Bright
ISBN 978-1-57344-367-8 $16.95

Bestselling Erotica for Couples

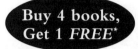

Sweet Life
Erotic Fantasies for Couples
Edited by Violet Blue

Your ticket to a front row seat for first-time spankings,
breathtaking role-playing scenes, sex parties, women who
strap it on and men who love to take it, not to mention
threesomes of every combination.
ISBN 978-1-57344-133-9 $14.95

Sweet Life 2
Erotic Fantasies for Couples
Edited by Violet Blue

"This is a we-did-it-you-can-too anthol-
ogy of real couples playing out their fantasies." —Lou Paget, author of *365 Days of
Sensational Sex*
ISBN 978-1-57344-167-4 $15.95

Sweet Love
Erotic Fantasies for Couples
Edited by Violet Blue

"If you ever get a chance to try out your
number-one fantasies in real life—and I assure you, there will be more than one—say
yes. It's well worth it. May this book, its
adventurous authors, and the daring and
satisfied characters be your guiding inspiration."—Violet Blue
ISBN 978-1-57344-381-4 $14.95

Afternoon Delight
Erotica for Couples
Edited by Alison Tyler

"Alison Tyler evokes a world of heady sen-
suality where fantasies are fearlessly ex-
plored and dreams gloriously realized."
—Barbara Pizio, Executive Editor, *Penthouse Variations*
ISBN 978-1-57344-341-8 $14.95

Three-Way
Erotic Stories
Edited by Alison Tyler

"Three means more of everything. Maybe
I'm greedy, but when it comes to sex, I like
more. More fingers. More tongues. More
limbs. More tangling and wrestling on the
mattress."
ISBN 978-1-57344-193-3 $15.95

Ordering is easy! Call us toll free or fax us to place your MC/VISA order.
You can also mail the order form below with payment to:
Cleis Press, 2246 Sixth St., Berkeley, CA 94710.

ORDER FORM

QTY	TITLE	PRICE

SUBTOTAL _____

SHIPPING _____

SALES TAX _____

TOTAL _____

Add $3.95 postage/handling for the first book ordered and $1.00 for each additional book. Outside North America, please contact us for shipping rates. California residents add 8.75% sales tax. Payment in U.S. dollars only.

* Free book of equal or lesser value. Shipping and applicable sales tax extra.

Cleis Press • Phone: (800) 780-2279 • Fax: (510) 845-8001
orders@cleispress.com • www.cleispress.com
You'll find more great books on our website

Follow us on Twitter @cleispress • Friend/fan us on Facebook